BENEATH
THE
ABBEY WALL

Also by A. D. Scott

A Small Death in the Great Glen
A Double Death on the Black Isle

BENEATH THE ABBEY WALL

A Novel

A. D. Scott

ATRIA PAPERBACK

New York   London   Toronto   Sydney   New Delhi

ATRIA
A Division of Simon & Schuster, Inc.
1230 Avenue of the Americas
New York, NY 10020

ISBN 978-1-62090-889-1

To Glenn McVeigh

BENEATH
THE
ABBEY WALL

PROLOGUE

Ten past nine on a mid-September night, everything in the town was tight shut, including the sky. It must have known it was the Sabbath.

The stone staircase leading from Church Street to the suspension bridge was not the man's usual way home. But after a long cold shift in the railway marshaling yards he was weary, and cycling the long way round, across the Black Bridge in the rain, would chill a man to the bone.

Since he was a child, taking the stairs down to the river made him uneasy. It could be the graveyard above, the tombstones rising above eye level. It could be the wall, the ancient remains of the Abbey of the Black Friars. It could be the rumor of a ghost— the ghost of the Black Lady, but more likely the ghost of a Black Friar in cloak and cassock.

He always told his wife he didn't believe the old stories— *old wives' tales*, he called them, but this night, in the dark, in the drizzle, and the lamp above the back porch of another church halfway down the steps was broken—it was even more eerie than usual.

He hugged one side of the long flight, keeping close to the iron banister that ran down the middle, his bicycle hefted on his left shoulder.

He saw the bundle on the porch step without thinking much. Later, when asked, he recalled an impression of abandoned coal sacks—the hundredweight size, he said. But for the hand, lying upturned, reaching out in a gesture of supplication, still warm, unlike that of the angel in the graveyard opposite, he would have hurried on.

The wife waits up till half past nine, he told the police sergeant; one minute late and he would have to warm his supper himself.

He knew it was a body; he'd seen enough of them in the war. He dropped his bike, felt for a pulse, found none, then sprinted up the street to the police station. And no, he told them afterwards; he hadn't lifted the sacking, somehow he couldn't, and no, he hadn't seen anything or anyone. Nothing at all.

He had felt an absence from the bundle of sacks and a presence from the graveyard over the wall, but that was not the kind of thing a man could tell anyone.

He saw a flicker, a movement, something, dancing between tombstones, hiding behind the largest, one so old it was leaning at an angle like a drunk.

It was that, more than the discovery of the woman's body, that made him hare up the street so fast he had to stop outside the police station to clutch his side, a painful stitch stopping him from taking another step.

When he had his breath back, and when he reported what he saw, he didn't mention the ghost. But he never forgot how terrified he had been.

The theft of his bicycle from where he dropped it on the steps beside the body nagged at him for months. The hand, reaching out, haunted him for the rest of his life. And ever after, even though he didn't believe in ghosts, he cycled the long way home.

CHAPTER I

After twenty-five years as a journalist, McAllister was used to late nights, so when the doorbell rang at twenty past eleven he was awake, reading, and on his third single-malt whisky of the evening. As he put down his book and rose to answer the door, he felt uneasy. Who would be awake in this Scottish Highland town this late on the Sabbath?

Police Constable Ann McPherson stood on the doorstep. "Mr. McAllister. We've found a woman. She's dead. One of my colleagues thinks she works—worked—at the *Gazette* . . ."

WPC McPherson saw a flash of dread cross McAllister's face. "It's not Joanne."

Ann McPherson knew McAllister and liked the editor of the *Highland Gazette*; liked his wit, his intellect, and secretly admired his tall dark brooding elegance. She had also guessed at his fascination with Joanne Ross, a reporter on the *Gazette*, a woman fifteen years younger than his forty-five, a woman whose smile and changeable-as-the-ocean-blue-green eyes and ever curious mind had entered his dreaming—awake and asleep.

"Come in." Not waiting for an answer, he went straight to his sitting room to pour another dram.

"Who is she?" he asked after he gulped the whisky down.

"That's why I'm here. We need your help to identify her."

He noted she did not say what had happened and knew this was not good. "I'll get my coat."

Until now, September had been glorious. A late burst of warmth and color and crystal nights, the glens and mountains orange and red and ochre, the islands in the river that cut the town in half, were decked out in an outburst of beauty that made the heart glad. But this Sunday, winter gave advance notice with a grey dreich-damp cold shroud, covering the town and mountains, spiced up by a steady nor'easterly straight off the North Sea that sent even the seagulls inland. It seemed a fitting day to end in death.

McAllister was grateful that on the short journey across the river, WPC McPherson said nothing.

The car park for the mortuary was at the back of the building and dark except for a single faint light above a door marked "Entrance." The exit was not marked, but McAllister was aware of the tall robust brick chimney and wondered if it was the exit, or perhaps entrance, to the underworld.

"McAllister."

"Detective Inspector."

They said no more. Detective Inspector Dunne led the way down a corridor and held open the thick green doors to the high-ceilinged room, where a mortuary attendant was waiting beside a trolley. A rubber sheet—green, color-coordinated to match the door and tiles—covered the figure awaiting McAllister's verdict. He mentally blessed the deities, in which he had little faith, for the three shots of malt he'd had earlier. Or was it four?

He took a breath through his mouth, then nodded.

The light was harsh, making shadows. It highlighted the look of surprise that McAllister fancied he saw on the brow of her clearly dead face. He never understood that epitaph on tombstones, "Only sleeping."

"Enough," was all he managed to say, before turning and walking out into the corridor.

"I have to ask you formally . . ." DI Dunne came up behind him.

"Can I smoke?" McAllister asked.

"In here." WPC McPherson indicated a waiting room.

The police officers waited until McAllister filled his lungs, exhaled, before putting the formal question.

"Mr. McAllister, do you recognize the deceased?" the inspector asked in a formal policeman's voice.

"I do. It is, was, Mrs. Smart, business manager at the *Highland Gazette*. I don't remember her first name."

As he said this he felt a rush of guilt. This was the woman he had worked beside for a year and a half. This was the woman who made sure the *Gazette* functioned, the woman who was as essential to the newspaper as the printing press.

"I'm sorry, it's the shock."

He knew it wasn't, and he knew he would be ashamed of this lapse of memory for the remainder of his life. He turned away. He wanted to remember her differently—alive, clearheaded, calm, an anchor in the newsroom, an older woman, once pretty, who had grown into a handsome understated elegance. He wanted his vision of her, hair in a chignon, never a stray strand, no makeup and the only touch of vanity a perfume that Joanne had assured him was called Joy, to remain intact, not sullied by the sight of her in death. And he needed to breathe, to affirm he was alive.

"I need air," he said. He didn't add that the mortuary was thick with the presence of death, and he could only breathe through his mouth, and he needed a cigarette, and he needed a whisky, and he wanted to talk to someone but he was too old to talk to his mother, and he was once again regretting his aloofness, his self-isolation, facets of his character he never saw as a fault, until lately.

Mrs. Smart is dead.

DI Dunne walked with McAllister along the corridors, out into the fresh air, saying nothing. The detective was a good man. And sensitive. He knew when to say nothing.

McAllister refused the offer of a lift home. He wished DI Dunne a good night, knowing it would never be that. WPC McPherson had left. *Probably off to break the news to the husband. That seems the lot of a woman police officer.*

McAllister took the Infirmary footbridge across the river, the quickest way home. Halfway across he thought, *Her husband— all I know is that he is a retired military man.* Again he tasted the bitter tang of guilt. *I know so little about that splendid woman, and now it is too late.*

A church bell was striking one o'clock as he opened his front door. He went to the kitchen, put on the kettle. Remembering his mother's recipe for shock, he added sugar to his tea. Taking his mug to the sitting room, he added a slug of whisky—his recipe for shock. He threw a log on the embers of the fire, settled down to search for the name. Still the answer eluded him.

She was a private woman. I've worked with her since I came to the north from Glasgow, I liked her, I respected her, but I could never say I knew her. She was always Mrs. Smart to everyone—even to Don, but I should know her first name.

A calm efficient woman, he had inherited her and his deputy, Don McLeod, when he was brought in as the editor of the *Highland Gazette*. It took only one day for him to recognize that he did not need to tell them their jobs, and that they could run the place without him.

McAllister was there for a different reason—to bring the newspaper out of the nineteenth century and into the nineteen fifties. It had taken more than a year, but 1957 was the rebirth of a newspaper unchanged for more than a century.

Why in Heaven's name would anyone want to murder her? It must be a mistake.

He had always thought her name appropriate—Mrs. Smart—the model of an efficient office manager; quiet, well-mannered, capable, able to grasp his new ideas for the *Gazette* and implement them without fuss. She was fine-looking in an elderly, middle-class way. She seldom offered an opinion until asked, did not gossip, and kept her private life private.

Wasn't her husband a war hero from somewhere in the Far East? Don will know. They've worked together since before the war. Should I tell him? Is one o'clock in the morning too late? Who would want to murder her? Why was she in town at nine thirty on a Sunday night? How are we going to get the paper out without her?

And in the maelstrom of thoughts he kept returning to the question that bothered him most—what was her first name?

McAllister had had little sleep, but he wanted to be early; he felt it his responsibility to break the news to the others on the *Gazette*. He walked down St. Steven's Brae, brain not quite in the land of the living, the homing instinct guiding him to the office. The incoming tide of Academy pupils on their way to school in their blue blazers, chattering like a flock of starlings, in groups or dragging bicycles, in solitary despair because they were not part of a popular group, in panic over homework not done, dragging their Monday-morning feet up the steepness, parted around and oblivious to the gaunt man.

He continued down Eastgate in the suitably Monday-morning

dreich. To a passerby who knew him slightly and who was ignored when he lifted his hat to McAllister, the man seemed to be searching for something or someone. Which he was; he was searching for an answer.

He reached the ornate eighteenth-century town house that loomed over the end of the High Street and paused to light a cigarette. He would need all the nicotine his body could absorb to get through this morning.

Climbing the spiral stone staircase to his office, he heard the clatter of what sounded like a bucket. Through the half-open door of his office he saw a cleaner mopping the floor. He knew the *Gazette* employed a cleaner, he had seen the payments in the budget, but he had never been in early enough to meet her.

"I'll no' be a minute," she said without looking up.

"Fine." He walked the five steps across the landing to the reporters' room, where the floor was still wet. He took a tall chair at the end of the long High Table, as Don McLeod, his deputy, referred to it. He lit another cigarette and waited.

As he stared out of the solitary window at the dark grey cloud cover, he started to mentally compose the obituary. *A nice woman, with an impressive bosom; can't put that in an obituary.* He half smiled, his first since seeing the chrysalis of her body, covered by the sheet, her hair still tight in that immaculate French roll she had worn as long as he had known her.

A good woman—no, that doesn't do her justice.

"Goodness, you gave me a fright." Joanne Ross stood in the doorway. "Never expected to see you in so early."

McAllister busied himself stubbing out a cigarette in the metal ashtray with "Souvenir from Ayr" stamped around the edge.

She stared at him for a moment, seeing the darkness around and in his deep, almost navy blue, eyes. "What's wrong?"

"Let's wait for the others."

She knew that was all she would hear until Don McLeod, deputy editor; Rob McLean, her fellow reporter; and Mrs. Smart, the business manager, turned up. She took off her Fair Isle beret; finger combed her heavy chestnut hair, hung up her scarf and coat, stuffing her gloves into the pockets. It might be mid-September, but cycling across the river, the North Sea wind could penetrate right to the bone.

"Tea?" she asked.

"No thanks."

Joanne and McAllister were awkward alone with each other. The sound of Rob running up the stairs was welcome. Following him came the wheeze of Don's breathing, clearly audible from a half-flight of stairs above.

Sitting at the reporter's table that filled up most of the narrow room, facing the Underwood typewriter that she thought of as ancient and unforgiving and imbued with the spirit of John Knox, Joanne grinned at Rob as he came in.

Rob grinned back, shook the wind out of his overlong straw hair, threw his motorbike jacket at the hatrack, which wobbled but stayed upright, and holding his hands in the air, declared, "Goal!"

Don McLeod had to climb into the tall chair beside McAllister. They always made an incongruous pair—he short and barrel shaped, the editor long and pole shaped. He sat for a moment to get his breath back—the climb up the stairs on Monday always seemed steeper than on other days. His glance at the railway station clock registered the editor's early attendance, he winked at Hector Bain, *Gazette* photographer and serial nuisance who had crept in, taking the chair next to Joanne, knowing she at least would not shout at him, he muttered *Good morning, lass,* to Joanne, ignored Rob—it being too early for a twenty-two-year-old's version of wit—and began the search of his numerous pockets for his little red pencil, the one that kept the *Gazette* reporters up to the mark. He found it and put it behind his right ear. Now he was ready to start the week.

McAllister stubbed out yet another cigarette. "I have some news . . ." he started.

"Well, we are a newspaper," Rob pointed out.

Joanne threw a scrunched-up ball of paper at him. He ducked. She missed. They grinned at each other like small children misbehaving behind the teacher's back. Don McLeod looked at them as though he were their teacher not editor. He started to waggle his finger at them, then realized what was wrong.

"Where's Mrs. Smart?" he asked, knowing that for the ritual Monday-morning news meeting she was always in before the others.

McAllister saw he had lost control of his hands. He put them under the table, holding on to the underledge.

"Mrs. Smart won't be coming in. She's . . ." He couldn't continue.

It was Don who understood first.

"Has she had an accident?"

Before McAllister could reply, the sound of voices echoed up the stairwell.

"You can't go up without an appointment." *Gazette* secretary Betsy Buchanan's voice, although shrill, was completely ineffective—the two sets of footsteps were already halfway up the stairs.

Detective Inspector Dunne hesitated in the doorway. The uniformed policeman behind him was visible only as a navy blue blur. But the detective, in a smart wool jacket, white shirt, regimental tie, raincoat open, hat respectfully removed, with the face of an off-duty funeral director, made everyone instantly nervous.

"Mr. McAllister, can I have a word?" Detective Inspector Dunne asked.

"Where's Joyce?" Don stood, his body tensed, ready for a blow.

Joyce. Of course. McAllister was furious with himself.

Rob had a flash that this was going to be bad. Joanne's face went pale, emphasizing her freckles. Hector looked as though he was about to cry. And DI Dunne realized that Mrs. Smart's colleagues had yet to learn the news.

"Say what you have to say to all of us," McAllister told the inspector.

DI Dunne took a step into the room. He took a deep breath as though he was about to announce the next psalm, and, looking up at the high window, the one decreed by the original architect to let in light but not the stunning view of castle ramparts, said, "At approximately half past nine last night, the body of Mrs. Archibald Smart was found on the steps off Church Street leading to the Greig Street Bridge."

Then, ever-vigilant police detective, he shifted his gaze downwards to take in the reaction of Mrs. Smart's colleagues.

There was a distinct moan, like a beast lowing in pain. It came from Don. He leaned forward, elbows on the table, head in hands, rocking backwards and forwards as though at prayer.

Joanne stared at Rob, who put his arm around her shoulder.

"How did she die?" Rob asked.

The police inspector paused for a moment to consider whether to tell, then answered, "She was stabbed. I've been told she died instantly."

More as a puzzle than a question, Rob blurted out, "Why would anyone kill Mrs. Smart?"

"We don't know yet," the detective answered.

"Late last night I was asked to identify the body and—" McAllister began.

"And you never told *me*?" Don turned on him with a ferocity that made Joanne shrink back in her chair.

"It was early morning when I got home." The editor knew his mistake.

"We need to talk to all of you. I'll send someone back in an hour or so—give you all time to digest the news." DI Dunne had barely finished the sentence when he felt himself being propelled to one side.

"Mr. McLeod. Sir." The uniformed policeman called down the stairs. There was no response, only the echo of heavy footsteps.

"We'll need to speak to Mr. McLeod, as he worked with her the longest." DI Dunne nodded at McAllister, giving him the responsibility for his deputy editor.

When the policemen left, the silence stretched, no one knowing what to say.

"Does this mean Mrs. Smart was murdered?" Hector was the first to speak.

"It would seem so," McAllister answered.

The crack in McAllister's voice frightened Hec. "That's no' right," he said to one in particular. He rubbed his hands through his sticking-up carrot-colored hair, and sniffed. "That canny be right. She was a really nice woman."

"McAllister, how did it happen?" Rob looked at the editor, the man who knew almost everything—in Rob's eyes. "And why?"

"I don't know. All I know is I saw her body. That she was stabbed is news to me."

McAllister looked at Joanne, who was sitting with her head in her hands saying nothing. Rob too looked lost, fiddling with his pencil, staring at the table. Hector was sniffing, trying his best not to cry.

The shrill ring of the telephone made everyone jump.

"*Gazette.*"

"Rob. Beauchamp Carlyle here. May I speak with Mr. McAllister?"

Rob thought that Beech, as he was known, had no need to introduce himself. His voice alone—that educated upper-class born-to-rule drawl—would identify him. His guffaw that passed for a laugh and always made the listener join in even when they didn't get the joke endeared the man to all he met. Rob passed the receiver over.

"There's a disturbance at Mr. and Mrs. Smart's house," Beech said. "I'm at my sister's—she lives next door. It seems Mr. McLeod is involved."

"I'll be right over." McAllister hesitated before asking, "Have you heard? No? Mrs. Smart died last night. Yes. Terrible news. I'll see you in five minutes."

"I'm coming too." Rob was off before McAllister could stop him.

"Joanne. Could you hold the fort?" McAllister asked. "Any calls about Mrs. Smart—just say nothing."

It took Joanne a minute or so to realize Hec had sneaked out. She looked at the long expanse of empty table, wondering how they would be able to meet this week's deadline without Mrs. Smart, when the phone rang.

"*Gazette.* Oh, hello, Betsy. No. Mrs. Smart won't be in." Hearing the panic in the *Gazette* secretary's voice, Joanne knew she would have to break the bad news. Knowing that Busty Betsy, as the printers called her, hated climbing the narrow stone stairs in what Joanne considered too high-heeled shoes for a workday, she said, "You'd better come upstairs."

Thanks a lot, McAllister; dealing with a hysterical Betsy Buchanan is just what I don't need. But deal with Betsy she must; she had assured McAllister that knowing that her husband, Bill, was living with Mrs. Betsy Buchanan, war widow and assisted blonde, was not a problem.

It keeps him away from me, she had told McAllister. She would never admit her niggles of resentment; Betsy could wind Bill Ross round her little finger, whereas all Joanne had managed in ten years was to rile him, provoke him into hitting her—and worse.

The disturbance was over by the time Rob came roaring down the hill on his red Triumph motorbike. He parked on the pavement and went through the open gate leading to the back garden. The back of the large turreted mansion house faced the road leading to the south side of Loch Ness. The substantial gardens, bound by high stone walls, faced the river.

When he came in the garden gate, Rob saw three policemen: one talking to Mr. Beauchamp Carlyle, the other two talking to a man in a wheelchair. Holding onto the handles of the wheelchair stood a slight, Asian-looking man who seemed half the height of Mr. Beauchamp Carlyle's six foot five. Beech wrote the "Countryside" column for the *Gazette*, and unknown to most, he was a major shareholder of the newspaper. There was no sign of Don.

Rob waved to Beech, who mimed *Two minutes.* Rob saw the man in the wheelchair, guessed he was Mrs. Smart's husband, and wondered if it would be too crass to approach him. The arrival of a police car with Detective Inspector Dunne and a taxi with McAllister solved his dilemma.

Wee Hec, hiding behind a broken rhododendron bush, was pointing a camera, clicking so fast it sounded like a mad metronome.

McAllister waved Hec away with a shooing gesture but, ever the journalist, not before he was satisfied Hec had enough shots of the scene. McAllister also watched Rob prowl the perimeter of the lawn, taking in the people, the back door that looked as though it had been attacked with an axe, the broken garden pots, and remains of geraniums, chrysanthemums, and lavender shrubs lying like casualties on a battlefield.

Rob came over to him and asked, "Whatever happened?" The editor shrugged in a "search me" gesture. He took out a packet of Passing Cloud and lit up. *Whatever happened*, McAllister was thinking, *was done in great anger.*

"There's nothing much for you here, Rob. Get back to the office; you and Joanne can cobble together the basic pages for the next edition."

Rob looked at him, the question obvious on his face.

"I'll write up . . ." McAllister hesitated. "Murder" was the worst swear word in the world, he always thought. "I'll write about Mrs. Smart. Front page obviously."

"And Don?"

McAllister stood for a moment, sighed out a long stream of smoke, and turned away, his head shaking slightly from side to side.

Rob knew this was all the answer he would get. But as he sat astride his bike, he had to put both feet on the ground and hold tightly to the handlebars, unable to kick-start the engine. The reality of what had happened hit him. *Mrs. Smart is dead, murdered. Who the hell would want to kill her? And why the hell has Don McLeod vandalized her house?* When he eventually drove off, for the first time ever he drove well within the speed limits.

"I can't bring myself to believe it," Beech said as he showed McAllister into the next-door house belonging to his sister— another substantial mansion built in grey stone in the Scottish baronial style, with crow-step gables and French doors opening onto a front lawn large enough for a bowling green. "Mrs. Smart dead."

"A police officer thought he recognized her in connection with the *Gazette*. I was asked to identify the body, so I know she is dead. But murdered . . ." McAllister too was having trouble with the idea.

"Quite." Mortimer Beauchamp Carlyle had witnessed many deaths—even murders in his time as an administrative officer in the Sudan, but the murder of a family friend, in this quiet town—this was different.

Beech ushered McAllister into a sitting room the size of most people's houses. "Last night, I heard someone call next door—very late, nearly midnight. The police no doubt."

"Aye."

"My sister will be devastated. She and Joyce Mackenzie—Mrs. Smart—have been friends for about twenty-five years, ever since they both returned from abroad." He saw the question on McAllister's face and went to elaborate. What he didn't see was McAllister searching for an ashtray, wondering if he could light up in such a splendid sitting room.

"My sister was in China . . ." Beech started.

"I can see," said McAllister, looking at the Oriental furniture, such an odd contrast to the heavy wooden paneling and the equally elaborate paneled ceiling. But he could spy no ashtrays.

"Joyce Smart was in India. Came home in the early thirties. A few years later, her husband, Archibald, had an unfortunate accident with an elephant—so the story goes—and he too returned to Scotland."

McAllister detected a twinge of doubt in that remark.

Beech paced across the room as though measuring the dimensions of the faded Persian carpet. "Look here, McAllister, do you think it too early for a dram? I don't mind admitting I'm pretty shaken."

"Shaken? What's happened? And why is there a police car parked next door?"

A tall slim woman who could be mistaken for Beech's twin, not his elder sister, had come quietly into the room without the men noticing. Elegantly dressed in tweed skirt and moss-green jumper, her hair in a loose knot at the nape of her neck matched the plentiful silver frames of the photographs of groups of Asian children crowding the top of the baby grand piano. She did not seem nervous, but it was obvious she knew something was amiss.

McAllister had met her before but could not say he knew her. He stood. "Countess Sokolov."

"Please, no formalities, I prefer to be know as Mrs. Sokolov. Even though I am legally a countess, it sounds so pretentious."

As she smiled, McAllister saw that her eyes, as pale blue as a duck's egg, had that ethereal quality which, in a photograph, would make the eyes seem empty.

"I can see by your dram it must be . . . unfortunate." She said this to her brother. "Do you want to tell me now or shall I make tea first?"

"Tea first, please." Beech believed not so much in tea for shock, more in the tea ritual.

The three sat around a small table set by a window overlooking a profusion of flowerless shrubs that McAllister, being a Glaswegian, guessed to be azalea, the only garden plant he knew.

Rosemary Sokolov poured, saw her brother stir two spoons of sugar into his cup, and knew this was not going to be good news.

"Mrs. Smart has been killed." Beech was gentle but direct in his speech. They were both of an age where they had seen too much of death to use platitudes. "There is no way to soften this—my dear, the police are saying she was murdered."

Rosemary looked into her cup as though searching for an explanation in the tea leaves—or perhaps to hide the salt water in her eyes. "That poor woman—after all she has been through . . ."

They were silent for a moment, the pause like the one minute's silence on Armistice Day, to reflect on the dead. The phrase would stick in McAllister's mind. *After all she has been through.*

"I'm sorry," McAllister said putting his teacup carefully back into the delicate saucer, "there is not much I can tell you. But if and when I do hear more, I'll let you know." He stood. "Please excuse me, I must get back to the office."

Beech saw him out. "I'll come in this afternoon," he said, "see if I can be of any help."

"I'd be grateful."

They shook hands. The idea of Beech in the office was reassuring. The much older man had a calming presence and a good sense of the milieu of a newspaper. He knew all the casual correspondents and contributors. His name alone was enough to calm the most querulous complainants. His voice, when he telephoned to ask a favor or two from recalcitrant councilors or noble lords, made the listener believe that their opinion mattered. Plus, the family name, and that of the matriarchal lineage, made him a formidable figure in Highland society.

Thank goodness I can rely on Beech, was McAllister's thought as he strode off along the river to the town and the next edition of the *Highland Gazette. We will surely need all the help we can get.*

CHAPTER 2

Betsy Buchanan was at the front desk when McAllister arrived at the *Gazette* office. She looked frazzled.

"Hold the line please." She put down the receiver and said, "Mr. McAllister, Sergeant Patience has been here looking for Mr. McLeod, and Inspector Dunne has called I don't know how many times, and . . ."

"Did you write up an ad in this week's paper for a junior receptionist?"

"I did, but I don't know how I'll get through this week." Betsy was trying her best not to cry, worried she would ruin her mascara, but tears were always close these days.

"Ask around, see if you can find anyone to help out," he said. "And thanks, Betsy, you're doing a grand job."

McAllister feared that after the achievements of the last six months, the *Highland Gazette* would fall apart. The new design brought more advertising, that meant more pages, more content, and he was determined to keep up standards.

Yes, he had Rob, but the events of the last week had dampened what made Rob the successful reporter—his good cheer, happy grin, the ability to ask anyone anything. McAllister imagined that when in front of Saint Peter, Rob would be asking the awkward questions about war and famines and pestilence and the human condition.

Yes, there was Joanne, but then again, she had been so shaken she seemed to be walking around in a dwam. McAllister knew that Joanne was never one to doubt her ability to fail. Sometimes he felt like shaking her. "You're a good reporter," he wanted to say, "and a lovely woman." Then again, his former life as a senior journalist with a prestigious national newspaper had taught him that battered wives never scored high in self-esteem stakes.

Hector the *Gazette* photographer was doing his job fine. It was his bursting into tears whenever the murder was mentioned that was driving McAllister round the bend.

And Betsy Buchanan, the office secretary—all she could do was wring her hands and say, "There's a maniac out there. Maybe I'll be next." *If she keeps going on like that, I'll be the one to do for her,* McAllister thought.

Don McLeod going missing was hard to cope with. McAllister had often had the rhetorical thought—*What would we do without Don?* But he had never imagined that day would arrive. Don seemed as much a part of the *Gazette* as the printing press—and as indestructible. *And,* McAllister acknowledged, *I don't know how we can run the paper without Mrs. Smart.*

He stirred himself. *This will not get the next edition out.* He went to the door of his office and yelled across the landing to the reporters' room, "Hector, go and fetch Mr. McLeod from the Market Bar. Now!"

The reply was pitched in a high screechy wail, "He'll no' listen to me."

McAllister heard Rob intervene. "For goodness sake, Hec, Don's not going to bite you."

"He said he would kick me into the river if I ever again interrupted his drinking."

Rob could see how Don had that idea. Hec had a look about him; the look of a dog waiting for his master to come home drunk and angry, and eager to take it out on the dumb creature.

The Market Bar was Don's regular. Up an alleyway that led to the meat, fish, and vegetable section of the covered Victorian market, it was a drinking-hole-in-the-wall type of bar. Salubrious it was not.

Rob pushed his way past three men who had obviously finished a night shift, and this was their equivalent of an evening's pint or three. Hector stood outside in the alley, refusing to come in. The public toilets opposite were not a good place to hang about, but Rob left Hec to discover that for himself.

A few minutes past eleven in the morning and the bar was busy, smoke filled, and stinking of stale beer, tobacco, and another unidentifiable overlay—a stench from rotting fish or fowl or beast perhaps, but more likely the drains.

Don was hunched over the far end of long wooden bar. It was obvious he was sozzled.

"What'll you be having?" Don asked when Rob appeared at his side.

"Too early in the day for me."

"A whisky for the lad."

"You know I don't drink spirits." But Rob was ignored. "Don, we need you back at the office. We can't do the layout without you."

"McAllister can do it fine."

"Aye, but he doesn't have your touch."

"True." Don took the unwanted whisky and poured it into his pint. "Aye, I always had an eye for the layout." He tried to grin at Rob, but failed, his face looking more like that of a stroke victim. "Tell McAllister I'll be along in a whiley, I just have some business to see to first." He reached for his pint. Drained it. Ordered another.

Rob knew that was that. He wanted to do or say more and couldn't find the words, shocked at how shrunken the deputy editor had become. Turning quickly he left, scared he was catching Hec's crying disorder.

When Rob and Hector returned, mission unaccomplished, they saw Beech had joined the meeting. His offer of help—chasing up the correspondents' copy, proofreading, council reports—McAllister had gratefully accepted.

Joanne always looked forward to the ritual "Monday Morning News Meeting," an event she saw in capital letters, but today there was none of the usual joking and bad puns, mostly because of Mrs. Smart's absence, but also because Don McLeod was not there wielding his wee red pencil, shooting down the more irrelevant stories, correcting facts, eliminating stray adjectives and adverbs, and keeping them all, including the editor, in line.

"Is there any news about Mrs. Smart?" Joanne's voice was quiet, and asking the question on everyone's mind.

"I haven't had a chance to speak to DI Dunne . . ." McAllister spoke through a fog of cigarette smoke.

"Perhaps you should." Joanne's voice was gentle, the remark said not in judgment, more as a suggestion, but McAllister felt it keenly.

"You're right. I should." The silence in the room stretched. "She was one of us, a good woman . . ."

"And what about the funeral arrangements?"

McAllister said, "The Procurator Fiscal will want an expert witness to testify for the Crown. A professor from Edinburgh is coming to assist in the postmortem, so I expect Mrs. Smart's body will be released in a few days."

"Let's hope the funeral is not on deadline day," Rob quipped. He took in the psychic shudder that ran around the table. "Sorry, not in the best of taste."

McAllister was actually glad that someone was trying to lighten the mood and get them back to as near normal as possible. "I'm sure Mrs. Smart wouldn't have minded—she was used to journalists' appalling sense of humor."

They let that remark settle, all remembering Mrs. Smart—sitting at the table, presiding over the sometimes frantic proceedings, never flapping, never angry, her steel-grey hair never out of place, lipstick never smudged, the way she would look down at her papers, tidy them into neat stacks before picking out the relevant page and smiling at the corners of her mouth—the only indication she had something to say.

"I know the Aberdeen daily is splashing the murder on their front page," McAllister told them, "and so far, it seems no one knows about Don's altercation with the widower." He lit another cigarette from the butt of the still-lit one. "I'll cover the story of the death, but let's keep Don out of it." He saw the nods from all of Don's friends. "So, tell me what else we have for the edition."

"Lord Lovat and the council are at loggerheads over a septic tank," Rob told them, glad of the change of subject. "It's becoming personal."

"Good. Follow it up and get an interview with Lord Lovat if possible."

"I might be able to help there," Beech offered. Rob grinned his thanks.

"Joanne?"

Joanne hesitated. "It's not much of a story," she started, unaware that it was this hesitancy that annoyed McAllister, never the content of her ideas, "but some of the ladies of the town are gossiping about the provost's wife and the upcoming trip to Canada." She opened her notebook and read the quote from the Provost's Office: "The Provost will be studying 'aspects of the cinema business arising out of television . . .'"

"What?" Rob laughed.

"And promoting tourism to the Highlands," Joanne finished reading.

"Sounds like a fiddle to me." Rob wished he had this story. It would be a chance to make mischief.

"It's a good story, Joanne," McAllister said. "It gives an innocuous lead into what some might see as a fiddle, as Rob so aptly put it." He turned to the photographer.

"Hector?"

"I've football photos and some people getting their trophies from the bowling club."

"Write a few lines to go with the pictures, and make sure you get the names right."

Hector looked terrified at the idea he might have to touch a typewriter.

Rob sighed, knowing he would end up doing the writing, with Hec waving his arms, windmilling the action. "I'll help him."

"Right." McAllister was not in the mood for any more chat. "Let's get through this edition, and hopefully Don will be back soon." He gathered his notes. "Let's hope Betsy can cope with the advertisers until we appoint a new manager. In the meantime . . ."

"We will all help as best we can," Joanne spoke for all of them.

That week, the *Gazette* was produced without Mrs. Smart and Don McLeod, but barely. The compositors pointed out the more glaring changes in style, McAllister being out of practice at marking up the layout.

"I'm sorry," he said to the father of the chapel—a formidable man with a formidable title, who was in charge of the printers and also their union representative. "I haven't done this since I was a cadet."

"Aye, I can see that," the man replied. As McAllister turned to go he added, "I'm right sorry about Mrs. Smart—she was a good woman."

A good woman, that's what everyone says, McAllister thought. *Yet I still know so little about her.* He had written up the story of her death but ended up asking Beech to compose the obituary.

The Fatal Accident Enquiry had declared the death "Killed by person or persons unknown," and ordered the Procurator Fiscal to investigate. The *Gazette* front page contained the bare facts. The Aberdeen press coverage was much more sensational.

McAllister knew DI Dunne was telling the truth when he said there was no new information. "Sorry, McAllister, but we have no more other than the fact she was stabbed. Not that I want that published."

There was a good relationship between McAllister and the new detective inspector—unlike with the previous incumbent, a venal man, corrupt, cruel, incompetent, who had met an unfortunate end—an end known only to McAllister and two McPhee brothers.

"I'll write the usual 'Anyone with any information' appeal, then."

"That would be good. One other thing, could you tell Don McLeod we need to interview him? From what I've heard, he knew her the longest of anyone hereabouts."

"I'll try." McAllister was thoughtful after he put down the phone. He picked up the copy of the yesterday's *Gazette*, didn't like what he saw—lightweight, was his opinion—and reread the obituary.

When he had finished, McAllister still felt none the wiser. The facts of her birth, marriage, and career gave no real impression of the private person. *I presume that is how she wanted it,* he thought, *but death, violent death, is no protector of secrets.*

Somehow it seemed crass to find a replacement for Mrs.

Smart so soon after her death, but he knew it must be done. He walked across to the reporters' room.

"Joanne, we need your help."

At those words she was immediately on her guard.

Joanne went with McAllister into the editor's office. She had noticed the dark under his eyes a few days before but assumed it was overwork. It was more than that; McAllister feared the unraveling of all he had striven for, dreamed of, all he had come to the Highlands to achieve.

"Betsy Buchanan needs help. Since you know most of the advertisers from before you took on reporting duties, could you give her a hand?" He was waving his cigarette in the air as he spoke. "I realize it's extra work, and we'll run an advert for a replacement for—not that anyone could replace Mrs. Smart . . ."

Joanne felt a lurch in her stomach. Her first thought was, *No, I don't want to give up working as a reporter. I've come too far and I love my job.* What she was yet to acknowledge was that the job gave her a sense of self-worth; something her father, a minister of the strictly John Knox branch of Scottish Presbyterianism, had tried to discipline out of her; something her husband had tried to beat out of her. Plus, she needed the money; supporting their two daughters was not something Bill Ross remembered very often—unless it was to bribe them for information about their mother.

"Of course . . ." she heard the hesitation in her voice; her second thought, coming over her left, the devil's, shoulder, was saying, *Who do you think you are? You? A reporter? Up there with the professionals?* The voice, or rather voices, had been with her her whole life—first from her father, then from her husband, and often from herself. "If you want me to help . . ." Her voice trailed off.

McAllister saw her struggling with the idea. "You've come

on so much in the past six months, and you've the makings of a good journalist ..."

Don't patronize me, she thought, but he didn't catch her flash of anger.

"We'll advertise for a manager," he continued, "but in the meantime the *Gazette* needs someone on the business side. We have to ensure we have the revenue to pay for all the changes plus pay the wages."

No pressure then, she felt like saying. "I'll do it," she said.

He would never know it, but if he had only used a different tense, an "I" instead of a "we," it would have been different; she would have felt valued by him, not the organization.

"I know it might be hard for you to work with Betsy ..." McAllister had offered to ask Betsy Buchanan to leave when learning of her ongoing affair with Joanne's husband.

That's not fair, Joanne had said. *Besides, I'm grateful to Betsy for keeping him out of my hair.*

Women, I'll never understand them, had been McAllister's comment to Don. Don had agreed.

"I know how to deal with Betsy." She smiled when she saw his reaction. "Don't worry. I'll be all sweetness and light. She'll never know my manipulating ways."

"We can't afford to lose another member of staff." As soon as he said it, he regretted it. *Even the words coming out of my mouth are wrong—along with everything else.* "Thanks, Joanne. As I said, it's only temporary ..." But she had left before he could say more.

Joanne ran down the stairs. The phone was quiet for once. She didn't see the unplugged leads on the switchboard—Betsy's way of dealing with the volume of calls.

"Betsy, can you come upstairs?" Joanne asked.

Joanne could see Betsy was nervous as she came into the reporters' room.

"Joanne, I'm sorry. I know you must be angry at Bill for leaving you ..." Her voice had gone up a register.

Joanne said nothing to this remark. *If it salvages his pride saying he left me rather than the other way around, let him.*

"We're really in love," Betsy was saying.

All Joanne could think was, *You poor thing.* She knew she had married a damaged soldier who'd been through a terrible war. But she thought she could heal him. She failed.

She remembered the beatings from Bill Ross, her soldier laddie, her beautiful beau turned wife-beating-bully-boy husband. She remembered hiding the black-and-blue marks from her children, her colleagues, until one day, when he had hit her too hard, she ended up in hospital, and she was the one who felt ashamed—of being a battered wife.

"Betsy, I really don't care about you and my husband, some things are more important." She saw Betsy didn't understand. "Mrs. Smart ..."

"Oh. Right. I know. It's terrible ..."

"Mr. McAllister has asked me to help you look after the business side of the *Gazette* until a replacement manager is found. But I can't do that without you."

"That would be great, only ..."

"Really?"

"Mrs. Smart being killed is so terrible. I can't stop thinking about it. But I was hoping ..." Betsy couldn't look directly at Joanne. It was obvious she wanted to say something. Joanne waited.

"I was hoping ... maybe ..."

Joanne guessed what Betsy was hoping but did not feel like being generous.

"The advertisement for a manager will be in next week's *Gazette*. In the meantime, I will help if I can. But Betsy, you know the ropes, everyone likes you, you'd be so much better talking to the advertisers than me."

Betsy Buchanan couldn't help it. It *is what she is*, Joanne thought as she watched Betsy cock her head to one side, put her hand to her hair, smile in that oh so annoying little girl way, and say, "Do you really think so?"

"I do." Joanne sat down. "So tell me what needs doing."

"I'll visit our major advertisers, and get the ads off them. Mrs. Smart always said the personal touch was best."

And I bet you're good at that, Joanne didn't say. "That's great, Betsy. I'll help with the layout and coordinate with editorial." Joanne found she liked being decisive. They decided that McAllister would sign off on any major financial contracts Betsy recommended, and in less than an hour they had decided who was to do what.

"One thing, Joanne. Mrs. Smart paid me a commission on the advertising I sold. I'm happy to stay on the same wages if I get paid the extra."

Betsy was not the most educated of women, having left school at fifteen, but she had no doubt that she could do very well with a commission-based career.

Joanne laughed. "Ask McAllister. But I can see the *Gazette* will do very well with you in charge of sales."

"I'll need a title. I was thinking 'Advertising Manager.'"

Manager? Joanne thought, and then saw that it was only a title. "How about Advertising *Executive?*"

"I like it." More than anything it was the idea of a title and a business card that thrilled Betsy Buchanan—and the extra commission she was sure she would make.

When Betsy left, Joanne was pleased with the way she had handled the situation—professional and businesslike. Plus she had achieved her aim—to make sure that helping Betsy did not interfere with her job as reporter. *I can do both*, was her thinking. *After all, I'm a working mother, able to do half a dozen things at once.*

Mortimer Beauchamp Carlyle was seldom surprised by human nature, but the news he was about to convey to the staff at the *Gazette* had disturbed and dismayed him and his sister.

As he walked into the reporters' room, seeing the bent heads, hearing the clatter of the ancient Underwood typewriters, he fancied he felt the air vibrate as the words formed on copy paper, waiting to be edited, typeset, proofread, printed, the black type making the news and stories real, ready for the denizens of town and county to digest, to discuss, to sense that they were part of the Highlands of Scotland 1957. This was their world—a world changing too rapidly for many.

They needed their local newspaper to touch on the changing postwar world, but mostly the readers wanted reassurance, wanted to know that the schools were educating their children, the hospitals tending their sick, that the auction marts were busy, that the roads were being mended, and that the Church, of whatever denomination, still ruled their community.

Rob sensed the presence of Beech in the doorway. He looked up and grinned at the tall angular figure. "Hiya."

"Good morning, young man. Picking up the lingo from our American cousins?"

"And the music. You must come and hear our band next time we play."

Beech had heard the new American music that was sweeping Great Britain and found a startling resemblance to the chanting and singing of the tribes of Abyssinia and the Sudan.

"I'm not sure I would appreciate it." Beech remained standing in the doorway. "No, I'm here on a much less pleasant matter, I'm afraid."

There was a sudden lull in the chatter of typewriters. "I have information about Mrs. Smart's funeral."

"When is it?" Joanne asked.

"Today," Beech replied.

"Today? Where? When?" McAllister, Joanne, and Rob and Hector were speaking all at once.

"It was held this morning." He saw the looks of astonishment. "I've only just found out myself." Beech apologized. "My sister went next door to ask about the arrangements. Sergeant Major Smart said the body was released late yesterday afternoon and taken directly to Assynt, where Mrs. Smart is being interred in the family plot."

McAllister was the first to ask the obvious. "So why is the man still here in town when his wife is being buried on the other side of the country?"

"Ah. Yes. My sister asked the same. The sergeant major told her it was a private funeral. That he was unable to go all that way . . ." Sergeant Major Smart had also said that it was none of anyone's business and had shut the door in Rosemary Sokolov's face. Beech told this to McAllister later, in private.

"Does she have family over there?" Joanne asked.

"No one still living—as far as I know. Her mother died when Joyce Mackenzie was a child, her father died some fifteen or so years ago."

No one knew what to say, except Hector.

"That's no' right," he said, voicing everyone's thoughts. "No one should go to their grave alone."

"Why would her husband do this?" Joanne was shocked; funerals were big affairs in the Highlands, the size of the send-off giving comfort to the living and respect to the deceased.

Beech too was keenly aware of the breach of etiquette. He was aware of a second wave of bereavement, hurting Joyce Smart's colleagues and friends.

"When the time is right . . ." Everyone looked up at Beech, his voice and stance those of an elder statesman. "We'll find her grave. We all will go there, and hold our own commemoration."

"Yes, we will." As McAllister spoke, murmurs of agreement filled the room, and he knew the time would be right when the *Highland Gazette* had published the name of Mrs. Smart's killer across the front page.

CHAPTER 3

The lack of progress in the police investigation infuriated McAllister, and the reading of the will obsessed him; the death of Mrs. Smart came about because of her life, not some random act committed by a madman, of that he was certain.

I owe it to her, he told himself when he started delving to better understand why she was killed. But really it had been that terrible night when he couldn't remember her Christian name that had stabbed his conscience. And McAllister had a deep conscience—when it mattered to him.

"I'm off to see your father," McAllister told Rob.

"What about?" Rob asked knowing that his father, a respected local solicitor, would never divulge information on his work or clients.

"Mind your own business."

"Really? I thought a journalist's job was just the opposite."

McAllister stepped out into a grey September day, an opalescent grey, not a slate-grey, so, for this part of the world, at this time of year, a good day. The cheeky grin from the bright-young-going-places-self-styled-star of the *Gazette* had cheered him. *That young man will go far. I hope we can keep him a year or two more.*

He hurried to the solicitor's office, only a short walk away. He was curious about the meeting, and had no idea why he, albeit editor of a newspaper, should be invited to the reading of Mrs. Smart's will.

✦ ✦ ✦

From all his years as a prominent local solicitor, Angus McLean was used to strange wills. It was his opinion that many, from beyond the grave, wanted to influence the living out of jealousy. *They are alive, I must be dead, so let's loose some mischief,* Angus imagined the soon-to-be-deceased thinking. But he could not imagine such pettiness from Mrs. Smart. So, he concluded, there must be good reasons for her having made the bequests she did.

The will was businesslike. Not drawn up by himself but by a solicitor in Edinburgh. He had been named sole executor. He was about to discharge his duties—he glanced at the carriage clock atop the solid cabinet where he kept his law books and the whisky decanter and glasses—in ten minutes' time.

McAllister was the first to arrive. He came in, took a seat, the one that would give him the best view of the other attendees at the reading of the will.

Next to arrive was Jenny McPhee, accompanied by her son Jimmy. The three of them acknowledged each other, and the surprise on McAllister's face made Jenny laugh.

"I know no more than you, McAllister," she said. "All I know is this letter asking me to turn up, here and now."

"But we're right curious," Jimmy added.

Jimmy helped his mother settle in to her chair, treating her with the deference due a duchess—or the matriarch of the Traveling people that she was. Her small wiry body and dark skin showed her many years on the road. Her coat and her scarf and her rings showed a woman who kept the traditional life but was not averse to a bit of luxury.

The sound of a kerfuffle and a well-bred-commanding-the-troops voice came from the reception room. The secretary

opened the door, announced "Sergeant Major Smart," then stood
to one side with the look of a woman whose cat has just presented her with a rat.

A small, wiry, hazelnut-brown man, in neatly pressed khaki
trousers and shirt, pushed a wheelchair into the room. There sat
Sergeant Major Smart with what remained of his legs covered
by a tartan blanket. He did not introduce his companion but
looked at the others sitting in a semicircle, and took in the sight
of Jenny and Jimmy McPhee.

He tried to cover his shock and, McAllister fancied, his fear,
by blustering, "Damned if I can see why we couldn't have conducted this meeting at my house." He glared at Angus McLean,
blaming him for the presence of the tinkers. He would never
admit to knowing a Traveling person, far less the legendary
Jenny McPhee. And he was scared of Jimmy McPhee.

"How are you, Archie?" Jenny McPhee asked in a sugar-and-
spice-voice, the spice being the dominant flavor. "Joyce's house—
are you sure it's yours now?"

"Why is this *person* here?" The way the sergeant major
screwed up his face, the way he spat out the word "person," made
Angus McLean worry he might be having a stroke; a person of
the former soldier's status would never expect to be questioned
by a tinker.

Angus McLean ignored the sergeant major. "There is one
other person expected, and then we can begin the reading of
the will." He had recruited his son to make sure Don McLeod
appeared, but was uncertain he would succeed.

But a noise in reception announced their arrival. Rob ushered another almost-invalid to a chair. He was startled to see, but
knew not to comment on, the attendance of Jenny and Jimmy
McPhee. As he was leaving, Rob looked at the secretary, then
changed his mind; no one in the solicitor's office would tell him

anything, not his father and especially not the office gorgon, so he would have to wait.

I'll find out soon enough, he said to himself. *McAllister will fill me in. Or Don—providing he's drunk enough.*

McAllister had not seen Don for almost two weeks, leaving his deputy to do whatever he needed to, to recover from the shock of Mrs. Smart's death. Don's solution was to search for, and not find, the answer at the dark end of a whisky bottle. Sober or not was hard to distinguish with Don McLeod. McAllister watched Jenny McPhee close the gap between her chair and Don's, seemingly without movement, and he was glad.

Don had seen Jenny and Jimmy when he came in, but to wonder why they were there was beyond him, and nodding to acknowledge their acquaintance would hurt his head. But he was grateful they were there.

Angus McLean picked up a document. Everyone came to attention. "This is the last will and testament of Mrs. Archibald Smart, née Joyce Eileen Mackenzie," he began.

"As far as you know," the sergeant major interrupted.

"Do you know of the existence of another will?" Angus asked. But both he and Sergeant Major Smart knew it was a rhetorical question; the late Mrs. Smart had been meticulous in keeping her affairs in order.

"The will is a straightforward list of bequests with no extraneous codicils. Firstly: the sum of one hundred pounds per year is bequeathed for a scholarship, to be used for the training and education of a young journalist at the *Highland Gazette*. The terms state that the person must be under twenty-five, be from a disadvanted family . . ."

"You mean poor," Jimmy McPhee said. He had no time for those who didn't call an elbow an elbow.

"Precisely. And be a native Gaelic speaker. The editor of the

Highland Gazette will choose the candidate in an open competition, held to coincide with the annual Mod."

"Most gracious." McAllister nodded towards the sergeant major. He also tried to catch Don's eye, but Don's eyes were closed, his body motionless, as though any movement might set off a hangover, or worse.

"Second. All jewelry and a set of Highland dancing swords are bequeathed to Mrs. Jenny McPhee."

"Never!" Sergeant Major Smart shot up in his chair, his legs making a distinct clank. His Nepali caregiver stepped forward, then retreated back into the corner, watching his master like a guardian temple dog from his Himalayan kingdom. "Some of that jewelry is worth a fortune. Make note, McLean, I shall be contesting this."

"That is entirely up to you. However, your late wife's will is legal and unequivocal." As Angus McLean said this he saw Jenny McPhee whispering to her son Jimmy. She did not look at all happy at the news. Even among Travelers, who were known to keep themselves to themselves, Jenny McPhee was a secretive woman. No one knew what bound her to Joyce Mackenzie—as she always called her friend. Neither woman was ashamed of the friendship, and no one, not even Jimmy McPhee, knew of their shared past. Until now.

Angus McLean too was curious as to why Jenny McPhee was a beneficiary but would never ask. He looked down at the document and continued, "The sum of two thousand pounds is left to Bahadur Gurung in recognition of his devoted service to my late father."

Jimmy whistled when the substantial sum of money was read out. The Gurkha soldier remained as impassive as a painted deity from his homeland.

"Next"—Angus was holding up the document in front of

him as though to ward off the venom wafting across the deck—
"the marital home at Ness Walk is left, unencumbered, to Sergeant Major Archibald Smart."

No comment from the sergeant major this time.

"Next. All monies in the bank account in the name of Joyce
Eileen Smart are bequeathed to the local orphanage. Joint bank
accounts revert to the widower."

"What bank accounts? I know nothing of a separate account.
How much is in there? I have every right to know."

What an auld eejit, Jenny thought.

"We can discuss that later." Angus wanted to get on with
the reading, knowing there was worse to come. He took a deep
breath. "The estate in Assynt, Sutherland, is left, in its entirety, to
Donal Dewar McLeod."

This time Angus began wondering if Sergeant Major Smart
would need an ambulance.

"I knew it! That man." Sergeant Major Smart pointed at a
now more alert Don, or at least a man with his eyes only half
shut. "That man murdered my wife."

Don was immediately on his feet. Jimmy put an arm between
him and the sergeant major, who was attempting to rise from
his chair. The Gurkha jumped between him and Don. McAllister was saying, "Calm down, calm down." Jenny was sitting back
enjoying herself. And Angus was glad of the width of the partner's desk between himself and chaos.

"If you don't need him anymore, I'm taking Mr. McLeod wi'
me," Jimmy said.

Angus nodded gratefully. "We can go over the details another
time."

Jimmy's grip on Don's arm and the strength he was using to
propel him out the door left Don with no choice. There was no
energy left in him; three weeks of steady drinking had seen to that.

"I shall be reporting this to the police," Sergeant Major Smart called after them. "This proves motive, you know." But everyone ignored him.

Angus McLean wanted the gathering over and done with. "I have informed all the beneficiaries of the contents of the will, as is my duty as executor. My office will be in contact to sort out the details."

"I will fight this." The sergeant major's voice was still loud but had lost a little of the arrogance.

"The will is properly drawn up and will be properly executed." Angus had never liked the man, and not for the first time wondered how a person as obviously decent as Mrs. Smart had married such a popinjay. "To fight the will would be expensive. The law will take into account your inheritance of a property of substantial value, worth more than fifty percent of the total value of your late wife's estate."

"I will do everything in my power to see that that McLeod man inherits nothing." He next turned on Jenny McPhee. "As for you, I will make certain you do not inherit a single piece of her jewelry."

"I canny stop you, Mr. Smart"—Jenny's nonuse of his title was deliberate—"but know this; she was a far better woman than you ever deserved, and she is sorely missed."

When the sergeant major had been wheeled out of the room, Jenny waited a minute to avoid meeting him again, then she too rose to leave.

"Thank you, Mr. McLean. What happened to Joyce is beyond belief and pains me greatly, and this"—she gestured to the papers on the desk—"does not make me any happier."

McAllister saw the back of her hand, brown and wrinkled, and he knew she was much older than she seemed. *Don's age,* he thought. He also noted her saying "Joyce," and considered that she might know the secrets of Mrs. Smart. Not that Jenny McPhee was likely to share her knowledge with anyone other than her son Jimmy.

"I'll miss the woman." Jenny lifted a handbag that resembled a badly cured reptile, pulled down a hat that resembled a tea cozy, and added, "But I wish she hadn't landed me with this inheritance. It'll only lead to trouble." She nodded—"Mr. McLean, McAllister"—and made for the door.

"Could you give me an address where I can write to you?" Angus McLean asked.

"Care of the Ferry Inn will get me."

When he and the solicitor were alone, McAllister sat down and lit a Passing Cloud, hoping the fragrance would clear the malice from the air.

"I suppose you are used to it," he said, waiting as the solicitor filled and lit his pipe, setting off enough smoke to kipper a good dozen herrings. "But from all I know and read, wills bring out the worst in everyone, and this will is certainly intriguing."

"I couldn't pass an opinion on a client's mind." Angus smiled. "All I do is administer their wishes. In this case I fear it may be a long-drawn-out, perhaps bitter, process."

"Rather you than me." The banality of the comment covered McAllister's curiosity. He knew he would get few answers from Angus McLean—but maybe a few discreet directions. "It was good of her to leave a scholarship to the *Gazette*."

"She was a good woman."

"She and Jenny must have been close."

"Indeed."

"An estate in Sutherland—does that make Don a laird?"

"Quite a thought." Angus McLean smiled, but he was giving no more information than absolutely required of him by law.

They shook hands. McAllister left to walk to the *Gazette*

office. In the act of walking he did his thinking; he would consider yet another layer of complexity in the character of the much-missed Mrs. Joyce Eileen Smart, née Mackenzie, of the Assynt Mackenzies.

The scholarship for a young person from the Gaeltachd was novel and welcome and much needed. The bequests to Jenny McPhee and Don McLeod were perplexing.

In former times Jenny and Mrs. Smart must have known each other well. McAllister had not been aware of a connection between them; the friendship seemed unlikely—one being a tinker, the other a lady. Although he could say he knew Jimmy McPhee and his mother, he could not say he *knew* them; the Travelers were secretive, and knowing the hostility towards them from the majority of the population, he didn't blame them for distrusting outsiders.

As for an estate in remote Assynt—what would Don do with it? There was nothing there but heather, peat bogs, lochs, and lochans, fortified by fiercesome mountains. In McAllister's opinion, summer in the Northwest, with its nine-and-a-half-month winter, did not make it the Highland paradise of song and legend and maudlin expatriate memory. A Glasgow public house was his idea of real Scotland.

Not that he knew the area well. When a young journalist in Glasgow, he had been as far as Lairg once, in June, and had been driven back by rain interspersed with occasional sleet. Two years later, in August, he had driven up the west coast to Ullapool and on to Lochinver, on some of the most beautiful roads in Scotland. The purple-heather-clad hills were spectacular, though the shocking clouds of midgies that could bite through cowhide made walking nigh impossible. The way the locals examined a stranger as though he was a green man from Mars, the absolute ban on any activity on the Sabbath, and the desolate glens with abandoned crofts overgrown with grass a brighter green than the surrounding moorland depressed him. He knew the history of the Clearances and the stories still hurt.

Yes, there was something majestic about the ancient scarred mountaintops, particularly Suilven. Yes, the late-night-never-quite-dark light was enchanting, but he was a city man then, too young and self-absorbed to fall in love with landscape. So he went scuttling back to the warm comfort of his beloved hard man land of Glasgow.

McAllister thought again about the woman he had worked with but barely knew. He hadn't known her husband was wheel-chair-bound. He hadn't known she was wealthy. He hadn't known she had lived in India. There was much he hadn't known. But he agreed with the many people who'd said, "She was a good woman." *Such an old-fashioned phrase that,* he thought, *and in Joyce Smart's case, absolutely true.*

He had reached the *Gazette* without being aware he was there. Climbing the staircase, he thought, *Jenny McPhee is right, there's trouble brewing.*

Chapter 4

✍

Once more, settled in his armchair with the fire blazing and the wireless playing Mozart, McAllister was startled out of a good book and a good malt by a late-night visitor. This time it was Saturday, but again the thought came to him, *It's almost the Sabbath, who on earth is about in this town, this late at night?* Again, he knew it would not be good news.

The visitor was Sergeant Patience, a man whom all considered most inappropriately named.

"Mr. McAllister, sir, you're needed down the station," the policeman told him.

"Nothing serious, I hope?"

A big barreled bulk of a policeman, the sergeant was not always popular but had lately formed an odd alliance with Rob McLean over motorbikes.

"It's Donnie McLeod and it's no' serious—yet," the sergeant said, "but if he carries on like this much longer, there's no saying what might happen."

"I'll get my coat and meet you at the station."

Don was in a cell, but the door was open. The smell of drink and vomit and stale urine was nasty, but what really appalled McAllister was the state of the man; he looked like one of those lost souls who had suffered in either or both of the wars, wandering the country, living a half-life, surviving on the kindness of strangers and the Salvation Army.

"Are you charging him?" McAllister asked.

"No' this time," Sergeant Patience told him, "but it's no' always me who finds him and I canny vouch for some o' the other police officers who don't know him like I do."

"Would you help me get him to my car?"

"Nae bother."

On the short ride home, McAllister worried Don might vomit. He wasn't scared for his car, just afraid Don would choke. *One death at the* Gazette *is enough.*

It took McAllister much more effort than it had the policeman to get Don out of the car, down the garden path, and inside the house. At the doorstep, while McAllister was fiddling with his keys, Don leaned against the porch door, then slid to the checkerboard tiles, and collapsed in the middle like a sad Victorian sponge cake. All the while Don was muttering, arguing with himself, in Gaelic. To McAllister, who knew no Gaelic, the words washed over him like a Highland burn, running to the sea.

Getting Don upstairs to bed was beyond him. Getting him to the bathroom was difficult, but McAllister managed. Stripping off trousers, jacket, and shirt that had been slept in since the day of the reading of the will, a week ago, was relatively easy, as Don was snoring on the kitchen floor; getting him into the sitting room and onto the sofa was achieved without putting McAllister's back out. He tucked a blanket around his deputy; then, in case of accidents, he spread old newspapers around the floor near Don's head before retreating to his armchair to sit the night out, on watch for the man he admired and cared for sleep the sleep of the unready.

The ringing of his doorbell awoke McAllister.

"Not again," he muttered as he massaged the crick in his neck from sleeping in the armchair. He had slept in fits and starts, had

woken in the grey dawn—which was not that early this time of
year—to help Don to the bathroom, had made a cup of tea, then
dozed off again. By the sound of various church bells, from a
simple toll to a full peal from the cathedral, he knew it was now
mid-morning.

"Good morning, Mr. McAllister."

"Is it?" McAllister peered at the bruised sky and smelt immi-
nent rain.

"I won't come in . . . I don't suppose Donnie McLeod is still
with you . . ." The big man shifted uncomfortably on his small
neat feet.

"He . . ." McAllister did not have a chance to elaborate.

"No, I don't suppose he's here." Sergeant Patience was speaking in a deliberate, penetrating voice, knowing it would carry
down the hallway. "And I don't know where he went to last
night . . ."

McAllister waited, knowing he would soon know why the
policeman was blethering on.

"We, I mean Detective Inspector Dunne, has been wanting
to speak with Mr. McLeod for some time, and always seems to
miss him. So, since he was in the cells last night . . ."

"With the door open . . ."

"A precaution in case he chocked or summat . . ." Sergeant
Patience took McAllister's nod as agreement and continued, "So,
if you should see Mr. McLeod, maybe you can persuade him to
come in, volunteer-like . . ."

"Not a word about last night will come from me," McAllister
told him. "But wasn't Mr. McLeod booked in?"

"Nothing like that, I, we, was only helping him off the street,
just in case . . ."

"Aye." McAllister wanted to say he was grateful, knew
this wasn't needed but also knew that Don was now in the

policeman's debt. "If I should see Mr. McLeod, I'll tell him to contact the police."

The slump of relief on the man's face made McAllister reassess him. He knew the sergeant would do *him* few favors, but his concern for Don McLeod was laudable. Then he remembered the old newspaper saw about good subeditors of long standing—and that was his deputy—"They knows where the bodies are buried."

McAllister made tea. He considered cooking bacon and eggs and his favorite Stornaway black pudding, then decided against it; the state of Don's stomach might not be ready for a good Scottish fry-up.

It took three large mugs of tea, the first one fortified with a slug of whisky, before Don was ready to slump upright. It took a long bath and a change of cloths three sizes too big for him before Don looked half alive. But the real talking had to wait until late in the afternoon, after McAllister had lit the fire and served them his culinary masterpiece—cock-a-leekie soup.

"You look like a ghost of yourself," McAllister remarked. "An improvement. Last night you looked like the ghost of some long-dead clansman from Culloden."

Don made a noise, no words.

"I know it's none of my business . . ." McAllister continued.

"You're right. It's no."

"But if you are going to kill yourself slowly, can you let me know so I can make other arrangements." He let that remark lie between them as he served his guest another bowl of soup.

They took their time and after washing up, they went back to the sitting room. The rain had set in dark and heavy and steady, real Sunday weather, so McAllister switched on the standard lamp, a dark wooden piece whose base was carved with what looked like overlarge misshapen vine leaves, the parchment shade trimmed with yellowing tassels hanging unevenly around the rim. It had come with the house and McAllister had kept it, as he enjoyed the well of golden light it made in the high-ceilinged room. When the uneven electric flow made the lamp flicker, he thought of campfires and starry nights and times past, drinking with friends in hidden camps in the foothills of the Pyrenees, resting before the next round in the losing battles against Franco's fascists.

"Thanks."

The sound of Don's voice made McAllister jerk back to the here and now.

"Thank Sergeant Patience."

"He's no' a bad manny under all that flesh and bombast."

A long five minutes passed before Don spoke again, but McAllister didn't mind.

"I'm no' coming back."

"Fine," McAllister said, "but I'd appreciate it if you could come in and help out until we find a replacement."

"I'll do that." Don was beyond noticing McAllister's apparent lack of sympathy, beyond seeing McAllister's dismay.

"There's a bed made up . . ." was all the editor could think to say.

"No. I'm off home."

McAllister doubted that. The nearest public house was the most likely destination, he thought. "Don, I need your help to find whoever killed Joyce." As he said the name, he saw the flinch, the shudder, the pain. It was as if a knife, the same knife that had killed her, had penetrated between Don's ribs straight to his heart. The shaking, the trembling, the snorts were not an alcoholic aftermath; he was crying. Don was holding his head between his square ink-stained hands, sobbing in heaving silent spasms. McAllister went to the drinks cabinet and brought out the big gun, a Glen Farclas 110 proof, a whisky he called the Lazarus cure.

He put the glass into Don's hand and poured a lesser measure for himself, and sat out of sight of his friend, gifting him the invisibility to recover. He waited. When the sobbing subsided into sniffing, into blowing the nose, into finishing the dram, McAllister took the analyst's role, asking, "When did you first meet her?"

"Right after the first war."

With the patience of a heron stalking minnows in a lochan, McAllister waited.

"I had bad burns." Don didn't say from what. "She was only a young thing, nineteen, born on Hogmanay on the last day of the old century, 'a foot in each century,' she'd joke. She was a volunteer nursing assistant in a place for wounded soldiers—in Stirlingshire it was. She was staying with family friends, hoping to get in to university." He didn't tell McAllister it was a castle with titled gentlefolk she was living in, and there was no need to explain how unusual it would be for a young woman of any class to go to university in those days.

"I was the only sailor there," Don continued, his voice faint, speaking through the thick yarn of time. "When I was admitted, I was delirious, only speaking the Gaelic." He took a sip of the whisky, the water of life. It acted better than a blood transfusion. "Not that her Gaelic was great, but she's from the Northwest, she'd heard it enough around the estate. Spoke it wi' the local bairns."

"And you became friends."

"Aye. We became friends. I recovered and was going back to Skye but somehow got waylaid here and found myself on the *Gazette*. I think they gave me the job out of pity and because I could spell and besides, I was the only one the printers would listen to."

"Right Bolshie lot printers can be sometimes." McAllister laughed.

"That's rich coming from a Glaswegian."

McAllister heard the lift in Don's voice. "So you met up with Joyce again here?"

"Aye. She was in India, came back in the early thirties. Thon soldier fellow came back five years later and not long after, Joyce came to work at the *Gazette.*"

That the wife of Sergeant Major Smart, a decorated and wounded former soldier, took a job was highly unusual. That a woman of Mrs. Smart's wealth and background and education had done so was more than unusual, it was a mystery. *One of the many mysteries surrounding Mrs. Smart,* thought McAllister. Then he remembered the sergeant major's bullying and decided that was why she had taken a job.

"So how does, did, Mrs. Smart know Jenny McPhee?"

As soon as McAllister spoke, he knew his mistake; he had broken the bond between them. He saw the slight shift in the way Don held his glass; noted the way his friend licked his lips, took a deep breath, let it out slowly, then set his shoulders back as though he were about to face a firing squad.

"That's for Jenny McPhee to tell, that's if she wants to." Don was definite in his answer. *Which I very much doubt* was the unsaid remainder of the response.

McAllister knew there would be no more real information that evening—if ever. "I told Sergeant Patience you'd present yourself at the police station for an interview."

"Aye, I owe him."

"We'd all like you back at the *Gazette.*"

"No." Don eyed the bottle sitting on the side table next to the hearth, but McAllister didn't take the hint, so he stood, hitching up the ridiculous trousers, so long on him he looked like a scarecrow.

"I'll give you a lift home," McAllister offered, but Don shook his head and immediately regretted the gesture. He walked out of the room practicing the steps—one foot, then the next.

"Thanks," Don called out to McAllister, who stood on the doorstep, watching him shuffle up the garden path like an old man in slippers two sizes too big.

"Anytime. There's always soup on the hob in this house." McAllister knew that if he were the crying kind, he would burst into tears at the sight of Don McLeod passing under the pool of lamplight down the street back to his own house, where, as far as McAllister knew, Don lived with not even a wee dog for company.

If he wants to tell me anything, he'll tell me, McAllister thought as he prepared for an early night. *I only hope he doesn't drink himself to death before then.*

Rounding up the Monday morning news meeting, McAllister told them all that Don would be off for a while longer.

Joanne said, "We miss him."

"I know he's upset by Mrs. Smart . . . I mean we all are, but . . ." Rob was floundering, not knowing how to put his gut feeling that there was more going on than he, as the resident know-it-all, knew.

"How will I know which team to photograph?" Hector asked. "Mr. McLeod always knows who'll win." As usual he was ignored.

"I doubt if Don McLeod has had a holiday from the *Gazette*, ever," McAllister told them. "So let's just see this as a long over-due holiday." The meeting had been businesslike, none of the usual banter, and over earlier than usual. He looked around. "Anything else? No? Okay, we'll check where we're at tomorrow morning."

He was not in his private office more than five minutes when his phone rang.

"Thanks Betsy, send him up."

When Detective Inspector Dunne came in and had shut the door, McAllister saw the detective's face and wondered if he should pour them both a dram. No, not yet eleven. Too early on a workday.

"I've come informally, more as a courtesy." DI Dunne perched on the visitor's chair, a chair deliberately chosen by McAllister to make meetings as short as possible. "I value our relationship with the press . . ."

"Spit it out, man."

"Donal McLeod has been arrested for the murder of Mrs. Smart."

"Never." The word came out like a cannon shot, and McAllister jerked back with the recoil. "You *can't* believe he did it."

"The Procurator Fiscal believes we have enough evidence to charge him with murder in the first degree."

McAllister caught the implication in the policeman's words. "Thank God hanging has been abolished."

DI Dunne said nothing, just stared at the floor.

"You said the fiscal says he has enough evidence—how about you?" McAllister was pointing his finger directly at the policeman's heart. "Do *you* believe Don capable of murder?"

"I believe everyone is capable of murder under the right circumstances. I believe the evidence against Don McLeod is strong. But cold-blooded premeditated murder? A careful, accurate stab with a knife? Let's just say I am not entirely convinced."

"What evidence do you have?"

"McAllister, as I said, this visit is informal, to let you know one of your employees is charged and . . ." Dunne was struggling with how much he should tell.

McAllister watched the struggle play out in the detective's hands, not his face. *He'd be no good at poker,* was his irrelevant thought.

"Sergeant Major Smart is well regarded in this town," DI Dunne started.

McAllister knew what that meant; it meant he had all the right people, including the Chief Constable and the Provost and all the ex-servicemen in the British Legion, on his side. He knew the *Highland Gazette* had ruffled feathers and rattled bones, especially recently, but to believe Don McLeod killed Mrs. Smart, that made no sense.

"I want this to go no further for now—although it will come out eventually . . ."

McAllister nodded.

"The sergeant major has made a statement saying Don McLeod had a close friendship with his late wife going back decades."

"Friendship?"

"Aye." He was unable to use any other word. A man in his mid-forties, the idea of people in or near their sixties being lovers was unthinkable. "Maybe there was more to it when they were young. They spent every Sunday evening together for years . . ." He hesitated. To share the content of a witness's accusations could cost him his job, but he trusted McAllister and valued his intelligence.

DI Dunne had heard the ramblings of the sergeant major with great distaste. The retired soldier had constantly reminded everyone in the police station of his powerful friends.

"Sergeant Major Smart says that Don McLeod is a known gambler, about to retire . . ."

"Really? I never knew that." McAllister believed Don would

retire when the clansmen were resurrected from their graves in Culloden.

"And that, having prior knowledge of her will, he plotted to kill Mrs. Smart in order to benefit."

"Plotted?"

"With Jenny or Jimmy McPhee—or both."

"Can any of this be proven?"

"Jenny and Jimmy McPhee have firm alibis—almost all the public bar, plus the landlord, in the hotel in Muir of Ord swear the McPhees were there all evening. Mr. McLeod has no one to vouch for him, and he admits she left his house minutes before her death. Also, her leaving a valuable estate to him—the fiscal thinks that shows motive."

"That proves nothing." McAllister sighed and reached for his cigarettes.

"You'll find out eventually, so . . ." The inspector knew he was about to break so many rules he would be back in uniform as a lowly constable if found out. "The knife. We've recovered it. It was hidden in a crevice in the courtyard wall outside Don McLeod's house."

"He wouldn't be so stupid!"

"He's admitted it's his knife—an old filleting knife he says belonged to his father. But it's sharp and clean and . . ." *And still had traces of blood on it.*

McAllister stood. He needed to pace. With the inspector there, there was little space. He pored a dram without offering the policeman one. He downed it in one, then went back to his chair. Elbows on the desk, head in his hands, he said, "None of this makes sense. Don cared for Mrs. Smart . . . greatly." He was unable to say the "love" word.

"He also admitted he was drunk that night. Add all these things together and the fiscal sees a good case."

"What about you?" McAllister was not hearing certainty in DI Dunne's voice, but the inspector only shrugged. "Will you pursue this further? Try to find the real killer?"

"Ah well. You know how this operates." They both paused to consider Dunne's words, both knowing indeed how the system operated. "Being the lead detective and a person having been charged, all I can say is, a cold-blooded killer who knew what he was about did this." That it could be a she never entered his mind. "If anyone should show me good reason to investigate further, I would be duty bound to do so." The policeman had resumed formal policeman speak, then his voice dropped an octave, went softly confidential, and McAllister was reminded of the story that Detective Inspector Dunne had been destined for the Church before the war changed his plans. "Don's not helping himself."

"What does he say?"

"That's it, he's saying nothing, and the sergeant major's shouts are loud."

DI Dunne knew he had said more than was needed. He stood. "I'll bid you good morning, Mr. McAllister. I'll see myself out." He said this partly as a formality and partly because, seeing McAllister's face, he doubted the editor could move from his chair.

Once alone, move from his chair McAllister did—straight to the decanter. He took the Talisker he saved for serious occasions and poured a healthy dram. Still standing, he gulped it down. He poured another, and took it to his desk. Five minutes later, and none the wiser, he picked up the phone and dialed.

"McAllister at the *Gazette* here. May I speak with Angus McLean?"

Five minutes after that, he walked into the newsroom where Rob and Joanne were working steadily at their typewriters. Even

Hector was picking away, two-fingered, listing the weights and the winners of a trout-fishing competition.

"The front page." McAllister had their attention. "I'll be doing the lead story." He leaned against the high table, feeling the effects of the whisky on an empty stomach, or so he told himself. "Don has been arrested for the murder of Mrs. Smart."

The babble of "no" and "never" and "that's not right" and "the polis are stupid"—this last from Hector—filled the room, echoing up to the high ceiling and back down to the high desk, permeating walls that had absorbed much in one hundred years, but nothing as scandalous as this.

"I know, I know"—McAllister held up his hand—"but we must cover the story. So be prepared for the onslaught of gossip and innuendo."

"And Don?" Joanne looked at him, her eyes huge and, McAllister noticed, startlingly green, as though emotion had washed out the bluish tint he normally saw and loved.

"Don McLeod did not kill Mrs. Smart," McAllister told them with total conviction. But the cold-blooded journalist part of him flashed the thought, *But nothing is certain except death itself.*

CHAPTER 5

The *Highland Gazette* was the news and everyone, right down to the printer's boy, hated that.

Rob was particularly annoyed at being waylaid on the steps outside the *Gazette* office by a gleeful rival from the Aberdeen daily broadsheet.

McAllister fended off phone calls from other newspapers with a brusque "No comment," but he gave a brief phone interview to a colleague from the Glasgow national, knowing it would be reported accurately.

The front page of the *Gazette* carried the full facts of Don's arrest and the charge. "We report this as we would any other case of this significance," McAllister told Rob, Joanne, Hector, and Beech.

They had worked early and late, pushed themselves until exhausted, and the newspaper had come out on time, with full content.

Friday morning, and the regular postmortem meeting was taking place. No one knew how to express the delayed-until-after-the-deadline shock. The hush around the table was dense. Like the crew of a sinking ship, they wanted the captain to announce the rescue plan.

"First, I'd like to thank all of you," McAllister started. "We managed to put together a newspaper minus two of our key staff. Thanks also to Mrs. Buchanan for looking after business so efficiently." He glanced across at Betsy, thankful she had had the tact not to sit in Mrs. Smart's usual place at the head of the table, not knowing Joanne had pre-empted Betsy Buchanan by taking the seat herself. "This saga is likely to go on for some time unless . . ."

"Until we can find who really killed Mrs. Smart." To Rob, Don was the consummate newspaper hack, accused of a crime he did not commit, destined to be proved innocent by the dashing young hero, himself. Only, Rob could find no way into the case. No one he knew, knew anything to help his investigations.

"Aye—until the real killer is found," McAllister agreed, but the exhaustion in his voice, the slump of his body, his lighting one cigarette from the butt of the previous one did not inspire confidence.

"McAllister, how could Don be charged . . . I mean, what evidence . . ." Joanne was stumbling over her words, her brain refusing to contemplate.

"All the evidence is circumstantial—but you never know." He saw the faces of his staff, each in their own way expressing their horror that Don might be found guilty. He started to cough to cover his emotions. "Let's start early on next week's edition."

The mumbles of *Fine* and *Sure* and *No problem* were all anyone could muster. But work—a refuge from thinking about Don McLeod, locked up, awaiting trial and the judgment of fifteen of his peers—saved them.

As Friday was normally a slow day on the *Gazette*, it was Joanne's library day. Today, it felt like an escape to an oasis of tranquillity. In order to borrow two books of fiction, two books of nonfiction had to be checked out. She thought the system patronizing, but because she was forced to, she had discovered travel books, which she would share with her girls, especially those with pictures.

The books were heavy. Joanne had left her bag in the office and was attempting to wrap her coat around to protect them from the intermittent drizzle that had been falling for the past three days, making the cobbled surface of the steep brae of Castle Wynd treacherous.

"Careful there."

From a step above, she was level with and much too close to the man she had almost collided with. From this step, she could see directly into his hazel eyes, see his even white teeth in an open, I-know-I-am-a-good-looking-man grin. She thought she felt his breath on her cheek, but perhaps that was wishful thinking. His other attributes, good haircut, good teeth, good but unostentatious tweed jacket and cavalry twill trousers in a shade of brown that spoke quality, made him instantly recognizable as not Scottish—or at least not Scottish of the class that she belonged to.

"I'm so sorry, I was in a right dwam." She knew she was blushing and hated it.

Again the stranger's grin made her feel off balance.

"My mother used to say that."

"Oh really?"

"She used to say 'a right dwam,' usually referring to me when I was lost in a book—like you." He pointed to her finds from the library.

She couldn't quite place his accent. "You're not from here," was all Joanne could think to say, knowing that to mistake a Canadian for an American was as terrible as calling a Scotsman English.

"No. But my bones are from hereabouts. I'm Neil Stewart." He held out his hand, then laughed. "Sorry, I can see you're laden. Would you like help with those?"

"Thanks, but I'm not going far. I work down the street at the

Highland Gazette." This was said with obvious pride, and she was delighted when he whistled in appreciation.

"A journalist, eh? I was a journalist before becoming an academic. Started at my hometown newspaper in Nova Scotia; now I live in Ottawa." He glanced up at the Church Street clock tower. "Have you time for a cup of tea? I'd love to pick your brains about the town."

"I'd love to. But I'm late and it's crazy in the office right now . . . why don't you call me at the *Gazette?*"

"I'll do that." Again his smile. "So, what do I call you?"

She saw him glance at her wedding ring.

"I'm Joanne Ross." It was suddenly important to her to state the facts. "I hate the *Mrs. Ross* bit—I *was* married, I'm now separated, and I want to be known as *me.*" Even saying the words felt daring.

"Pleased to meet you, 'Me.'"

It was a silly joke, and she was glad of it. Again he offered his hand. Clutching her books in the crook of her elbow, she took it. "Pleased to meet you too." She smiled back. "Sorry, but I must get back to work."

"Can we meet again?"

Yes. Yes please, she was thinking. "Call me at the *Gazette* office," she said, and hurried off, anxious to hide her embarrassment.

Did I really do that? Ask him to call me? Joanne was amazed at herself. *Anyhow, I don't suppose he will.*

Neil Stewart had worked and planned and saved for this journey for seven years. He had arrived in Scotland two months ago and had spent the time in Edinburgh, mostly in the National Library. But the focus of his journey was the Highlands.

Expecting Scotland to be like the stories that permeated his childhood—stories from school, from books, stories told by his émigrée mother—was, he knew, unrealistic. But from the moment his train had reached the lowland hills to its steady climb up and across the faultline of mountains, his enchantment with the highland scenery grew and grew. He felt, right to his bones, the visceral pleasure of a prodigal homecoming, knowing that passing burns, rivers, crags, glens, were as much a part of him as that other indelible mark of a true Scot—freckles.

And from the moment he arrived in the Highlands town, stepping off the train and crossing the station square with its statue of an unknown soldier from a forgotten war and seeing the stone terraces lining the wide street, Union Street, aware of the air and the harsh light and the faces and walk and dress of the passersby, familiar yet poorer than he had imagined, he felt he belonged here, because that was why he had come—to belong.

"Where to?" Even the accent of the taxi driver was familiar. It was his mother's intonation, cadence, the way the *wh* in "where" was pronounced as softly as a whiff of wind.

"Seventy-three Crown Terrace, please."

"You'll be staying wi' Mrs. Wilkie then."

It wasn't a question, it was a statement. The way the man said it, as though he was announcing the Apocalypse, did not fill Neil with confidence.

"So where are you from?"

"Canada." He wanted to say, *From here.*

His name—Neil Stewart—came from here in the Highlands. He knew his late mother, Chrissie, was born in Sutherland but not where. She had always been reluctant to talk of the details of her past. His dark sandy hair, his hazel eyes, and his freckles were marks of a Highland man and although he did not know it, having been born and raised after the diaspora of Scots to Nova Scotia, he had the trait of those raised in a time warp; they did not recognize that their homeland had changed and moved on. *Brigadoon* was Scotland to many of them.

The journey was short. The taxi driver pulled into a semicircular driveway and stopped in front of a glassed-in porch sheltering a double door painted a shade of brown reminiscent of a medical sample.

The guesthouse was a large Victorian edifice with a lawn, herbaceous borders, and not one ounce of warmth showing in the shrubs or the curtains or the paint. It seemed that all the life had been drained from it in its transformation from family home to lodging house. Respectability dictated that net curtains shroud every window; convenience meant the removal of trees so all that remained were churchyard cypress evergreens.

Neil took his suitcase, asked the fare, paid, and added a tip.

"Here's yer change, sir," the man said.

"It's for you."

"I don't need a tip. Sir."

Neil saw the friendly face turn cold, registered that the man was offended. "I'm sorry, I . . ."

The driver slammed the door of the taxi and was off before Neil could finish the apology. There was a note attached to the door. *Please enter and ring bell.* It made no sense, but after ringing the doorbell a few times, Neil went inside, found a small brass handbell on a table, and rang it. As he waited he read the framed list of all things disallowed. Not a propitious start.

Down the green linoleum-lined hallway came a tall grey woman with grey hair, grey dress, and grey demeanor.

"Mrs. Wilkie?"

"Mr. Stewart." Her inflection was as grey as the rest of her, and Neil felt another of his illusions shatter. *Where is the warm Highland welcome?*

Perhaps comfort is not respectable either, Neil thought after ten days of chill and damp and excruciatingly bad breakfasts where even the porridge was horrible, lumpy, and occasionally burnt. Dinners were worse; every meat, fowl, or vegetable was boiled into submission and coated with a grey sludge he presumed was gravy.

Only his research gave him joy. One half of his book, set in the Canadian diaspora, was written. Now he needed to finish researching the Scottish part.

The public library became his refuge. It became a habit to start the day with the newspapers. First he would read the *Scotsman,* the biweekly *Courier,* and finally the weekly *Highland Gazette.* He admired the *Gazette.* Unlike the newspaper he had worked on in Halifax, he saw it as a paper for the times. *They know it is 1957,* was his judgment, *and they must be doing it tough reporting the murder of one of their own.*

As he was folding up the *Gazette,* he thought, *Why not? It would help me financially and maybe give me access to their archives.*

Joanne was struggling to proof the pages the printers had set and sent upstairs for approval. "I'll never get the hang of reading upside-down!" she wailed. "And I can't read back to front."

"I can."

It was a scene from a romantic comedy except Joanne was a brunette, not a blonde. And the stranger in the doorway was not the proverbial American abroad but Canadian.

"Hello again." He smiled at Joanne. "I'm Neil Stewart. We bumped into each other at the library. Remember?"

"Aye. I mean—yes. Hello." She blushed. Then was furious with herself—*The sight of a good-looking, interesting stranger and you're behaving like a schoolgirl fainting over Elvis—grow up, Joanne.*

Neil looked across at McAllister, sensing he was the man in charge. "I was wondering if there is any part-time work available."

Again that North American grin demonstrated his confidence with strangers.

"I'm John McAllister, the editor." McAllister rose to shake hands. "Are you a journalist?"

"I was on a newspaper in Nova Scotia for ten years. Worked on everything—reporting, subediting, and occasional staff photographer."

"When can you start?"

Neil stared at McAllister, then laughed. "That's it? No interview? No references?"

"It'll take half a day to find out if you're for real." McAllister gave his trademark one-eyebrow-raised-lips-tight-shut grin and pushed a pile of copy across the desk. "Right you are, Neil, start subbing these."

The stranger took in the ancient Underwood, wishing for a moment he had his brand-spanking-new Olivetti, rolled in a fresh piece of paper, then looked up. He saw three faces that had either survived a particularly rough sea crossing or else were in shock. He saw that the phone was off the hook—in a newspaper office. He didn't ask; he'd read the news. He started to type. The others did the same.

The sound of the hooter from the iron foundry bounced off the ring of hills surrounding the town. Most businesses took that as a signal for the lunch break. Most small shops and businesses closed at one o'clock, opening again at two. Most people went home for the midday meal. Others, Joanne among them, brought a flask of tea and sandwiches. She liked having her break alone; it was one of the few times she could enjoy solitude—a rare treat for a working mother.

But she was intrigued; she had never met a man who was not Scottish, except for the Frenchmen who came to town every autumn selling onions tied into long string. Onion Johnnies was their nickname. But as they spoke little English or Scottish, they didn't count. She had never met a man who seemed so at ease with a woman. And she was vulnerable to charm.

"What are you doing for dinner, em, lunch? Sorry, I don't know what you call it in Canada."

"My mother called it dinner. But in smart academic circles we call it lunch and right now I usually call it a sandwich—and not a very nice one at that."

"Do you fancy a coffee and a decent sandwich? There's a great place on Castle Street."

As soon as she'd asked, Joanne looked away, embarrassed by how forward the questions must seem. Neil hadn't noticed.

This is the second time I've asked him for something. He'll think I'm a loose woman. No, I can pass it off as Highland hospitality.

"Really? Take me there this instant. I've been searching for good coffee ever since I arrived."

To Joanne, even walking down the flight of steps and through the car park and across busy Castle Street felt daring. *What if anyone sees us?* she was thinking. *So what?* She told herself. *He's a colleague.* But among her first impressions of Neil Stewart was a sense of irresistible danger.

The small café was narrow and long and a favorite amongst staff from the offices in the town. The worst of the lunchtime rush over, a black-aproned waiter, with what was left of his hair combed across his pink skull looking like it had been stuck there with glue, gestured to a window table before whipping out his notepad, to which was tied a pencil on a grubby length of string.

"Can you make an espresso?" Neil asked.

"We certainly *can*." The man straightened his back and talking down his nose said, "And we *do*."

"A double then." When he had gone, Neil leaned across the table and in a loud whisper said, "I think I offended him."

"You did," Joanne agreed. "So if you're wanting a decent coffee from now on you'd better tell him how good it is."

When the coffees arrived, Neil sipped his and declared loudly, "This coffee is exceptional."

"I know." Their waiter, who was also part owner of the café, replied, honor satisfied.

Waiting for the toasted sandwiches, Neil said, "Tell me about working on the *Gazette*."

"Well . . ." Joanne began. To her frustration, tears welled up.

"Idiot!" He smacked his forehead. "I'm so sorry. I read the news about your colleagues."

"Mrs. Smart's death was horrible. Don McLeod's arrest doesn't feel real. He would never have—" She shook her head as though tossing her hair around would dislodge the memories. "I walk into the office and expect to see Mrs. Smart sitting at the head of the table, pen in hand, ready to take notes . . ."

"After my mother died, I kept seeing her out the corner of my eye." Neil was staring out the window, not seeing the passersby. "More than once I thought I saw her disappearing round a corner, shopping bag in her hand. Or I would imagine I could hear her climbing the stairs to bed—after she had checked the front and back doors twice to see if they were locked—something she said she never did when she lived in Scotland." He leaned forward slightly. "And something I've never told anyone—I still talk to her, especially at night. I tell her about my day, I tell her of my achievements, knowing how proud it would make her. Some would think I'm mad, but it's comforting."

It was this more than anything that made Joanne warm to this stranger, drop her guard; the way he confided in her, the way he told her the small things in his life; it made him vulnerable, human, more of a man. He was intelligent, an attribute she admired, and knowledgeable. It was what attracted her to McAllister, but with Neil she did not feel intimidated.

"Heavens, we'd better get back." Joanne was surprised that the time had passed so quickly. She put a half a crown on the table. Neil pushed it back and laid a ten-shilling note down. The waiter appeared and took Neil's money, saving the embarrassment of a discussion. "Thanks." Joanne smiled.

"You're welcome," Neil replied.

She hurried across the road. For a woman who went to church on Sundays, who was reared on the Ten Commandments, who had known no one but her husband, even being alone in the company of an unknown single male was not the done thing; for a woman from this town, this society, it was verging on sin—and she knew it.

His long strides easily kept up with hers. They climbed the steps back to the office, back to the deadline, back to sorrow and a difficult edition of the *Highland Gazette,* reporting the tragedy and naming one of their own as perhaps a murderer.

Chapter 6

Mortimer Beauchamp Carlyle had instructed Angus McLean to find the best Queen's Counsel available for the defense. Who was to pay for this, Mr. McLean did not know, nor did he ask. It would be an expensive legal bill, that he did know. Along with a QC, an assistant advocate would have to come north as part of the team.

The trial was ten weeks away. Then the full panoply of the High Court of the Judiciary would convene at the trial of Donal Dewar McLeod for the murder of Mrs. Archibald Smart, née Mackenzie. The lack of cooperation from the accused journalist made Angus McLean believe the likelihood of a guilty verdict being passed.

As promised, he telephoned the Procurator Fiscal to ask permission for McAllister to visit Don McLeod.

"Mr. McLeod has no close relatives. Mr. McAllister is a friend as well as a colleague . . ." Angus had told the fiscal, whom he knew well, the legal fraternity of the town being small and what might be described as incestuous—the families having intermarried for generations.

A half-hour visit granted, he next phoned McAllister, hoping that he could persuade Don McLeod to help in his own defense.

The only good thing about the prison, although the neighbors would dispute this, was the location, a short walk from the middle of town and a short drive from the courts.

McAllister had gone through the red stone arch of the main prison gate before and again felt a cerebral drop in spirit and, he fancied, a physical drop in the temperature of the mid-autumn midafternoon.

"Mr. McLeod is waiting in the visitors' room." The lilt in the guard's Scottish English placed his antecedents as west coast, or perhaps Western Isles. McAllister could never tell the difference.

The guard had left them alone with an ashtray. McAllister knew this was against regulations, but he had caught the murmur in Gaelic between them.

"I'm right outside the door," the guard said, "but I have to leave it open."

"How are you? I've brought cigarettes." McAllister rushed his words, the sight of the sunken eyes and the deep lines etched into his deputy's forehead, as if drawn in printer's ink, disconcerting him, making him remember that Don *was* past retirement age, although never before had seemed more than sixty.

"Whisky?" Don asked.

"Not allowed."

"Aye, that'll be right."

They lit up.

"We're getting a paper out," McAllister started, "it's adequate . . ."

"Aye, I saw it." Don was deep in a cloud of smoke and looking at the faint light from a window set so high prisoners could see the sky but not have the joy of a view.

"I want to help but I can't help unless you help me first." McAllister knew there was no room for fancy talk with Don.

"I didn't kill her."

"I know that. So I have to find who did."

"Her husband."

"Why? And why now?"

Don shrugged.

"Come on, man." McAllister was exasperated. "This is serious."

"You listen to me, McAllister. I will never say anything that will blacken the reputation of . . ." He couldn't bring himself to say her name. "She married Archie Smart in India and soon found out he was only interested in her money. He treated her like dirt their whole marriage. She came back to the Highlands to get away from him. He stayed on in India with his regiment, only returning after his accident climbing out of a whorehouse window. And it wasn't girls he was visiting. His smashed legs went bad and by the time the ship docked in Southampton, they couldn't be saved. He survived the amputation, more's the pity. Joyce nursed him until he could get about, with him treating her like his slave. Then her father, Lieutenant Colonel Ian Mackenzie, just before he died, came up with the idea of employing a Gurkha from his regiment to look after Archie Smart."

Don took another cigarette, striking a match with his thumbnail—a prison gesture—then McAllister remembered it was probably a legacy of Don's years in the merchant navy.

"So"—Don spoke through an outbreath of smoke—"much as I'd like to think Archie did it himself, it's no' possible. And Bahadur, he never killed her either. He was right fond of Joyce and he loved her father."

McAllister remembered the next puzzle in the life and death of Mrs. Smart. "Why did Mrs. Smart, Joyce, leave a bequest to Jenny McPhee?"

Don shrugged.

"Were they friends?"

"You'll have to ask Jenny that."

"For God's sake, Don, will you do nothing to help yourself?"

Don shrugged again and looked away. It was only the flash of despair that passed quickly over Don's face, to be just as quickly replaced by his usual nonchalance. Only that stopped McAllister from reaching over and giving him a good shaking.

"A knife was found in your courtyard."

"Aye, a filleting knife that's been there for years. Well used it is, too—that's why it's so sharp. Next to where the knife is kept is a tap, and a drain, and a slab o' marble. You canny fillet fish indoors. Of course no one will listen, no one believes me . . ."

"Time's up, Mr. McAllister." The guard stepped into the room.

"Can you think of anything that would help get you out of here?" McAllister asked.

"All those secrets." Don was staring at his fists, speaking to himself. He looked up as McAllister stood. "I'll no' betray her confidence, even though she's gone. But ask yourself why thon waste o' space o' a man was in such a hurry to bury her. Start there." The anger in Don's voice was quiet with the rage of someone who, although not guilty of this murder, might become guilty of another.

Probably a good idea to have him out of harm's way, thought McAllister, *for now.* He nodded a farewell.

Don nodded back, saying, "Next time, see if you canny sneak in a wee drop o' the hard stuff."

"I didn't hear that, Donnie McLeod," McAllister heard the guard say as he was walking away towards another guard waiting with another excessive bunch of keys.

Thinking Sunday might be a good day to track down the McPhees, McAllister was driving out of town, against the flow of the Sunday-church-kirk-chapel-meetinghouse traffic. Walking to worship, no matter the weather, was the custom. But the old ways were vanishing, more and more people driving. Heading down the road, the ferry his destination, and the eldest McPhee son's council house. No one was in.

"Do you know where Mr. Keith McPhee is?" he asked a lad with a runny nose and constant sniff who was sitting astride a bike, staring at him.

"What's it worth?"

"Thruppence."

"Gie me two cigarettes and I'll tell you."

Since he had started smoking at thirteen himself, there was not much McAllister could say, so he shook out two cigarettes, and the boy told him that Keith McPhee and his wife were in Glasgow. He grinned up at McAllister, then seeing the way the man's eyes narrowed, he added, "Mrs. McPhee, the auld one, and Jimmy McPhee, they've *been* staying here, but they left."

"Where did they go?" Two more cigarettes were held out.

The boy said, "Try Muir of Ord. The tinkies' camp."

Next time I'll bring Woodbines, my good cigarettes are wasted on boys, McAllister thought.

It was only when the stranger was getting into his car that the boy noticed the strange shape and smell of the cigarettes.

"Hey, what's this foreign rubbish?" he shouted. But the car had taken off to catch the ferry.

It took some time for McAllister to find the Travelers' camp, as there were few people around to give directions. When he arrived at the strung-out collection of vans, lorries, three caravans, and five traditional benders, it took some finding to get anyone who would point out Jimmy McPhee's caravan, which was slightly apart from the others, with two ponies hobbled nearby.

"I'd like to talk with your mother," McAllister said when Jimmy opened the caravan door.

"Aye, there's many a person who'd like a word with my mother—but few she'd give the time o' day to."

"I visited Don McLeod in prison yesterday."

"Oh, aye?" Jimmy took his time in considering the request before deciding to hand over the decision to his mother. "Ma won't be far along the road. We'll take your car."

Jimmy didn't say, but McAllister guessed that DI Dunne would be one of those wanting a word. The solicitor for Sergeant Major Smart another. The connection between Jenny and Mrs. Smart had not been known, and McAllister knew the matriarch of the Traveling clan wished it had stayed that way.

Jenny McPhee had endured the police interviews with patience, knowing that what she had to hide was her secret alone; Joyce Mackenzie had taken her part in the story to the grave.

Jenny McPhee had nothing against DI Dunne; what she had learned of him in the past had made her think of him favorably—or as favorably as a tinker could think of a policeman. He said he believed her when she had told him she was completely unaware of Joyce's intentions, and not particularly happy about the bequest. "To be left anything, far less her jewelry, is not what I wanted," she had told the inspector. "And no good will come of it, no good at all."

Jenny McPhee, like most tinkers and Highlanders, was superstitious. But it was not superstition that made her take to the road—it was a sense that the ripples from Joyce's death were spreading.

She had told her son Jimmy her destination. No one else. She was headed to a Travelers' camping place, one renowned for peace and beauty and fresh running water. She needed solitude, but her youngest son Geordie was with her; he was good with horses. Traveling alone was no longer an option; her knees hurt and her back was not what it once had been. But, as she did not want to be noticed, a single canvas-covered cart was less conspicuous, less likely to irritate the lorries belting northwest-ward on the main road to the farthest ends of Scotland.

Jenny McPhee had a fine sense of obligation. She owed Joyce Mackenzie her life and the life of her sons. Not life as in death, but life as in freedom; freedom to be a tinker woman and raise her family without living in terror of the welfare taking her children from her to abandon them in an institution "for their own good," with no word to the parents about where their offspring were, no hope of ever getting them back. That was what Joyce Mackenzie and her father had done for Jenny McPhee. What she had done in return had been so little, Jenny thought, and what that was she would never tell.

She hated the sergeant major and wanted him found guilty of killing Joyce, Mrs. Smart, whether he had done it or not. But with his disability, she accepted it was highly unlikely he had done it.

"No, lass," she muttered to herself as the cart negotiated the ups and downs and twists and elbows of the road, "leave it be. It'll only bring trouble."

Jenny was found eighteen miles farther up the road. The sight of McAllister did not please her.

"Jimmy." Her voice, like a sharp bark from an old vixen to her cubs, made McAllister jump.

Jimmy grinned at his mother. "I already told him you didney want to talk to anybody."

Jenny was seated at the front of the high dray, the horse's reins resting lightly in one hand. Geordie was walking behind leading the spare horse. The cart was the same as those used by the milkman or the coalman or the rag and bone collector; honest, sturdy, no decoration, little paint. But the tinkers' cart had a shallow roof made from tarpaulins slung over metal hoops high enough to sleep under or sit up, but not stand. String, rope, and baling twine weighted with river stones held the canvas down. A collection of pails and tin tubs were slung underneath and off the back. A misshapen bundle wrapped in blue wool that might contain anything from firewood to artificial limbs was secured to the back by a very substantial rope—a hangman's thickness of rope.

The whole catastrophe, including Jenny, was not picturesque, not a sight tourists would want to point their box Brownie at; there was little romantic about the lives of the Traveling people of the North.

"Don McLeod could be facing the rest of his life in prison." McAllister spoke in a flat voice, neither asking for help nor expecting any, only stating a fact, but knowing that to a Traveler this was worse than death.

"I'm making for the auld camp about a mile further up," Jenny said. "Meet you there."

McAllister and Jimmy reached the place where the river made a semicircular loop around a flat area strewn with gravel, driftwood, ferns, and flood debris. The sound of water running over rocks drew them over to the border of hazel and willow and birch. Large lichen-splattered boulders as large as giants' marbles lay along the edge of the riverbed, some in, some out of the water.

They lit up.

Standing smoking, looking at the light dancing through the gold red bronze lime last of the autumn leaves, McAllister's eye was drawn to the high hillside where pines stood in ranks determined to give neither shelter nor solace to flora or fauna.

Across the road the lower slopes of Ben Wyvis looked equally uninviting. The long slow incline of heather and bog cotton gave a lie to the name mountain; it looked like, and was a similar color to, a squat toad.

But the campsite between the desolations had grazing for horses, clusters of trees for shelter, and a well-blackened circle of stones—the site of centuries of campfires. More than that, the place had the calm of a great cathedral.

As they waited for Jenny to catch up, they did not speak much. They were not friends, but there was respect. They shared a highly developed sense of justice that did not necessarily involve the law, and had collaborated once in a highly criminal act of justice. McAllister knew he and Jimmy, and Jenny for that matter, would help Don, legally or otherwise.

When the horse and cart arrived, Jenny climbed down and handed McAllister a large blackened kettle.

"Make yerself useful." She nodded towards the sound of water.

The only other contribution McAllister could make was to fetch the whisky from the car.

With the horses settled, the tea made, the bread and cheese and onion handed around, and the gloaming giving way to the first stars, they were glad of the fire. With whisky warming inner parts and the dimming of the light, the conversation could begin.

"How's he holding up?" Jenny asked, not needing to say who "he" was.

"Asking for whisky."

"Speaking of which . . ." Jenny held out a tin mug. McAllister obliged.

"Another thing Don said was to ask myself why Mrs. Smart, Joyce, was buried in such haste." He did not expect an explanation, just throwing out a line.

"Archie Smart knows the answer to that. Ask him what he's hiding."

"Do you know?"

Like all of her clan, she avoided direct questions. "I'll no' break my word," she said, "but start at the beginning and poke around. After all, isn't that what you do for a living?"

He could feel but not see the grin in her voice.

"Joyce Smart, Mackenzie, was your friend." He was provoking her, wanting her to say more.

"Aye, she was. And her old father, bless him, he was a good man too."

"Not just to us," Jimmy joined in, "they were good to all us Traveler folk."

"The Mackenzie family did far more for us than we ever did for them." Jenny was emphatic on that point. "If it hadn't been for Joyce we'd have lost more children. But I sorely wish she hadn't put me in her will."

They were quiet for a moment, but McAllister had to ask. "Lost them?"

It took a long noisy silence—running water, wind in leaves, the seashore sound of pines, the night birds, the furtive deaths of small creatures at the mercy of larger small creatures, before Jenny could bring herself to start her story. She fixed her eyes on the distance or perhaps the Evening Star.

"When your child dies, you put them in the ground. You visit their grave, lay flowers, lucky white heather. You can talk to them, sing to them, you know they are there. But when your child is taken from you . . ." She left the sentence hanging.

It was not that she didn't know what to say, how to describe the years of searching, imagining what they looked like, how they had grown up. It was rather that, if expressed in words, it would lighten the blackness, cheapen the pain, and the lost boys needed her to hold onto that to keep them alive.

No, she thought, *no one can know. So there is no point in telling.*

She stood. She brushed off her skirt as though the gesture would banish the memories. "Be off with you, McAllister. I'm up with the dawn so I'm needing ma bed." But she knew she would not sleep well.

As the sound of the car disappeared over the hill, Jenny went to douse the campfire. But the bloodred embers cast their spell, and she found herself mesmerized, staring into the remains of the fire. She took an unlabeled flat bottle from the depths of her skirt pocket and poured another dram into the tin mug. Sipping the colorless liquor that tasted of heather and seaweed and pine, she looked up into the Milky Way. A shooting star in the northwest quadrant of the sky—over Assynt, she thought—fell earthward. She smiled.

"I promise," she told Joyce. "It may take a whiley, though. And lass, much as I appreciate you remembering me, I wish you hadn't let the world know."

Geordie saw and heard his mother muttering as she poked at the fire, the sparks flying heavenward to join those other glowing embers. He kept his distance. He had no idea why they had set out on a trip so late in the year, and he would never ask. She was his mother, but he too had a healthy fear of the legendary Jenny McPhee.

"Jimmy, I know you and Don go way back," McAllister started. He was concentrating on the road so fiercely that his knuckles gleamed white against the steering wheel. "Can you not tell me something, anything that might help set him free?"

"If I could I would."

"What did your mother mean when she said she owed Mrs. Smart—"

"Joyce Mackenzie. Use her real name." Jimmy's voice resembled the camp dogs growling at unknown night noises. "As for her and ma mother, that's their business."

It took another five minutes or so before McAllister, his mind overwhelmed by the story, could bring himself to ask his next question. "Your brothers? The ones who were taken?"

"Have you no' heard o' the bairns that were—and still are—stolen from tinker families?" Jimmy asked. "No, you and everybody else are no' concerned wi' the likes o' us."

McAllister's foot involuntarily lifted from the accelerator. The thought gave him the shivers.

"The welfare declares them neglected," Jimmy continued, "grabs them, and that's the last we see or hear of them."

Everything in McAllister made him want to stop the car, but he knew that the anonymity of the dark, of sitting side by side, not able to see faces, gestures, pain, made a story easier to tell.

"We're well liked, mostly, in the North West. People around Ullapool and Lochinver, and Sutherland, they treat us well. But there are some do-gooders working for the welfare who believe our bairns are better off in institutions, going to school, being sent to homes in Australia and Canada, having life on the road beaten out o' them, and worse."

Jimmy's voice seemed to be coming from far away; he had spent some time in one of those schools and had seen the evil that those caring men could inflict on small boys locked up in their care.

"What Joyce Mackenzie and the auld Colonel did was give us a wee but and ben on the estate. It was basic but much more than four walls and a roof; it was an address, and we bairns could go to school, and that kept the welfare away."

It was then that McAllister knew the magnitude of the debt Jenny felt to Joyce Mackenzie. A home, an address, the privacy of a cottage, no matter how basic, on a private estate, where the welfare would be loath to invite the wrath of a landowner, an old soldier, a family of the Highland gentry. But it still didn't explain the bequest. *It should have been the other way round,* he thought, *but perhaps it was friendship, pure and simple.*

"Drop me off at the Longman camp outside the town." Jimmy barked out the order. The memories of that time, at that institution, when he was twelve or so was not a place he wanted to revisit.

They continued along the firth into town. Their arrival started the camp dogs barking. Jimmy let out a roar that cleansed the memories and stopped the barking, except for one puppy that would not last long if it continued yelping.

Jimmy leaned in the car door before shutting it. "Talk to thon Beech character. He knows a thing or two—or at least his sister does."

On the drive home, McAllister considered Jimmy's suggestion; it threw up more questions than answers. But he would ask, knowing that with the prurience of a good journalist, he would not let this story go.

When he reached home, McAllister was surprised to find how late it was—nearly midnight. He took a book to bed but could not concentrate. He put it aside and tried to make sense of what he had discovered.

It was Joyce Mackenzie's father who had sheltered the Travelers, so why would *she* leave a bequest to Jenny? Perhaps it was no more than what it was—a gesture, a simple act of kindness; jewelry was not an item Archibald Smart needed, and there were no children, daughters, daughters-in-law to pass the jewelry on to. As far as McAllister knew, the line stopped with Joyce and her husband.

Children stolen from their parents he had vaguely heard of, and he did not doubt it happened. A wicked iniquitous practice, but what does it have to do with Mrs. Smart's death? He was drifting in and out of sleep, the bedside light still on; only when his book hit the floor did he reach out to turn it off.

Waking next morning to a tangle of sheets and eiderdown and the metallic taste of spent fear, he remembered only fractals of his nighttime visitation from marble angels and lost boys and drowned boys and gunshots at dawn and falling, endlessly falling, down the long flight of steps beneath the abbey wall.

As always, McAllister dismissed it as a side effect of too much reading and one too many whiskies.

CHAPTER 7

McAllister was exhausted; the Monday morning news meeting was a drudge rather than an adrenaline-fueled let's-get-a-good-paper-out delight, so he focused on composing the edition with the least possible fuss.

"Joanne, you're covering council business; anything important?"

"Problems with the town water supply from Loch Duntel-chaig—I've an interview at council chambers later."

"Good. Rob?"

"I'm covering the trial of the drunken driver who hit and killed a schoolgirl out west."

"Hector?"

"The usual."

"Neil? How're you managing?"

"I'm getting the hang of it," Neil replied. "I'm finding out that Canadian English is not Highland English."

Joanne laughed when he said this.

He's not that funny, McAllister thought as he watched Joanne watching Neil.

"I'd like to finalize my hours," Neil continued. "Monday, Tuesday, and Wednesday until paper the goes to bed; is that okay?"

"How long can we count on you?"

"A couple of months should see me finished with my research."

McAllister nodded. "Fine. Don McLeod will be back by

then." He sounded as though he was trying to convince himself of the truth of this. "I saw him on Saturday, he's . . . he asked me to sneak in some whisky next time."

The brightness of Joanne's laugh, the extra-wide grin from Rob, and Hec's "That's great" annoyed McAllister, though he was unable to think why. "This week's edition." He moved on, annoyed at his annoyance. "Neil, could you help Mrs. Buchanan? She's booking all sorts of advertising but has no idea how to draw up the layout."

"Sure. I'm happy to show her," Neil said. Betsy gave her signature smile, the one that reminded Joanne of her youngest daughter's doll's painted-on smile.

"Can I sit in?" Joanne asked. "I'd like to learn how to make up the dummy."

"If you're covering stories, plus helping cover Mrs. Smart's duties . . ." McAllister was aware how peevish he was sounding. "Just make sure you have the time." He turned to Betsy Buchanan. "Mrs. Buchanan, how are you managing?"

"I'm managing very well, Mr. McAllister." Betsy was booking in the ads, indeed increasing the advertising space. What neither she nor anyone else realized was, her paperwork was shambolic. In the case of some clients, nonexistent.

"Hector? Any problems?" McAllister asked out of duty, though he was nervous that the photographer might give him an answer that threw up tribulations needing the judgment of Solomon.

"It's hard without Mr. McLeod. He can always pick the winner in the football so I know who to photograph." His wee bright-face-bright-hair-bright-grin seemed on reduced wattage since Don's arrest. "Maybe I can get to visit him in the gaol for next week's away game. It's Thistle against Forres."

"You can't get a visitor's pass to talk about the Highland

League football," McAllister told him, ready to move on to serious matters.

"Why not?" Joanne asked. "It might do Don good to see Hector. Take his mind off . . ." She went pale. She was about to say, *Take his mind off a life sentence,* and was appalled at the thought.

"Hector always drove Don to distraction." Rob saw McAllister was considering the idea. "I could ask my father if he could arrange it."

"Do that." McAllister wanted to finish the meeting but knew, as editor, he had to rally his staff. "Last week was bad; it may not get better for a while. Remember, we are a bloody good newspaper and will continue to be, so ignore the stories in our daily rival. I will report, *and investigate"*—he was aware of every face looking closely at his—"Mrs. Smart's death, the accusations against Don, I will be covering those stories—and the trial. So, to give me time, I'm appointing Rob as acting deputy-editor."

Rob looked up from the playlist he was scribbling for his band's next gig. He nodded agreement but did not look as delighted as he would have been in happier times.

"Neil, you're the chief and only subeditor. Joanne, reporting duties as usual, but do you need help since you're also dealing with administration?"

"Beech has taken over chasing up the casual contributors, and Betsy is doing a good job. So I'm fine. But we really need a typist cum receptionist."

"See to it. I'll be in my office for an hour or so, then I'm unavailable. If you need anything, ask Rob."

When the editor had left, Neil sensed it was time to change the atmosphere. "So, Rob, tell me about this band of yours."

"It's brilliant," Hec answered, "you should hear them, all kinds of American rock 'n' roll stuff. Great for dancing."

Joanne smiled. She had seen Hector dancing, looking like an out-of-control puppet with three of the vital strings cut, including the one for his head.

"For once I agree with Hec," Rob said. "I'm singer and lead guitarist and we're pretty good—for around here. Do you play?"

"I play a pretty mean blues harp." Neil joined Rob in the spitting contest.

"A harp?" Hec snorted. "Only lassies play a harp."

"Idiot." Rob laughed. "Harp is short for harmonica, a mouth organ, a mouthie to you."

Joanne was glad of the explanation too, as she had had no idea what Neil meant.

"We're rehearsing this Saturday afternoon in the Scout Hall. Why don't you sit in?" Rob asked.

"I'd like that."

Rob left to cover the Sheriff Court proceedings, and Hector got on checking the names on his sports shots. Joanne typed up county council proceedings. Neil checked copy, occasionally querying a spelling, a name, an occasional point of geography, and the morning passed, the bones of the next edition falling into shape.

"I'm off," Hector announced just before midday. "I've printing to do so I'll see you tomorrow."

Joanne finished her work. She watched as Neil finished checking the last of the copy.

"How's the research going?" she asked. She was interested in everything about him, and the neutral topic of research might lead to the more personal questions she was dying to ask.

"It's going well," he replied. "Or at least it was." He stretched, flexing his fingers. "Boy, this old machine is tough on the hands and shoulders." They smiled. "My research." He leaned back in the high chair, a gesture characteristic of McAllister. "I knew what I wanted to know before I came to Scotland," Neil continued. "I've verified my ideas. But reading the old records in the library, a lot of new information has come up. Now the manuscript needs serious rearranging and editing."

"That sounds daunting."

"A little. It's more exciting than anything. I was concentrating on the nineteenth century but I'm now finding early-twentieth-century emigration equally fascinating." He grinned at her. "You don't want to hear me on my pet subject, I could drone on for hours, completely bore you."

"No, I find it really interesting." She looked at him thinking, *You could never bore me.*

"Tell you what, why don't we have a drink after work—no, sorry, no respectable women allowed in bars—a coffee, after work."

"Tonight is difficult . . ."

"Of course. Your children. Girls, aren't they?"

"Yes, Annie is ten, Jean nearly eight."

"Do you go to band practice?"

"Sometimes." *Liar,* she told herself, *you've never been before.*

"I'm looking forward to it. It should be fun."

"I'll see you there then. My girls are staying the night with their grandparents so we could have a drink afterwards." She made that up but knew the Rosses would love to have the girls stay the night.

Later, when thinking over the conversation, Joanne's thoughts were a confusion of *Why did I mention I'd be free for the night? Why did I? Why?* She reassured herself, *Seeing him with Rob and the band will be fine, then Rob will join us for a drink, we won't be alone.*

"I have to go shopping." She was panicking. She stood. "See you later."

She fled, not noticing him smiling at her subterfuge.

Up until breakfast next morning, Rob had been confident Don would be released. He was accustomed to his father being remote when involved in a complicated case. But the furrows on his father's forehead and the absentminded way Angus McLean backed his car out of the driveway, almost colliding with the coalman, terrifying the poor horse, made Rob reconsider. His father was not a man to panic.

Once at work, Rob finished an article on a local baker who insisted on prosecuting a child for stealing a sausage roll. He angled the story to expose the baker as the skinflint most knew him to be, without being libelous.

"This is for you, Neil." Rob put the finished copy into the sub's tray. "I'm away out for about an hour." He could have spoken to the moon for all the attention he got; Joanne and Neil were engrossed in a conversation about Labrador or Nova Scotia or other cold, cold places that held no interest whatsoever for Rob.

"Can I have a quick word with my father?" Rob asked the dragon cum secretary cum receptionist who guarded his father from clients who, her expression said, must have committed some unfortunate deed if they were in need of a solicitor.

"I will see if Mr. McLean is available."

A person more icy than Artic Canada, was how Rob always thought of the woman.

"What can I do for you?" his father asked when Rob came in and took the visitor's chair.

Rob knew not to waste his time. "Don McLeod. Is there anything I can do to help?"

Normally Angus McLean knew Rob only wanted reassurance that all was well, and his reply would be, no thank you, but thank you for asking. This time he said, "Perhaps you could help."

The solicitor had not been enthusiastic in his son's choice of career, would have preferred that his only child attend his old university before settling into a career in the law. McLean and McLean had been his dream. However, after nearly three years at the *Gazette*, he acknowledged his son was a talented reporter, excellent at ferreting out information.

"Don McLeod lives in a close near the Old High Church," he started.

Rob knew the place. "Opposite the stairs where Mrs. Smart was killed."

"Quite. According to the police, the neighbors neither saw nor heard anything that night. However, Mr. McLeod's next-door neighbor is a student nurse. I haven't been able to contact her. Apparently she works shifts. I'd like to know if she has any information that might help the defense, specifically if she knew of the whereabouts of the knife." He then went on to explain the significance of the knife, the one used to kill Mrs. Smart.

Rob felt the hair on his arms tingle when his father described the filleting knife. "Leave it with me," he said when his father finished.

"Thank you, Rob." Angus McLean turned back to his papers. "I must continue with this"—he tapped a document—"and I needn't tell you how essential it is we follow every lead, no matter how tenuous . . ."

As Rob stood to leave, his father, in a voice soft with the Highland sibilants, said, "Perhaps you and McAllister could . . . you know." He made a circular motion with his hand as though bringing an orchestra to attention.

Rob did know. He and McAllister had worked well together in the past, discovering information that the police had overlooked, or perhaps it was more a case of employing methods the police were not allowed to use. *But,* he thought as he walked back to work, *McAllister shuts off when I ask about Don McLeod—and Mrs. Smart. But I'll do as my father suggested, I'll investigate.*

That evening, as McAllister was on his way to dinner with the Beauchamp Carlyle siblings, he found himself passing the home of Mrs. Smart, or Joyce Mackenzie as he now thought of her.

He looked up at the high crow-step gables, the Ballachulish slates glistening in the light of a gibbous moon; the mansion looked like an apt setting for an Edgar Allan Poe poem.

"The date on the masthead gave me a real shock, only two months to Mr. McLeod's trial," Beech said as he and McAllister sat with a whisky by the drawing-room fire.

His sister, Rosemary, was in the kitchen finishing off dinner, glad to escape the tobacco fumes. "Tobacco destroys the taste buds," she told her brother, often.

Twenty minutes later, she summoned them. "Dinner is ready."

In the dining room, a long table that would sit sixteen comfortably was set at one end. A table candelabrum, as bright as a Halloween bonfire, set the numerous items of unfathomable silver serving dishes sitting polished on the sideboards aglistening.

An elderly woman came in with a tureen. Her hands trembled as she filled their bowls, but not a drop of soup was spilled. She had ignored Countess Sokolov, as she always called Rosemary, not *Mrs.* Sokolov as Rosemary requested, when told there was no need to get out the best china. So, the overelaborately decorated best china it was.

The soup was chicken, but the spices and herbs were nothing McAllister could identify. He shared his cock-a-leekie soup recipe and asked for her secrets. Rosemary Sokolov said she grew her own Asian herbs and told him her traumas of gardening in the Highland climate.

"I found Himalayan plants do best," she said, "and I've taken advice from Mr. Bahadur next door on tending the plants."

"Mr. Bahadur?"

"He looks after Sergeant Major Smart. He was in the Gurkha Rifles under the command of Colonel Ian Mackenzie, Joyce Mackenzie's father."

"Ah, I see," McAllister said, although he didn't completely.

All through dinner, good manners prevailed; the real reason behind the invitation assigned its time and place—the drawing room.

The drawing room, another large space, was at the front of the house with French doors opening onto the lawn. High stone walls hid the river, but there was always the sense that it was there, bearing the waters of Loch Ness to the sea. After serving her brother and McAllister with coffee, Rosemary settled into a deep armchair opposite the journalist. She was not looking forward to the "inquisition," as she thought of it.

"I caught up with Jenny McPhee on Sunday." McAllister went straight to the heart of the matter, sensing there was no need to prevaricate with the countess. "She told me about the boys taken from her by the welfare authorities and that Joyce Mackenzie and her father had helped her keep her other boys."

"Jenny would not have told you that without a good reason," Rosemary said. "She is a very private woman."

McAllister waited for her to elaborate. She said nothing. How the matter of stolen Traveler children was connected with the murder intrigued him, but Rosemary was as opaque as Jenny when it came to explanations.

"I am doing all I can to free Don McLeod," McAllister said, "and to find who killed Mrs. Smart. To do so, I have to ask questions that might not seem relevant."

"I prefer to call her Joyce Mackenzie," Beech interrupted.

"Joyce was proud of her name, proud of who her people were. And the sergeant major was never much of a husband."

"That is not our business, Mortimer."

Beech smiled, used to being chided by his elder sister. He looked at her—how she sat, her swanlike neck, her straight posture, her hands clasped on her lap, the impossibly correct portrait of a gentlewoman—knowing this appearance disguised a woman of steel. He thought of his sister as a warrior woman.

"Old Colonel Ian Mackenzie, Joyce's father, indeed most of the people of the Northwest, have a good relationship with the Traveling people." Beech continued the story, knowing his sister's reticence but also keenly aware that they must provide any information that might help Don McLeod. "Remote communities rely on them for news of neighbors, they buy their goods, use their labor; tinkers are good seasonal laborers and are excellent tinsmiths and can repair most things. Also, Jenny McPhee's first husband, a Stewart from Sutherland, had been in Mackenzie's regiment in World War One and was killed in France."

Rosemary took up the story. "Colonel Mackenzie came back to the estate in Assynt for a visit before being posted to India. Joyce was there and she, with her father's agreement, made crofthouses emptied by the Clearances available as winter quarters for Traveling families. They weren't much, apparently, four walls and a heather-thatched roof, but shelter nonetheless."

She was looking out into the night-dark sky but all she could see was their reflections in the window. "I knew Joyce Mackenzie when we were girls; our families were friends. I did not meet her again until I returned to Scotland in the mid-thirties and she was living alone in the house next door. We resumed our friendship. Joyce told me of local-authority welfare officers removing children from tinker families and putting them in institutions.

Some were adopted, others sent to the colonies, others . . ." Shaking her head, she gave a slight shudder as though a sudden draft had crossed over her shoulders.

"*'For their own good.'*" Beech quoted the expression governments, colonialists, conquerors used to justify their actions. "As though their lives locked up in those appalling places were an improvement on life on the road."

"With the Mackenzie estate giving them winter quarters, the children went to school. Keith McPhee, Jenny's eldest, did so well, he was the first Traveler known to go on to university. Most of the children receive a basic education as they are only in school for the winter, but it all helps." Rosemary Beauchamp Carlyle had spent most of her life helping others gain an education. It mattered to her.

"I have heard that tinkers are accused of stealing children," McAllister commented.

"Quite the opposite." Rosemary was firm in her reply. "Many an unwanted Highland or Island child has been taken in by them."

"Were you yourself involved in helping the Traveling families?" McAllister asked the siblings.

"No," Rosemary replied. "Over the years, Joyce told me about growing up as an only child on a remote estate in Sutherland. Her mother died when she was four, so no wonder she welcomed the company of the Traveler children."

"I know of some of the pipers," Beech said. "There are one or two first-class musicians amongst them and they keep alive the old tunes—and compose new ones. There is nothing I love better than taking to the road in my old jalopy and sitting by a campfire hearing the bagpipes played by a master like Sandy Stewart."

Since McAllister knew the "jalopy" in question was a Bentley, he thought it must be an incongruous sight to see it parked at a tinker camp. He moved on to his next query.

"I was wondering if maybe his man, the Nepali Gurkha, could Sergeant Major Smart have persuaded him . . . paid him to kill . . ."

"Never." Rosemary was firm. "Never. The Gurkha regimental motto is 'Better to die than be a coward,' and what is more cowardly than stabbing a defenseless woman. No, Bahadur is a good person. Colonel Mackenzie asked him to look after the sergeant major, but really it was to protect Joyce. The man has given up his homeland to help her. And . . . and this is only speculation on my part, I wouldn't be surprised if he returns to Nepal as soon as the will is executed."

"The police might want him here for the trial," McAllister pointed out. "Do you think I could to talk to him? I'm floundering here, desperate to find anything that might help Don."

Beech and his sister looked at each other. "I will ask," she said. "Now if you will excuse me . . ."

McAllister and Beech stood.

"Thank you for dinner," McAllister said.

"I'm sorry we can't help you more," she replied and walked from the room as though her feet were treading air.

He turned to Beech to thank him and said, "I will keep searching. There has to be a reason for someone to commit murder."

The evening's conversation had had an edge to it. McAllister had a sure and certain feeling that the Beauchamp Carlyle siblings knew much more but had not decided what, if anything, they would divulge.

"Leave it with me," Beech said as they shook hands. "I'll talk with my sister. Sometimes promises have to be broken."

McAllister was glad of the walk home. Leaving behind the

sheen of the river and the quiet sound of fast-running water, a sound just a note above silence, he tried to organize his thoughts. All he could think of were the questions not asked; not asked not because he was too polite; unasked because the questions were insensitive in such a setting as the Beauchamp Carlyle drawing room.

So he asked himself.

Did the brother and sister know about Joyce Mackenzie's relationship with Don? Did they know of the Sunday-evening trysts? *No knowing the answer to that.* Did they know why she was buried in such haste? *I should have asked.* He resolved to ask Beech when they were alone.

As he reached his garden gate, one other thought came to him. *Did Rosemary or her brother know that Don McLeod and Joyce Mackenzie knew each other before she set off for India?*

After he switched off his bedside light, the final thought that would accompany him in his dreams came.

Is Bahadur a first or surname in the Gurkha tradition? Or is it a title? And what does Mr. Bahadur know? In that moment between awake and asleep, McAllister convinced himself that the man knew a lot.

CHAPTER 8

Late on Friday morning Rob finally managed to talk to McAllister. He caught the editor coming up the stairs, a sheaf of what looked like accounts in his hand, and the look of a man about to read his own death warrant. "Can it wait?" he asked Rob.

Rob saw the state of McAllister's hair—it needed washing and cutting, he saw his shirt was unironed, his shoes shabby, and replied, "No, it can't wait."

McAllister sighed. "Right then, my office."

"Why don't I come round to your place later? I'll bring some pies, and we can have your famous soup."

"I haven't had time to make any."

"In that case, I'll bring the supper, you supply the tea." Before McAllister could object, Rob left and drove straight home to see what the housekeeper had left in their larder.

Two hours later, his mother's picnic basket balanced on the petrol tank of the motorbike, Rob drove across town to McAllister's house. He rang the bell, then let himself in, shouting, "Supper's up."

"In the kitchen."

Rob could smell the pine logs burning in the kitchen range as he walked down the unlit hall. McAllister pushed away the chaos of reports and accounts covering the kitchen table. He had stacked them into piles: dealt with, read, and undecipherable—by far the biggest pile. He gestured to them, saying, "My admiration for Mrs. Smart grows by the day."

Rob said nothing, but the thought hurt. He put the basket down, found the gadget to light the gas oven, put the steak and kidney pie in to reheat, and started to lay the table with the ease of a waiter in a high-class hotel.

McAllister watched, and only when Rob produced a bottle of wine did he find the energy to get to his feet and fetch glasses from the sideboard. It took a good half hour for them to eat, drink, clear the table, and get down to the point of Rob's visit.

"I was talking with my father . . ." Rob started.

McAllister lit a cigarette.

"He didn't say, but I get the feeling he hasn't found much to help with Don's defense."

"That makes two of us," McAllister said.

"So what I was thinking was this . . ." When he became intrigued by a story, Rob was never put off by anyone or anything—not McAllister, his father, nor his obsession with who was in the 1957 Top 20 music charts, nor his motorbike, not even the disintegration of his long-distance relationship with a girlfriend in Glasgow—got in the way of his pursuit of a scoop.

". . . I'll start by talking to the people who live in his court and the neighbors along that part of Church Street." Rob spoke as though McAllister was the subordinate, not him.

"The police have already . . ."

Rob ignored this. "Then I'll talk to the man who found the . . . Mrs. Smart."

"He works in the railways."

"Aye, I know. And, as I'm the only one who can get sense out of him, I'll talk to Hector."

"Hector?"

"He knew that Mrs. Smart and Don were . . . seeing each other." It was the only phrase Rob could think of; "having an affair," "courting," "lovers" seemed inappropriate terms for people of their age.

"Hector did?"

"Aye. What's more, his granny knows more about Don McLeod than anyone—though getting information out of her might be hard."

"You can always remind her that Don is about to be locked up with perverts and murderers for the rest of his natural life."

Rob was shocked by the callousness of McAllister's statement. He reached for the wine bottle but found it was empty.

"McAllister, despair is not going to help. We have to do what you taught me, what we've done in the past—with spectacular results, I might add—we will investigate. We can ask questions without scaring people." *Or at least I can,* he thought. "We can take shortcuts if we have to." *None immediately come to mind, but bending the law might be necessary to clear Don's name.* "So, what have you discovered so far?"

It took a moment for McAllister to consider where to start. Then habit kicked in. He reached for a blank sheet of paper, picked up the pencil he had been marking the accounts with, and wrote the heading, INTERVIEW. Underneath he wrote: *neighbors, man who found body, Hector, Granny Bain.*

There he stopped. "The will puzzled me . . ." he started.

"The will?" Rob had been waiting for this; he knew he would find out the contents sooner or later.

McAllister had forgotten or not realized that Rob knew only of Mrs. Smart's bequest to the *Highland Gazette.*

"Perhaps it is better if you don't let your father know I told you, but . . ." McAllister explained to Rob the bequest to Jenny, the bequest to Don, the leaving of the mansion in town to Sergeant Major Smart. He told Rob of Jenny's unhappiness at being left the inheritance, of the sergeant major's vow to fight the will, the Mackenzie family's sheltering the Traveling people, and Jenny's advice to *start at the beginning.* But he did not mention the stolen boys; that was Jenny McPhee's business.

Rob was fascinated by the whole saga, and when McAllister ended he commented, "Good luck to the sergeant major taking on my father in a legal stouch." He stretched out his legs, sighed, and said, "We'll need a load of luck, too. Mrs. Smart's will is certainly . . . provocative." It was the only word he could think of to describe such a strange list of bequests. "Though I can see Jenny McPhee in Mrs. Smart's pearl necklace, I can't see Don McLeod as the laird of an estate in Assynt." McAllister could almost see Rob's brain ticking in double time. "*Start at the beginning,* Jenny said. What beginning?"

"I'm not sure. Mrs. Smart was a Mackenzie . . ."

"A well-known and well-liked family in Sutherland," Rob supplied.

McAllister had forgotten that for all his youth and obsession with the new era, Rob McLean was essentially a product of traditional Highland gentry, related to half the other gentry of the north.

"Joyce Mackenzie met Don in a convalescent home for those wounded in the Great War," McAllister started.

"Really?"

"In the early twenties, Don started work at the *Gazette,* and Joyce Mackenzie, as she was, went to India, where she married Archibald Smart." McAllister was writing down a timeline as he spoke. "In the early thirties she returned to the Highlands— alone. Her father dies, in India, shortly after her return, so Beech told me, and Mrs. Smart, as she then was, inherited the estate and the town house."

"And probably a pretty penny in the bank," Rob added.

"Mrs. Smart started working at the *Gazette* in 1937 . . ."

"Most unusual for someone of her social status—especially as there was no financial need," Rob commented.

"Archibald Smart was invalided out of the army in . . . Actually, I'll have to check that," McAllister said. "Rosemary Beauchamp Carlyle, Countess Sokolov, or Mrs. Sokolov, as she prefers to be called, was a neighbor and friend of Mrs. Smart. She had also returned from overseas, Shanghai, in 1936, and it seems she is the only person to have a close relationship with Mrs. Smart."

"Apart from Don."

"Aye. Apart from Don."

"Start at the beginning . . ." Rob considered the conundrum. "You know, for us Highlanders the beginning is always, 'Who are your people?'" Rob said this in perfect imitation of a Gaelic speaker speaking English. "So maybe Jenny meant it literally. Start with the births, deaths, marriages, who inherited what—isn't that the classic stuff of disputed wills and murders?"

McAllister had his elbow on the table and was rubbing his thick back hair with his hand, staring and not seeing.

Rob saw the weariness. "We'll talk again when we find out more." He stood, took his jacket off the back of the chair, zipped it up, saying, "McAllister, Neil is doing a great job, and Joanne; even Hector is helping, although I'm having to correct his English. We're using more pictures, and Beech is a handy proofreader—so leave the work to us. You concentrate on getting Don out of prison." *And spending the rest of his natural life locked up* was what he didn't need to say. "I'll see myself out."

Hearing the roar of the bike fade into the night, McAllister reached once more towards a stack of accounts awaiting his scrutiny, then pushed it back to join the chaos. "Not tonight," he muttered, and without washing up, he walked upstairs to bed and nightmares.

* * *

It took only one phone call but a long wait for Rob to talk to the man who had discovered Mrs. Smart's body. Someone had to go down to the railway marshaling yards to pass on the message, outside calls being forbidden to workers, but the man returned the call.

"I can meet you tomorrow, I work a half day on Saturday. One o'clock? The café at the bus station?" Mr. Kenneth Grant asked.

"Aye, that'll be grand." Rob echoed the man's accent, lapsing into the Highland way of expressing himself. This was a part of Scotland where the dialect was light, it was more a way of speaking English as though directly translated from the Gaelic; the circuitous roundabout way of the sentences had a good-mannered graciousness; "Would you be having a cup of tea?"

"No, I didn't see anyone," Mr. Grant told Rob when they met.

"No, I never heard anything," was his answer to the next question.

"No, I'd never seen her there before that night."

"No, I wouldn't know her from Adam. Or Eve."

"No. And how would *I* know what she was doing there?"

Rob was stumped for another question, but there was something—a hesitation, a glance into the distance, the way the man shifted in his seat—that had made Rob certain there was *something*.

"Sorry to keep pestering you"—Rob gave one of his "I'm just a young lad doing his job" looks—"but Mrs. Smart was one of us, and everyone at the *Gazette* is pretty shaken up."

"I can see that." Mr. Grant lit a cigarette but said no more.

When Rob spoke, it was not to Mr. Grant directly, more in the way of an observation. "You know, sometimes when I *think* things over, I don't get it. But when I'm driving my motorbike or dropping off to sleep, I remember some little thing, something that I'm not even sure I really saw . . ."

"Aye. I ken what you mean." They did not look at each other, just sipped their cold tea. "Sometimes, in the railway yards, 'specially when you're on the night shift, the light plays tricks, bouncing off wet rails, or a red lantern winking in the wind between carriages, stuff like that . . ."

"I can imagine."

"You know thon steps?"

"Aye." There was no need for Rob to ask "which steps?"

"I never saw nothing that night—excepting her body. But the churchyard up above . . . a right spooky place it is."

"Especially on a dreich night."

"Aye." Mr. Grant leaned forward, as though delivering a secret. "I thought I saw something—it was no more than a flicker moving through the tombstones. Gave me a right good fright."

"It would have scared the living daylights out of me"—Rob grinned—"'specially since some say there's a ghost from the time of the Blackfriars Abbey."

"Aye, I've heard that. I canny say more because that is all it was—a flicker out the corner o' ma eye. Not something I'd swear to on the Bible."

"Did you sense it was a person there?"

"Now don't be thinking I believe in ghosts." The man was so indignant at the suggestion that Rob understood he *was* wondering if he'd seen a ghost.

"I don't believe in ghosts either," Rob told him, "but I've seen and I've felt some things I can't explain."

"Aye, that's it. A wee bit o' movement, a glint o' something you canny be sure of, canny explain." He glanced at the clock, then stood. "I must be off."

Rob knew that Mr. Grant was uncomfortable; this was women's talk, not the sort of thing a grown-up former member of the Lovat Scouts decorated for bravery at Anzio should be talking about.

"Thank you for your time, Mr. Grant."

"Aye. Well. As long as you don't make a song and dance about it in the *Gazette* ..."

As they shook hands outside the café, in a haze of diesel fumes, to the noise of buses and a child's wailing, Rob knew the man *had* seen something. But what?

Tossing up whether to return to the *Gazette* office or continue his search, Rob found his feet had made the decision. Standing at the narrow passageway to the court where Don's tiny terrace, the end one of four, hid from passersby, he peered in. No one, nothing, moved.

He crossed Church Street, where the oldest buildings in town, mostly churches, were grouped together, to the top of the steps where Mrs. Smart had been found. At the back of the building on the right, a solid squat eighteenth-century affair with crow-stepped gable ends, there was a black iron gate set in a sandstone arch. It was a back entrance to the churchyard of the Old High Church, built on the site of, and probably using stones from, the ruins of the Abbey of the Black Friars. He looked, saw nothing remarkable, but noted that it was not locked.

He continued down the steps, trying to avoid staring at the back porch on his left, the back doorway into the church of a different denomination, trying not to picture Mrs. Smart's body abandoned not just to the dark loneliness of death, but to the horror of murder. Instead he examined the churchyard wall opposite, examining the moss, the lichen, the dark stains, not knowing what he was looking for, but knowing that as the tombstones were above, the bodies must be level with his eyes.

He found nothing.

Bereft of ideas, he retraced his steps. Almost at the top of the stairs he had a glimpse, a flash of moving white, an echo of the railwayman's sighting; "a flicker out the corner o' ma eye," he had said.

Rob grinned in relief when sense told him that what he had seen was not a ghost but someone ducking into the close leading to Don's house. He ran up the steps and across the street, startling a horse standing waiting as his master delivered coal.

"Hello," Rob called out. "Hello!" His voice echoed in the narrow passageway. He ran into the courtyard, almost tripping on the very old and very uneven cobblestones, and found himself staring at a vision in white who was staring back.

"I'm Rob McLean," he said.

"I know," she said, "I've seen you in thon band of yours."

"Really? Did you like us?"

"Loved it, couldn't stop dancing."

"You're a nurse."

"Obviously." She flicked her nurse's cap with middle finger and thumb and smiled. Rob was instantly smitten. He liked the way her mouth turned up at the corners. He liked the way her hazelnut-brown hair struggled to escape the band that held it tight to comply with uniform regulations. He liked her skin, pale from not enough sun or too many night shifts. Most of all he liked her eyes, an extraordinary bright blue, and ready for mischief.

"Do you fancy a coffee?" He came straight out with it, no fear of rejection, as so far, he had never been refused by any women, pretty or plain.

"I've just come off early shift and I have to change out of this." She pointed to her uniform, and Rob thought, *Pity, I love a nurse in uniform.* "And I can't ask you in as my parents would kill me if they found out I had a man in the house."

"How about the coffee bar next to the post office? I'll wait for you here."

"Five minutes." She wiggled her fingers in a "cheerio for now" and managed to put her whole body into the gesture—not that Rob noticed; all he could see was this sexy lass who obviously fancied him, something he was used to.

As he waited, Rob looked around. The terraced houses were narrow, two-storied, solid stone. The backs of other houses formed the courtyard. The passageway was the only entrance and exit. Rob went to Don's house and tried to peer through the window, but the lace curtains, with what looked like velvet curtains behind, closed off the sitting room from the courtyard and the world.

"No point peering in there. The man is in the gaol." The coalman, a sack on his back, glanced at Rob before going to one corner to open a door set in the wall, then pouring the coal in.

"Do you know him?"

"One o' the best men you could hope to meet," the man said. "And that's all I'm saying."

Out of the blackened face the man's eyes glinted, and Rob knew to ask no more. The glare lasted only a second, but Rob was relieved when a door opened and a lass's voice said, "Ready?" and the coalman left.

Before walking to the coffee bar, the nurse turned to Rob and said, "I'm Eilidh, by the way."

"I'm Rob—but you know that already." He considered whether to tell her, then decided yes. "Look, I'd better explain . . ."

"It's fine. I know you work at the *Gazette* with Mr. McLeod."

"Is there anything about me you don't know?"

"Well, I know who your father is, and I know where you

work, and I really like your music. And I hear you don't have a girlfriend." She said this, grinning, looking straight into Rob's eyes.

He laughed.

They took a booth in the café well away from the door. They talked about their favorite music, found they both liked films, discovered they both went to the dancing in the Caledonian Ballroom whenever they could—"which is not often enough," Eilidh told Rob, "but I broke up with my boyfriend as he's studying in Glasgow and I never see him, so I've no one to go with unless with a group of nurses." She was not consciously hinting, but he knew she would not refuse him should he ask, and he really fancied the idea.

"You must be really upset about Mr. McLeod." It was Eilidh who brought the conversation around.

"More than upset. We're all devastated."

She liked him all the more when she saw his eyes go bright.

"Were you at home that night?" Rob asked.

"I knew nothing about it until the next day when the police came to interview me."

"It must have been a shock."

She said nothing.

"Did you see—or hear . . . ?"

"Can we change the subject? This is so depressing."

He caught a glimpse of an impatient seventeen-year-old. "Sorry. It's just that Don McLeod is a friend and I'd like to help anyway I can." Rob had heard the church bells strike three in a pause between records on the jukebox. "And it's time I was off."

"Maybe one night we could catch the film at the Palace." She looked across at him and smiled. "They're showing the Marlon Brando. He reminds me of you."

"That's me, I have the bike and the jacket and the attitude— but a haystack for hair." She had it right; Rob fancied himself as a Highland Marlon.

"I'll check my shifts and give you a call." Eilidh had the reputation of being a pushy wee thing. Rob didn't notice.

"Great. And if you can think of anything at all that might
help Don McLeod . . . Sorry, I really have to run, I've got a band
rehearsal at four thirty."

Arrangement made, they left, Rob to fetch his motorbike to
drive to the Scout Hall, Eilidh to sleep.

She watched him as he strode up the street. She was watching his hair down to his leather jacket collar, his boots scruffy
but fab—her latest word picked up from the television—his
black trousers tighter than any she had seen, and thinking, *He's
a much better catch than the last one.* It was decided; Rob McLean
would be her new boyfriend.

CHAPTER 9

Joanne was trying to hurry her daughters. She had brought them home to collect their Sunday-best coats and shoes and hats, her in-laws having agreed that they could spend the night with them.

"Do we have to?" Annie asked for perhaps the seventh time. "Why can't we stay at home with you?" It was not that she wanted to stay at home, rather that she was suspicious of her mother's private life, which she thought her mother was not entitled to, or at least, not entitled to keep secret from her eldest daughter.

"You haven't had a Saturday night with Granny and Grand-dad for ages," Joanne pointed out. "Granddad is really looking forward to seeing you."

"But we were with them this morning." Annie would not relent until she discovered where, when, and with whom her mother was spending Saturday night. The afternoon she did not care about, only the hours after dark, which she considered to be the time when adults were naughty.

"Jean, your teddy, your nightie, your Sunday-school Bible, clean socks . . ."

"And my coloring-in books," her youngest daughter added.

"No wonder your bag is so heavy." Joanne smiled. "Right, out we go. Annie, I'm going to lock up whether you're ready or not."

She opened the front door, jangled her keys, and stepped out into the weak October sun valiantly trying to penetrate the blanket of clouds the color of dirty washing. She ignored Annie's wails, put the key in the door. The eldest girl rushed out, accidentally on purpose shoving her sister out of the way, and went ahead, out the garden gate, down the street, pretending to make her own way to her grandparents', pretending she wasn't with Joanne and her sister but always keeping them within sight, just in case.

"Thanks, Mum, thanks, Dad." Joanne smiled but the look from her mother-in-law made her realize she was overdoing it, making her mother-in-law look suspiciously at her, as though she guessed Joanne was up to no good.

"I'll see you all at church tomorrow." That should remind them that even though she had left their son, she was still a decent woman.

"What are you doing here?" Bill Ross had come in by the kitchen door and was staring at his wife, ignoring the fact that she saw far more of his parents than he did.

Joanne wasn't ready to look at him, but she had no choice. She switched on a smile. "Hello, Bill." She was momentarily upset by how well he was looking.

He looked at her, looked at his girls, said nothing, then turned to leave.

"You'll stay for a cup of tea." Granddad Ross was not asking.

"I'll put the kettle on." Granny Ross went into the kitchen.

"Say hello to your dad," Joanne told the girls.

"Hello, Dad," Jean said, then scuttled off to join her grandmother.

"Hello, Dad." Annie pitched her voice in exactly the tone she knew would make him want to hit her, knowing he wouldn't dare in front of her granddad, and not caring if later she would have to face the consequences.

"Annie," her mother said, "why don't you help Granny?"

Annie heard the plea and decided to relent; it would be her mother who paid for her defiance, not her.

Joanne looked across the room to where Bill, still standing, was trying to have a conversation with his father about football. He had his back half-turned, deliberately, Joanne thought, but all the same, she could see the change in him. His shirts were new. His heavy brown hair was cut too short for her liking; he was spruced up as though he was going somewhere, wearing a tie that she would never have chosen. And there was something about the set of his shoulders, strong ex-army, now builder's, shoulders—they seemed to have dropped an inch or so, no longer in their former position of a bull about to charge.

She liked the change in him and knew it was all Betsy's doing. To her surprise, instead of feeling guilty about their marriage, she thought, It wasn't his fault. We were wrong for each other. He looked across at her as though reading her thoughts. And she saw him, the father of her children, the boy who had been sent to war, who came home healthy in body, wounded to his soul. Her upbringing and education had taught her that forgiveness was the essential Christian message; she did not forgive him for the mental and physical abuse that she had endured throughout their marriage, but she felt sorry for him. And she no longer believed the abuse was her fault; no longer believed she had deserved it.

Granny Ross served tea to her husband, her son, and her daughter-in-law, then went back into the kitchen to be with the girls, leaving the door open so she could hear the conversation. But little was said.

"How's work?" Joanne asked her husband.

"Fine," Bill replied. He put the teacup back in the saucer, which rattled. He looked at the clock on the mantelpiece, as though it would magically ring out a reprieve. He put a finger under his shirt collar to ease the newness, the sharpness of the collar, and Joanne could read the thought, *Why am I still here, why am I not off to the football?*

Silence.

"How's life at the *Gazette?*" Granddad asked but immediately regretted his choice of words as he, like the entire county, was aware it was more a matter of death than life at the newspaper.

"We're managing as best we can," Joanne replied. "Just waiting for Mr. McLeod to be released." Her husband's snort of skepticism annoyed her. "Yes," she continued, "we're all working hard to keep the paper going. I'm even having to help Betsy Buchanan with the advertising and business side of things." She was well aware of what she was saying but doubted Granddad was.

"I have to be off." Bill stood, gave her his signature, I'm-the-boss-of-you stare, and finding it had not the usual effect, left without saying good-bye to his mother or his daughters, but taking time to slam the front door, the garden gate, and the door of his van.

For the rest of the weekend, and well into the week, until Granny Ross was able to find out more from a neighbor and notorious gossip, she puzzled over Joanne's reference to Betsy Buchanan, a woman Mrs. Ross senior was not particularly fond of, but respected, her status of war-widow absolving Betsy from the normal sobriquet of "flighty." When Granny Ross heard the rumors of her son's fling with Betsy, she didn't know what to think, as secretly she considered Betsy a much better match for her son than Joanne: Betsy was one of them; she came from the same housing estate; she had gone to the same school as Bill—not the academy, the technical high school; her father worked in the post office; she only went out to work because she had to—unlike her daughter-in-law.

It had taken many difficult years, but Mrs. Ross now had a

soft spot for Joanne. At first she thought Joanne was too *above herself*. She respected that Joanne's father was a minister in the Church of Scotland and better educated and in a different class from them. She did not like it that Joanne's parents had disowned her for becoming pregnant and having to marry in a hurry; she took it as a slight on her family. But, she reasoned, Joanne's father is a man of the cloth and has to stick by his principles, else who in his parish would respect him? She thought Joanne a good mother, although working when she didn't have to was not what good mothers did. She also knew her son beat his wife. Her opinion on that she never shared. Only her husband knew her deep shame.

And Mrs. Ross was not happy that once more her family was the subject of gossip, especially from the likes of Mrs. Ishbel Cruickshank, her informant and rival in the best flower display for their church stakes.

Earlier that morning, well before anyone else was in, Joanne had phoned her friend Chiara from the office.

"Are you going to band rehearsal this afternoon?"

For Chiara, who worked evenings in the family chip shop and café and was six months pregnant, half past eight on a Saturday morning was early.

"I'm only half awake and you're asking about band practice? What's the real reason for the phone call?" Chiara was yawning and muttering in Italian to someone—not her husband, Peter, who spoke only English and German and Polish and French; probably her aunt Lita.

"I thought I might go along to hear how the boys are improving."

"Joanne, it's me, your best friend . . ."

"Can't hide anything from you, can I? Neil Stewart is

going to sit in, he plays mouth organ, or 'blues harp,' as Rob calls it."

"In that case, I'll be there. I want to meet this mysterious stranger. Pity I'm pregnant, I might have taken him for one of my many lovers—me being Italian."

Joanne was still laughing when McAllister came in. One look at the tiredness exuding from every part of him stopped her.

"Sorry, that was Chiara . . ."

"Don't apologize. We could do with some good cheer in this office."

"How's Don doing?"

"Angus McLean is seeing him this morning, an official visit. And so far, we can only get permission for me to see Don." He was looking at her as though he wanted to say more but couldn't think what.

"Right, I'll see you on Monday morning."

With that he was gone, and Joanne knew there was nothing she could do to help McAllister. Unless he asked. She knew that, him being a clichéd strong silent Scotsman, he was unlikely, or unable, to ask. Perhaps, at another time, she might have confronted him, made him talk, share his pain. But she was distracted. Neil's voice, as he greeted Betsy Buchanan, and Betsy's answering twitter, were echoing up the stairwell.

"I'm only here for a minute," Neil told Joanne as he stood in the doorway, his hat pushed slightly back, an expensive-looking briefcase, the type solicitors usually carried, in one hand. "I'm off to the library archives. What time and where do we meet for the practice?"

"Four thirty," Rob answered as he squeezed past Neil. "The scout hut opposite the Royal Academy playing fields."

"I'm none the wiser," Neil said.

"Not one of the dirty-old-man brigade who watch hockey practice then." Rob laughed. "I'll pick you up."

"Good, here's my address in town." Neil scribbled on the back of a business card.

Rob looked at Neil's card with his address in Canada, his title, and qualifications. "Wow, an associate professor."

"Full professor if I get my PhD. Talking of which, I have work to do and must dash."

"I'll pick you up around quarter past four. You can hold my guitar for me."

When Neil was safely down the stairs, Joanne made a grab for the card. "Let me see that."

"Please!" Rob held the card high. "And why so interested? Because you fancy him?" He saw her blush, one of the many things he loved about his friend; an almost-middle-aged woman—to him, anyway—a mother of two, and she still blushed. "You do. You do. You fancy Neil." He said this in a sing-song eight-year-old-in-the-playground voice, elongating "Nee-il" into two syllables.

Joanne ignored him. She was looking at the card proclaiming Neil Stewart's title, the crow-black print, the weight of the stock, giving him a status she had not considered before now.

"He's . . ." *Far and away beyond me,* she was thinking.

"He's been to New York and he's here in town for only a wee while, and I intend to pick his brains about the big wide world beyond the Grampians." Rob was relieved to be having a cheerful conversation. "Maybe he'll know some new numbers for the band."

"I'm sure he will." Joanne was sure Neil knew a lot about many things, how to treat a woman included.

"Come on, let's sit outside for a minute, I can't hear myself think." Chiara led Joanne to the grassy bank outside the hall.

They sat on her coat, taking in the last of the diminishing sun. The sound of the band counting in the seventh—or was it the eighth—version of "Roll Over Beethoven," was faint but clear, sounding as though they were playing inside a box, which was all the Scout Hall was, a large wooden box with a tin roof.

"That Neil makes a big difference to their sound," Chiara said.

"He does," Joanne agreed.

"He's certainly enjoying himself, and enjoying the adoring looks from the audience."

It took Joanne a moment to realize Chiara was talking about her. "Chiara, I was only listening to the music." But she started to laugh when her friend pursed her lips and shook her head as if to say, *Who are you kidding?*

"He's gorgeous, he's talented, he's a mysterious stranger . . . fatal." When Chiara saw her friend's faraway eyes, a sensation that no good would come of any involvement with Neil Stewart made her shiver. The sun falling behind the hills, late-afternoon dampness gathering, added to her chill.

"Let's go back." Chiara stood. As they walked up the track to the door of the hall, she looked up at her much taller friend. "I hope you're not falling for Neil." There was recklessness in her friend that few saw—except Chiara. *Never been anywhere, or seen anything—sheltered upbringing, domineering father, an unlucky encounter with a man just back from the war who couldn't believe he was alive . . . * That was Chiara's explanation.

"Don't be silly," Joanne was too quick to protest. "He's great fun, good to be around, and he's leaving in two months."

"Aye. Just don't forget it."

Rehearsal came to a stop. It was obvious everyone had enjoyed themselves.

"I have to run," Chiara said. "I'm helping Papa out in the

chip shop. Let's hope the home team has won; there's nothing worse than a disgruntled lot of football supporters on a Saturday night."

Peter Kowalski, Chiara's husband, held open the door for his wife as solicitously as a prince escorting his princess. Joanne knew this was not because Chiara was pregnant—it was how Peter always treated his wife. And in another life, his life before the war, he was not a prince but a Polish count.

Rob and the drummer were packing up. Neil jumped down from the stage. "That's what I like about my part, all I have is this." He held up a harmonica, removed a box from his pocket, and stowed it away. "So, Mrs. Ross, plans for the evening?"

"I'm not sure . . ."

"Good, because I was wondering if we could find this mysterious Jenny McPhee. I'd really like to meet her. I've come to the part on my history where the input of a tinker—sorry, Traveler, would be invaluable. And I hear Mrs. McPhee is a legendary storyteller as well as singer."

"Well . . ." Joanne had a good idea where to find Jenny early on a Saturday night—if she was in town, that is, but she worried that if Clachnacuddin had been playing at home, and if they had lost, which was not unusual, the bar near the ferry, which the McPhees frequented, was not a good place to be.

"Where are you two off to?" Rob intervened.

"I was asking Joanne how I might meet Jenny McPhee," Neil replied.

"We could check the bar down the ferry," Rob suggested.

"I thought of that, but aren't Clach supporters a bit wild?" Joanne was nervous of drunk men, singly or en masse.

"Clach are playing away"—Rob laughed at her—"there is no way I'd be down there on a Saturday otherwise. Tell you what; why don't you two get the bus and I'll meet you there in say an hour? I want to get my guitar home." He stroked his Fender Stratocaster.

"Great." Joanne had to force a smile; the fantasy of Saturday night alone with Neil had all but vanished.

Despite there being no legal documents to prove it, there had always been rumors that the Ferry Inn was owned by Jenny McPhee or perhaps her son Jimmy. Whoever owned it was not big on interior decorating. On the outside, iron bars, spaced to give the solid unadorned building a resemblance to a prison, protected the windows. Inside, the floor was scattered with sawdust, and the brass rail around the foot of the bar was green, sticky and stained with what could have been corrosion but was most likely dried blood.

Rob had left his bike at home, borrowed his father's car, and parked it a good half mile nearer town.

"I'm meeting Joanne and Neil," he had said when his father asked where he was off to.

The possibility of the car disappearing from outside the Ferry Inn made him lie, indirectly, to his parents about his destination. Even in their circle, the Ferry Inn was synonymous with riots, stabbings, and the after-hours lock-up where patrons were supposedly guests of the publican, not men breaking the licensing laws.

Jenny McPhee had arrived back in town that afternoon, her thinking done. Or at least that was what she told Jimmy. Her real reason for coming back was that the damp was getting into her bones, and she knew autumn (which was really early winter in these parts) was coming to an end—not a good time to be on the open road.

She was in the tiny room at the back of the bar that served women and those too afraid to join the mêlée out front. Sitting

at a table, hat resplendent with grouse feathers, she was looking as though she was about to conduct a séance, waiting for
the spirits of the dead to come through, although the only spirit
likely to be found would be in a bottle of The Glenlivet.

"Here comes the young Pretender," Jenny announced when
Rob walked in, Neil and Joanne following behind.

Rob bowed. As he expected, Jenny told him, "Mine's a Glenlivet, a double."

"Let me get it," Neil offered, and Rob did not refuse. "And
you?"

"A shandy."

"Me too," Joanne said.

Seeing the look on Neil's face, Rob explained, "I'm driving."
He did not feel like having the usual discussion about why he
did not have a beer with whisky chaser habit.

"Mrs. McPhee," Neil started when they had settled around
the table, sitting close, as this was the only way to hear one
another over the noise from the public bar, "I'm interested in the
folk tales of the Traveling people."

"Are you now?" Jenny took a good draught of the dram,
smacking her lips in an exaggeration of an old crone, before sitting back and staring into the depths of Neil Stewart. Taking
her time, she asked the Highland greeting, "So tell me, Mr. Neil
Stewart, who are your people?"

Rob grinned and nudged Joanne before sitting back in his
chair to enjoy the contest. His family, the McLeans, were origi-
nally from the Isles, and he knew the "who are your people"
question. He knew that when and if Neil could establish his cre-
dentials, Jenny McPhee might, just might, consider telling him
whatever she thought Neil needed to know. Or not.

"My mother was from Sutherland. She died three years ago,"

Neil started. "She was a widow when she emigrated to Canada. I never knew my father." He did not tell Jenny that after his mother's death, he had had months of anger, fear, shock, even the edges of a light insanity that had blurred his thinking in the time after he had buried her in Canada, not her beloved Scotland, where she had always wanted to die. And that week, the week when she lay dying, she had told him.

I have tried to be a good mother, she had said, and he had assured her over and over that she was the best mother anyone could wish for. And after two or three of these conversations, and his constant reassurance, she told him, *I'm no' the woman who gave birth to you. You were someone else's bairn.*

I'm your son, you're my real mother, nothing else is important, he had assured her, stroking her hair, which was still dark and thick although no longer shining. He had no further explanation; she went into a coma. It was as though she had emptied her body and soul and had no more to tell.

As the years passed, he had admired his mother even more for bringing him to Canada, hiding the truth of his birth, saving him from a childhood of being a bastard child.

"So, you're a Stewart frae Sutherland." Jenny was staring intently at him as though memorizing the map of his face. "That's no' a load o' help, the place is hooching wi' Stewarts."

Rob did not know if Joanne or Neil noticed, but Jenny could speak a Scottish version of the Queen's English as well as most. So why was she slipping into the vernacular?

"She told me she was born in Strath Oykel."

"That's a long glen, that one."

"I have a picture of her, taken before she left Scotland."

The snapshot was about two and a half inches by three; the color less sepia than dirty ivory, and whoever had taken it did not have a steady hand. In the foreground was a smiling woman wearing a tightly belted coat and a head scarf. Not much of her hair was visible, and her smile showed no teeth, just a nervousness at having her picture taken.

"My mother told me this was taken before she left."

"Oh aye?" Jenny McPhee was doing her best to look disinterested but her body seemed stiff, on alert, waiting for a blow to strike.

"See, there in the background." Neil pointed to the faint smudge of an odd twin-peaked mountain lurking on the horizon. "That's the mountain called Suilven. The Sugar Loaf, she sometimes called it."

"Is it now?" Jenny handed him back the picture. She made no mention of the Travelers' caravans just discernible in the far corner of the photograph, but she surely saw them.

Neil was about to ask Jenny more when Jimmy McPhee came into the saloon bar.

"Ma. Rob." He nodded. "Mrs. Ross." He looked at Neil.

Rob introduced them. "Jimmy McPhee, Neil Stewart. Neil is from Canada and working at the *Gazette* for a couple of months."

Jimmy did not offer to shake hands—it was not his custom. He looked at Neil, sizing him up—that was his style. He wasn't sure of what he saw, except that this stranger obviously had money and education, could look after himself in a fight, and although Scottish on the outside was something else inside. And Jimmy knew that although Neil might be bigger, he was softer, and he, Jimmy, could take him in a fight.

"Neil Stewart," Jimmy repeated. "My ma was a Stewart . . ."

"I must be off now." Jenny stood. "Thank you for buying an auld woman a drink, Mr. Stewart."

If Jimmy was as surprised as the others at how quickly Jenny left he did not show it, only followed her out like the faithful watchdog he was.

She moves surprisingly quickly for an old woman, Joanne thought.

"I obviously didn't make a favorable impression." Neil smiled.

"Of course not." Joanne was indignant at the thought of anyone not taking to Neil.

Rob too had been puzzled by Jenny's reaction but dismissed it as another of her eccentricities. "Jenny McPhee takes some time to warm to strangers, that's all."

"Good, hate to think my charm isn't working," Neil said, giving her the little boy lost smile that always made Joanne's stomach lurch. "Another drink, anyone?"

"Not here," Rob said, "this place has all the charm of a mortuary." He stopped. "Sorry, sorry. Me and my big mouth."

But his words had put a damper on the evening, and as they left and stood in the street, the drizzle and the sound of a shouting match further down the street—probably Clach supporters arguing over another defeat—made for miserable company.

"Come on," Rob told them, "I borrowed my father's car. I'll give you both a lift home."

Joanne sat in the backseat watching her evening disappear and the drizzle turn to rain. Rob drove to her prefab first.

"Thanks for the lift." She smiled. "I enjoyed band practice." She waved at the departing car, but Rob and Neil were laughing at something and didn't see her. As she opened the garden gate, her head caught an overhanging branch of the lilac tree. It showered her with rain and the slimy remains of autumn leaves.

"Damn and blast it." She had been meaning to trim the bush, one of the many jobs not done around her tiny refuge, the postwar emergency house that was supposed to be pulled down in two years' time. Through the tears it was hard to find the keyhole. "Damn and blast," she said again, but with no real anger, only tiredness.

Making herself cocoa at twenty-five past eight on a Saturday night, she couldn't shake the insidious internal voice that kept whispering, *Why would he want to spend an evening with you anyway?*

So she did what she always did: turned on a classical concert on the BBC Third Programme; read her library book; fell asleep in the chair; came to at the sound of the national anthem that ended the evening's broadcasting; went to her single bed in the smaller of the two bedrooms; slept until the dawn chorus, the persistent song of the blackbird that lived in her garden not allowing her to go back to sleep.

CHAPTER 10

It was not that Joanne Ross was being heartless over Don McLeod's plight, more that her heart was occupied by Neil Stewart.

Every day she was reminded of Mrs. Smart's death, of Don's absence, of the forthcoming trial, but a veil of enchantment enveloped her, shutting her off from reality.

Joanne was not neglecting her children, had not forgotten her friends, was not indifferent to her parents-in-law's concern about the collapse of her marriage, and she was working well in the still-unfamiliar role of reporter on the *Gazette*. It was rather that with the appearance of Neil Stewart, everyday life seemed less interesting, less vivid, than time spent with him. The hours alone with him, in the office, sharing sandwiches, which she provided, at her favorite thinking spot—the castle forecourt— weather permitting, were beguiling.

What no one, not even Joanne, knew was that she was in the grip of an obsession that might be called love. It affected her sleeping, her ability to acknowledge that Neil would leave, back to his life in the university. She read and reread Annie's favorite geography book about Canada; she even reread the Anne of Green Gables series and loved the ending. She collected the brochures from the man from the Canadian High Commission who had come to town to recruit Highlanders to the emigration program. She dreamed of her new life in a custom-built ranch house with picture window and wooden floor and a large stone fireplace. She imagined a kitchen with a washing machine and refrigerators full of exotic fruit like melons and pomegranates, though she did not quite know what a pomegranate was. She had redecorated an imaginary bedroom at least six times. She planned and planted a garden with flowers and vegetables and maple trees—she knew no other Canadian tree except endless varieties of pine.

The dreaming was no longer confined to her bed: filling her daytime, her work time, her alone in the evening with her knitting time; the dreaming crowded out all sense and all reality; crowded out Mrs. Smart and Don McLeod and John McAllister.

Her daughters found her singing more often, dancing with them in the garden, playing silly games, always ready to tell a story, to take them for ice cream, where they usually bumped into her friend from Canada. They went on picnics with him to Cawdor Castle, to Castle Urquhart, to Culloden. He seemed to know more of Scotland than a Scot. He told stories about battles and empty glens and people leaving to live in Canada and America and New Zealand and Australia—which seemed a fine idea to Annie, especially Canada—she wanted to meet grizzly bears and Mounties and red Indian chiefs and visit Anne of Green Gables.

At work, McAllister did not notice; he was often absent from the office, and when he was present, his mind was elsewhere. He thought Neil was not a stylish journalist—his ability to pitch his stories at a small-town audience lost in all his education—but he was hardworking, capable, and competent, all McAllister needed. He envied Neil's ability to talk lightly and amusingly yet be a serious academic—in less fraught circumstances they might be friends. He noticed Joanne around Neil, thought it a foolish flirtation, but it irritated him nonetheless. And he thought less of Joanne for being so easily charmed; they all knew Neil was only passing through.

Rob was distracted by the extra work, plus rehearsals for his band's upcoming first night in front of an audience of more than fifty-five, but he enjoyed being around Neil, saw him as a man of the big wide world, a man who had crossed the Atlantic on an aeroplane.

Hector had spent the past weeks scuttling around like a demented guinea pig. Now responsible for all the content of the sports pages, plus his usual work covering school events, town and county council gatherings, and the occasional accident and emergency, he still had time to notice Neil. And have reservations.

Neil paid him no heed and, although used to being ignored, Hector was used to being ignored in an inclusive way, as though he was the *Gazette*'s mascot, or resident genius, as he thought of himself. No, Neil's charm did not work on Hec, because Hec had never been caught in Neil's searchlight.

"Have you time for a coffee this afternoon?" Joanne phoned Chiara, catching her as she was about to leave for the café.

"For you—always." They laughed. "But no coffee, my wee one kicks enough as it is." Despite her pregnancy, "slow down" was not in Chiara's vocabulary, so work continued, a glass of red wine with dinner stayed; only her five cups of coffee a day changed.

Later, sitting in their favorite window table, Joanne told Chiara about the plan for the trip to the west coast.

"Of course the girls can stay with us. Why don't you leave them on Friday evening, that way you can set off without rushing."

"That would be great. They hate getting up in the dark, Jean especially—she is still scared of the dark and Neil says we should be on the road by seven."

"Oh well, if Neil says seven then it's seven."

Joanne did not catch the sarcasm; she was too busy thinking about Neil.

"He's looking at the more recent migration to Canada—turn of the century," Joanne was telling Chiara. "He laughs about a people who leave one stretch of barren rock for another, in places like Newfoundland and the southern tip of New Zealand."

"Very attached to barren rocks, you Scots," Chiara teased.

"And Neil says . . ." Joanne saw Chiara rolling her eyes. "What?"

"Have you any other topic of conversation? Like . . ." Chiara saw what she had done to Joanne; like a bright wee sailing boat hurtling along and suddenly the wind drops, her smile, her happiness, came to a standstill. "Oh, Jo, I'm sorry. I was teasing. It's only that . . . I don't want to see you . . ." *Make another mistake* was what she was going to say. "Me and my big mouth." Chiara mock-slapped herself. "You know you're the sister I never had, you're family. And I'm wrong. You're right. Life is short. Go off with your gorgeous Canadian and enjoy yourself."

Joanne was blushing. "I'm still in shock over what happened to Mrs. Smart . . . but it also makes me want to *live* my life."

"And life is precious." Chiara took her hand. "I mean what I said. Enjoy yourself. You deserve it." She stopped herself from saying, "Be careful," but only just.

Chiara had reservations. Not about Neil but for her dearest friend. She watched Joanne falling. She knew Neil was passing through. She saw Joanne dreaming. She could see Neil's charm. She also saw he was ambitious. She did not know but she suspected her friend's fantasy; the one where Neil proposed and they all went to Canada and lived happily ever after.

Chiara knew a divorce was almost impossible for a woman; a man was more easily forgiven. She knew that for a woman, the financial consequences were often dire. She knew how the town would label Joanne—and her children. She was completely certain that Neil Stewart cared for Joanne, but for him this was the working equivalent of a holiday romance. And she was scared for her friend.

Neil had been telling Joanne of the trip for a week or so.

"I'm off to the west coast via Strath Oykel," he had said. "I want to look up the parish register in a tiny church near Lochinver."

"A wee kirk"—she laughed—" 'tiny church' makes you sound English."

"Heaven forbid!" He held up his hands in mock horror. "Why don't you come? You can be my interpreter."

"I'd love to." She meant it; the rain and the cold and the dark of the Northwest in late autumn did not matter; being with Neil was all that mattered.

The trip arranged, the girls taken care of, Joanne was watching Neil sorting papers on the table. It was clear he knew what he was looking for and where to look. He had names of arrivals to Canada and relevant dates, lists of families and familial relationships and the parishes they came from, names of ships, ships' manifestos, all neatly typed in columns, with space between questions allowing for the answers. What he needed was to confirm his research in the Scottish parish records.

To one side was a photograph.

"That's your mother." Joanne recognized the photograph Neil had shown Jenny McPhee.

Neil pushed it towards her. "It was taken a week before she left the glens for the last time."

The photograph in the cardboard folding frame was protected by tissue paper but had yellowed. The lucky white heather his mother had brought with her to Canada had long since disintegrated. He had promised himself to pick more, but it was too late in the season for heather, and very few knew where white heather grew—only the tinkers know, his mother had told him.

Joanne examined the picture, but the woman's face was hard to read, her eyes squinting as she looked into the sun. Her clothes looked as though she were about to go to church, her hat her Sunday best, was pulled down—*to hold it tight against a ferocious wind, most likely,* Joanne thought. In the background, the twin peaks of the distant mountain were distinctive and strange. On the far edge of the picture, although faint and faded, was the unmistakable shape of Travelers' caravans and two horses. She didn't like to mention them, although she didn't know why.

"Where was this taken?" Joanne asked.

"At the far end of Strath Oykel, so my mother said. This was before she was married; 'just a lass' was how she put it. And that mountain is called Suilven."

"It's certainly striking."

"It is. And we will see it on Saturday." He looked at her, and she looked back but could not hold his gaze for more than a fraction of a second before turning away, knowing that her face was growing pink.

"Looking forward to it?" he asked.

"Of course. But I wouldn't count on seeing the mountain. There's so much mist and rain in those parts you sometimes can't see more than a few yards."

"Maybe. But we'll have fun anyway."

She looked away. The significance of her decision was completely lost on him. But she was going on this trip, no matter the consequences. A cocktail of guilt, pleasure, excitement, and dread made the skin on her arms tingle, and she crossed them, hugging herself, telling herself over and over, it's just a harmless day out to the west coast. That's all.

Joanne had asked Neil to pick her up on the riverbank near the Islands. It was not that she was ashamed, just that she did not want to be seen getting into his car this early on a Saturday morning.

When he drew up in the borrowed car, Joanne felt a flash of doubt. Too late for cold feet, she told herself.

"Right on time." She smiled as she got into the car. "I thought you hated early mornings."

"Not hate, more not used to them." He smiled back. "After years on a daily newspaper where I was lucky to finish by midnight, my body is not used to early."

They followed the river back to the main road north, crossed the canal, passed through the fishing village strung out between the road, the railway line, and the firth. The sight of a famous battle, Neil told Joanne.

She laughed, saying, "You know more about my town than I do."

Saturday mornings, the roads were busy in the opposite direction; people coming into town from the glens and the coastal villages to shop. Many came into town from Beauly and Strathconon and Strathglass, from Kiltarlity and Conon for a big shop or for clothes and shoes, new washing machines and televisions. The border of Ross & Cromarty was a mere fifteen miles away, and the people from there went to their own county town, not only to shop but to catch up on the gossip. And Dingwall was fine for Wellington boots and farmwear but not for fashion and teashops and staring at electrical appliances you couldn't afford.

Neil laughed when he saw the first major road sign. "'North,'" he read. "Well, that's simple. I suppose we'll meet another sign and it will say 'West.'"

"Or 'North-west.'"

"Or 'North-north-west.'"

The banter lightened the trepidation she was feeling at being on such a momentous adventure. All her senses acute, the air in the car seemed charged with lust—although that was not a word she would acknowledge, as ladies did not feel lust, and besides, lust was a sin.

"The turn-off should be marked Bonar Bridge or maybe Ardgay, or hopefully both." Joanne had the map and as navigator she was happy to have something to concentrate on.

"Ardgay." He sounded the name as though it were a spell. "My mother talked of visiting relatives around there."

"Just past Evanton on the main road, there's a shortcut to Ardgay, but it looks pretty winding and steep—over the hills not around them."

"Over the hills and far away . . ." Neil chanted. "The road will be no problem in Countess Sokolov's car."

"Countess . . ."

"Mr. Beauchamp Carlyle's sister, Rosemary, married a Russian count in Shanghai in the nineteen thirties, I believe. Although she prefers plain Mrs., I love knowing that I know a countess."

"How do you know them?"

"I had a letter of introduction from a solicitor. She and her brother have given me access to their family archives. There is such interesting material in it from the late eighteenth and early nineteenth centuries . . ."

Joanne half listened as Neil rattled on recounting births and deaths and marriages along the Fraser matriarchal line of the Beauchamp Carlyle family, feeling altogether inadequate. *Much too elevated company for me,* she was thinking when the sign for the turn-off appeared and they almost missed it.

"Left," she called out, "left here."

With a squeal of tires and the engine moaning, he changed down gears, propelling the car into a much narrower road. Fortunately nothing was coming the other way.

"I'm sorry." Joanne was shaken.

"I enjoyed it—gave me a chance to show off my driving skills." Neil was laughing. He reached over and patted her on the thigh. "Not too much of a shock for you?"

Not the driving, she thought. But the hand on her knee burned her skin, or so she fancied. And once again, she was scared by the momentousness of the journey.

"I'm fine," she replied, "and the road is really bonnie."

The minor road wound up over hills, down into glens, crossed stone bridges, climbing higher and higher until they reached an open stretch of moor and forest. The sky was vast and grey. The firth spreading below was a lighter shade of grey, the hills a green-grey and the outlines of mountains on the horizon to the north a deep dark foreboding grey. Only a splash of yellow on a gorse bush next to the roadside, and the sulfur-yellow patches of lichen on the drystone dyke that measured the hillside into quadrants, broke the monochrome of the vista.

They clambered out of the car, pulling on raincoats.

"Well, I see what you meant about the visibility," Neil said.

"This is nothing," Joanne told him, "at least we can see. And at least it's not real rain, only a light mist of a rain."

He laughed. "Only a light mist of a rain . . . I'll remember that when I'm soaked through."

The journey down to Ardgay and Bonar Bridge was short, so they decided not to stop but to push on up Strath Oykel hoping the weather would clear the farther west they drove.

Crossing the bridge over the narrow end of Dornoch Firth, they crossed into Sutherland. For the length of the glen—a fault line stretching from east coast to west coast—the road was mostly in Sutherland, but sometimes in Ross & Cromarty; the contours of the rivers and history had made manifest the ancient boundaries.

At first the glen was indeed bonnie. Drystone dykes were everywhere. Joanne was counting the miles of them—*Are these Scotland's version of the Great Wall of China?* she was thinking— counting the hours, the days, the years of backbreaking labor they must have taken to build.

They reached the Oykel bridge and the end of the walls, the end of "bonnie." Now it was a landscape that could well be described as a terrestrial version of the moon, and the higher and bleaker the landscape became, the quieter Neil was.

Joanne did not notice; she was half dozing in the warmth and the leather seats and the comfort of his company, dreaming half-dreams, unable to fall completely asleep—being this close to him, shut in against the weather, the past, the future, being here with him alone on this dreich Saturday in the wilds of Suther-land, made every part of her, skin, hair, heart, and knees, feel she was as enchanted as a faerie princess briefly in this realm to cap-ture a lover.

Neil, feeling as desolate as the land they were driving through, did not take in the dancing white heads of the bog-cotton. He did not see the pattern and color and texture of the lichens. He did not notice the beauty of the tiny plants and minuscule flowers and shrubs on the verge of the road, in the bog, growing in cracks in the rocks, clinging to life as surely as the people had and did. And in the emptiness, in the vast open-ness not broken by tree or by man, he did not feel the joy of the proximity to heaven, or the heavens.

He felt cheated.

This is what those displaced Scots were longing for; this is what they were devastated to leave behind. Moors are so barren they're pitiable. The leaving of this wilderness broke the hearts of those clansmen and women. It made them, their songs, their stories, their music, this landscape that continues to haunt every generation of the scattered diaspora, the progeny of the Highland Clearances.

Were all my mother's memories exaggerations, falsehoods?

At first he thought it a mirage. Then the shroud lifted and he saw it again, this time for more than a minute. He kept driving. There it was again, no mistaking it. Suilven.

He pulled over. Switched off the engine. Joanne sat up. The mist parted. She saw the mountain, and said nothing. This was his moment.

He stared at his touchstone, his nemesis, his mountain. He got out. Joanne watched him standing, staring, as still as the silence and the air around them. For once the landscape did not echo to the sound of running falling water, nor the frequent croak of carrion crows or the cough of sheep or the rustle of wind—there being nothing to rustle. Leaving space for him to absorb the encounter, she stared at the twin peaks and her heart was glad. Glad for him, but also inspired by the sight.

There is something about that mountain, she thought, *and like his mother's photograph, it will be forever imprinted on my memory.*

But, as he contemplated the sight of his pilgrimage, he found it wanting; too round, too bleak, no color. His sacred mountain was not high enough, not sharp enough.

"It's just as it is in your mother's picture," she said as she walked over to join him. "Really bonnie."

"Joanne, this could never be called bonnie. Stark, threatening, menacing, ominous, never bonnie."

"Aye, you're right, not bonnie, but beautiful and . . . *primordial.*" Joanne was staring into the distance, her back to him. She felt he had been reprimanding her for a lack of vocabulary, but no matter what he said, she saw the mountain as spectacular and yes, beyond bonnie. It was beautiful.

The clouds were not lifting, but the light started to brighten, blue shafts waving through the slipstream like carnival streamers, widening, until there was more sky than cloud.

Suilven, with rounded mountains framing it and thin silver slivers of loch, their beginnings and endings unclear, lay on the horizon shining clear.

Suilven all sparkling; caught in a shaft of light of biblical dimensions, the mountain seemingly growing taller, sharper, the twin peaks revealing themselves as one fractured ridge with deep dark rivulets running like guy ropes to anchor it to the land.

Yet still it did not satisfy him.

Neil shook himself, shivering like a dog shaking off water.

"Let's drive on a little further. See if we can find the exact spot where the picture was taken."

Over the next few miles, Joanne, sensing his detachment from the surroundings, assumed it was her. She was desperate to please him, searching out the window for some rock some lochan some cleft in the landscape that might please him. Suddenly she saw it. "Neil, is this where the picture was taken?"

"Maybe."

He got out. He walked towards the shore of the lochan. He lifted his head to stare at the mountaintops, sniffing the wind like a wolf investigating new territory. Now, not only could he see it, he began to feel it, feel the day, the sunlit day. *More likely the sunny quarter of an hour,* he thought, *and equally cold.*

He could not dismiss the sensation. He *could* feel it. And he could feel her, the woman he had known as mother, see her raise her hand to her brow to squint into the camera, laughing, probably saying, *Hurry up, it's freezing in this wind,* to the photographer, a person whose name she said she couldn't remember.

A small cluster of trees bent at the waist by the winds, huddled at the far end of the lochan. Joanne thought she recognized the spot from the photograph—yes, she was sure, this was where the tinker's horse-drawn caravans had stood. The only place of shelter for many a mile, it was a good place to set up camp, make a fire, fetch water, rest the horses, catch brown trout. And the view of Suilven, sitting plumb in the middle, was a marker, a pyramid, a giant standing stone, as spiritual as any in civilization.

Neil looked at his watch. "I'm meeting the elder of the Old Parish Church at Inchnadamph at two, so we'd better get a move on. I hadn't realized it would take so long to get here."

His impatience brought her down from the mountain to the reality of the car; taking time was what a journey was about for her. "That's because we've been traveling Highland miles, not Canadian ones," she joked.

But still, she was curious; this should have been his Damascene revelation. *The photograph, his native land, did he not feel the pull of the mountain?*

"I'd love to stop at the hotel for a beer and something to eat, but I'm not sure we have time." Neil was already holding open the car door for her.

"We can have tea and a sandwich at Inchnadamph. I've packed all we need, including gingerbread."

"You're a marvel."

It was only three words; the only three words that had ever come near to him saying what she wanted to hear. She had to turn away to hide her blush and her joy and her shame at behaving like a schoolgirl with a first crush.

Neil never noticed. He put the car into gear, and with Suilven still ahead of them, they continued westward, meeting the
main road at a T-junction. Through a series of loops and twists
the road descended rapidly. The parish church where Neil was to
check the records was clear from some miles distant.

They had fifteen minutes to spare. Joanne unwrapped the
waxed paper and offered Neil ham or egg sandwiches, hoping
they were adequate for a person from Canada. She unscrewed
the flask, poured the tea; he didn't say much but was quick
enough to finish all the sandwiches plus two scones before a tap
on the window broke the quiet of the picnic.

"Mr. Stewart?"

Neil got out but didn't introduce Joanne, even though the
elderly man was peering at her with undisguised curiosity. They
nodded at each other, both aware of the breach of good manners.

The two men left towards the small white church, and
Joanne packed the remains of the picnic before heading out for
a walk.

The wind from straight up the loch where the kirk and
graveyard stood at one end was fierce, cutting through her
wool coat and jumper and blouse, chilling her to the bone. She
decided to explore the churchyard, hoping to shelter behind the
walls and a large rectangular stone erection that was surely a
family vault.

It was no good. Rain now accompanied the wind. Just as she
was about to go back to the car, a flash of color made her look
towards a freshly filled grave tucked away in a far corner, the corner nearest to the loch shore.

She didn't know, but intuition told her; this was the grave
of Mrs. Smart. They were in the right area, probably in the right
parish. *How many churchyards can there be in this empty landscape,*
she thought as she walked over the slate slabs that led to the kirk

door, which Neil or his contact had wisely closed against the day.

The grassy path leading the rest of the way was sodden, and Joanne's shoes were quickly wet through. *Folly,* she thought, *walking in good shoes in this land of bog and rock.*

There was no headstone, nothing to mark the grave, only a solitary bunch of flowers, but not bought flowers, just a small gathering of gold chrysanthemums. At the foot of the grave, someone had planted heather. There were no flowers showing, but again instinct made Joanne guess, *lucky white heather.*

"There's not much in the way of flowers at this time o' year."

The voice made Joanne start. She turned to look at an old woman, not much taller than her eight-year-old, dressed entirely in black except for a cream knitted scarf in a Shetland lace pattern—*print o' the waves, one of my favorites,* Joanne thought.

"Who is buried here?" Joanne asked.

"A dear, dear lass," came the reply, the voice so faint, it was carried away in the wind, and Joanne was not sure if the woman had said more than this.

"I knew a lovely woman from around these parts," Joanne started. "We worked together, and it was only after she died that I realized I was fond of her." She was surprised at her words. "Her name was Mrs. Joyce Smart."

"No, lass, her name was Joyce Mackenzie."

Joanne knew how proud Highlanders were of their family names and, having heard much about Sergeant Major Smart from Rob, she too felt that her married name was not what Joyce Mackenzie would want to take to her grave. It was as though the murdered woman was a shape-shifter: Mrs. Smart, the epitome of an efficient, reticent, tasteful woman; Joyce Mackenzie, a Mackenzie of the wilds of the Northwest, only child, Gaelic speaker, friend to many, beloved by many, known by few.

"Thon soldier she had the misfortune to marry didn't even

turn up to see her to her resting place. Nor did he inform anyone of the funeral arrangements. But she is a Mackenzie from this parish, a good woman, and she is honored as such."

"I know," Joanne said. "Sorry I've forgotten my manners. I'm Joanne Ross. I worked on the *Highland Gazette* with Mrs. . . . with Joyce Mackenzie."

"Mrs. Mary Stewart—pleased to meet you." She smiled up at Joanne, and it was as lovely as the sun coming out over Suilven, and her face just as craggy. "That your man over there?" She nodded towards the porch of the kirk, where Neil was shaking hands with the verger.

"A friend," Joanne said and, seeing the look on the woman's face, added, "A colleague."

"Oh aye. Your friend, he's from these parts?"

"He was born here but brought up in Canada. His name is Stewart, the same as you. Neil Stewart."

"There's that many Stewarts and Mackenzies around here, and we're no' all related." She smiled a smile so sweet and so sad, and Joanne suddenly saw that the woman was not as old as she looked. *It's the harsh life up here in the wilds,* she thought.

"*Sealbh math dhuibh,* good luck to you." The woman laid her hand lightly on Joanne's arm as though offering a benediction, then walked off across the grass and up the slate slabs, opened the gate, and was up the hill at a surprising speed, off to what looked like nowhere.

She looked right into me, Joanne thought later.

Seeing that Neil and the kirk elder were shaking hands, finishing their meeting, Joanne walked towards them.

"I'm right sorry you had a wasted journey," the older man was saying.

"Not at all. The parish registers are fascinating historical documents." Neil was reassuring him. "Thank you again for allowing me to see them."

Neil walked over to join her, leaving the man to lock up. "Let's find the nearest hotel, preferably with a bar and a fire."

She wanted to share her discovery; she didn't see how distracted he was. "Look over there. That's where Mrs. Smart— Joyce Mackenzie that was—is buried." She pointed to the fresh grave.

"Really?" He stared at the gravesite but made no move. "Now you can reassure everyone at the *Gazette* that she is resting in a 'bonnie' place. Or wouldn't you use that word for a graveyard?"

She knew he was teasing but felt a hurt nonetheless. "Yes, I'd use the word 'bonnie.'" She looked around at the loch and the hills on three sides and another sharp mountain in the far western corner. "Especially when the sun comes out."

"If."

Just like all the men Joanne knew, he had to have the final word.

Back in the car, Joanne looked at the map. "It's about three-quarters of an hour to Ullapool and a much quicker road home. Why don't we stop there for a meal? There's bound to be a fish-and-chip shop."

"Or maybe even a proper hotel with proper food."

She felt vaguely put down by this remark. *What's wrong with fish-and-chips?* And dinner at a hotel was not something she could afford.

The hotel was a three-story building with small windows deep set into the whitewashed stone overlooking the pier. The fire in the bar big and bright, Joanne took a chair on one side of the hearth. Neil went to order drinks. The curious glances from the locals no longer bothered her. She knew she would be taken as a visitor, so the unwritten law of Scotland—no women in a public bar—would not apply.

Neil is taking a long time, but as soon as she thought it, he turned from his conversation with the landlord and came over with a whisky for himself and a glass of port for her.

"*Sláinte mhath,*" he toasted.

"Yes." She did not use the Gaelic, always slightly embarrassed when a non-native mispronounced the words, the same as she hated it when English people tried to speak with a Scottish accent and ended up sounding as though they were mocking the Scots.

But then, he is from the Gaeltachd, so he has the right, she thought, as she held up her glass to see the fire dance through the ruby-red liquor. The first sip filled her mouth with warmth and sweetness and a sense of wonder. Here she was with the man who made her heart lurch. Here she was, in a place unknown, away from her children, away from her past. Her smile across her glass said it all, encouraging Neil that he had made the right decision.

"It's all been a bit overwhelming," he started. "Really knocked me for six."

The hurt from the oh-so-small slights she had sensed ever since they set off on the trip vanished. "No wonder," she agreed. "This place has haunted you for years."

"Even before she died, all she really talked about was the glens." There was a wistfulness in his voice. Or perhaps disappointment. "My mother was not what you would call a conversationalist." He raised his glass to contemplate the fire through the golden spirit.

"Now you've seen the moors and the mountain, you know where your ancestors came from."

"Maybe." He took a sip of the whisky, glanced out to the dark and the invisible loch across the street and sighed, then shivered so imperceptibly Joanne wondered if she'd imagined it.

"Joanne, it's late, it's dark, and it's raining again . . . and I've had one too many." He held up his glass but he was far from drunk. Being drunk, loss of control, was not something he enjoyed. "How would you feel about staying here tonight?" He did not tell her he had already asked for a room.

"I . . ." She was blushing. As red as this ruby port, she feared. This is what she had dreamed of. But the reality was terrifying. And the small voice from the left, the Devil's side, was urging her on, saying, *This is what you do to keep a man.* The voice on the right, the righteous voice, was saying, *This is a sin.* But it was faint, as far away and as faint as the Summer Isles on the far horizon at the far end of the sea loch, lost in dark and mist.

"I want you." He had considered saying how much he needed her after the day's events, but instinct told him there was no need.

"Yes. I want that too." She couldn't look at him, and the noise of conversation around them had grown in proportion to the drink consumed, but he caught her "Yes."

It was the sound of barrels knocking together that awoke Joanne. She moved slowly, almost scared to open her eyes and see the sleeping head on the pillow next to her. The completely familiar hair, the dark shadow of beard, the unfamiliar body, and most of all the sense of wonder at them being together at last made her tremble.

He's mine, she said to herself. *And I now know what it means to truly love a man,* was her next thought.

His breathing changed. He opened his eyes. Grinned. The rush of emotions, love, lust, danger overcame her. The awareness of her folly she dismissed but could never banish. She looked at him, in the white bed in the white room, the sounds of seagulls filling the Sunday morning, and this time, she reached for him.

It was only on the journey home that the thought came to stick in her brain like a burr; *I wish he would tell me he loves me.*

CHAPTER 11

The same Saturday Joanne and Neil were wandering the glens of the west coast, Rob came into work and found the reporters' room empty. Although it was a half day and slow, Joanne would normally be there at the typewriter banging away. He had a vague recollection of her saying she would not be in. "Chasing a story," she'd said. *Wonder what it is*, he thought.

Hector appeared from nowhere. Rob fancied that Hec knew the secrets of an H. G. Wells time machine and could transport himself from place to place by no visible means. But he knew Hec usually used the St. Valerie Avenue bus when he didn't have his granny's car.

"What are you up to today?" Rob asked.

"Since there's no one to tell me what to do, I'm taking pictures of a Highland dancing competition, then off to the football as usual."

"Don't tell me; your granny told you to photo your wee sister for the paper or else?"

"How did you know?"

"Because I'm a genius." Then Rob remembered he wanted to ask Hec's granny about Don McLeod, but Granny Bain was notorious for not coming forward, and when she did, she was as enigmatic as a soothsayer deciphering the entrails, so it was best to be in her good books. "Would you like me to come with you to the dancing? Maybe write a wee story to go with the picture?"

"Really?" Hector stared at Rob. "Why would you do that?"

"Slow news week. We need to fill the space." He watched Hector's face shine bright enough to mark a shipping channel in the thickest haar. "And Hector, you need to cover the Caledonian match today; you've featured Clach's last three matches."

Hector was so chuffed his sister would get a mention in the paper, he agreed to cover a match featuring the archrivals of his beloved Clachnacuddin FC.

The competition was being held in the Northern Meeting Rooms. Rob cheered to discover Mharie Bain was in the sword dancing section even though it was usually men and boys who did sword dancing. He had enjoyed watching one of his uncles dance—until Rob was forced to learn it to please his grandmother. Fortunately she died, so he gave it up.

The panel of judges sat below the stage. Rob noticed one of them was the wife of the chief constable, so he would include her name in his article. It would be an all-round winner of a morning—if he managed to get something out of Granny Bain.

Luckily Mharie Bain's section came early. Luckily she won. When Hector disappeared with his sister to find better light for the photo, Rob had a chance to speak to Granny Bain. They went to the hallway, took a bench, and Rob told her what he wanted. *There'll be no fooling her, may as well come straight out with it.*

"Mrs. Bain, my father has asked me to try to find anything at all that might help his defense of Mr. McLeod."

"He didn't do it." She almost barked the reply.

"I know, but the police have a good case."

She looked at him. He saw where Hector got his eye color, but there was something disturbingly knowing about the stare in Granny Bain's eyes. "Does your father think Donal stuck the knife in her?"

Rob's pencil clattered to the floor. As he bent to pick it up he felt a wave of nausea. He tried to compose himself and straightened up. "No, he believes Mr. McLeod is innocent."

"Aye, and sorry, laddie, I can be a wee bit direct sometimes."

"Direct" was not the word Rob would have used, unless maybe "direct as a heart attack."

"So, how do you mean I can help Don McLeod? I don't know nothing about what's happened."

"Mrs. Jenny McPhee said it was all in the past, she said to start at the beginning. Only I don't know where to find the beginning."

"Her mother had her here in town, that's the beginning, then her mother, God rest her soul, died when Joyce was a bairn, that's another beginning. The old colonel kept Joyce at home, sending her to the local school wi' crofters and, aye, tinker bairns even, until she was eleven or thereabouts when she was off to school in Edinburgh and the colonel off to India. I never knew her then. Next thing, she appeared back in town when she was twenty or thereabouts, same time as Donal came back. They'd met somewhere when he was convalescing from his wounds, burns it was, in the Dardanelles he was when his ship sank. Of course I never knew her that time neither, just to say hello to, her being right friendly with Donal."

"And you knew Don, Mr. McLeod . . . ?"

"His granny and my granny were cousins."

"And he and Mrs. Smart were . . ."

"None of your business." She was thinking it over, trying to see how all this, from all that time ago, could be relevant now. "Aye, they were good friends. Not that their friendship could amount to anything, she being gentry, the only child of a well-to-do laird, him being a crofter's son, never mind that he was a clever one, ending up at the *Highland Gazette* and doing well for himself. No, it would never do."

"Is that why she went to India?" Rob had a vision of thwarted love, broken hearts, and wretched farewells.

"How should I know?" Granny Bain's voice was sharp and scary.

"Because it might help Mr. McLeod if you did know, and you told me."

"So you can make up a story for the newspaper?" She said this as she was standing, gathering her cardigans and coat around her, and what looked to be a baby's lace shawl but was probably a scarf with many holes not in the right places, ready to do battle with the wind. He had already noticed a number of hatpins holding down a misshapen piece of felt to her grey-white hair and was suitably intimidated by their deadliness.

"Sorry, lad, you've stirred up the memories. My man went down on that same ship."

He was looking down at her; so tiny she was, in a formidable kind of a way. He liked Granny Bain; he wished she were his granny.

"Granny Bain, sorry, Mrs. Bain . . ."

"Granny Bain is fine."

"If you can help my father help Mr. McLeod . . ."

"I will."

Walking into the empty reporters' room to write up the story, Rob was glad to hear the radio on in McAllister's office. *Some sign of life*, he thought, even if it is just the Third Programme. When he realized the music was Wagner, he began to worry again.

"What?"

Even across the landing, even above the radio, he heard McAllister roar like a wounded lion.

By the time Rob recovered, McAllister was already halfway down the stairs. He ran after him but stopped when he saw Betsy holding the telephone receiver away from her, glaring at it as though the instrument was responsible for the shock.

"What is it?" Rob asked.

"I wasn't listening in." She dropped the receiver. It missed the cradle. She put it back. Not looking at Rob, she gave a most unladylike sniff. "I don't listen in, not anymore."

"Betsy, I don't care if you did listen in, tell me why McAllister rushed off. It sounded really important."

"I put the call through," Betsy said, "that's all."

"Betsy, *who was it?*" Rob shouted, and as Rob never shouted at anyone, she burst into tears.

"It was Detective Inspector Dunne."

"Get me the police."

Betsy dialed, handed the phone to him, then backed away into the secretary's cubbyhole of an office to hide.

Rob knew immediately the voice that answered. "Sergeant Patience, it's Rob McLean. What the hell is going on?"

"I don't know if I should tell you."

"I'll be round the back lane in one minute."

"Mind, you never heard the news from me," Sergeant Patience said for the third time as Rob ran off to get his motorbike.

The hospital was on the outskirts of town, and Rob decided the quickest way was by the longer main road rather than through the winding back streets and suburbs of town, fighting his way through the Saturday-morning-shopping traffic.

He overtook lorries laboring up the hills and through the twisting bends. A dark road, enclosed by steep hills and thick trees on both sides, it was treacherous in winter black ice and treacherous in flickering summer light. He passed slow vehicles recklessly, sounded his horn futilely. He lost all sense of his own mortality. Don was "at death's door," as the sergeant had put it.

Leaving his bike parked illegally, Rob ran towards the emergency department doors. He spotted McAllister pacing, smoking, making tracks in the narrow strip of grass that bordered a bed of withered wallflowers. "Is he alive?"

"Aye," McAllister told him, "just."

"What happened?"

"Tried to hang himself."

Rob could barely take in the notion. "Don? Hang himself?"

"The doctors are with him. He can't speak. And they're worried about brain damage. Technically he died, but the guard resuscitated him." McAllister had a flash of the man, the Highlander, the gentle big man who spoke to Don in the Gaelic, and was grateful.

Rob sat on the grass, put his head in his hands.

McAllister threw his cigarette butt into a patch of weeds to join the dozens of others, discarded by those waiting for the good the bad and the tragic news that was the lot of hospital emergency departments. "No visitors allowed. The police have posted a guard outside his room. Anyhow, Don can't talk, so there's no point in going in."

"Yes, there is." Rob stood. "Just go in there." He was shouting. "He'll know somehow. He'll sense a friend."

"Aye." But McAllister could never admit he was not up to the sight of his old friend so diminished he would try to take his own life. "Maybe you should go."

Rob thought for all of one second. "I will." He rubbed his hair, his head, as though the massage would set his brain cogs working. As he left through the swing doors into the Valhalla of the hospital accident and emergency department, he thought, *Don really must believe there is no escaping a guilty verdict.*

McAllister was asking himself a similar question. "What the hell would make you want to end it all, Don McLeod?" he muttered to the heavens. He refused to consider that Don might be guilty.

The woman behind the admissions counter looked as friendly as Cerberus at the entrance to the underworld, so Rob stood in the corridor searching for someone who might give him news of Don's condition. He saw the nurse in the distance, and even though her back was turned, he was certain it was Eilidh.

He hurried down the corridor trying in vain to diminish the clatter from his motorbike boots.

"Eilidh."

She turned. She looked around. The corridor was still empty.

"If I'm caught talking to you, the matron will have my guts for garters." But she was smirking as she said it.

"Do you know anything about Don McLeod?"

"Aye, but you'll not be able to see him. There's a prison guard outside his room."

"Blast." Rob shook his head as though that would clear the darkness.

"He'll be fine. The guard caught him in time."

Her voice sounded oddly callous. *No*, Rob decided, *she sounds like a nurse. They're all pretty matter-of-fact about death and injury.*

"I'm sorry, Rob, I really do have to go."

"Can we meet later?"

"I'm on late shift, so not really. But I'm coming to the dance to hear you play."

"Smashing. I'll leave your name on the door." He called this after her, as she was hurrying off, having caught sight of a sister bearing down on them, her nursing headdress making her look like a galleon in full sail.

"Can I help you?" her voice implied that she knew he was up to no good.

"Rob McLean, *Highland Gazette*. I'm wondering if I can visit our deputy editor, Mr. Donal McLeod." He tried his signature grin without much hope, and he was not disappointed.

"He is not allowed visitors." And she sailed on.

Off to intimidate other targets, Rob guessed.

When he went out to find McAllister, the editor had vanished. When he went home, his parents were out. He made himself some tea, warmed up the supper his mother had left in the oven, switched on the television, switched it off again; he couldn't stand shows with big bands featuring big-haired singers.

He went out again. He drove to Joanne's house. He found the place empty, no lights, no music, no shadows behind the curtains. He was on the edge of desolate when he remembered. *Hector lives around the corner; he'll be in his studio cum washing shed. He'll be developing film. He'll keep me company.*

He went round the back of the house. Hector wasn't in the studio. But there were light and noise coming from the kitchen. He knocked. Granny Bain took one look at him and said, "Best come in."

She took his bike jacket. She handed him tea from the pot on the stove, then said, "Tell me what's happened." So he did. When he had finished, she said nothing, just sighed.

The kitchen clock, big and round like a single frame of a giant's wire spectacles, was ticking away Saturday night, a night when a young man should be out enjoying himself, not sitting in despair with a Highland granny.

When she started speaking, her accent thick with soft Gaelic sibilants, it was as though the sea had decided to speak.

"I remember that time as though it was yesterday, because Donal was the only one who could give me the whole story. The ship went down, holed by a German battleship. But before she sank, she went on fire. Terrible. Only a few survived. And it was three years after it happened before Donal got back to tell me, him having to recover because he'd lost most of the skin off of his back."

What is it about this century? Rob was thinking as Granny Bain went into another silence. *All these deaths, all this war?* He knew of his own family members lost in both world wars; he knew every village, every town had its war memorial, breaking your heart as you read the long columns of the names of the fallen, often several from the same family. He knew Armistice Day was almost upon them and how somber his family and their friends and the towns and villages became on the eleventh day of the eleventh month.

He had been terrified he might be conscripted when Prime Minister Sir Anthony Eden declared war on Egypt over the Suez Canal. He had listened to what little news there was from the invasion of Hungary, watching the newsreels in the cinema in horror. But instead of feeling safe in his Highland hideaway, it made him determined to leave, *as soon as possible* he was now thinking. *I need to get out into the world. Become a real journalist.*

"... loved each other," Granny Bain was saying. Rob was not sure who she meant, was it her and her husband; Don and Mrs. Smart?

"But it was impossible. One thing I do know is that he regretted it all his life."

Rob did not feel he could interrupt the tide of memories with questions. Rather, he felt that by letting it go, the story would unfold. And it did.

"She was prepared to give up everything, her name, her reputation, her home, her inheritance, so Donal told me, but he said no, he told her he couldn't ask that of her. It was like *he* was the snob, no' her—even though she was from the gentry." She shook her head at the folly of it all. "So, he sent her away."

She reached for her tea. She would never tell anyone that after Joyce Mackenzie left town, Don had drunk himself stupid, that he only told her his miserable story because she had picked him up from the gutter outside his wee house in Church Street, that at that time, just as now, he was well on the way to killing himself.

"Later, after she came back from India, he never said, but I know he blamed himself for her ending up with thon Smart fellow. A jumped-up-too-big-for-his-boots manny thon—and his father no more than a beater on an estate in Perthshire—so I've been told."

"So what's all this to do with . . ."

"Rob?" Hector stood in the doorway staring. They hadn't heard him come in. "What're you doing here?"

"Come to check on the story about the sword dancing competition," Rob answered. "Your sister is a star."

"And out too late for her age," Granny Bain said. "Hector, off with you and fetch her from Mrs. Grigor's house."

"But it's only half past eight."

"Hector."

Hector fled. Granny Bain handed Rob his jacket. He knew he would learn nothing more.

"Thank you. And if you should think of anything . . ."

"I'll let you know."

And, Rob knew, she would if she could.

Chapter 12

I don't want to pressure you . . ."

"But the trial is only four weeks away." McAllister completed Angus McLean's sentence for him.

They were in the solicitor's office. It was nine thirty on Thursday, publication day, and McAllister had not even bothered to glance through that day's *Gazette*.

He looks terrible, Angus McLean was thinking.

He looks like he needs a good night's sleep, McAllister was thinking.

"So Don's still in the hospital?" It was more a rhetorical question, as Angus knew McAllister had been to visit Don late the previous night, after the *Gazette* had been put to bed.

"I was told I was not allowed to see him," McAllister said, "but the sister relented. I think she felt sorry for Don."

McAllister's eyes glazed over as he remembered the visit to the hospital. Angus saw his anguish. He began to fill his pipe, knowing to wait until the editor returned to the here and now.

When McAllister had arrived—to find the lights dimmed, the ward silent except for the hush of feet moving behind the screened-off bed McAllister guessed was Don's—he pulled the curtain to one side and looked in.

"Do you know the time?" the ward sister had asked.

"How is he?"

"He'll survive."

"Aye, but for how long?"

The woman, who at first glance appeared to be a caricature of a ward sister—all starch and no comfort—took McAllister by the arm and led him out into the corridor. The ward doors closed behind them with a sigh of compressed air.

"Mr. McAllister . . ."

"How do you know my name?"

"Wheesht," she shushed him. "Of course I know who you are, the same as I know Mr. McLeod. It's a small town. And a big murder. Everyone's talking, and not everyone credits Don McLeod with Mrs. Smart's death."

"You know, knew, her?"

"No, but my mother did." She sighed. "She was a good woman. Everyone knew about them . . ."

I didn't, but McAllister was too ashamed to admit it.

"He couldn't have killed her. He loved her." But the way she said it, the way her voice took on a misty tone, annoyed him.

"Not everyone thinks that way."

"You're right. Many always want to believe the worst." She shook her head. The white headdress crackled. "Come back tomorrow during visiting hours, you can see him then."

"You're keeping him here?"

"Aye. The doctor knows Mr. McLeod, and we'll find reasons to keep him here as long as possible. But you didn't hear that from me." She smiled and patted him on the arm. The touch of her hand, through the layers of coat and jacket and jumper and shirt, made him realize how long it had been since someone had touched him with love.

"Can I not just peek in to see him?"

She thought for a moment. "The guard is in the canteen on a break. If he finds you, you never got any permission from me." She turned away, disappeared through a door into some hospital netherland that could have been a cupboard or the secret entrance to Brigadoon.

McAllister tried to walk quietly, but that only made more noise, the leather of his shoes creaking in the unaccustomed position. Peering around the screens, he saw Don's head, his thick grey and white and black hair lit by the night-light shining from the wall above. His eyes were closed. The neck was not bandaged, but even in this light McAllister could see the dark semicircle of bruising. He saw the hand hanging outside the sheets, caught the glint of the bracelet of steel where Don was handcuffed to the frame of the bed. The feeling that he needed a chair overcame him, but the chair was at the end of the bed, and all he wanted to do was to sit and hold his old friend's hand.

"Did you bring a dram?" It came out as a garbled croak, but McAllister understood.

"You're alive." It was meant as a joke, came out as surprise.

"Aye."

McAllister bent down, touched Don's hand. "I can't stay. I'm not supposed to be here."

"Aye." Don gripped McAllister's hand. The grip was not strong. "Ask thon nurse, the young one, if she . . ." Don started.

"I'll have to ask you to leave, Mr. McAllister." Although the guard, the same man McAllister had met in the prison, spoke softly, McAllister knew he would have to go. He squeezed Don's hand again.

"He wants the nurse," he told the guard as he left, unable to look at the shriveled old man who was once Don McLeod, cock o' the North.

When McAllister eventually went home, he spent the rest of the night reading, sleeping, awakening, making tea, adding a dram to it, taking the mug to bed, trying to read but rereading the same paragraph or sometimes a whole page over and over, all the time the words of the nursing sister coursing around his brain. *He loved her.*

And he knew he was jealous. To truly love someone, for that love to survive on only one Sunday evening a week alone together for two decades . . . he was jealous.

"McAllister." Angus McLean summoned McAllister back from his contemplations. He had smoked one pipe to McAllister's two cigarettes, watched the editor staring out the window, had seen his face, particularly the minute shifts of the eyebrows, reflecting pain and loss and puzzlement. Now, Angus decided, they needed to plan.

"As I was saying," the solicitor reminded McAllister, "the advocates for the defense are coming up from Edinburgh next week. I'd like to have something to tell them."

"I have nothing. No ideas. Nothing."

"Mrs. McPhee, has she information that might help the case?"

"I don't think so." McAllister shuddered. The proverbial ghost had walked over his grave. "I'll talk to Jimmy McPhee again." His voice had changed. There was a hardness to it that made the solicitor look up, see the grim set of McAllister's mouth, and he took comfort from it.

"Let me know if you hear anything, anything at all."

They shook hands, and McAllister walked out to fetch his car. He would never tell Angus McLean, but he would find Jimmy, they would plan, scheme. If he had to lie and cheat and plant false evidence he would. *And Jimmy will help me.* This McAllister knew.

It took a day and a half to find Jimmy through the elaborate system of leaving messages in various drinking establishments.

Late Saturday afternoon, McAllister was at home, having visited Don again, only for Don to keep his eyes tight shut and growl, "Go away." So he did. But he'd keep visiting whether Don wanted or not.

When Jimmy McPhee phoned him at home in the late afternoon saying, with no word of greeting, *Jimmy McPhee here*, McAllister told him, "I need to speak to you."

"I'll be round your place the night, but it might be late."

Jimmy McPhee was late—half past ten at night late. He was sober, which surprised McAllister, and he was carrying a briefcase, which surprised McAllister even more. A second glance and McAllister decided it was not documents Jimmy was carrying, so he said nothing. He went to the shelf and selected a Dalmore single malt. Jimmy saw the bottle and grinned; it was a bottle produced not many miles from the McPhee encampment, and a bottle that Jimmy himself had once presented to McAllister.

"A fine taste in whisky you have," he said.

"And a fine taste in friends," McAllister replied. They raised their glasses. They drank. There was a comfortable silence as they savored the peat coursing through the veins.

"Your mother well?" McAllister broke the hush.

So it's to be the Highland way, Jimmy thought. *Must mean some big favor he's wanting.*

"She's well, feeling the cold in her bones, though."

"Aye, my mother's the same."

They contemplated the fire.

"The defense doesn't have to prove who did it," McAllister started, "just raise enough doubt . . . maybe only show an alternative . . . the Procurator Fiscal, he'll have to show . . . 'Beyond reasonable doubt' . . ."

" 'Specially in a murder case," Jimmy finished.

"So have you thought more on Don's predicament?"

Jimmy liked how McAllister did not ask him for his mother's thoughts on the matter—although it was Jenny McPhee who would know the secrets of that time and that place, when Joyce Mackenzie and Donal McLeod were courting, and whatever else had happened—or not.

"Two thoughts," Jimmy replied. "Who knew where he kept the knife? And could the sergeant major somehow have done it—because my mother is certain he is her killer."

"Aye, the sergeant major." McAllister was pleased Jimmy had brought up the subject. "I know he can walk, I've seen him. But with his legs, could he manage the steps?"

"Now that's what I was thinking." Jimmy leaned forward, elbows on his thighs, both hands around the tumbler as though the liquor would warm his hands along with his insides.

"You know where she was found? On the back porch of the church?" McAllister's voice was too casual, and Jimmy too alert not to notice. "Suppose he somehow had a key to the church, was hiding there waiting . . ."

"The police must have checked." Much as Jimmy liked the theory, he couldn't see DI Dunne neglecting to check such a simple scenario.

"Really? When they were convinced from the beginning they had their man? Convinced by Sergeant Major Smart's accusations? By the contents of the will?" McAllister did not raise his voice, did not show anger; it was this that convinced Jimmy that he was right—McAllister *was* on to something.

"Aye, it's a possibility, but the higher-ups of the constabulary are quick to blame anyone as long as it's not one of their own. I'm sure they're sorry there was no convenient tinker around that night."

"I'm sure they checked." They smiled at each other when

McAllister said this. "I'll have to think this through, but could we suggest that the sergeant major might have been there that night?"

"Suggest?" Jimmy laughed. "You'd need to do more than *suggest.*"

No more needed saying, so McAllister got up to recharge their glasses.

"I met thon Canadian gadgie who's working wi' you," Jimmy commented. "Seems decent enough."

McAllister was now the one on alert. It was something in Jimmy's tone, not his use of the word "gadgie," which McAllister now knew was not an insult, just the Northerner's word for a man.

"Aye, him and young Rob and Joanne Ross came to the Ferry Inn two Saturdays past, but ma mother was unsettled by him."

"Really?" *What was Joanne doing on a Saturday night with Neil Stewart,* was what McAllister wanted to know. "Why was that?" was what he asked.

"There's no knowing what my ma thinks o' anything or anyone." But he had a wild idea, and it was not one he wanted to think about. He drank the dram in a single gulp, stood, and saying only, "You know how to find me," he left.

The sound of the front door closing and Jimmy's car starting and the clock chiming midnight made McAllister aware of how tired he was.

He checked the fire; he took the glasses into the kitchen and rinsed them. He went to switch off the lights but sat down again. One answer and one question, he thought; whatever was needed to raise doubts in the mind of a jury, Jimmy would help; whatever it was about Neil Stewart that has unsettled his mother, Jimmy was asking for help.

But what was Joanne doing out on a Saturday night with Neil

Stewart? He had noticed that Neil and Joanne had become friends. He knew they had had the occasional coffee together, shared a sandwich sometimes.

Maybe shared more than a sandwich. His attempt at a lightness he did not feel wasn't working. A slow sinking black despair had crept over him, pinning him to the chair.

Joanne. Neil. No. Never. It can't be.

He kept trying to persuade himself there was nothing between Joanne and Neil. And he kept coming back to a picture of them, in the newsroom, sitting just a little too near, their faces a little too close, laughing in that way lovers do.

He eventually fell asleep in the chair and awoke, cold-tired and unable to get back to sleep for a long time.

"It's open," McAllister yelled. He had heard Rob's motorbike even though he was in the kitchen, and as he had toast under the grill, he didn't want to leave it. He hated burnt toast.

"Not at church, then," Rob said as he came in carrying the Sunday papers, which he had collected off McAllister's front porch.

"Keep your facetious remarks for a career in tabloids."

"Not me, I'm going into television—remember?"

Without asking, McAllister put out an extra plate, broke two more eggs into the frying pan, then cut more bread for toast. "Help yourself to tea."

"Did you see Joanne yesterday?" McAllister asked, hating himself for being so greedy for news of her.

"No. Have you seen Don?" Rob knew Joanne was not in town but he was not going to be the one to tell McAllister.

"Seen him, spoken to him, but got no answers."

"If the sergeant major killed Mrs. Smart, he's had a long time to plan it."

It did not surprise McAllister that Rob went straight to the very point he had been thinking himself. "Aye, so but why now? What changed?"

"I've no idea." He had not asked his father about the will, he knew there was no point, but something about it bothered him. "Do you know when the will was drawn up?"

"No," McAllister said. "Why?"

"I've no idea why I asked the question," Rob said. "It's just that murders are often to do with who inherits what ... in books and films at any rate."

"Another point, how would whoever did it know about Don's filleting knife?"

"Unlikely the sergeant major knew." Rob was annoyed when he said this. He wanted the man to be guilty, especially as he was causing his father all sorts of problems, pestering him, setting another solicitor onto him to question his handling of Mrs. Smart's will. "Eilidh—I told you about her, the nurse who lives next door to Don—she might know. I'll ask her."

"As soon as possible. Do you know if the sergeant major has an alibi?"

"He's legless, I would imagine that's his alibi."

McAllister couldn't help it. He laughed. And he couldn't remember the last time he had laughed. "No seriously, what alibi ..."

"McAllister, I know it's serious, but we have to laugh occasionally or else we'll all try to hang ourselves." Rob was speaking through a mouthful of toast. "Alibis." He swallowed. "Right, the sergeant major; he was at home—alone, or so he told the police; the Gurkha, let's not completely dismiss him as a suspect, he was out, walking he says, alone, in the dark, on a brisk Sunday night."

"He was a friend of Mrs. Smart and her father ..."

"And he inherited a sizable sum of money. How much was it?"

"Two thousand pounds."

"That much?" Rob whistled. "That's a fortune, especially in Nepali terms . . ."

"We have so much to check up on, and not nearly enough time."

"You'd better tackle the Gurkha man, and maybe ask Beech's sister, Countess Sokolov, if she knows whether the sergeant major really was at home that night. I'll talk to Eilidh." He stood. "I'll try to track her down today."

"Good, and I'll call round to see Beech and his sister." McAllister turned to the sink and ran the hot tap for the washing-up. His back to Rob, he said, "I hear you and Neil met with Jenny McPhee and Jimmy recently."

"I'd hoped to shock Neil by taking him to the only louche place in town, but it didn't bother him"—Rob grinned—"I'm sure he's seen worse. And Neil's sitting in on our next gig, he plays a mean blues on the mouth organ."

Don't ask, don't ask, McAllister was telling himself. "Joanne was with you?" The words absconded like a rat from wreckage.

"Yes, but we didn't stay long; Jenny wasn't in form so Neil didn't get to hear the legendary McPhee songs and stories. He was a wee bit disappointed; he's hoping to pick Jenny's brain for his book."

"Then where did you go?" The minute he said this McAllister regretted it. *I sound so petty.*

Recognizing jealousy even from this unlikely source, Rob was tactful. "Joanne went home and Neil and I made an early night of it." His voice was light, his face casual, but he understood what it had cost McAllister to ask.

"Do you want that last piece of toast?" It was all Rob could think of to change the subject. And it worked.

McAllister sliced off two more pieces of bread, set them

under the grill, and no more was said about Joanne Ross, Neil Stewart, and Saturday night.

McAllister waited until early afternoon before calling Rosemary Sokolov. It was her brother who answered the telephone.

"Come for afternoon tea," he replied in answer to McAllister's question.

Once more McAllister found himself taking the path along the river. Once more he found himself peering over the wall into Sergeant Major Smart's garden, or rather Mrs. Smart's garden— it was only her husband's by dint of her death, and if he were to be found guilty, he would not inherit it. McAllister was thinking this as, finding the garden deserted, he walked around to the main road to come in the street entrance to the Beauchamp Carlyle residence.

"Which tea do you prefer? Earl Grey or Lapsang souchong?" Rosemary Sokolov asked.

McAllister would have preferred Typhoo, extra strong, but he replied, "Lapsang, please."

And once more he marveled at the vast contrast between his life as the son of a Glasgow fireman, a scholarship boy, a man who had made his own life, and that of the Beauchamp Carlyle siblings, born into aristocracy and wealth and the divine right to command outposts of empire.

But this is 1957, he reminded himself, *and all is changing, especially after the debacle of Suez.*

McAllister discovered he liked the tea, and he said so.

"I don't drink, and I certainly don't smoke." This, Countess Sokolov said to her brother, who was sitting opposite her on the sofa at right angles to a generous fire. "So tea is my passion. I send for it from a tea merchant in London. I'll give you some if you'd like."

"I would like that very much." McAllister was also finding he liked Rosemary Sokolov, which was good, as he admired her brother, had great respect for his humor and intellect. "I was hoping you could ask Mr. . . . . Bahadur, is it, a few questions."

"Why don't you talk to him? His English is fluent." The countess was not going to intervene.

"I'd also like to ask you about the night Mrs. Smart . . ."

"Was killed." She did not believe in euphemisms; having seen much of death, she saw death as a natural process, except in this case. "What would you like to know?"

"Was the sergeant major at home that night?"

She hesitated.

"He says he was," McAllister explained, "but he has no one to vouch for him."

"He has a car," she told him, "one of those new three-wheeler machines for the disabled, the ones with hand controls. It has rather a distinctive engine noise. It went out early that evening, but I have no idea when it came back."

McAllister noticed the pronoun. "*It* went out?"

"I have no way of knowing who was driving."

"The logical supposition would be that Sergeant Major Smart was driving." McAllister said this quietly, politely, in no way questioning her choice of phrase, echoing her open-mindedness.

"Mr. McAllister, I have always made it my business to mind my own business; what went on in the house next door is not for me to discuss."

"Mrs. Sokolov, our friend and colleague Mr. McLeod's life depends on finding out who murdered Mrs. Smart. The police believe they have their man, they are looking no further."

Brother and sister looked at each other. "I can tell you the little I know," Beech offered, "and, my dear, the rules of civility have been broken by a murderer. We must help if we can."

She nodded once and started speaking with barely a pause between sentences. "Ever since the sergeant major came back to the Highlands to live in her house, there was always a terrible commotion early on Sunday evenings when Joyce went to visit Mr. McLeod."

She did not think it pertinent to recount the numerous other times when the sound of the sergeant major's cursing could be heard clearly over the garden wall—particularly in the long summer evenings, when the nastiness of the language drove her indoors, away from enjoying her beloved garden and herbaceous borders and the sounds and scents of the river.

"He would follow her up the pathway out into the street, screaming abuse, calling her terrible names. Anyone passing by would clearly hear him. Often he would follow her, walking as close as he could and as far as he could. When he bought the car, he'd follow her, but she told me she always took the steps between the churches and the abbey wall. She had a key to the gate into the courtyard where Mr. McLeod lives, and they always kept that gate locked."

Joyce had told Rosemary this in a joking, despairing conversation one afternoon when it all became too much and she had stayed with her friend and neighbor for a week, needing a refuge and a good night's sleep.

"So the sergeant major knew where Don McLeod lives? He knew they were friends?"

"Joyce Mackenzie and Mr. McLeod had been friends since just after the Great War. They resumed their friendship when she came back from India. She made it clear to the sergeant major that she would not give up the friendship, but agreed to contain it to one meeting every week. She agreed not to . . ." She looked across at her brother, who nodded. "Joyce agreed to continue living with Sergeant Major Smart, in her house next door, but on the Sunday-evening meetings she would not give way."

"But why?" He saw the question was too vague. "Why would she agree to continue living with a man who so obviously hated her? She was wealthy enough to leave him. And the house belonged to her."

"Yes. Her father made certain that the deeds were in her name only. If the sergeant major made a claim on it, the property would revert to the colonel's regiment as a rest home for retired officers." She leaned forward and lightly touched the teapot. "I'll make a fresh pot." It was clear that she was not going to say more.

"Let's go onto the terrace." Beech stood, holding an empty pipe in one hand, reaching for the tobacco tin with the other.

McAllister was grateful. It had been nearly an hour since his last cigarette, and he was restless.

"I saw the sergeant major smoking a pipe. Strange-smelling tobacco he uses."

McAllister saw Beech's reaction and, afraid Beech might think he had been spying, he quickly added, "I was out for a walk, I happened to catch a glimpse of him over the wall."

Since Beech was six foot five, it did not occur to him McAllister might be spying on his neighbor. "Didn't you recognize the smell?"

"It wasn't Turkish tobacco."

"Ah yes, you've never been to India." He smiled at McAllister's confusion. "Our neighbor is rather partial to opium. A habit he picked up in the East. Probably a good thing. Keeps the pain away. Keeps him subdued."

"Subdued?"

"He has a temper."

"Would he have killed his wife?"

"Would he? Possibly. Could he? Possibly."

McAllister was becoming frustrated with the conversation, one that was lacking long joined-up sentences, and shedding more mystery than light.

"On Sunday nights . . ." McAllister started.

"Joyce Mackenzie would visit with Mr. McLeod. Gurkha Bahadur had a night off. Sergeant Major Smart sometimes followed her, but more often of late he would entertain friends, mostly ex-servicemen, in a game of cards, and from the noise, it would appear that a large quantity of drink was consumed."

"Why was this never mentioned before?"

"Probably irrelevant." Then Beech added, "And some of the participants were policemen, or at least one, to my knowledge. Sergeant Patience," he added, reading the question in McAllister's eyebrows.

"What time did Mrs. Smart return?"

"I don't know. Late, I presume. On one or two occasions over the years, she would stay a night or two with my sister. Not that I know Joyce's household arrangements; it is only in the last year that I have taken to staying more frequently in town—to work on my small contribution to the *Gazette*."

"Much appreciated." McAllister meant it. The presence of Mortimer Beauchamp Carlyle was reassuring, not just to McAllister; the younger staff, especially Hector, were always asking casual questions of Beech, always receiving helpful answers.

"So, what do we have?" Beech continued. "A relationship between Mr. McLeod and Joyce Mackenzie that began circa 1919, 1920. Why would Don want to end it now after all that time? Why would Smart want to end it now? Who else would want to end her life?" The light was fading. A light but chill northeast wind was blowing upriver. The men did not notice.

Rosemary Sokolov watched them through the French

windows and left them to it, going into the kitchen; she did not want to see or hear anything about her friend's death, it hurt too much.

"It must come down to the will," McAllister said.

"Why?"

"Money is the classic motive for murder."

"And passion."

And again McAllister was feeling the frustration of not getting anywhere; all these meetings, all these conversations, nothing being resolved, the questions remaining the same or throwing up more questions. And the "start at the beginning" that Jenny McPhee had thrown out—he'd done that, he now knew how long Don McLeod and Joyce Mackenzie, Mrs. Smart, had known each other . . . Mrs. Smart, *Joyce Mackenzie—was that it?*

He suddenly knew where he would be looking tomorrow, first thing, or at least first thing after the news conference.

"One final question; how well do you know Neil Stewart?"

"Neil?" Beech was surprised at the change in subject. "He has been researching in our family archives. He seems an intelligent, likable man, and he's been a godsend to the *Gazette.*" Beech looked at McAllister but could read nothing in his face. "Is there any reason I should believe different?"

"None whatsoever. Put it down to a journalist's morbid curiosity." McAllister had to look away as he said this.

They bade each other farewell on the porch, and as McAllister walked down the pathway to the gate leading out onto the main road, Beech took his sister's hand and linked it over his arm.

"No matter what was promised, I think we owe it to Mr. McLeod to help all we can." He spoke quietly, but there was no mistaking the resolve in his voice. "Nothing will harm *her*, but if one believes in justice for the dead, we must help Mr. McLeod."

Rosemary Sokolov said nothing. But her brother felt her

grip tighten. Then she slipped her arm out and went back into the house.

Beech walked around to the side of the house to the area outside the coal shed where they kept the dustbins. It was the night to put them out for the "scaffies" who came early on Monday mornings.

He heard the door knocker at the neighboring house. He opened the coal shed door to find the gardening gloves. He heard the door knocker again. This time louder and longer. He put on the gloves and dragged one bin onto the path. He heard the door open and the sergeant major's voice.

"It's you. Get off my doorstep. Get out of my garden."

"I'd like to speak to Mr. Bahadur," Beech heard McAllister saying.

"He has nothing to say to you."

"That's up to him, isn't it?"

"Get off my premises or I'm calling the police!" The sergeant major's voice was at parade ground pitch, his anger unmistakable.

There followed a strange sound—perhaps a scuffle, perhaps a blow. Next came a yelp of pain, followed by a moan, then someone swearing. From the Glasgow accent that lessened the effect of the words, Beech knew it was McAllister.

"What's wrong?" he called out.

"I think my foot's broken," McAllister called back. "Smart slammed the door on it and it hurts like hell."

Beech knocked against the bin in his hurry, and the lid clattered onto the paving stones. He ran next door, where McAllister was sitting on the doorstep, the door ajar. Down the hallway, Beech could see and hear Sergeant Major Smart on the telephone.

"I want a police car here immediately. A man has attacked

me on my own doorstep. Yes, I've told you already. I'm Sergeant Major Smart, Ness Walk."

As he bellowed orders down the receiver he seemed not to notice, or perhaps did not care to notice, the slight figure of Mr. Bahadur slip past him, out onto the porch, where without a word he put his shoulder into McAllister's oxter. With Beech on the other side, they walked the crippled editor, still swearing like the Glasgow East End boy he was, out into the street.

As they were about to pass through the gate to Rosemary Sokolov's kitchen, where the first aid kit was kept, a police car came down the street at well above the speed limit, catching the trio in flashing blue light and the full beam of the headlights.

Knowing it was best to face the police, they stopped and waited. McAllister leaned against the wall and pulled out his cigarettes. Mr. Bahadur held out a lighter, as McAllister's hands were too shaky to flick open his own. Beech stood in front of his friends, legs akimbo, arms folded, on guard.

Neither Beech not McAllister knew the constables who climbed out of the car. Nor did the constables know them. But somehow, Major Mortimer Beauchamp Carlyle, retired, managed to persuade them that all was well but McAllister must be driven to the emergency department of the hospital immediately, or they might face demotion. And all this was accomplished without once raising his voice.

"And could you let my sister know where we've gone?" he asked Mr. Bahadur.

Not only did Mr. Bahadur let Mrs. Rosemary Sokolov know, he put out the bins and accepted her invitation to stay the night, but not before having a long and emotional conversation with Rosemary, whom he refused to call anything other than Countess.

CHAPTER 13

As is often the case, calamity had not struck but was creeping up in small increments. And no one at the *Highland Gazette* had an inkling.

The assistant in the grocery on Union Street—the high-class purveyor to the gentry—was serving Mrs. Angus McLean.

"That will be all, thank you," Margaret McLean said. "And I'd like to settle last month's account." She produced the account and the money. He screwed it into the pneumatic system, and it whizzed off upstairs to the accounts department.

As he was wrapping her tea and sugar into neat brown paper parcels, he said, "We like prompt payers like yourself, Mrs. McLean, and we pride ourselves on being the same." He looked cross as he said this, as though Margaret was somehow responsible for his problem. "Take the *Gazette*; first you can't get them to give you an account, next you get a bill in *red writing*"—he spoke as though this was a summons from Saint Lucifer himself—"and our establishment *always* pays on time." He glared at Margaret for not showing an appropriate response at the very thought of red ink. "I expect it's taking time to get back to normal after . . . if you can get back to normal after . . ."

"Such neat parcels," Margaret McLean said, putting them in her wicker basket and thanking the assistant once more as he handed her her receipt and change. As she crossed the street to the car, she wondered if she should pass the conversation on, then decided it was none of her business. Even though she wrote an occasional gossip column, *About Town*, for the *Gazette*, she was not a gossip.

On the west coast, Mr. Graham Nicolson, the *Gazette* correspondent, heard of an incident regarding nondelivery of the newspapers to the Isle of Skye.

The van that picked up the newspapers off the train had had a puncture and missed the island ferry. Mr. Nicolson wasn't told that the man had gone off to the pub to forget his cold hands and wet britches, that the rain got under the van's tarpaulin, ruining that week's edition, that the remaining newspapers were dumped at the local tip, and all calls to the *Gazette* had gone unanswered. Mr. Nicolson felt it a personal insult when the *Gazette* was criticized, but even he had to admit it was gaining a reputation for unreliability.

These are difficult times, he kept telling himself and others. And with his old friend and fellow Gaelic speaker and lover of fine single malts Donal McLeod in gaol charged with murder, he too was not sleeping well.

No one at the *Gazette* noticed that far fewer people were giving birth, marrying, or dying; when Neil laid out the "Hatched, Matched, and Dispatched" columns, knowing they were the best-read part of a local newspaper, he couldn't know that lately they were abnormally short.

No one knew that the results of a contentious bridge tournament had appeared with the names of the winner and the runner-up reversed, until the winner himself confronted Betsy and left with apologies for having made her cry.

A quarter-page advertisement, canceled for lack of funds, appeared in three more editions free of charge, but no one noticed except the very happy haulage contractor—and he wasn't about to tell Mrs. Betsy Buchanan her mistake, as he was still hoping she would pose for his company calendar as Miss April.

No one recognized that without the sharpness of Don McLeod's wee red pencil, the standard of the copy was declining. Rob was the worst offender, being a devotee of adverbs, which, in Don McLeod's stylebook, was a capital offense. No one monitored the decline in circulation. No one had the figures. And the accounts—no one had sat down and done the simple arithmetic because there were no numbers.

The *Highland Gazette* was slowly slipping to a standard below everything McAllister had worked towards and, for a short five and a half months, had succeeded in achieving.

Another Monday morning meeting was due to begin. Then Betsy Buchanan arrived and announced from the doorway of the reporters' room: "Mr. McAllister will be in late. You've to start without him."

Rob said, "Thanks, Betsy," and Neil smiled at her.

Joanne saw the smile and snapped, "Is there anything I need to know about the advertising, Mrs. Buchanan?"

"What do you mean?" Betsy thrust out her bosom like a wee cock sparrow, her face flushed. "I can cope fine." She fled down the stairs.

Joanne turned back to the typewriter to finish writing up a report from the Highlands Tourism Authority. She was trying to keep her face in neutral, suppressing the temptation to smile, to laugh, to shout out, *I'm in love. He chose me!* She tried to ignore the tingle in her arms and her knees that crept up whenever she sat in the same room as Neil, typing in rhythm with Neil, leaning over the table to check a document, when saying anything—even hello and good-bye. She felt she was in a cloud of static electricity, and wouldn't have been surprised if her hair stood on end.

Ten minutes later, she rolled the article out of the Underwood, popped it into Neil's tray for subbing, and the thought came to her, *There's something wrong with Betsy*. She sighed and went to check, only because Neil was working and only because she had to get away from him in case anyone noticed how different she was, how much she had changed, how much her whole life had altered.

Joanne went downstairs to the tiny office behind the reception desk, smiling at Fiona as she went in, but getting no response back. The fifteen-year-old was straight out of Technical High School with a proficiency in typing and bookkeeping, and Betsy's cousin's daughter.

But perhaps she can't talk in joined-up sentences because of her terrible pimples. Joanne immediately felt guilty about having such an unkind thought and looked around the dismal room. Lined with shelves holding accounts folders from probably the last fifty years, a two-bar electric fire, scuffed and stained desks, and semi-broken and obviously uncomfortable chairs, Joanne felt sorry for Betsy. *This is no place to work.* She sighed and, turning to Betsy, saw the tears she hadn't heard.

"Betsy, what's wrong?"

"I can't cope." She waved her hands at the three piles of paper in front of her, all substantial. Joanne saw that some were envelopes that hadn't been opened, and she was scared to check the date stamp.

"I've that much to do"—Betsy was sniffing now, most unlike her usually smart, perky self—"and I'm that much behind . . . and I can't afford to lose my job. Not now. If Mr. McAllister finds out, he'll kill me." Her hand flew to cover her mouth. "Heavens! I'm so sorry. I didn't mean that . . ."

"Sit down, Betsy. Start at the beginning."

"It's the accounts. They're all over the place. And I can't find half the invoices and . . . the bookkeeper says I have to make them all tally by the end of this month or she'll tell Mr. McAl-lister . . . And I'm . . . I can't tell Bill . . . I don't know if he'll stand by me . . ."

"Betsy, what on earth are you talking about?"

"I . . ." Betsy looked at Joanne. She had never liked her rival much. Like Bill Ross she thought Joanne was *too big for her boots*—Betsy's mother's phrase—and all because Joanne spoke with an educated almost non-Scottish accent and used linen napkins at meals—so Granny Ross had told everyone in the Church Women's Guild.

But her instinct told Betsy that Joanne had much to lose and much to gain from her predicament, and might turn out to be an unexpected ally.

"Joanne, I'm in a right mess," Betsy said, and a single large tear escaped, running down her Max Factor pancake makeup that Joanne considered more appropriate for evening than day-time.

An hour later, Joanne returned to the reporters' room half worried, half elated, but with no clear idea how to help Betsy out of a sizable pickle. *But I will help.* Joanne surprised herself with the thought.

"Serves me right for sticking my foot in the door," McAllister had said to Beech on the previous evening as they waited in the emergency department for the results of the X-ray.

"At least it is a Sunday, not a Saturday night after the pubs have closed." Beech's loud voice and his hearty clipped accent rang around the empty waiting room and cheered McAllister up immensely. He could well imagine Mortimer Beauchamp Carlyle facing ravaging tribesmen of the Abyssinian Highlands and ter-rifying them off with his voice alone.

There was only one small bone broken in his little toe. The bruising was extensive, the pain intense, and next morning McAllister found he needed a stick to walk. Changing gears in the car hurt far more than a break in the small toe would suggest. After climbing the stairs to the reporters' room, he held the Monday meeting with his foot up on a chair and a glass of whisky in his hand.

Rob immediately asked, "What happened?"

McAllister had to admit that he had put his foot in the door in an attempt to speak to Gurkha Bahadur.

"He is unavailable," the sergeant major had said before deliberately swinging the door shut on McAllister's foot.

"The rotten swine . . ." Joanne said as she came into the reporters' room, catching the end of the tale.

McAllister lit a cigarette. "Good of you to join us, Mrs. Ross."

"But I was . . ." It was her turn to flap her wrists.

McAllister had an enormous capacity for intellectual reasoning and a limited capacity for emotional self-analysis and could not believe how painful it was to be with Joanne. *It hurts worse than my foot.*

He turned to Rob. "Sergeant Major Smart has charged me with assault. Your father thinks he'll drop the charges in return for me not countersuing *him* for assault."

Rob grinned. "I'm sure my father will win the argument. But what happened?"

"What have we for this week?" McAllister did not want to discuss the ignominy of a broken toe.

"'Editor of local newspaper charged with assault?'" Rob suggested.

The silence that followed, the absolute stillness of McAllister—apart from the curl of smoke coming from the cigarette dangling from the corner of his mouth—made them all hold their breath.

"Is there any news on Mr. McLeod?" Hector broke in. "Any progress on the case?"

"He's in hospital. He's as well as can be expected, but it's hard for him to talk. And no, there's no progress in his case."

"Why no'?" Hector looked across at McAllister. "Why aren't we doing anything?"

"We will get this newspaper out. We will do all we can. We will—"

"Most of the pages are filled with the usual," Neil broke in, "but we need a front page." He hesitated. "I'm assuming the rival press will report Mr. McLeod's attempt to . . . his being admitted to hospital." Neil looked around. "It *is* news." He held his hands out in a half apology.

"See if the story turns up in the Aberdeen daily. If it does, you write it up, you're neutral in all this." McAllister got to his feet. Winced at the pain. His stick clattered to the floor. Hec retrieved it for him. All four of them looked at one another as they listened to his shuffle down the stairs.

Rob was about to turn on Hec, but the photographer got in first. "I'm no' sorry for asking. Mr. McLeod will be before the judge in three, no, four weeks." He gathered up some contact sheets, put them into his schoolbag, and left.

"I have the front page for you, Neil," Rob told him. "An old acquaintance of ours—Mrs. Janet Ord Mackenzie—is up for sentencing this morning. She killed a farmhand on her estate. Although everyone knows the story, I can spice it up enough for a front-page splash plus a full inside-page story." He shook his motorbike jacket off and put on the smart blazer he kept on a hanger for court-reporting duties. "Joanne will fill you in on it." He smoothed down his hair. "See you later."

They waited about thirty seconds, then Neil reached out for her hand and pulled her to him.

"Good morning, Mrs. Stewart."

"Don't say that."

"I'm joking." He leaned his head on her shoulder.

That's why I don't want you to say it, Joanne was thinking. But she said nothing. His hand strayed to her lower back, was caressing her, making her shiver. She stood back a pace. "Neil, not here."

"Where? When?"

That was the problem. "I don't know," she said. "Certainly not at my place. No, wait, maybe you could come over on Wednesday. The girls stay with their grandparents on press nights." She was breaking her self-made rule: never have anyone male in her house, her refuge; not because she might be found out, more because it was her sanctuary.

"I'll try to keep my hands busy typing until then . . . Now, the sentencing of Mrs. Double Barreled, what's that about?"

"Mrs. Ord Mackenzie, right, well, a few months ago, last Easter . . ." And she told him the story of the double death on the Black Isle estate of her friend Patricia, not forgetting to mention her front-page scoop, her very first lead story, and he was duly appreciative. *I love him,* she thought, *and he's leaving.* But now, there was a glimmer of hope. *So I must ask Hector as soon as possible.*

It was early afternoon before Joanne managed to find herself alone with Hector. "Hector, I was wondering if you could do something for me? Something personal."

"Oh aye?" He didn't mind doing favors and assumed it was the usual—taking pictures of children—and he liked Joanne's girls, especially Annie, who was friends with his sister.

"It's a bit tricky." She hesitated, then came straight out with it. "I want you to take compromising pictures of my husband, Bill, with Betsy Buchanan so I can get a divorce."

"What?"

It was not that Hec hadn't heard or didn't understand, it was that he did not do that type of work, no matter that it would have made him money. He had been asked to do this before, usually by solicitors who specialized in divorce—although divorce was rare, and he had always refused. In Hector's opinion it was tacky, there was no artistic merit in it, and he would have to appear in court to verify when and where he had taken the pictures.

"I can't do that, Joanne." His voice was quiet, but the underlying hurt was clear. "We work with Betsy."

"Betsy wants this too. *She* will tell you when and where to take the pictures."

"What?" Now he was completely confused.

"But my husband mustn't know. Or anyone else."

"If my granny hears of it, she'll throw me out." Hector was jiggling from foot to foot, completely confused by the request. "Ma granny, she said *no smutty pictures,* and she'll find out, 'cos I'll have to go to court and tell how I got the pictures."

"Really?" Rob was standing in the doorway. "What have you done this time?"

"Mind your own business, Rob McLean," Joanne snapped.

"Sorry I spoke."

He looked at her. She looked away. She ran down the stairs, out into the wind. It was nearly November, and the chill was getting to her bones. But her face was hot. She pulled her cardigan tight, crossing her arms, tucking her chin in, but the wind still penetrated the layers of cardigan and jumper and cotton vest.

"Damn and blast," she was muttering when McAllister appeared, seemingly out of nowhere, saying, "I agree."

"McAllister, don't sneak up like that! You gave me a fright."

"I'd ask you to have coffee with me but I don't think I can walk across town. Maybe later?"

"Maybe. I have to get back, I'm freezing out here."

He watched her run into the *Gazette* office and once more agreed. *It is freezing,* he was thinking, *and it's more than the weather.*

McAllister's only positive news came at the end of the day from Angus McLean.

"I'm phoning to let you know Sergeant Major Smart has dropped the charge against you."

McAllister thanked him.

"I have a meeting on Thursday with the advocate from Edinburgh. He and his assistant will be here to prepare the defense. Would you care to join us?"

McAllister agreed. He started to make notes for the meeting, then called out across the landing for Rob.

"Shut the door."

Rob did and took a chair.

"Have you spoken to your nurse friend?"

"Tonight. She has a day off and is sleeping for most of it, she said."

"Ask her about the knife—who would know where it was kept. And anything that might be useful."

"Yes, sir."

"Sorry, Rob. I know you know what you're doing. I only wish I did." He lit another cigarette, the first of his third packet of the day. "I have no idea what's wrong with me. I can't sleep, I can't make decisions, my judgment is haywire, I feel powerless, I can't find anything to free Don."

"This advocate from Edinburgh has a good reputation," Rob told him. "Let's put together all the information we have, and hope he can make more sense of it than us."

"Let's hope so." McAllister did not sound optimistic but at least it was a plan.

That evening, as Rob drove over the Black Bridge to see Eilidh, he remembered McAllister's instructions: ask about the knife. *Of course,* Rob had thought, *that's obvious, but what else might Eilidh know?*

He had been shocked by the editor's lack of clarity; he was used to McAllister's insight, he couldn't believe how his hero was floundering. He knew the situation with Don was dire, so why was McAllister so indecisive? Neither Rob nor McAllister himself was aware that Joanne's abandonment might be contributing to the editor's overwhelming sense of loss. All Rob could see was how slowly the man thought and moved, as though wading through emotional and spiritual tar.

He arrived at the end of Church Street and switched off the bike engine. As instructed, he parked on the opposite side and further down from the passageway leading to Eilidh's terrace.

The gate was closed but unlocked, just as she said it would be. He hesitated before pushing it open and turned to look again at the path leading to the steps down to the footbridge—the steps between the church and abbey wall, the steps where Mrs. Smart had been murdered. It was raining slightly. Just as it had been on that night. A damp misty rain, which, if you looked out a window you couldn't be certain was rain except for the shine on the slate roofs, the paving stones, the cobbled street, weather that made driving a motorbike horribly dangerous, and made murder or a haunting no surprise.

He went down the passageway between and under the first floor of the buildings, where the roof was not high. Wide enough to get a coffin through; that was the saying about these old buildings. In the courtyard—the size of the sitting room in a grand house like that of Countess Sokolov—Rob stood looking at the empty windows in Don's house. Less than two months empty, and the one-down, one-up terrace felt as desolate as a cottage from the Highland Clearances.

He knocked on Eilidh's door, needing warmth and light and hopefully some cuddling.

"Hiya." She opened the door and pulled Rob in. "It's freezing out there." She had a quick look around, saw no one, and shut the door. "I don't want anyone to see you. My parents would make me live at home if they knew I had a man visiting."

"Do you want me to lock the gate?" Rob asked.

"Please." She pulled open the cutlery drawer and handed him a brass key that looked as though it would open a pirate's treasure chest. "With the house next door empty and Mr. McLeod's house . . . I'm alone here, so I keep the gate locked."

"When did the house next door become empty?"

"Oh, two years or so ago."

Damn, Rob thought, *no witnesses there.*

When he came back in, Eilidh had put the kettle on. "Coffee?" She shook the tin of the co-op's own brand of instant coffee. Rob's heart sank. "Love some."

"This wee place belonged to my mother's mother," she explained, "and when she died, my parents let me have it for as long as I'm at the hospital." *Then they expect me to train as a district nurse, and return home or at least marry someone respectable, preferably a doctor who will settle somewhere in my father's parish and we can all go to his church together and listen to his endless sermons about hell and damnation and . . .* "Sorry?"

"And here was me thinking you'd be hanging on to my words of wit and wisdom." Rob laughed. "Listen, before we go out—or stay in—I want to ask about Don's fish knife."

"I know nothing about his stupid knife." She was fed up with questions from everyone—from the police, from her parents, from colleagues, from the woman in the co-op where she did her shopping, and now Rob. "I keep saying, I've never seen the knife."

"Aye, but do you know anyone who might know?"

"I suppose the people who lived next door might. They were friends o' Mr. McLeod, so he said. Then there's the usual—the coalman, the binmen, the meter reader, I don't know . . . I suppose Mrs. Hoity Toity must have known, but then again, she didn't stab herself."

Rob was disconcerted by Eilidh's description of Mrs. Smart until he remembered how correct she could be, how proper and prim she might have seemed to outsiders.

And when Eilidh put the record on the Dansette, he could understand that perhaps there might have been a problem with neighbors over the volume. When Eilidh started to dance or, rather, thump about, he well understood that Mrs. Smart or Don might have said something. When she joined in the chorus—she knew all the lyrics and could manage a fair American accent—Eilidh was loud, and completely tone-deaf.

"Wow," Rob said when the record had finished, "that was incredible." He meant it. She went to play it again.

"I'd love a Dansette but it's too expensive for me." He was lying. He had one. They cost three hundred guineas, and his mother had paid for it to keep the peace, or at least her husband's health; Angus McLean went into the garden whenever Rob played his music on their big record player, and as winters were nine months long, she was happy to indulge her only child if only to prevent her husband from catching pneumonia.

"I haven't paid for it yet." Eilidh was stroking the case as though it was a pet. "I got it on hire purchase."

She saw he didn't believe her; hire purchase if you were under twenty-one was impossible.

"I forged my mother's signature as guarantor, else they wouldn't give me the credit." She took Bill Haley off and put Elvis on. "Mr. McLeod's lady friend once told me she thought the music was too loud, especially on a Sunday, but I told her to mind her own business. *You ain't nothing but a hound dog, cryin' all the time . . .*"

Rob endured it for the three minutes and something seconds it took to finish, then grabbed her in a clinch and started to nuzzle her neck.

"Hey, you're not backwards in coming forwards." She giggled, did not resist, and after a minute or so, joined in with a passion to match her dancing. It was Rob who was overwhelmed by Nurse Eilidh Davidson of Kiltarlity, not the other way around, so he didn't get to ask her any more about the night Mrs. Smart was murdered. And he completely forgot to ask about the knife.

Chapter 14

Jimmy McPhee was a man whom many knew of, but few knew. He was an outsider. An observer. A man who thought human frailty a weakness. He would take note of people and their conversations, of objects, of places, and squirrel them away in the recesses of his memory. And like most people born into an oral culture, he had a prodigious memory. When the time was ripe, he would retrieve stored memories and impressions, the taste of the place and the weather, and his timing was very good indeed. That is what made Jimmy McPhee a man never to be underestimated.

His mother's withdrawal into silences longer than usual, her wanting to be on the road even though she well knew that rain or sudden snow was likely, concerned him. The anniversary of the theft of the boys was in November. And that anniversary was soon. And that was why his mother was not herself, or so he kept assuring himself.

Then there was Neil Stewart. Here he was, noseying around, asking his mother to help with the book he was writing, on the same subject as his older brother Keith—why should his ma help a stranger? *The cheek o' the man,* Jimmy thought.

Then there was the notion that Neil might be a relative. *Nah,* Jimmy told himself at first, *I'm sure I'd know.* As the weeks went on, he was less certain.

He believed he had inherited some of his mother's sixth sense, and would know if this man was of his flesh and blood.

But, he remembered, he had been a child, nearly five, when the young ones, babies really, were snatched, and he retained only an impression of them. Neither of them had his red red hair, but hadn't the older boy been golden-headed? He couldn't remember the boy's face—he mixed it up with the younger brothers who came along later when his mother remarried.

What he could remember was the crying, the screaming, the gut-wrenching keening from his mother for days after.

He was not yet five. He could only stand and stare as a woman reached into the big coach-built pram that someone had given them. He remembered that when he was wee, he thought that's how babies arrived: in a pram.

The baby was wailing a high-pitched squeal—like the seagulls when you went stealing their eggs. His mother came running up from the lochan. She started screaming at the two men and the woman, who was now in the back of the car doing nothing to comfort the baby, who cried as though he knew what was happening, filling the car with his anguish.

He remembered the grim face of the woman, who he later recalled looked like a prison warden, and the wailing, drowned out by screeches, from his mother, who was held back by one man, a constable, as the other grabbed his next brother, three he was, and his mother was shouting, "Run, Jimmy! Run! Hide! Run, Jimmy!"

He ran, but when he looked back he could see that the men had their hands full of one kicking struggling child and one kicking struggling biting screaming woman, until the constable holding her gave her an almighty shove, and his mother tumbled into the heather while the policeman ran to the car, where the others were locked in the backseat holding onto the howling bairns.

The constable, not a local man, started the engine, and by the time his mother recovered, Jimmy still watching from his hiding place behind a big boulder, the car had disappeared down the track, away from their encampment, away for forever, and never forgotten.

And he saw, as though he was back there in that place and time, the papers the man from the welfare had given his mother, the papers she had thrown back at him, blowing in the wind, down the track, trying to catch the departing children, white papers like tiny ghosts trying to catch the wee souls they had formally inhabited.

"They gave me a receipt for them as though they were parcels," Jenny had told Joyce Mackenzie. Jimmy had overheard the conversation and it had puzzled him, and whenever the postman came with a parcel for them, which was rarely, he wondered if it might be one or other of his brothers coming home in a box. What made him the hard man he was, was his mother; there was nothing he could say to her, or do for her, except to be close to her, waiting, enduring, being her shadow son. And that was the day, even though he was only four and three-quarters years old, that Jimmy McPhee vowed, *No one will ever capture me, never capture my body nor my soul.*

On Tuesday, at half past eleven on a morning that was weeping at the loss of autumn, Jimmy walked into the bar on Baron Taylor's Lane.

"Thon McAllister fellow was asking after you," the barman told him.

Jimmy left without stopping for a drink, crossed to the Station Square, went into the telephone box, inserted the pennies, and dialed the *Gazette.*

"Your place at seven the night," he told McAllister. Without waiting for a reply, he walked back to the bar. This time he ordered.

*   *   *

"Rob," McAllister yelled without getting out of his chair. The yell carried across the landing into the reporters' room, then spiraled down the staircase, so that the new junior, Fiona, heard only the roar. A nervous girl with black hair and a fresh crop of pimples, she considered phoning her mother, who worked as an assistant at the bakery and provided her daughter with a constant supply of day-old doughnuts. Fiona wanted to say she couldn't take another day at the *Highland Gazette*, but she didn't, only because it was a toss-up as to whom she feared most—McAllister or her father.

"Yes, master," Rob said as he shut the door behind him.

"The advocate from Edinburgh will be here on Thursday."

"Not you, too," Rob complained. "My father's so jittery you'd think he was practicing tap-dancing."

McAllister rubbed his eyes with one hand and said, "Thank you, Rob, I needed that." He smiled, but the smile did not lift the sadness from his eyes.

Rob knew that all he could do was to be practical. "What are you and my dad going to tell the Grand Panjandrum from the Faculty of Advocates?"

"That's why we need to talk."

"The advocate has asked if he and his assistant can walk through the crime scene before they interview Don."

"Who is now back in prison." McAllister felt his skin crawl at the thought of the dank cell with little light and far less comfort than a hospital bed. "Jimmy McPhee is coming to my house tonight. I'm hoping he has more than 'look in the past' stuff to tell me. Because I've looked till I'm blind and I've seen nothing."

"Maybe you should ask Neil if he came across anything when he was searching the parish records in Inchnadamph . . ."

He saw he had lost McAllister. "That's Mrs. Smart's—the Mackenzie—parish church. Joanne said they saw her grave. Apparently there's no headstone, but people have been laying flowers and . . ."

McAllister had turned his head away, but Rob saw it. McAllister looked as though he too had been stabbed in the heart.

It took Rob half a second to realize what he had said. *They. Neil. Joanne.*

And he had enough sense not to dwell on the subject. "Firstly, the gate to the close where Don lives . . ."

He watched McAllister take up a pencil, making an effort to concentrate.

"Was the gate locked that night?" Rob continued. "It seems Mrs. Smart made a point of making sure it was locked on the nights she visited, probably to keep her husband from confronting them. Apparently she had her own key."

"So, point one, did she lock the gate, did she have the key on her? If she locked the gate, did the killer take the key so he could return the knife to the hiding place?" McAllister was doing all he could to forget what Rob had said, but, like an attack of tinnitus, the words echoed in the periphery of his hearing—*Joanne, Neil, they.* "You said the railwayman thought he saw something in the churchyard?"

"He might deny it, but I'm certain it wasn't a ghost that he saw."

"So, in the time it took the man to run to the police station, the killer could have gone to the courtyard and put the knife back in the wall."

"Aye," Rob agreed, "we're back to the knife. Eilidh, Don's neighbor, says any number of people might have known where it was kept."

"Who also had a reason to kill Mrs. Smart?"

"Which brings us back to her husband. Two motives—jealousy and greed."

"The same motive could apply to Don." McAllister tipped his chair back into his thinking position. "I still keep thinking, why now? This situation had been going on for years."

"I have one more thought. The Gurkha. Everyone says he was devoted to the Mackenzie family, that's why he's not a suspect. But what if he'd had enough of the sergeant major? What if something ordinary became too much and he snapped? What if he knew about the legacy—it's a fortune in his terms, enough to last him the rest of his life. He has no alibi. He knows how to use a knife. I've looked them up in the library—Gurkha soldiers are fiercesome killers."

"I'll talk to Beech again, but they say he was devoted to Joyce."

"Maybe I could join you and Jimmy tonight."

"Fine, but if he tells you to go . . ."

"I'll be gone." Rob stood. "And we've still to get out a newspaper, so have you done the op-ed yet?"

"Later."

When Rob returned to the reporters' room, he decided that later might be never, so he called Beech, asked him to write the editorial and two obituaries, and when asked why, said, "McAllister isn't feeling too well." When he put down the phone he saw Joanne and Neil had been listening.

"Is McAllister okay?" Joanne asked.

"No, not really—but I'm glad you've noticed."

He saw her flush, then look away. Rob hadn't meant it callously; he was just stating the world as he saw it. Plus, he was busy searching his pockets for a ten-shilling note, all he had to last him until payday at the end of the week, and couldn't find it, so he did not notice he had hurt her.

The remark cut, making her shiver, making her, for a brief moment, grasp the fugue she was in, reality gone. Rob was her friend. McAllister was a friend, a man she more than liked, and although she had fantasized that he might one day look at her in more than friendship, she had scorned the idea.

McAllister thinks I'm not too bright, she told herself, forgetting the times when they had talked and laughed as though they had known each other their whole lives.

"Hello, is anyone there?" Rob was waving the ten-shilling note at her, found inside his spiral-bound reporter's notebook.

Joanne's eyes came back into focus.

"I'm off to interview a visiting Canadian evangelist. See you when I see you." Rob left her to her doubts, and ran down the stairs two at a time.

Neil had been mostly ignoring their exchange, focused on the correct spelling of a Gaelic name. He looked at Joanne and said, "It must be hard for McAllister. Were he and Don McLeod close?"

She grabbed on to the question, dismissing thoughts of her own culpability in McAllister's descent into melancholy, and answered, "Yes, I suppose they were, are—in an odd, bickering old couple, way."

"The best we can do is get this paper out." Neil smiled and went back to typing.

His smile worked—as always.

"Good idea." She did the same.

It's nothing to do with me, she tried telling herself as she sorted out the community notices for the next edition. But she knew this was not true—*We were once more than colleagues. We came close to.* . . . She tried not to think how close she had come to spending a night with McAllister—until common sense had come to her rescue. And she tried to push away the awareness that she was not being a good friend to him when he was obviously in distress.

Some months back, when her husband, Bill, had beat her so badly she ended up in hospital, she needed a friend. And McAllister had listened to her, helped her stick to her resolve to leave the marriage, had not once been judgmental. But not once had he indicated he cared for her—except as a good friend and colleague.

No, she chided herself; *I know he is interested in me. But why does he never say anything?* It didn't occur to her that she was the one who had discouraged him; all her talk of freedom and friendship had made McAllister—an inarticulate man when it came to expressing feelings—even more reticent.

Now there was Neil; another man who had made no commitment but who made her forget everything and everyone—even McAllister, even her family, even her reason.

Jimmy arrived at McAllister's house at twenty to eight, no apologies for being late, but a bottle in his hand.

"You." Jimmy looked Rob up and down, mostly up, as he was a good six inches shorter. "I suppose you're here to help Don McLeod—no' being nosy for the sake o' it."

"I'm helping my father with the defense case."

They sat around the kitchen table, the bottle and two glasses in the middle and a jug of water, which was ignored. Rob had made himself a pot of tea, and the discussion began.

"Does he know about ma brothers?" Jimmy jerked his head towards Rob.

"No. Is it relevant?" McAllister asked.

"No idea. Then again, I've no idea about much of this shambles. But Joyce Mackenzie left money to the orphanage."

It took Rob a moment to connect Joyce Mackenzie to Mrs.

Smart. "What has the orphanage got to do with anything, and why do you keep calling her Joyce Mackenzie?"

Jimmy looked at Rob, gave him the long stare for which he was notorious, and said on the outgoing breath of a lungful of cigarette smoke, "You want to use her legal name? The late Mrs. Donal Dewar McLeod?"

"They're married?" One look at Jimmy's shrug, and McAllister knew it had to be true. "Great God Almighty." He said the words as though only the Almighty, in whom he didn't believe, could make sense of the secret.

"I can't believe it." Rob stared at Jimmy, hopeful that reading the lines and scars on the tinker's face might shed some light on the bombshell. But no. "Are you sure?" he asked. No reply. But Jimmy's face said a lot. "Sorry, yes, of course you're sure . . ." Rob was sitting down, leaning back in his chair, shaking his head as he spoke, disbelief extending to his open, palms-up hands. "Who told you?" The look in Jimmy's eyes told Rob he had stepped over the boundary of Traveler etiquette. "Sorry," he muttered.

"All the times I've spent with Don and he never once let on that they were close, never mind *married*." McAllister was talking to himself, rolling the information around his brain, his tongue. "Married. Don. Mrs. Smart was . . . Mrs. McLeod."

"I'll always think of her as Mrs. Smart," Rob said. "It really suited her."

Rob looked from Jimmy to McAllister and back again. He saw neither of them was going to say it, so he said, "They're bigamists."

"Maybe," Jimmy answered. "Don't know for sure."

"No," McAllister said. "Legally it would be Mrs. Joyce McLeod, as we now know she was, who was the bigamist, and only if she went through another marriage ceremony." He knew he was being pedantic, but words were his refuge in times of distress. "But where does this get us?" McAllister was asking himself, not looking for an answer.

"With more questions," Jimmy said. He didn't tell them, and he would only have told McAllister if he could articulate the will-o'-the-wisp thought, but there was something more, something his mother couldn't bring herself to say.

He thought it was about the brothers, but maybe not; he felt, rather than saw, her distress, the way his mother's shoulders rounded, the way she held her cardigan or her coat tighter to her, the way she complained about the cold and the damp and the old ways vanishing; all this from a woman who never complained, who would give you a clip round the ear if you complained, even when there was only tatties with eyes and beards to eat until the next pennies or halfpennies or farthings came in. She would say, *Be thankful for what you have, Jimmy McPhee. There's a lot worse off than us.*

Although happy to help anyone escape from the law, Jimmy also had a vested interest; Don McLeod was a valuable source of information, *the keeper of the town's secrets he had called himself more than once.*

Knowing a person's secrets gives you power, his mother had taught him. And Jimmy knew the reverse was true. *The less anyone knows about you the better.* His brother Keith, the clever one, had once thought that that would have made a good clan motto, in Gaelic of course.

"I'm off." Jimmy downed the remains of his whisky. "I'll be in touch."

McAllister was not completely surprised at Jimmy's abrupt departure—that was the way of the man—but he had wanted to talk more.

"I'll see maself out." Jimmy needed to leave, to avoid a conversation with McAllister. He needed to think about what he had previously dismissed as unthinkable. He needed to talk to his mother.

With the sound of the front door shutting, all Rob could think to do was to make another pot of tea.

"Have a drink, for goodness' sakes." McAllister caught Rob watching him pouring another dram.

Rob ignored him. "I presume I can tell my father this . . ." He was about to say "news" but "revelation" seemed more appropriate.

"Jimmy didn't say not to."

"It's late. I'll see you tomorrow." What Rob meant was, he needed to talk to his father, immediately. Needed his father's calm steady unshockable voice.

McAllister, his eyes glazed as though looking down into an invisible dark cavern and seeing nothing but blackness upon blackness, only nodded.

Rob left.

The fire shifted in the grate. The bottle steadily diminished. Still the blackness did not clear. But flickering forms appeared and disappeared; foremost Joanne. McAllister was unable to articulate the sense of loss; he who prided himself in being a wordsmith could not find the words for the visceral pain he experienced when he recollected her laughter when in Neil's company, the way her body bent towards him when they were talking.

He had a vision of her hair; the way it fell half over her face when she was unsure of herself—which was less and less, he now realized. *I wanted her to fly*, he remembered, *I encouraged her, but not to fly so far away from me.*

He became aware of the chill creeping in from under doors and floorboards and through the invisible gaps in the hundred-year-old house. He reached for the bottle, found it empty. He reached for a cigarette but his mouth felt like the full ashtray sitting on the table. He went to the sink, drank water straight from the tap, a habit of his childhood when he could never stand still enough to find a cup and fill it.

He went to bed. This time he slept. But in the morning, he wished he hadn't. The dreams were not the usual—not the ones where he was running to catch his brother before he, or sometimes another little boy, fell over and over into the river the canal the loch the water.

This time in his dream he was a Glasgow Professor Henry Higgins—teaching his Eliza, his Joanne, how to behave. And once more he was running, as the more she learned, the further he was left behind. He was running. She was laughing. She was running. He was desperate.

When he awoke, and even though the dream was only half remembered, he told himself he had no right to judge her, no right to tell Joanne whom she should love.

When he went to the kitchen to face the debris of the previous night, the sight of the ashtray he had forgotten to empty left him miserable. And no further in his quest to free Don McLeod.

Angus McLean went to the station to meet the advocate and his assistant off the Edinburgh train. As he watched the passengers disembarking from the first-class carriage he instantly knew which was Mr. William Brodie, QC. Angus examined the short stout man—"compact" was the advocate's own description of his roly-poly shape. Although the QC was clad in a sharp midnight-blue suit cut by a most expensive tailor to minimize the client's width, the local solicitor, much to his surprise, saw that the advocate's tie was of such a virulent scarlet-verging-on-pink, it was a beacon on an otherwise drab day. Angus also fancied he had caught a glimpse of socks of the same color. He confirmed the sighting as he ushered the visitors into the Station Hotel, where the lawyers were staying for the night.

A table had been booked for luncheon. Mr. Brodie, QC, had communicated that business would not begin until after they had eaten. Angus McLean knew that no business could be conducted during meals, in spite of his son's assertion that that was a business practice in the United States of America.

After a meal where the advocate had praised the fish and his deputy had said nothing, Angus McLean suggested they walk the length of Church Street to gain an idea of the geography of the crime scene.

"Good," replied Mr. Brodie, QC. "I need to walk off the train journey. Mind you," he added, "the kippers at breakfast were very good indeed."

As they reached the intersection between Church and Union streets, Angus pointed eastward towards the scene of the crime and westward towards the police station. The assistant opened a sketchbook and started to draw a diagram.

"So," said Mr. Brodie, "the man who discovered the body ran all the way up Church Street to the police station . . ."

"Then up a steep brae . . ."

"Then he ran all the way back with a constable in tow . . ."

"A sergeant . . ." Angus said. But the idea of Sergeant Patience running struck him as unlikely.

At the top of the stairs beneath the former abbey wall, they paused to allow the artist-lawyer time to catch up on his sketching. They examined the gate to the churchyard, then walked slowly down the steps to the back porch of the church that bordered the other side.

"This is where the victim was found?"

"Yes."

As Angus watched, the advocate examined the door handles,

the lock, the iron balustrades, the stone wall with the grave-stones towering above them, oblivious of the curious looks from passersby. Angus also watched the deputy advocate hold up his pencil to judge the distance between objects, mutter approximate distances, and note them beside his sketch of the scene. The team of garrulous advocate and silent deputy advocate were working as professionally as a pair of music-hall artists who had been treading the boards, perfecting their routines, for decades.

Angus glanced at the sketchpad and saw the detailed plan with the river, the churches, and the steps, all in reassuring detail.

"I can help you fill in the names of the landmarks," he offered. He received a nod in reply; not from impoliteness, but his was concentration so intense, soaking up every detail of the surroundings, the artist-advocate dared not look up to speak.

"Now." Mr. Brodie, QC, was wiping his hands on a hankie, which, Angus was pleased to observe, was traditional white. "Let us now examine the location and home of Mr. Donal Dewar McLeod."

They crossed the street. A man in black who looked like an usher from one of the many churches on Church Street stood and stared at the strangers. He did not look as though he approved of the trio of lawyers, especially one with a pink tie.

Angus produced the key to the gate, which his secretary had tied to the house key with a piece of twine, a brown cardboard label attached.

Mr. Brodie pounced. "Did the keys come like that?"

Angus was startled. "Like what?"

"Tied together, man."

"No, my secretary . . ."

"Please instruct her not to interfere with evidence."

Angus put the key in the lock of the iron-barred gate, and

tried not to show his discomfort. *Of course, he is correct,* he was thinking, *but there's no need to lecture me as though I was his junior.* They walked down the close, the deputy advocate measuring the length in strides. "Twenty-three feet," the deputy announced, and noted it on his diagram of the scene of the crime.

"Is the gate normally locked?" Mr. Brodie asked Angus.

"At night, yes."

"Did Mrs. Smart have a key?"

"I . . . Yes. I believe so." But the mention of her name had made Angus hesitate.

"Spit it out, man."

As the advocate said this, Angus heard the faint resonance of the accent of a man from Moray—a neighboring county of phlegmatic farmers not known for flights of fancy, and he immediately felt confident.

"She is, was, not Mrs. Smart. Not legally." Now he had the attention of both advocates. "I only heard of this last night. My son, Rob, is a journalist. He occasionally helps me with research and he will bring us copies of the relevant documents. It seems that Joyce Mackenzie married Mr. Donal McLeod in 1920."

"That information will support the prosecution." Mr. Brodie saw Angus McLean nodding. "If McLeod is her legal husband, he inherits everything. Premeditation for monetary gain would be my argument if I were prosecuting."

Angus was looking at his shoes; brown brogues, he saw they could do with a polish. What he was hearing from Mr. Brodie, QC, had been his own thoughts when Rob had told him of Don McLeod's marriage.

"Miss Joyce Mackenzie, who was perhaps Mrs. Donal McLeod, left for India, alone, in 1921?"

"Early 1922, so I have been informed," Angus said.

"I see." Early in his career William Brodie, as he then was, had adopted a policy to use the neutral phrase "I see" even when he had no idea what was happening. This had added to the reputation of omniscience that attached to the name Mr. William Brodie, QC.

Angus held up the keys and said, "Shall we go inside?"

"The courtyard first, if you don't mind." Angus was again surprised, this time by the man's accent. *Not Scottish*, he was thinking, *public school definitely, Eton perhaps.* He was delighted when he later asked the deputy where he went to school and his guess was confirmed.

A tap came out of the wall above a drain in the far corner of the courtyard. To one side there was a block of granite, its upper surface polished smooth. Behind it, a crevice in the wall looked right for the storage of a knife and big enough to store a cleaver. The wall above was the only one not part of a building, but as it was at least one and a half stories high, and of a smooth construction, they thought it unlikely anyone would come into the courtyard over the top.

"This is where Mr. McLeod prepared fish," Angus informed them.

"Sensible fellow." Mr. Brodie was ferreting around the niche with his hand. Finding nothing except dried fish scales, he nodded and walked to the front door of the narrow terrace. Angus produced the key, opened the door, and stood aside to allow the Edinburgh lawyers first entry.

Facing the door rose a staircase where many policemen's boots had left mud on the carpet. At the left of the staircase was a coatrack, to the right a door leading to the sitting room. At the back another door lead to a galley kitchen. There were the remains of a fire in the grate, the remains of a newspaper on the table and a bottle of whisky—empty. On top of a bookshelf, crammed with titles familiar to the advocate, sat a vase with the remains of what looked like roses.

Roses in September, Angus McLean thought, *they must have been expensive.* Then he remembered Mrs. Smart's walled garden.

Angus could not bring himself to join the others upstairs in the bedroom. As he waited, he thought the house felt forsaken. *But not as terrible as the cell where Don is now in residence.*

Not more than a quarter of a mile away, Don McLeod was scratching an itch in his memory.

It was the nurses and the medical staff, particularly the students, who had dislodged the fragment; the student, a medical student, Don seemed to remember, a student whom he had only met once before when the young man had knocked on his door asking for change for the electricity meter. *I've an idea he was Eilidh's boyfriend. Had he been there that night? Or was it the night before?* The harder he tried to remember, the less certain he became. *No, I must have it wrong,* Don decided. *If he were there that night, the lass would have said so when she was questioned about Joyce.*

The name did it. Saying her name, thinking her name, remembering the small and the large instances of their friendship, made him hurt to the bone. He would have cried were he not Donal McLeod from Skye, where only the heavens wept.

CHAPTER 15

No, I haven't time, I'm meeting Angus McLean and the advocates from Edinburgh this afternoon." McAllister did not look up from his writing. With a leaky fountain pen, he was attempting to make notes for the meeting, as he did not want to join the others at a typewriter in the reporters' room.

Joanne could not look at him either. She felt the tension and was not able, or willing, to ask the cause.

"Fine. I'll write you a memo." She turned to go. "But someone needs to look at the accounts and letters . . . there are complaints . . ."

"Can I help?" Beech stood in the doorway.

"No," McAllister said. "Joanne can deal with it." He looked up. He saw her waiting, wanting him to say something more. And he wanted her to know his hurt so he lashed out. "Will that be all, Mrs. Ross?"

She didn't reply. He went back to scribbling in his notebook. He heard her leave and did not look up. When he did, he saw Beech watching him. Which made him even more surly. "I can't give you long. I'm preparing notes for Angus McLean."

"That is why I'm here." Beech shut the office door, the Do Not Disturb sign to all at the *Gazette*. He sat down. Taking his time, he reached for some sheets of folded writing paper. He smoothed them open. He cleared his throat. McAllister was beginning to wonder if this pantomime was meant to further annoy him. But he sighed and put down his pen. Then Beech began.

"I have here an account of a conversation my sister had with Gurkha Bahadur. The information may help with Don's case."

Now he had McAllister's full attention.

"Firstly," Beech began, "Sergeant Major and Mrs. Smart . . ."

"Were not legally married."

Beech, although surprised, was too polite to ask McAllister how he came by his information. "In 1920, Joyce Mackenzie asked her father's permission to marry Mr. Donal McLeod." Beech glanced at his notes, although there was no need; he knew the contents almost word for word.

"It took months for her to hear back. Her father was upcountry with his regiment and letters to and from India sometimes took months to arrive, sometimes never arrived. Joyce Mackenzie waited more than six months, to no avail. Then she and Mr. McLeod married in the local parish church in Sutherland. When a letter finally arrived, apparently shortly after the marriage ceremony, Colonel Mackenzie denied his permission. Not because Don McLeod was the candidate; he wanted his only child to wait because of her age, and he wanted to meet the future husband."

Beech sighed. He himself had never married, he had married his career, and the vagaries of matrimony were a puzzle to him.

"A year or so after the marriage, Joyce McLeod, née Mackenzie, went to India to join her father. It took her months to get there. When she arrived, she was ill—weak, thin, in distress, according to Bahadur, who at the time was Colonel Mackenzie's batman. The colonel arranged for her to stay with friends in a hill station in Simla for the climate. But apparently it was another year before she regained her health, and even then, Bahadur said, she was fragile."

This McAllister found hard to believe. Mrs. Smart, as he

still thought of her, had seemed so strong, so independent. "Why would she leave for India so soon after marrying?"

"All Bahadur knows is that Joyce once told him that Mr. McLeod left her. Told her to find a way to have the marriage dissolved."

"Now, that really surprises me." McAllister thought about this. "From what I know, they loved each other."

Beech made no comment. He glanced at another page of the notes and continued. "In India, Joyce lived very quietly, not part of the wives' brigade. But her father was away a lot, and she must have been lonely. She became a volunteer at an orphanage clinic. Then Sergeant Major Smart began to pursue Joyce Mackenzie. Smart was persistent, Bahadur says, and, apparently, he was thought of as a most charming man." Beech did not add that his sister had also made a side note that Bahadur had never trusted the man.

"After about two years, they married. Joyce told my sister that she agreed in a moment of weakness, in the heat of a particularly hot summer. Smart announced it to all the army set, and it was done. Her father was not unhappy about the match but not thrilled either."

"They were married when?" McAllister was taking notes.

"March 1930."

"So it was a bigamous marriage?"

"Maybe. Maybe the first marriage was indeed dissolved. I don't know."

"Then . . ."

"Then . . . Not long after the marriage it became obvious that Smart was treating his new wife badly, physically and mentally. He'd discovered that although her family was rich, she herself had no cash. He had gambling debts and other unsavory habits. The colonel paid off some of the debts and hushed up a scandal . . ." Beech paused. "I don't think we need go into that . . . So, when Joyce Mackenzie left Smart to return to Scotland, it was with her father's tacit blessing."

McAllister had not forgotten Don's remark about the sergeant major's fall from a brothel window and that it hadn't been girls the soldier was visiting.

"Mrs. Smart, as she was known when she returned here, she and Mr. McLeod resumed their relationship. My sister, recently widowed, returned from China in 1934. She and Joyce became friends. All was well until . . ."

"Until Archibald Smart returned."

"Without his legs."

McAllister looked at Beech. "That was a remark worthy of Rob."

"Or Mr. McLeod," Beech agreed.

McAllister suddenly saw it; Mortimer Beauchamp Carlyle's resemblance to a wolf; not a big-bad-fairy-tale-I'll-blow-your-house-down wolf, but a lone noble savage intelligent wolf. *Never get on the wrong side of that man*, McAllister told himself.

"From the day he came back until the day she died, Smart made Joyce Mackenzie's life hell on earth," Beech said. "My sister and Mr. Bahadur will attest to that."

"So where does all this get us?" the editor asked.

"It gives Smart a motive."

"Don too."

They were silent for a moment, then Beech stood. "If you don't think I'm interfering, I will talk to Joanne and Mrs. Buchanan, see if I can be of help with the accounts, et cetera."

"I'd be grateful." McAllister did not mention that as Beech and his sister were the major shareholders and Beech chairman of the *Gazette*'s board of trustees, he had every right to scrutinize the accounts.

"If there is anything else I can help with, do let me know." Beech was examining McAllister, and his concern came through in his voice.

"I will." McAllister meant it.

After Beech had left, McAllister knew he could not bear to stay in the office. He had a typewriter at home, so he left to write up the notes for Mr. Brodie, QC. He also needed to eat. He could not remember when he had last had a decent meal.

No, he thought, *I'll pick up some fish, I'll cook properly, then I'll type up the notes.* Somehow the thought of domesticity cheered him. And the knowledge that he could work without constantly straining to listen for Joanne's voice, without constantly tracking her movements, was, he knew, much healthier than his morning's behavior.

On the premises of Angus McLean, Solicitor, there was a room off the main office that looked more like a dining room than a meeting room. The secretary had laid pens, paper, and a bottle of black ink just in case the illustrious gentlemen from Edinburgh needed to refill their fountain pens. She had no time for the newfangled Biro pens and believed no real gentleman would ever use one.

Angus McLean went into the room, looked out the bay windows, spotted McAllister striding down the street, and was glad the editor was early.

"I thought we might catch up before the others arrive."

"Good," Angus said. "I must say I'm slightly nervous about the meeting—Mr. Brodie, QC, has a formidable reputation."

"Mr. William Brodie, QC?"

"Yes, but for heaven's sake, don't call him 'Deacon.'"

The reference to the infamous eighteenth-century jurist and burglar, Deacon William Brodie, who was hanged on a gallows of his own design, had plagued Mr. Brodie most of his life. Then again, it had been the spur to him taking the queen's silk.

McAllister and Angus McLean spent a short fifteen minutes going over the relevant points, such as they were, before the advocates were announced. Rob came in at the same time, and as the secretary said, "Mr. William Brodie, QC," as though she were announcing royalty, Rob, standing behind her, quipped, "Ah-ha, Deacon Brodie!"

Like Lot's wife, the secretary was pillar still.

McAllister looked out of the window, his shoulders trembling, trying his best not to laugh.

Angus McLean looked at the ceiling.

And Mr. Brodie, QC, turned to Rob and beamed. "No relation, I'm told, but it does my reputation no harm to never deny it." He held out his small hand, "McLean the younger, I presume?"

"Rob."

"You're the nosy reporter on the *Gazette*. Here, sit next to me, tell me the gossip, the speculation, everything; let me judge whether it is relevant or not."

They all sat, now looking forward to the meeting. Mr. Brodie told the secretary Rob would take notes. "You have shorthand?" Rob nodded, and she left in very high dudgeon indeed.

"Firstly, let me say that I believe the prognosis for Mr. McLeod is not good," Mr. Brodie started, "but"—here he paused for dramatic effect—"not beyond salvaging. If we are unfortunate and there is a guilty verdict, I am sure that, as the evidence is circumstantial, an appeal would succeed."

"Thank goodness for that." Rob spoke for all of them.

"That is more a reflection of the times; with capital punishment abolished, juries are less reluctant to return a guilty verdict. Now, let's review what we have." Mr. Brodie barely paused for breath between sentences. "This case calls for the 'Abelard and Heloise' defense."

McAllister sat up. He doubted a twelfth-century love affair, a French one at that, was a suitable defense strategy for a small Highland town in the mid-twentieth century.

Angus McLean agreed. "The McLeod Faerie Flag might be a better analogy," he suggested.

Mr. Brodie positively radiated approval. "Yes. Of course. Splendid."

"Faerie flags?" McAllister was even more doubtful.

"There are at least two versions, so take your pick," Rob explained. "The flag was either a banner from the Crusades or a gift to a McLeod chieftain from his faerie lover—another unsuitable match that ended in tears."

McAllister was reminded that as a Southerner, he was completely unconnected with the Highlanders from the Gaeltachd. But though he might not know the legends, he trusted the lawyer's theatrics would at best win over a jury of locals, at worst confuse them.

"The story of a love gone wrong means we must hope for as many women on the jury as possible," the advocate continued.

"How can you manage that?" Angus McLean was perplexed. Under Scottish law there was no say in who the jurors were.

"Pray," Mr. Brodie said, and turned and winked at Rob.

"Next, bombard the jury with possibilities, the husband for example." Again he turned to Rob. "Everything unsavory you can find . . ."

"There is a rumor he is not the war hero he claims to be . . ." McAllister put in. But he left out the rumor of the sergeant major visiting boys in an Indian brothel.

"Splendid." Mr. Brodie was tapping his dainty red-sock-clad feet in happiness.

"I heard Smart gambles," Angus contributed.

"Sergeant Patience is rumored to be one of the card circle." McAllister again.

"Even more splendid. He was the first policeman at the scene, he is a friend of the sergeant major—I'll give him the full grilling."

"The sergeant major behaved appallingly to Mrs. Smart. We have two excellent witnesses to this." McAllister again.

"Of course. Mortimer said he would be happy to speak in court."

It took McAllister a second to place who Mortimer was, then he remembered Beech must know the advocate, as it was he who had suggested him in the first place. Mr. Brodie sensed the confusion. "Beauchamp Carlyle and I are old acquaintances. My father was a footman on his family estate."

At the honesty of this, McAllister liked the man even more.

"Mrs. Jenny McPhee—would she make a good witness?"

"Splendid," Rob said, making Mr. Brodie chuckle and nudge Rob with his elbow.

"Next, we'll call the Gurkha chappie. Should make an interesting witness. And McAllister of course. You can attest to the sergeant major's temper."

"That might backfire. The sergeant major tried to have me charged . . ."

"I'm sure I can help the jury to see what a bully the man is. Next, do we know anyone from the church who could be a witness to Mrs. Smart's good works or something along those lines?"

"I'll find someone," Angus McLean said.

"And if anyone can find something that might muddy Smart's reputation . . . hand in the till, housemaid pregnant . . . that sort of thing . . ." Mr. Brodie went on. "Next, the key; a fine old mystery. We shall make much of that. The knife the same. Next"—he turned to another page—"the will. Mrs. McPhee's legacy. Mrs. Married-Name-Yet-To-Be-Determined was most generous in her bequest to a Traveler woman. The bequest to the Gurkha chappie the same. The estate in the Highlands; did Mr. McLeod know it might be worthless once death duties were paid? Mr. McLean, would you find out exactly how much Mr. McLeod might inherit, erring on the low side perhaps?" The questions were rattled off with the speed of a Gatling gun. "Next, I need the details of the sergeant major's financial situation."

"That will be difficult." Angus looked across the table hoping this guardian of the law was not encouraging his son to indulge in illegal activity.

"Come, now, one of you gentlemen must know a friendly bank manager."

"Don would have something on someone who might know. Or Jimmy McPhee, he knows everything," Rob told him.

"Marvelous, this boy of yours." The advocate's feet were dancing as he beamed at Angus McLean. "I shall ask Mr. McLeod when we meet. But I believe it may not be a good idea to have Mr. Jimmy McPhee in court." He looked around the table. "My next step is to interview the prisoner." He used the word deliberately, to remind them Don was a man charged with murder in the first degree. "With all your notes plus my own observations and more sterling work from young Rob here, we have a start. Now it is up to Mr. McLeod to start talking in his own defense."

"His secret is out," McAllister pointed out.

"Ah, but are there more?" As Mr. Brodie, QC, said this, he shut his leather-bound notebook—red, naturally.

McAllister spoke. It was not that he wanted to dilute the enthusiasm, it was reassurance he wanted.

"There is absolutely no evidence against Sergeant Major

Smart. And no matter how unsavory the man, it seems highly unlikely he could have killed Joyce Mackenzie."

Angus had been thinking the same, and he nodded his agreement.

"You are quite correct, Mr. McAllister. I cannot see how Smart could physically commit the crime. However, in the absence of other possibilities, we shall use him to distract from the most likely killer—Mr. McLeod."

McAllister did not find this at all reassuring.

"Well, gentlemen, we have plenty to keep us busy, and we will talk again after I have seen Mr. McLeod." It was as though he owned the room, his companions his chatelains, and now they were dismissed to do their master's bidding. But no one minded.

After handshakes all round, the advocate murmured to Rob, "Dinner this evening? Station Hotel?"

"I'll be there."

When the gentlemen advocates had left, Angus looked at McAllister. "No smoking in here, I'm afraid. Let's go into my office."

"That was splendid," Rob said as he watched his father pack his pipe and McAllister savor the first cigarette he had had in almost an hour.

"I don't know how a jury will keep up with him—he had me bamboozled," McAllister replied.

"Yes, but will the judge see through the tactic and clarify the arguments for the jury? It is often the summing-up that determines the verdict." Having put a damper on McAllister's hopes, Angus lit his pipe and puffed away like Para Handy.

"We'd better go. We have a newspaper to put out," Rob reminded his boss.

They walked back to the office in silence. There was much to think about, not least the next edition of the *Highland Gazette*.

* * *

"We'll have the wine list first, please," Mr. Brodie told the black-clad waiter, who, Rob thought, had probably been hired when the hotel opened in 1854.

"They have an acceptable burgundy," Rob said. "I believe Lord Lovat orders it when in town."

"Splendid."

Mr. Brodie sampled the wine. He nodded at the waiter, then at Rob. "You are a young man full of surprises."

They ordered dinner, ate, drank, made small talk, and then retired to a corner of the lounge.

Mr. Brodie went straight to the point. "I'd like you to be my research assistant." This time Rob nodded. "Write to me. Inform me of anything and everything: gossip, guesses, wild scenarios, wild women . . ."

"You mean Jenny McPhee." Rob was enjoying himself.

"I have heard that Beech's sister has a colorful past. Those girls that went out to India, there must be some in town who might have heard stories that could discredit the sergeant major."

"I'll ask my mother."

Mr. Brodie gestured to the barman. "Another bottle of the burgundy, please."

As the second bottle was opened Rob was wondering if he could leave his motorcycle in the Station's left luggage office.

"Sergeant Patience. He was first on the scene. He plays cards with Smart."

"I find him a decent enough man, he helps me out from time to time." Rob didn't like the idea of the sergeant as an enemy. "The other players are apparently former soldiers."

"Perhaps you could intimate to the sergeant—as a friend— that I intend to pull him apart in the witness stand. That would be most embarrassing, unless, of course, he has information that might help the defense. I'd also like to know why McAllister was summoned to identify the body. Surely someone in the police station knew who Mrs. Smart was? So why not call her husband?"

"I hadn't thought of that." Rob's admiration for the QC shone out of his face, and the man hitched up his trousers slightly, the better to show off the socks.

"Next, find out if Smart ever attended the church on the riverbank next to the stairs."

"I know the minister there was an army chaplain during the war."

"So the sergeant major was possibly of that congregation. Next, ask the good sergeant and anyone else you can think of about the sergeant major's mobility. Then find me someone willing to testify that Smart was physically capable of gaining access to the back porch by going in through the front door, the riverbank entrance of the church."

Rob was scribbling frantically, hoping he would be able to decipher his not-so-perfect shorthand.

Mr. Brodie paused. "Here, laddie, you haven't touched your drink." He lifted his glass in a toast. "To the befuddlement of juries everywhere."

Rob laughed and raised his glass.

"When I ask you to research these questions, I am not looking for proof perfect, only as many possibilities as you can suggest—no matter how wild."

"Then I'm your man." Rob was so excited at the idea of being Mr. Brodie's sleuth that he found himself jiggling in his chair, in imitation of the advocate.

"Splendid." One point dealt with satisfactorily, Mr. Brodie reached for his glass. "Now, what happened to the key to the gate into the courtyard? Again, we need to quiz Sergeant Patience.

The knife also. It is not so much who took it, but how did it get back into the niche in the wall?"

Rob wrote these questions in block capital letters.

"And thinking on the whereabouts of the key leads me to ask about the handbag."

"Handbag?"

"Very well said, young McLean." He refilled his glass, gestured to Rob, who motioned no, then made a toast. "To Mr. Wilde and handbags."

"Cheers." Rob was enjoying himself hugely.

"A woman would never be without a handbag, and none was found at the crime scene. Ergo, the murderer made off with it, or a passerby stole it, or . . ."

"Mr. Grant, who found the body, left his bike at the top of the steps. It disappeared. Maybe someone used it to get away."

"Thank you for reminding me." Mr. Brodie's knees, as well as his feet, were now dancing.

"Mr. Grant thought he saw something in the graveyard above. Just a glimpse out the corner of his eye, he said. I think he thought it was a ghost."

"Splendid indeed! And would your man make a good witness?"

"He seems a solid, dependable sort."

Rob realized that Mr. Brodie was not making notes. *I bet he has a memory like an elephant*, Rob told himself. He was correct. William Brodie, QC, could recall conversations, facts, faces, with prodigious accuracy. When a child, his parents would wheel him out at family gatherings to play the Memorize the Objects game. He was perfect every time.

"Now, tomorrow morning's meeting with Mr. McLeod; tell me about the man—just quick impressions."

"He's the keeper of the town's secrets," Rob started. He saw the interest in the advocate's small bright eyes. "He likes a bet on the horses. He likes a dram. He speaks Gaelic. He thinks Trotsky made some valid points. He's really good at his job. He's smarter than you'd think from meeting him."

"Good at keeping secrets too." Mr. Brodie was rolling this around as though tasting a good wine. "He kept the marriage secret all these years to protect the good name of his lady-love. How touching."

Rob heard admiration, not sarcasm. "So, if the sergeant major found out . . ."

"Precisely." Mr. Brodie beamed. "But *when* did he find out? Had he always known? Did he have to live with the knowledge for years, having his nose rubbed in it every Sunday evening?"

Rob could see how that would drive a man to murder.

"Had *she* decided she had had enough? Did Mr. McLeod persuade her at long last to come to live with him?"

"No, I don't think so." Rob was answering the last question. "There was no change that I could see in their behavior."

"Ah, but did you ever notice they were close? It seems no one on the *Gazette* did." He answered his own question.

Rob considered this. "You're right. I didn't do very well for a reporter, did I?"

"You'll learn. So now, ask many questions. Answers not always necessary. Remember, the defense must only prove, on balance of probability, that Mr. McLeod did not kill her. We do not need to find the culprit." Mr. Brodie stood. "It has been a pleasure." He held out his hand. "Please keep in touch. Telephone me anytime. Send a report as soon as possible. And don't forget an invoice for your time."

"But Don's a friend." Rob had never considered being paid for the work.

"I expect a professional job, therefore professional rates

apply. If Mr. Angus McLean should question this, refer him to me. But perhaps best not to mention it." Mr. Brodie winked, then set off on his red-clad feet, across the carpet towards the grand staircase, as though on his way to an assignation with a courtesan.

Rob decided to drive home, believing the cold would sober him. As he turned the bike around, the clock struck ten. He remembered the date. There were barely three weeks till the trial. That sobered him.

CHAPTER 16

The phone in his office started to ring when he was halfway up the stairs. He ran the last steps and regretted it. "McAllister," he answered, his breathing heavy and hoarse.

"Brodie, QC, here." The breathing from the other end of the phone reminded the advocate of a racehorse that had just won an eight-furlough steeplechase. "I have just come from the gaol. I'd like to ask your opinion on a number of points before I go back to Edinburgh. I will be here for . . ." McAllister could almost see the dapper wee gentleman consulting a pocket watch, but dismissed the notion as fanciful. "My train leaves in fifty-five minutes."

"I'll be right over." McAllister put down the phone and made for the stairs.

"McAllister," Joanne called out, "I need you to approve this . . ." She was waving some sheets of copy paper.

"Later," McAllister called from halfway down the stairs.

Beech appeared around the corner of the half-spiral stairs. "Can I help?"

"I need someone to sign off on these articles. The father of the chapel has already threatened me with a blank page if I don't get it down to the stone in the next two minutes."

Beech went into the reporters' room, unscrewed his pen, and signed the pages. "There. Done."

"Don't you want to read them?" she asked.

"And spoil the surprise when I read the *Gazette* over breakfast?"

"Will the printers accept your signature?" This question came from Neil, who knew how strictly the printer's union enforced their rules.

"Oh, I think so." Beech smiled. "Don McLeod is highly regarded. I think they will bend the rules until he is back." Beech sat at a typewriter, looked around. "Anything else?" Neil handed him some copy. "Ah, my favorite subject—council rates." He started to type, and the room came alive with morning-of-deadline vim.

Just before the seven-o'clock deadline, Rob announced, "That's all, folks. McAllister is checking the final proofs but, all being well, another edition of the *Highland Gazette* will roll off the presses on time."

"Well done, everyone." Beech clapped. Neil joined in.

Joanne blew an offending wisp of hair out of her eyes and leaned back in her chair, rolling her shoulders. "That was insane."

"But fun." Neil smiled.

Joanne had to look away. Thrilled that she had this secret, she was also terrified that everyone in the room could sense the current between them. Especially Rob.

"So, who's up for a drink? Beech? Neil? Joanne?" Rob asked.

"An early night for me, my boy." Beech was already up and putting on his coat.

"Not sure," Neil said. "Joanne?" He looked at her.

She looked away.

Rob saw the small smile—*She thinks it's a secret*, he thought, and he grinned. "Okay, I get it. Maybe McAllister will join me." He doubted it. McAllister had not returned until midafternoon—on deadline day and with two key staff missing. And even if he did fancy a drink, Rob wasn't sure he wanted his company—*more cheer at a funeral*. So he went home. He didn't mind; an evening transfixed by Radio Luxembourg, rock 'n' roll crackling over the airwaves, fading in and out as though it was coming from another planet, not a radio mast in not-too-distant-as-the-crow-flies Europe, was Rob's idea of heaven.

Joanne and Neil walked through town, Joanne pushing her bicycle. In the basket were cooking apples for a pie and eggs for custard.

I'll make you an apple pie, she had told Neil, not wanting to say, *I'm desperate for your company.*

"You must get on well with your in-laws," Neil said as they walked across the bridge.

"Granddad Ross is a lovely man," Joanne replied. "I'm not sure Granny Ross approves of me—but she loves the girls."

"And your husband? Is he still in the picture?"

"No, thank heavens."

"If life here is anything like a small town in Canada, it must be hard for you. My mother certainly found it so."

"Your mother was a widow. She didn't desert her husband."

"She was a widow for respectability. Her husband left her a few months after they arrived in Canada, so I was told." *Even that was a lie,* he remembered but did not share.

It was dark and the night was cloudy and the streetlights far apart, and the trees, especially those in front of the bowling greens, were big and bare, the many-fingered limbs creating a bower over them as they passed at a very slow pace, the weight of the story slowing Neil down.

He had never told anyone about that day.

"I was eleven, starting high school, when some busybody in the office saw my birth certificate and made sure everyone knew I had no father."

She could hear it in his voice. The pain and anger still fresh.

"At midafternoon break, John Rasmussen, the bully in the

form above me, whose father worked in the lumber mill and was also a bully, started the chant." What Neil remembered most clearly was that John Rasmussen, although from a Swedish family, was chanting in a strange mixture of Canadian, Scottish Canadian, and Gaelic accents.

They were almost at Joanne's prefab and, not wanting to break the spell, her bicycle against her right hip, she stopped, and Neil was talking, and she was listening, and the sound of the silent trees was the music the dirge the pibroch to the tale.

"He was saying, *Bastard. You're a bastard,* his voice low so the teachers wouldn't hear, and after saying it about half a dozen times, his sidekick, a daft fat boy called Eric, joined in." The sound of John Rasmussen's voice had stayed with him and would stay forever. He had heard it during the mortar fire at Monte Casino and it had made him stronger. He had heard it on the day he first walked into the university, an ex-soldier student on a scholarship. When he heard it, it made him stronger, *Bassstrd,* it sounded like, *basstrd, basstrd, you've got no da, basstrd, basstrd.*

"I was big for my age, and strong, and I hit him, so the head-master gave me and John Rasmussen six of the best and we became good friends." Neil kicked a tree root that had pierced the tarmac of the pavement. "He died right at the end—when most of Italy had been liberated and we were about to go home, he was shot by a sniper."

John Rasmussen was the only person he had ever talked to; about the resentment, the pain, the shock—not of having no father—but of being lied to. And on every birthday, in spite of his reading, in libraries and archives, in parish registers, how impossible it was for unmarried women to keep their babies— he could not forgive that. He told himself he did not hate her, his birth mother, the one who rejected him, gave him away, but no, there was no forgiveness.

"My mother, my real mother, who brought me up, who worked gutting fish until her hands were crippled with arthritis, who fed me, who told me stories in the long winter nights, who gave up her beloved glens for me, that woman was truly good. Whoever gave birth to me is not my mother."

He said it with a finality that made Joanne wonder whom he was trying to convince, himself or her.

"My parents threw me out when I became pregnant on the first and only time I'd drunk spirits, gin of all things, and . . ." She quickly came out with her story, to show him that she too had suffered. "My father is a minister. He could not bear the shame." She laughed, and it was her turn to hide the bitterness that had diminished over time but never completely vanished. "So much for Christian forgiveness."

They were speaking conversationally, trying to tell their stories lightly. But neither was fooled.

"I love your little house," Neil said as he held open the gate for her. "And your garden."

For once Joanne was glad she hadn't the time to trim the hedge, glad the lilac was overbearing, blocking the front door from the lane. She went round the back and put her bike away, opened the kitchen door, and was suddenly aware that the girls were away, that she and Neil were alone.

"Would you put the kettle on?" she asked, her hands covered in flour and butter for the pastry. Ten minutes later, the apple pie in the oven, she went to close the curtains in the sitting room. The thought of her husband made her nervous. *Never mind he's with Betsy,* she thought, *he'd still give me a good hiding if he found me with a man.* The double standard she did not think about, it was just the way it was.

She switched on the radio. Brahms swelled out into the room. She took off her shoes. She ran her fingers through her hair and wished she had time for a bath. She went to the bedroom to check the sheets were clean.

"Milk? Sugar?" Neil called out. He had the tea made and the mugs out on a tray.

"No sugar, thanks."

"Not very Scottish." The sight of the tray, the way he had put out the sugar bowl and milk jug, made her tingle. *What man does that,* she thought, and she knew for certain she loved him.

"And you're very well trained, milk in the milk jug indeed."

"My mother was once in service. She insisted everything was done properly. *No matter how poor we are,* she would say, *good manners and good habits cost nothing.*" He smiled. "I still have her most precious possession, her tea set. There are only three cups and saucers left, but I treasure it." He did not tell her that no matter how many times he asked, his mother never revealed how she came by the tea service. "Coming here, I feel I am paying homage to her. She was once a beautiful young woman, barely eighteen when she went to Canada, where she had a tough life, and I wanted to say thank you to the mountains and glens that she came from."

There was something artificial in the way he said this, but Joanne put it down to his being a scholar, a man whose words were better on paper. *Not that he's not silver-tongued, he could charm the birds from the trees.*

Joanne rose. "I'll make custard."

He reached out, put his hand on her wrist. "No regrets?"

"You asked me that before and the answer is the same—no, no regrets." But she wished that she did not feel so guilty. *Adultery, adulterer, fallen woman,* those were the words that would haunt her as surely as *basstrd* haunted him.

He pulled her onto his lap. She felt she had never been kissed properly until she met Neil. She felt she had never known what love was, until she had met Neil. And the guilt—she pushed it down deep into a well where her conscience could not penetrate. For now.

"Better switch off the oven," he murmured as he led her by the hand to her own bedroom, her narrow bed, her sanctuary that she had vowed no man would breach—until she met Neil Stewart.

It was late when they eventually had the apple pie and tea. Without custard. He ate half, and with every slice he told her again how good it was.

"So you can cook too," he teased. He loved the way she blushed so easily.

"And sew and knit and all the usual housewifely things."

"Your husband was mad to leave you."

"It was the other way round, I threw him out." This was important to her; Joanne was proud of remaking her life. No matter how many disapproved, this was a better life for her and her children. "And, although he doesn't know it, I am going to divorce him." *There, I've said it.* She prayed Neil would see what a divorce meant.

Neil looked at her, but with his mouth full of apple pie, he could only nod.

"Bill is living with Betsy Buchanan. And Betsy wants him to marry her." She hesitated. "Betsy is pregnant."

Betsy had been in tears when she made Joanne promise to tell no one. "Cross your heart you'll never tell," Betsy had said, and Joanne had to look away, scared she would laugh as Betsy invoked the *cross your heart and hope to die* promise she had last heard in the school playground. But Neil would never repeat the information.

"Wow," was all he said.

His reaction, or rather nonreaction, was not what she expected. *Can't he see what this means?*

"Betsy's not sure what Bill will do." She knew she was blethering but it was important he understand. "Betsy is helping me get evidence of Bill's infidelity. Then I'll apply for a divorce. We need a witness to stand up in court and testify, or at least have some photographs of them in a compromising situation . . . what? Why are you laughing?"

"It's all so ridiculous. Not you. The law. It's the same in Canada. You have to have proof of infidelity. I've even covered a case where dirty sheets were shown in court."

"That's horrible." Joanne found this distasteful and vowed to change her sheets as soon as Neil left.

He helped himself to another cup of tea. "I admire you, Joanne. You have made a new life for yourself, a new career. It will be hard living here as a divorced woman, but you are prepared to do it." He reached across for her hand. "And I know you can."

A numb sensation gripped her whole body, a deep-down chill, colder than any Scottish winter, gripped her toes—even in sheepskin slippers. She wrapped both hands around the mug of tea—but still the ice penetrated. Her shoulders in the cozy moss-green twin set, bought to bring out the color of her eyes, felt bare. She was as exposed as an unwanted daughter left out in the snow, and she knew it.

"You'll have no trouble getting back into the boardinghouse? I thought your landlady was an ogre." She needed him gone.

"I have a key." He was surprised but did not want to show it. "Maybe another time we can find somewhere to be together for longer? It was perfect in Ullapool."

"Maybe." She could hear his voice change, trying to reassure her. It didn't work. Fatigue hit her, and she wanted to cry.

Though why, she had no idea. Often, after a conversation was over, after the person had gone, when it was too late, it would come to her—the hidden heart of the matter.

"Sorry," she said as he put his arms around her, "I am exhausted, and these past weeks have been dreadful."

"I hope that doesn't include me."

"Oh no, of course not. It's just that Mrs. Smart's death . . . she was a good woman . . ."

"So I keep hearing."

"And Don McLeod is a friend."

"You want me to use the back door?"

"Please."

He leaned towards her to kiss her. She buried her face in his shoulder, the tweed scratching her nose, making her want to sneeze. She wanted to stay there safe and forever. *But there is no forever, to him I'm just a fling.*

"Sorry, I'm exhausted." She pushed him away. And if he sensed her distress, he didn't say.

She didn't hear the garden gate shut because she had oiled it in preparation for Neil's visit. She put out the milk bottles, locked the doors, put out the lights; she brushed her teeth; she went to put on the new nightgown, the new one she couldn't afford but had bought in the bridal department of Arnotts. She stuffed it back under the pillow and threw herself onto the mattress, pulling the eiderdown over her, and started to cry. She cried, she sobbed, she sat up, she told herself, speaking aloud, "This is ridiculous." She lay down. Sleep did not come.

She waited. The alarm clock on the bedside table showed twenty past two.

She got up, went to the kitchen for water, saw the two mugs, two plates, one remaining slice of apple pie and she sobbed, great burns and rivers of tears streaming out of her eyes and her nose. She washed the dishes, still sobbing. She wrapped the pie in waxed paper and put it in the pantry and went back to bed. When she picked up her library book and tried to read, she couldn't see the text.

She didn't register what she was saying, over and over the same phrase—she was saying, more a refrain than a conscious thought, *What have I done? What have I done?*

The next day wasn't any better. The day after deadline was usually a late start for Joanne, and she was glad of it.

"*Gazette*."

"How are you, Joanne? It's been ages since we had a get-together." Margaret McLean had hoped to catch up with her on deadline night, but Rob had said Joanne was with Neil Stewart.

"I know. We're so short-staffed, I never seem to have a moment." *Except for Neil*, she realized.

"Would you and the girls like to come over on Sunday afternoon?" Margaret asked. "We'd love to see you all."

"I'm sorry, I can't, I'm busy." The excuse sounded weak even to her own ears. She was not busy. But she would not commit to anything, in case Neil might want to be with her. The previous night was not forgotten, but the power of hope and illusion was formidable. "Once this case is over and Don is back, I'll have more time. Sorry."

"Maybe tea or coffee on your lunch break . . . I'll call you." Margaret was not upset when she hung up the telephone, only concerned. She knew an obsession when she saw one.

The next call followed the first by two minutes.

"Hello, stranger."

"Elizabeth. I know, I am so sorry, things are not easy here."

"Never mind. Stay for lunch after church on Sunday. We can catch up then."

This lunch there was no avoiding. For Elizabeth, Joanne's sister, church was not optional, and Joanne had not attended in three weeks. Although in no way overbearing, nor critical, Elizabeth kept her eye on her sister. She did not know of Neil Stewart, but she would not approve if she did. That was what kept Joanne away—fear that her sister and her husband the Reverend Duncan Macdonald would guess her adultery.

Joanne slumped in her chair. It was almost midday. She had work to do. She needed to call Chiara, whom she hadn't spoken to all week. She had laundry to do, shopping. She needed a haircut; she needed to finish sewing a dress for next week's dance. She needed to sleep.

Neil might be at the library working. Dare she interrupt him when she changed her library books? He was irritable the one time she had interrupted him in the archives. Maybe he was at the guesthouse typing up his notes. Or at the home of one of the illustrious families of the Highlands, reading their family letters and documents, ferreting out their secrets, their skeletons. She wanted to run to fly to his side. This passion was burning her up. She needed to ask, to know.

She put her elbows on the table, her head in her hands, and addressed her absent friend and mentor. "Don McLeod, where are you when I need you?"

"In gaol," McAllister answered.

She jumped. She let her hair fall forward to hide her face. Then looked up. They looked at each other. She saw how old he was looking. He saw how exhausted she was.

"Don and I, we used to talk. Nothing serious, he didn't do serious, but he had a knack of putting everything into perspective."

McAllister listened. That was what he too missed most about Don.

"I'd tell him something that was bothering me, he'd say it wasn't worth the time of day." What she didn't tell him was Don's exact phrase, *There's nothing worth getting your knickers in a twist over.* "I miss him."

"Me too."

They both hesitated. The moment passed.

"Right, I'll see you later," McAllister said.

"Right, I'll finish this." She gestured to the typewriter.

"Thanks for all the extra work you're doing."

"Not at all."

She started typing. He went into his office and shut the door.

And both of them, in their separate thoughts, in their separate lives, felt the loss of the closeness that could perhaps, so McAllister hoped, have become more.

CHAPTER 17

When Rob came in to work on Friday morning, the only person there was Hector. And he didn't count.

"Where is everyone?"

"Search me." Hector didn't look up from his proof sheets.

Rob ran back downstairs. "Hello, it's Fiona, isn't it?"

Fiona, who had returned to the *Gazette*, dragged back by her mother, after quitting for a day, couldn't look at Rob. She was not terrified of him the way she was terrified of McAllister and her dad, but she thought Rob was a dreamboat, so could barely answer.

"I'm looking for Mrs. Buchanan."

"I'm sorry, she's not here." She was sorry she couldn't help Rob McLean, singer with the Meltdown Boys.

"McAllister?"

"He's not come in. Mrs. Ross neither." Two sentences, one after the other—she was getting braver by the minute. "Mrs. Buchanan is with Mr. Beech sorting out office stuff."

The telephone rang.

"*Highland Gazette*, can I help you?" With an unknown caller her confidence was high, her voice clear. That changed when she identified the voice. "Oh hello, Mr. Stewart. Yes, thank you, I'm fine. Yes, he's here." She handed Rob the receiver and turned away to hide her crimson face and the unfortunate spot that had sprung up that morning, which she examined every five minutes in the lavatory mirror, leaving the phone unattended.

"Rehearsals? Yep, same time, same place." He listened. "I can put the word around, but the best place to find the McPhees is the Ferry Inn. Right, see you then." Rob put down the phone. "Thanks, Fiona. Hey, would you like two free tickets to the dance next Friday? Bring your boyfriend but don't forget to keep a dance for me."

Crikey, Rob thought, *she looks as though I've offered to strangle her not dance with her.*

Listening to Rob running up to the reporters' room, her heart still racing at the thought of a dance with him, she ignored the phone. It stopped, rang again almost immediately. She picked it up but didn't have a chance to say anything. "Yes, Mrs. Ross. I'll let them know." She wrote, *Mrs. Ross, not in until the afternoon.* Then a woman, dragging a three-year-old who kept kicking the counter, came in to place a classified, and Fiona forgot to pass on the note.

McAllister appeared at eleven thirty.

"Where is everyone?" He stood in his customary stance, filling the frame of the door to the reporters' room, but instead of reminding Rob of a watchful heron, he made him think of a scarecrow that crows were nesting in.

Rob took one sheet of paper out and put another into the machine, saying, "Hec was here. Now he's gone. Beech is working with Betsy, heaven help him. Joanne's not in yet."

"Why not?"

"How should I know?"

There was no reply. Rob looked up, saw McAllister. He took in the shirt that needed ironing, the purple shadows under the eyes, the pasty skin, and although he would not swear to it, there seemed to be a tremor in the editor's right knee. "What's happened?"

"I was at the gaol."

"Right." Rob nodded. "Your office? A drink?"

"My house. I need to eat."

"I need to get this off to Mr. Brodie, QC. Will it need an update?"

"Maybe. Wait until we've talked."

"Give me an hour."

When Rob arrived he walked straight through to the kitchen. He was carrying a bag of plums and some oranges.

"You look like you have scurvy, so I brought these." He found a bowl and put the fruit on the table. "And you need a haircut. You're not your usual Paris Left Bank suave self." He flung off his leather jacket.

McAllister immediately felt better. He liked Rob, appreciated his humor, and was dreading the day, which he saw as inevitable, when the young reporter would spread his wings and take off for parts foreign and south.

Lunch consisted of mutton pies, beans, HP Sauce, and sliced tomato garnished with parsley, a relic from McAllister's days on the newspaper in Glasgow—except for the tomato and parsley, as nothing uncooked would ever pass the lips of a Glaswegian.

When they finished, Rob started washing up, knowing it would be easier for McAllister to speak without the help of a drink if his audience had his back to him.

"Don's smaller."

Rob didn't interrupt.

"Thinner, too." McAllister took a long draw from his cigarette. "But he likes Brodie."

"Mr. Brodie, QC," Rob interjected.

"Aye. As Don tells it, the conversation was not long but made Don feel much better about his chances."

Don McLeod had searched his prodigious memory and could find only good things about the advocate Mr. William Brodie,

QC; he was not a Highlander but from the Carse of Moray, so almost. But Don had not expected the lawyer to bear a close physical resemblance to himself twenty years and many fewer drams ago.

"Brodie, QC."

"No need for me to state my name."

"Mr. Donal Dewar McLeod," Mr. Brodie recited. "Let us begin. I know the background to your marriage and the subsequent events when Mrs. McLeod went to India."

"Mrs. McLeod?"

"Is that not her legal name?"

"It is." Don had never heard her called this, and it broke his heart.

"The news of Mrs. Smart not being legally Mrs. Smart will be momentous enough," the advocate had explained. "The news of two elderly good folk of the town in bed together in the early hours of a Sunday evening? That will never do."

It took a moment for Don to recover. All he could think was, *It would have pleased her so much to be Mrs. Donal McLeod, and I denied her that.*

"Did Mrs. McLeod have her own keys to the house and gate?"

The questions came quickly.

"Aye, she did."

"The keys? Her handbag? Did she have them when she left?"

"Of course."

"Did Smart know about your marriage?"

"He did."

"When?"

"He knew in India."

"So why . . . ?"

"He wanted her money."

"And why did she agree?"

"She didn't want to break her father's heart." The lawyer stared, waiting. "Smart blackmailed her into it."

Mr. Brodie stared again, waiting. "Blackmail?" he prompted. Then, seeing Don would say no more, he moved on. "If Smart *were* the murderer, was he capable of it? And how did he manage it? And why now?"

"He was well capable of it, and he's much more mobile than he lets on." Don paused. "I've had plenty of time to think about it, but I just canny see him doing it—much as I'd like him locked up for the rest of his life." He rubbed his chin. He needed a shave. Mr. Brodie knew that his client would have to look immaculate for the court, and he made a mental note to see to it.

"He knows where I live," Don continued. "He's followed her often enough. Maybe he had a key to the back door of the church. He was a member there. But how did he know about my knife?"

"And what changed after all this time that would make him kill her now?" Even though his thoughts were not helpful, Brodie was pleased Don was talking.

"Search me." Don shrugged, but the flicker in one eye—as though a light had suddenly been switched on in the periphery of his vision—alerted the advocate.

"There must have been a reason Smart snapped—if he did."

"Not that I'm aware of."

Mr. Brodie knew Don was lying and knew there was no point threatening him with prison—the death of the woman he loved was a life sentence. "What about the Gurkha, Mr. Bahadur? Is he a likely candidate? He has inherited a large sum of money. He knows how to use a knife."

"Never. That man loved Joyce, protected her like she was his sister."

"I've never found love stops people from killing each other."

The way Mr. Brodie said this made Don look closely at him. The lawyer looked back.

"I didn't do it," Don said.

"Glad to hear it, Mr. McLeod. Now, defense strategy. I will do everything I can to discredit Smart. I will also do everything I can to cast doubt that you rose from your bed in a postprandial state, followed her, then killed the love of your life in a neat, cold, calculating manner, with your own knife, which you then returned to its usual niche in the wall."

"The fiscal will argue I was drunk." Don gave a bleak smile, knowing everyone would believe that.

"If you can tell me why the sergeant major was blackmailing her, that might help establish a clear motive."

"No."

From that emphatic negative, the advocate knew he would gain little more from the interview.

"I'll be back, Mr. McLeod," he said as he put his papers into a folder and tied it up with red ribbon. "You won't tell me now, but I'm sure you will, when faced with a life sentence."

Don doubted that, but when he was returned to his cell, he spoke to Joyce, a habit he had fallen into, as what he missed most about her was the conversations, having a person to talk about anything and everything to. That and having someone to put your arms around. "I promised, lass. So don't worry. I'll keep my word."

Don had told McAllister most of the conversation with Mr. Brodie, but left out Sergeant Major Smart's blackmailing Joyce McLeod née Mackenzie into a bigamous marriage. He did not want McAllister in the cell next to his.

McAllister told Rob most of the conversation between himself and Don, but left out the end.

"How is everything at the paper?" Don had asked.

"Muddling along," McAllister replied.

"How's the Canadian shaping up?"

"He's good at his job."

Don heard the unsaid. "What's he like?"

McAllister could only shrug. "He's intelligent, interesting, good-looking, gets on well with everyone." The bitterness in his voice alerted Don.

"Beech has been helping him in his research. He's playing harmonica in Rob's band. He has Betsy charmed. He is seeing Joanne outside of work. They went away to the west coast together."

Don heard the pain. He reached for a Capstan Full Strength. He offered one to McAllister, who took it and produced a lighter, then choked on a cigarette that, even to him, was one stop short of old rope.

"You know, I have one huge regret that will never go away." Don was speaking to the wall. "I sent her away. I let my stupid pride . . ." He turned. "Listen to me, McAllister. Don't make the mistake I made. Don't be so bloody Scottish. Tell her how you feel."

"It's too late for that." McAllister radiated defeat. His shrug, his wave of the cigarette, his stretching his legs out and exhaling through his mouth as he said *It's too late* . . . made Don furious.

"Do something. Tell her. Never ever leave it unsaid until it really is too late."

The heartbreak and the sheer frustration coming from Don penetrated McAllister's despair. And even though he had no intention of confronting Joanne, he had heard Don's cry of pain.

Rob was sitting at the table with a cup of tea, hearing McAllister's spoken and unspoken recount of the visit with Don. When McAllister finished, he sensed something important had been left out, but didn't ask.

"Well," Rob said, "at least Don is communicating." He started fiddling with his pencil, beating out a drum solo on the table. "I have some information—though how it helps I don't know."

McAllister raised his eyebrows. Rob stopped drumming. "Sergeant Major Archibald Smart is from Sutherland. His father was a gillie on the late Colonel Ian Mackenzie's estate before moving to Perthshire."

"So Archibald Smart would have known Joyce Mackenzie when they were children?"

"More than likely. She went to the local school until she was eleven."

"How does that fit in?" McAllister asked.

"No idea, but Mr. Brodie wants any and every . . ."

"Mr. Brodie, QC." McAllister grinned as he reminded Rob, making Rob grin back at him.

"I'll keep digging," Rob continued. "Neil is familiar with researching parish registers, he's promised to look for anything relating to the Smarts and Mackenzies of Assynt."

"Neil seems to be fitting in well."

Rob was putting on his jacket and did not catch the sarcasm. "Yes, he's really fast at subbing, and not as pedantic as Don. Good at research too. It was him discovered the sergeant major was from the Mackenzie estate. Plus he's a pretty good musician. I'm impressed. Come and hear the band play, a week today." Rob picked his keys up from the table. "See you in the office."

"You're not the only one impressed by Neil Stewart," McAllister muttered when Rob was gone. He tried not to be bitter—*Joanne has a right to see whoever she wants.* He reached for his cigarettes, decided to wait—his lungs were feeling like the inside of a kipper factory. He knew he needed to force himself back to the *Gazette,* to check on work, to be in the same room as Joanne, to see her face as she tried to avoid looking at him.

What had Don said? Don't be like me?

"You had your time of happiness." McAllister said this aloud. The words echoed in the almost empty house that was three bedrooms and a sitting and dining room too big for one man. "At least you had that."

"Glad you've decided to grace us with your company, Mrs. Ross," McAllister said when he walked into the reporters' room, and immediately wanted to cut his tongue out when he saw the hurt in her eyes.

"I phoned in to say I would be out at the hospital looking at the plans for a new wing."

"Sorry." He was standing close to her. He wanted to reach out, to touch her. To say he was sorry. Sorry about so much. But he didn't know how to begin. He tried to catch Joanne's eye, but she was hitting the keys of the typewriter as fast and hard as a boxer on a punching bag.

He left to hide in his office. He could not bear to be home in a house that was too big. He did not want to be in the office. He had no idea where he wanted to be. So he left. Again.

He walked up past the castle, down towards the river. He walked along the riverbank, past the mansions of Archibald Smart and the Beauchamp Carlyles. He crossed the swaying suspension bridge onto the first island. He tried sitting on a bench, but watching the river flow brought no comfort. He walked through the islands, crossed another suspension bridge, turned left, walked the northern riverbank path under a canopy of the bare creaking fingers and limbs of beech and oak and elm and sycamore. He reached the canal, turned left onto the towpath. And he walked and he walked, mile upon mile, until it was quite dark and he had no idea how far he had come, although he knew it was well beyond the town.

Below, he could hear a faint murmur. The river, he guessed. The silence of the canal did not fool him. There was life there too. And death. He looked heavenward. The sky was clear except for the multitude of stars as cold and as silent as himself. He began to pick out the constellations. The tidal pull of the almost full moon began to tug at him.

For the length of one cigarette he stood and watched the reflection of the stars barely moving in the soft undercurrent of the canal.

What had Don said? Pride—that was it.

What had Rob said? A haircut.

He had the beginnings of an idea, so he turned back and walked out the remains of the evening, and that night, slept soundly.

Rehearsal was over. Rob and Neil looked at each other. The adrenaline of the music still ran, and they needed to be anywhere but back in their respective rooms, alone on a Saturday night.

"Still looking for the McPhees?" Rob asked.

"Very much so."

"The Ferry Inn then."

Neil had no problem being a passenger on Rob's bike. He envied the younger reporter his freedom.

"It's early, but Jenny is usually in by seven," Rob said as they settled down in the saloon bar to wait.

Deep in a conversation about blues musicians, Rob didn't notice Jenny come in, but Neil did. He stood.

"Mrs. McPhee."

"Mr. Stewart."

Jimmy came in behind his mother. He did not look pleased to find company. "Is this aw'right wi' you?" he asked his mother.

"Fine." She sat down, nodded to Neil. "I'll have a double Glenfarclas."

There was something in the way she settled down, arms folded, face set, that made Rob think of a statue of Queen Victoria, and made Jimmy think the visitors should leave. Now. But Jenny said nothing except *Sláinte*, when Neil put the glass in front of her. Then she waited.

Neil felt like a student sitting final exams. "I was in Sutherland recently. I saw Suilven from the same spot the picture of my mother was taken."

"Aye, it's right bonnie up there."

Neil smiled. It was almost the same words Joanne had used. "A friend of mine said the same." He had a quick flash of her at home, and tried to remember if he had promised to see her tonight.

"How is Mrs. Ross?"

Neil was startled. "She's well." He sensed an accusation in Jenny McPhee's voice.

"You're here for a reason, Mr. Stewart?" Jenny wanted the conversation at an end. The past was the past. Nothing could be changed. Neil Stewart—she knew who he was, he was doing fine; healthy, educated, prosperous, that was more than enough. *It was all such a long time ago, I don't need ma heart broken all over again.*

"I'm curious about my mother." He produced the photograph, careful not to let the beer stain the cardboard frame. "Did you know her?"

"Chrissie Stewart. Yes, I knew her. She went into service in a big house in the town."

"Were you related?"

"You mean was she a tinker?" Jenny smiled. "Well, lad, that would be telling, and there's not many folk who would want to know a tinker was their mother."

"I was adopted."

"Were you now?" Jenny's voice sounded surprised. Her eyes opened wide. She had on a small smile. But Jimmy wasn't fooled.

Neil was uncertain. Rob looked closely at Jenny as she downed the last of her dram, so he couldn't see her face clearly. Something was not being said, that he knew.

"Chrissie was a nice wee soul. I'm sorry to hear she's no longer with us."

"Thank you."

Jenny gestured to her son. "Jimmy, we need to be getting back."

"I found out recently that Sergeant Major Smart was born and raised on the Mackenzie estate."

Jenny took her time looking him over. "Ma eldest, Keith, he's like you—always burrowing in the past. And like you, he sometimes doesn't have the sense to leave the past alone."

"My PhD depends on this—that means a professor's job."

"I ken what a doctorate is," she snapped, "my Keith is going for one."

Neil was reminded this was not an ordinary woman, this was Jenny McPhee. She might not have gone to school, but she knew much.

"Did you know the sergeant major as a boy?"

"Now what would the son of a gamekeeper be doing wi' tinkers?"

"Joyce Mackenzie had no problems with tinkers, nor her father from what I hear."

"Jimmy." Her son jumped. Rob jumped too; the voice was like the crack of a whip, the meaning as clear.

"Well, Mr. Stewart, I'm glad to have met you. Glad to see you're well. Though I doubt we'll meet again." She nodded slowly at him and he gave an almost imperceptible nod back, which only Jenny saw. "Thank you for the dram."

Rob saw a frailty in her that hadn't been there when she came in. He saw a sadness in her eyes, a momentary tremor in her chin, which she too noticed. And, matriarch of the McPhees she was, she stretched her neck, held her head high and, shoulders back, dismissed the passing weakness, waved a queenly wave. The audience was over.

Rob saw that Jimmy was looking as though he wanted to hit someone, and when the McPhees were gone, he realized he had been holding his breath. "That was a bit of a disaster." He laughed.

Neil wasn't laughing. He was playing with his glass, turning it round and around, looking into the remains of the golden spirit.

Rob, leaning back again the wall, was doing all he could not to shiver. "Time I was off too." His voice sounded unnatural even to himself. "Can I give you a lift?"

"Hey, that would be great." Neil grinned. "As I'm not too popular here, I may as well go where I *am* wanted." He downed the last drops of his whisky. "Can you drop me off at Joanne's?"

When Joanne heard the motorbike she thought it was Rob. But the sound of two voices, then Neil saying *Thanks for the lift,* came clearly through the still night.

She tried not to panic. *At least the girls are here,* she thought, *so nothing can happen*—a good thing or a bad thing, she couldn't decide.

Annie answered the door. "It's Uncle Neil," she said. She was still up. *Eight o'clock is for babies,* she told her mother every night, so, on Saturdays, bedtime was nine. And every Saturday night, her sister Jean tried to keep awake until big girl's bedtime. So far, she hadn't made it.

And every Saturday Joanne said to Jean, "You're getting too big for me to carry," but knew she would be sad when her youngest no longer wanted her mother to pick her up, tuck her in, and whisper silly seashell sounds in her ear.

"Is Uncle Rob not coming in?" She peered into the dark, but the noise of the engine and a flash of red taillight was her answer.

"He has to rush home to listen to his music on the radio," Neil told her.

"We say wireless."

"So you do. But I'm not from here."

"Annie, bed." Joanne smiled at Neil and smiled at her daughter, and for once, Annie did as she was told without arguing. Joanne knew Annie would read in bed with her secret torch, bought with her pocket money, but said nothing. She had done the same at boarding school.

"I'll put the kettle on." Joanne needed to be in the kitchen. She needed to recover from the hours she had spent waiting, listening, alternatively hoping for and dreading his visit. "So, what did you get up to today?" she asked when she brought in a tray with tea and shortbread, biting back *Where were you? I was waiting . . .*

"Working in the morning, band practice in the afternoon . . ."

Why didn't you ask me? I love being at band practice. She was remembering her miserable hours glancing at the clock every five minutes, wondering whether to look for him at the library, or at the boardinghouse, to accidentally on purpose bump into him, so she missed the beginning of his account of the meeting at the Ferry Inn.

"So Jenny took offense at my questions and left in a huff."

"She can be thrawn when she wants to be."

"My favorite word. *Thrawn*. My mother called me that. She said I was as stubborn as a Shetland pony."

"As thrawn as . . ." Joanne corrected him.

And in their laughter, in his reminiscing, they were comfortable again. They did not see the crack in the girl's bedroom door where Annie, sitting up in bed in the almost dark, was listening to every word. And when the laughter ended, when the voices sank to a murmur, she knew for certain that her mother was in love, like Anne of Green Gables. *But how can she love another man when she is still married to Dad?* She fell asleep to the idea of Canada, specifically Prince Edward Island.

It could have been the warmth of the room, or the sound of rain, or the three whiskies or Joanne sitting on the leather pouffe, listening in that way his mother had when, after his regiment had returned from Italy, he had told her about his friend being shot and his being unable to save him because he was dead before he fell. So Neil found himself saying all that he had bottled up, *since my mothers' death,* he thought, *or a lifetime.*

"I believed that coming back here, I would find answers," he started. "I had my lists, what I need to complete my thesis and hopefully a book. The work is almost finished, needs a good edit . . ." He paused. He did not know how far he could go. "But I will be leaving with so many personal questions unanswered, questions I thought were of no importance until I came here."

Joanne felt sick at the word. *Leaving. Is there no place for me in your life?* she wanted to ask.

"You'd love Canada." The change in his voice startled her.

"I'm sure I would." Her clouds were turning into rainbows.

"I thought when I came here, it would be different; the whispers about women alone, about a child with no visible father, the poverty, the narrow-mindedness, the sheer hard work to just stay alive. I didn't expect here to be the same. I believed all those tales about Highland hospitality, about everyone looking out for everyone, about the mountains and glens being so bonnie they broke your heart . . ." He laughed. "That's why I live in a city now." Joanne was lost. *What was he trying to say?*

"My mother was a completely selfless woman. She ruined her hands, her health, gutting fish to make sure I had all the books I wanted, all the things a normal boy with two parents had."

He remembered the new bicycle, the trip to Ottawa, the fountain pen when he was accepted at the academy.

I promised I'd look after you, she told him as she was dying.

"She didn't need to sacrifice herself." He was not looking at Joanne as he was speaking. His legs stretched out straight, and he was leaning back in the only armchair in the room, his eyes closed.

"When she died, a solicitor contacted me. There was money. Every year since she arrived in Canada, a deposit went into an account labeled Education Fund." He didn't tell her the deposit arrived on his birthday. "Mum had taken out sums here and there, always coinciding with the start of a new term. She had barely touched the capital and told me the extra came from over-time . . . Then the solicitor, a decent man who'd known me all my life, saw how much I blamed myself, believing that to pay for my education my mother had worked herself to death. He went against her wishes and revealed that the money came from a mysterious benefactor, in Edinburgh, Scotland."

Joanne reached over and put her hand on his knee.

He opened his eyes and smiled. "So . . . this is quite some journey for me."

"I'm glad you told me." Joanne hesitated, then asked, "Have you been looking for your . . . family?" It was the only word she could think of.

"No, not *looking* . . ." His lips tightened. "But it's strange what you come across when you're not looking." He looked as though he was about to say more, when Jean came into the room.

Joanne felt he was about to say more, when Jean interrupted him. Three-quarters asleep, she said, "I need a wee-wee." The child didn't see Neil. She went to the bathroom with her mother. When she was finished, she went back to bed, without completely waking. Joanne was glad her daughter no longer wet her bed.

Maybe it was the reality that Joanne was a mother that did it, maybe the remembering that she was still married, but when she came back to Neil, the connection had been broken.

"It's late," was all he said.

No it's not, she wanted to reply, but that sounded so childish.

He stood. "I'll see you soon."

When? She wanted to ask.

He went for his coat and scarf.

"Much as I'd like to, I obviously can't stay in your narrow bed tonight, Mrs. Ross." He pulled her to him, put his chin on her head. "But I'm really looking forward to next deadline night."

She kissed him inside the house but had to break off the kiss, as she was in danger of begging him to stay and she still had enough pride to know that begging was not somewhere she wanted to be.

When she was closing the front door after watching until he was out of her garden and down the lane, she heard him start to whistle. It was not a song, more a walking, or marching, or mending a broken machine or car or bicycle tuneless whistle, beloved of workmen and soldiers and those who had not a care in the world. And it broke her heart.

She went to bed quickly and quietly. She pulled the eiderdown over her head. It would muffle the sound of her sobbing.

The despair was salted with the understanding that she

was she was letting herself down—again. *Didn't you swear you would no longer let a man hurt you?* She turned the pillow over to hide a big wet patch. *It's not him, Neil; he's not the one hurting me. I'm doing this to myself.* She sat up, reached for the glass of water without switching on the light. *How can I even dream of marriage? He doesn't want that. Only sex.* She burrowed back down into her nest. She returned to the country of doubt and self-loathing and was too lost to see how mistaken she was.

CHAPTER 18

The sooner Don is back running this newsroom the better, Rob was thinking. But having typed up his notes for Mr. Brodie, QC, he had his doubts that would happen. *Because who else could have done it? The knife is Don's . . . he inherits . . . he has keys . . . he was there . . . he drinks . . . he . . .*

"Rob? Are you with us?" McAllister asked.

"Sorry." They got back to the business of the Monday meeting.

Rob noticed that this Monday morning, McAllister seemed marginally more aware of his surroundings. Neil was alert but quiet. Joanne was shifting about in her chair, chewing a strand of hair. Rob saw that she too needed a haircut.

What's happening to us all? he thought. He glanced across at Hector. Even he was not his usual chortling-at-jokes-that-only-a-nine-year-old-would-appreciate self.

The major contents of the paper decided, McAllister asked Rob into his office. "What was the name of your barber?"

Rob laughed. "Hairdresser. Mr. Raymond."

"Are you sure men go there?"

"Tell him I sent you." Rob checked McAllister as though the editor was going for a job interview. "You could also buy a duffle coat. All the best intellectuals and members of CND are wearing them."

"Out." McAllister grinned. "No. Hold on. Jimmy McPhee; have you seen him lately?"

"Ah." Rob closed the door. It took twenty minutes to tell McAllister about the second meeting, equally inconclusive, between Neil Stewart and Jimmy and Jenny McPhee.

"So you think the McPhees are hostile to Neil?"

"Jenny McPhee isn't. Wary would be a better word. And Jimmy was no more than his usual hostile-to-everyone self."

When Rob left to cover the Magistrates Court, McAllister fetched his hat and coat. He put his head around the door of the reporters' room.

"I'll be back by eleven. All okay?"

"If I've any problems they can wait till then," Neil replied.

"I'm fine," Joanne said.

The shadows under and in your eyes? No, you're not fine, my bonnie lass, McAllister thought as he went down the stairs.

The hairdresser was on the north side of the river. McAllister took a circuitous route, leaving messages for Jimmy McPhee in the three likely bars. He then took the steps down to the footbridge, hurrying, almost running down; he did not want to imagine Mrs. Smart dead. He wanted to remember her in her chair, in the newsroom, pen poised, eyes bright, head to one side as she listened, considered, giving a slight nod or a shake, and, McAllister remembered, that was the matter decided. And only now that she was dead did he understand that the small smile, hovering at the corners of her mouth, had been for Don, her husband.

McAllister hesitated at the salon door, checking up and down the street as though he were about to enter a house of ill repute. The first thing that hit him was the smell, all too familiar from his mother's home perm kits that Mrs. Muir the neighbor used to administer in the kitchen in their tenement house in Glasgow.

Mr. Raymond—McAllister was not sure if this was a first, last, or only name, insisted on a hair wash.

The "girl," as Mr. Raymond referred to her, was at least forty, revealing a bosom that would put Betsy Buchanan to shame.

Not quite the thing on a Monday morning, McAllister thought.

He was presented to the hairdresser wrapped in a gown a shade of apricot unknown in nature, suitably clean, smelling of perhaps lavender, perhaps freesia, perhaps a kitchen cleaning product. Mr. Raymond danced around him, scissors poised, examining his head as though he was about to sculpt it, and finally started. And the haircut was good; the editor looked his age again, and interesting.

"Thank you," McAllister said when shown the back of his head in the mirror. He went to pay.

"Really?" said the "girl." "Can't we do the usual arrangement?" She saw his bewilderment. "Mrs. Buchanan runs an advertisement for free instead of paying for her hairdo."

McAllister had no time to ask more about the arrangement; Jimmy McPhee was standing in the doorway.

"Very posh," Jimmy said.

The assistant went as still as the statue of Flora MacDonald in front of the castle. Mr. Raymond dropped a towel over an open leather folder of cutthroat razors.

"Jimmy." McAllister nodded. "You're not here for a haircut, I presume," he said before paying what he considered an astonishing amount. *No wonder Betsy Buchanan has done a deal.* But he would speak to her later.

They went and sat in Jimmy's car, parked on the riverbank near another church, the Roman Catholic one. Across the river he could see the churches bordering the fatal steps. *How many churches are there in this one small area? Three, four, maybe five? Plus the remnant of the Abbey of the Black Friars.*

In the weak November sun the river was a rich dark whisky

color, the outline of the Black Isle clear on the other side of the rivermouth.

"The new girl on the front desk told me where to find you." Jimmy didn't bother with pleasantries.

"And here's me thinking you had your crystal ball with you."

Jimmy laughed. "I leave that to ma mother."

"Neil Stewart." McAllister came straight out with it.

"Aye. Neil Stewart," Jimmy repeated slowly, carefully, the two names separated into syllables. "Well . . ." He lit a cigarette, rolled down his window a little. McAllister did the same. "I've been thinking on Neil Stewart, and I'm no' finished thinking yet."

Their voices sounded oddly intimate in the small space, their outgoing breaths of cigarette smoke mingling as they talked.

"He was adopted. The timing . . ." McAllister began.

"Is about right." Jimmy sighed. "And my mother is no' herself."

That means Jimmy is upset, McAllister thought. *Dangerous*.

"My ma had not much to say to him, but she knows who he is, I think."

"If he is . . . would she say so?"

"Now that's the question. Maybe. I don't know. She's a great one for letting things be. To know he's safe, educated, that might be enough." He threw his cigarette out the window. "Besides, who would choose to be a tinker?" He laughed.

McAllister got the point.

Who indeed would choose to be one of the sometimes despised, mostly uneducated, wandering tribe of Scotland, he thought. *You'd have to be born to it to want it.* The Traveling people he knew were a fierce proud people, but they were outsiders. No, he had never heard of anyone choosing that life.

"Sergeant Major Archibald Smart was born on Colonel Mackenzie's estate. His father was a gamekeeper," McAllister said.

Staring out of the windscreen, seeing nothing, Jimmy was trying to calculate how this related to anything, and failing. "So?"

"He must have known Joyce Mackenzie when they were children, even though his family left the estate when he was quite young. And your family—they were staying in an estate cottage, he must have known of you."

"A falling-apart croft house," Jimmy corrected him. "And a gamekeeper and his son, they'd have had nothing to do wi' tinkers, the opposite more like."

"I wonder if he ever heard about the children?" There was no need to say which children.

"It's a very small community. Then again, who cares what happened to tinkers' bairns?" He shrugged. But he was not fooling McAllister. The bitterness in his taut body oozed from every pore. "So you're not taken in by Neil Stewart's charm? Not like Rob McLean and Joanne Ross?" Jimmy needed to forget about the stolen boys.

"Mr. Beauchamp Carlyle thinks well of him. He is helping Neil with his research." As he said this, McAllister knew that, no matter what others thought of Neil, his opinion would always be shadowed by the memory of Joanne glancing up at Neil through that strand of hair that had a life of its own, her eyes brightening to that blue-green he so loved.

"What you need is his date of birth." What Jimmy meant was *we* need his date of birth: he needed it as much as anyone; he needed to know.

"He must have filled in something for the *Gazette* records."

"If he gave his real date of birth. Ask Joanne. It's the kind of thing women always want to know." Jimmy stared at a seagull sitting on the railing contemplating his car. "Vermin," he called out the window at it. The seagull gave him a "same to you" look before floating off to find some pedestrian to poo on. Jimmy put the keys in the ignition. "Can I give you a lift?"

"I need to think, so I'll walk," McAllister said. "All I want is to clear Don McLeod. Neil Stewart doesn't concern me," he said before he got out of the car.

"Aye." Jimmy nodded, not fooled.

He did not drive off until McAllister was halfway towards the red stone arches of the suspension bridge. And both men were thinking the same. *Neil Stewart, who the hell are you?*

"Ah, just the man," Beech called out as McAllister arrived at the top of the stairs. "We need to talk about the accounts."

"Yes, we do." McAllister continued to his office, not bothering to check the progress of the edition with Neil or Joanne or Rob.

When they were seated, McAllister recounted the incident at the hairdresser's.

"One mystery solved, but there are about fourteen other discrepancies in the accounting to solve," Beech said as he put a tick against a name on a list he had compiled over the weekend.

"Joanne is supposed to be supervising the administration side of things," McAllister pointed out. "Hasn't she noticed what's going on?"

"I think you are asking too much of Mrs. Ross. She is doing a sterling job holding the paper together."

"Sorry, you're right." McAllister was suitably chastened.

"If you don't mind, I'll work with Mrs. Buchanan on this until we appoint a new business manager." Beech tapped the papers.

"What about Betsy?"

"She is an excellent saleswoman, but a competent manager is essential."

McAllister heard that a decision had been made. Whether Betsy stayed or was demoted, all McAllister could think of was the tears that would flow. "I'll leave it to you, if you don't mind."

Beech nodded agreement.

"What do you know about Neil Stewart?"

The way McAllister asked, trying to keep his voice casual, alerted Beech. Yesterday, his sister had asked the same question. "Not a lot. I like him. He is intelligent, interesting. When we have talked, I recognized that he is not altogether the competent man-of-the-world he makes out to be. Like many colonials, he has a slight inferiority complex when it comes to Great Britain."

"That's all?"

"He is ambitious, determined to have a glittering career."

That surely rules out a divorced mother of two as his wife. McAllister was ashamed the moment he thought this.

Beech was watching the editor, a man he liked and respected. "Is there a relevance to the interest in Neil Stewart?"

They both knew the reference was to Don McLeod.

"I can't see one." McAllister rubbed at his new haircut. "Perhaps your sister . . . ?"

"We spoke of this yesterday. Rosemary does not want the tragedy of Joyce's death to be compounded by another calamity." He did not add that it had taken a long and charged conversation to persuade his sister that it might no longer be possible to protect Joyce's past.

"A man's life is at risk," he had said. His sister had listened to his argument, but he knew she made her own decisions. So he was waiting.

Mortimer Beauchamp Carlyle left the *Gazette* midafternoon. On the walk home, he was thinking about the previous afternoon. A long dreary Sunday afternoon, the sky, the river, the hibernating plants, trees and shrubs, all seemed glazed in grey, adding to the melancholy of an anniversary they were about to commemorate—Armistice Day.

Beech was spending more and more time in town, away from the simple and solid eighteenth-century, impervious-to-all-weathers house in Cromarty, a ferry ride and an hour's drive away. He missed it. His library containing rare historical documents and pibroch music scores made it more than a house; it was his retreat, his place for thinking, his place for writing his memoirs, which he had begun thirty years previous. And the walks along the cliffs and the seabirds and stars, he missed those too.

He needed to be in town to help the *Highland Gazette*. And to assist McAllister. He accepted that. He watched his sister in her grief. Joyce Mackenzie was one of the few people she was close to. He watched her wrestle with her conscience.

"Perhaps I should talk to Mr. McLeod?" she had said.

This morning, Rosemary Beauchamp Carlyle had an appointment with Angus McLean. Was his sister about to break a solemn promise, he wondered, and if so, would it help free Don McLeod?

That night after dinner, Rosemary came to join him in the study. She began, "The police raised no objection to me visiting with Mr. McLeod."

"In spite of his occasional curmudgeonly behavior, Mr. McLeod is well liked." He knew this was hard for her and wanted to lighten the conversation.

"What Mr. McLeod told me, he asked I not repeat."

"Would it help free him?"

"To share his and Joyce's private life is his decision to make. And he refused me permission to speak. I have agreed not to divulge what I know."

"And if you were asked under oath?"

She looked away. He saw her rub one hand over the other, noticed how translucent they were, the skeleton almost visible. He felt a chill on the back of his neck and knew it was not from the numerous drafts in the century-and-a-half-old house; what he would do if his elder sister died before him he could not contemplate.

"I believe I did achieve something. I told Mr. McLeod his wife should be honored in death. A memorial service and a headstone are her due. I promised that if he were not freed, we would arrange that. But I told him he should be there. To honor her. He agreed."

"I agree too."

She smiled when he said this. "I hope all turns out well." But the hesitation in her voice made Beech doubt she believed it would. "Good night, Mortimer."

"Good night, my dear."

Beech knew that what Rosemary had told him might just work: Don McLeod now had a mission; Don was like a terrier; he would never let go once he had his teeth into a bone.

Beech went around the house, checking windows, putting out lights, locking his study but not the doors—he had never adopted the habit, because burglaries were almost unknown in the town.

Although there was no real reason to be more cheerful about the upcoming court case, he went to bed feeling hopeful. His sister had spoken to Don McLeod and was not completely despondent after the visit, and his sister was a wise woman.

It was late afternoon the next day before McAllister had a chance to talk to Joanne.

"I like the haircut," she said when he came into the reporters' room.

"It still stinks of shampoo," he said, rubbing his hand over his head, desperate to be rid of the Boots the Chemist cosmetic counter smell. "Why you have to have your hair washed to get a haircut is beyond me."

Joanne smiled. "That's the best part."

"Do you know Neil's date of birth?" He was at a loss as to how to broach the subject, so he just asked.

"Why?" She looked at him and he saw her whole body tense like a dog on guard over a litter of new pups.

"For the records." But the way he mumbled and couldn't look back as she watched him made him regret asking. And she knew it.

"Ask him yourself, he's downstairs." The brevity of her remark, the way she turned away from him back to the type-writer, snapped him into Mr. McAllister, editor in chief of the *Highland Gazette*.

"Maybe you could clear up another mystery. The hairdresser said Mrs. Buchanan runs ads instead of paying for a hairdo. Do you have the time to look into that?" He couldn't help it. The accusation—meant for Betsy, not Joanne, but not coming out as intended—was clear.

"I'm not your spy." She was suddenly furious with him, her-self, Betsy, Neil, everything. And she didn't know why. "If that's all, Mr. McAllister, it's five o'clock. I must get home to my chil-dren."

He watched her grab her coat, heard her run down the stairs. He was sitting smoking, staring at the ceiling, when Neil came in.

"Where's Joanne?" he asked.

"Lost," McAllister said. He walked out, leaving Neil staring after him.

"Looks like I'm writing the editorial again this week," Neil muttered and sat down to type.

*   *   *

Two days later Joanne was alone in the reporters' room, slowly turning the pages of the new edition of the *Gazette*. She could sense there was something not quite satisfactory, but couldn't pinpoint exactly what.

Neil had stayed the night again. No matter how many times she told herself it was wrong, immoral, a betrayal of all her promises to herself, she couldn't say no. She became aware that she was slumped over the table. She sat back, shoulders straightened. She closed her eyes tight shut. *Pull yourself together.* The phrase reminded her of the sports mistress at her boarding school, shouting at her when she cried, her knee bruised and bleeding from falling over on a frost-hardened hockey pitch with snow blanketing the hills a mere half a mile away, and the memory made her feel better.

"Joanne, do you have a moment?" Betsy had come up the stairs without Joanne noticing.

"It's about . . . what we talked about."

Betsy looks nearly as tired as me, Joanne realized. "Let's go out," she suggested.

They went to the coffee bar next to the post office. They were unlikely to run into the housewives of the town, the volume of the jukebox would see to that, and it was too early for Rob to be around.

"I've been speaking to Hector." Betsy was sounding anxious. "He's not keen."

"I know." Joanne was stirring the froth off her coffee. "Look, Betsy, can't you just tell Bill? I'm sure he'll stick by you."

"Are you?"

"He wants a son."

"My mother does this thing with a piece of silver and string to tell if it's a boy or girl . . ." Betsy's eyes misted up. "But I can't ask her. Maybe you could do it?"

Joanne said nothing.

Betsy decided on another tactic. "It's in your interests too, Joanne. Bill knows nothing about you and Neil, but what if he finds out?"

"Betsy!"

"I'm sorry. I'm desperate. I'm starting to show. And you don't have as much to lose as me. Your reputation is already . . ."

"What?"

"I'm sorry." And she was. In spite of their rivalry, as Betsy saw it, and in spite of knowing they would never be friends, she liked Joanne. "Maybe Neil Stewart will take you to Canada with him."

"Maybe you and Bill could go to Australia. Or New Zealand."

"My brother is in Australia. He's doing really well. He has this building business . . ."

They stared at each other.

"It only costs ten pounds to get to Australia," Joanne reminded Betsy. "And they are always advertising for tradesmen. Maybe your brother would help you."

"I could write." Betsy was considering the idea of being away from all this—the cold, the job, the other wife, her child a bastard—all the future gossip, which she knew would shame her mother.

"If you get on well with your brother . . ."

Betsy nodded. "I do. And so does Bill. They played football together for Thistle when they came back from the war."

Joanne remembered that as another of Bill's fantasies— that he could have been a division one player if Joanne had not trapped him into marriage.

"Send him a telegram, tell your brother you're desperate. No, tell him it would break your mother's heart." Joanne saw that this had hit home. "But don't tell Bill. Not yet. Get your brother to offer him a job first."

"I'm always telling him how my brother has heaps of work and is desperate for qualified tradesmen."

"Say it's a partnership, not a job. That sounds better." Joanne had the good sense not to say what she was thinking, *Bill will want to be important.*

Betsy was nodding fiercely. "And I'll tell him we can build our own house. He really wants to do that."

And knowing how good a saleswoman Betsy is, Bill hasn't a chance. Joanne knew the telegram had to be sent immediately, before Betsy had second thoughts. "The post office is next door." But looking at the pale determined face with the sweet baby-doll eyes, she saw there was more steel in Betsy than she had thought. *I once told Rob that Betsy reminded me of a blancmange,* she thought. *I take it all back.*

They spent the next fifteen minutes composing the telegram. Joanne put a one-pound note on the table to help cover the cost of what would be a very expensive cry for help. They smiled at each other, went next door, and sent the telegram, both praying for a reply, soon.

Chapter 19

❧

"Aunty Chiara, you're ginormous," Jean said as Chiara opened the door.

"Jean!" Joanne scolded, but she was laughing and couldn't help agree that for a tiny person, Chiara's bump was indeed ginormous.

Chiara led them into the hub of the house—the kitchen. She was babysitting the girls, as she wasn't going to the dance.

"Dancing? In my condition?" she had squealed down the phone at Joanne. "Don't be daft!"

The Scottish Italian inflection in "Don't be daft!" was still ringing in Joanne's ears, making her feel much, much better.

Chiara had invited them all for supper, saying, "A plate of spaghetti and you can dance the night away."

After a bowl of ice cream each, Annie and Jean scampered into the sitting room to watch television.

"Thank goodness that 'Toddlers' Truce' is over, though the government should have called it the Parents' Nightmare." Chiara laughed. She had never seen the point of the government regulation closing television between six and seven in the evening to safeguard family life. But, as she had no children, she couldn't express her opinion. "We'll have at least an hour of peace before they get bored."

"Not my two," Joanne said. "We can't afford a television, so they'll have to be dragged away from yours."

"What time are you going?" Chiara's husband had left early

to help set up the stage. "And have a beer or two," she had said, and he agreed.

"Peter says he's getting too old for the band," Chiara told Joanne, "so this is his last night as a member of the Meltdown Boys."

"I can't be a Meltdown Boy," he had said. "I'm thirty-six. We're playing the Everly Brothers hit, and the oldest brother is twenty. No, rock 'n' roll is for youngsters."

"So why am I going?" Joanne laughed when Chiara repeated Peter's remarks. "I'm nearly thirty-one."

"You don't look it," Chiara said. But she was lying.

Her dearest friend had lost that bonnie Highland bloom—a phrase Chiara had heard from a customer in the café. The weariness she saw in Joanne reminded her of the refugees she had seen in her tramp across Europe after the war. It was the look of a person who had lost and was lost.

"I like your skirt." Chiara stood, rubbed her back. "And I envy you your waist. I can't believe I'll ever find mine again." She had noticed Joanne was thinner—one more reason to worry about her friend.

Joanne birled around, and the circular skirt with the stiffened petticoat crackled and swooshed. The white sleeveless blouse with a turned-up collar she had finished the night before, the buttons sewn on only minutes before leaving her house.

"Not too young?"

"Never. You look smashing."

As Joanne walked towards the ballroom that spread between Church Street and the riverbank, she agonized over her skirt. *Rock 'n' roll is for young people.* So what was she, a mother of two in her thirties, doing? Why was she rushing off to a

Saturday-night dance, without a partner, to pick up a free single ticket left at the door by Rob, ten years her junior?

She would have to go to the bar by herself, order, and pay for her drink—even if it was only lemonade—all by herself. She almost turned and fled back to her bungalow.

I promised Rob, so I must go. She was lying, and she knew it; the enchantment of Neil was drawing her to the ballroom.

She had timed her entrance for an hour after the dance had started, and she could hear the resident Harry Shaw Band blasting away with a Duke Ellington number. Although local, the band was surprisingly good, and had a big following in the town and county and neighboring counties.

She collected her ticket, left her coat and scarf in the cloakroom, and went in, keeping to the edge of the dance floor on the opposite side to the bar area, which was crowded.

She watched the safely married couples dancing like one body. She could tell the soon-to-be-married couples, holding each other in a tight clinch with a promise of more later—made permissible by the ring on the left hand. She watched women dancing with other women—their men, glasses in hand, at the bar, engaging in the immortal dance of drunks.

The young crowd congregated in clusters near the front of the stage, girls in one group, boys in the other, waiting for the real action of the evening, the Meltdown Boys. Joanne could see that a circular skirt with cute blouse and hair in a ponytail were all the rage. One stylish lass was wearing pedal pushers, a fashion Joanne had only seen on *Six-Five Special*, the new top-of-the-charts program on television. But seeing Shona, her occasional babysitter, and Fiona from the office with their girlfriends, and one of the lasses who, she was sure, was still in the Girl Guides, made her even more aware of the age difference.

I belong to the Highland Dance crowd, Joanne thought, *and I'm dressed for rock 'n' roll.*

When the band finished their last number, a slow waltz, the bandleader thanked the crowd, then announced, "For all you youngsters, the Meltdown Boys will be on in ten minutes." This rated a cheer from the front, and a tidy exit for the cloakroom from the back of the floor. Some of the men knew they too would have to leave with their wives, but the hard-core drinkers stayed.

I hope Bill is not there, Joanne prayed, glancing at the bar. She was surprised to see the long lean body of McAllister, his back to her, obviously buying a drink. When he turned, she saw he was carrying two glasses and making his way towards her.

"I bought you a sherry," he said without asking if she wanted it or not.

"Rob left me a ticket, I couldn't refuse," she blurted out.

"*Sláinte,*" he replied, holding up a double whisky.

They stood side by side. She sipped her drink, glad of it. He did the same. They were relieved when the lights dimmed and Rob appeared at the microphone. A spotlight clicked on, and the squeals from the girls at the front made her smile.

Rob, hair in a quiff in imitation of Tommy Steele, announced the first number. "'Singing the Blues.' Tommy's British version, not Guy Mitchell's old man's version."

Making me feel my age again, but Joanne smiled at Rob's cheek.

McAllister couldn't stop a foot from tapping. This wasn't his music, he was a jazz man, but some of it, the blues parts, he recognized and liked. Muddy Waters, B.B. King, he and Rob had talked and laughed and exchanged records that summer, before . . . McAllister felt sick. He knew that once again he was drinking without having had anything to eat since a sandwich in the office for lunch.

"I have to go." He turned to Joanne. "I'll see you on Monday." He had to leave. Immediately. He was afraid of falling, falling backwards in an effort to stop his hand from reaching out and smoothing that strand of hair that had escaped from the hairband and was falling over her left cheek where the freckles were faint and the skin much paler than her usual, out-on-her-bicycle-in-all-weathers, brown.

He didn't tell her he had to go because the fish-and-chip shop in Eastgate closed at nine, and it was now eight thirty and he was faint from hunger and whisky and longing.

He didn't tell her he had been glad to see her, to stand by her side, to remember the smell of her hair and the nearness of her skin. He didn't tell her because he, the wordsmith, could find no words.

She didn't tell him how miserable she was, how lonely, how out of place she felt. She didn't tell him, because she couldn't admit it yet, that she had made the biggest mistake of her life, even bigger than the mistake of her marriage, because this time she was all grown up, so, she would later tell herself, and him, she should have known better because she knew Neil was leaving, he had never pretended otherwise.

Neil was sitting on a high stool at the left of the stage, waiting for his songs. Rob had announced him, "All the way from America . . ." He ignored the looks that description got from Neil, "our blues harp player, Mr. Neil Stewart . . ."

With everyone else, she looked at Neil. The spotlight had switched back to Rob. But in that flash of spotlight, the image of Neil she had glimpsed, and would always come back to, was of a moderately tall, moderately good-looking man, wearing what he told her were blue jeans, a garment unknown in Scotland, a man grinning, holding a mouth organ in one hand, watching the band

and the spectators from the side of the stage. It was an image of a man on the edge of everywhere.

Then Rob stepped up and broke her heart.

"We'd like to play one of my favorites." He didn't announce the title. Peter strummed in the opening on acoustic guitar. It was enough to have the girls at the front let out a little cry, except for Eilidh, who gave a small scream.

Rob took up the refrain, also on acoustic guitar and both leaning in the microphone, they sang, "Bye bye love, bye bye happiness, hello loneliness, I think I'm a-gonna cry . . ."

On the second chorus Joanne fled. She forgot her coat, her scarf. She didn't notice the rain, that at first was a drizzle, quickly turning into hard rain. She had on ballet flats that she had dyed black. She couldn't afford new shoes. They soaked up the water like blotting paper, the dye turning her feet blotchy dark. Her new mascara made rivulets of coal down her face; hair escaped from the ponytail and stuck to her face. And she ran.

She ran and walked and ran, and when she reached her little prefab bungalow, she realized she had left the keys in her coat in the cloakroom. The spare was under one of the flowerpots by the back door. Which one she didn't know, as Annie never returned them to the right place. She knocked the pots over, spilling dirt and parsley and the remains of the summer pansies over the doorstep as she scrabbled in the dark rain, November freezing her fingers as she felt for the key.

It's always the last one, she sobbed, in what was now a storm, the trees in the lane shaking out the last vestiges of autumn, the sky warning it would be many months before real sun returned.

She ran to the bathroom. She stripped off her sodden clothes, leaving them lying at her feet, rubbing her skin hard with a small threadbare towel as though punishing herself. And still she couldn't stop shivering.

She hadn't the energy to run a bath. She went to fill a hot-water bottle. She was waiting for the kettle to boil when she had to run. She was sick. She kept being sick.

No, she kept moaning, as she bent over the toilet, *no, no.*

The band was packing up. Eilidh was waiting for Rob below the stage.

"Are you coming with us?" one of the girls asked. "We're going to a party in Hilton. One of the boys, his parents are away for the night." They were thrilled at the prospect.

"No thanks, I'm waiting for Rob." The way she said it made the other girl like her even less. Eilidh was popular with boys, not girls.

"Forgotten me already, have you?"

A young man, slightly older than the rest, stepped towards Eilidh, and taking her by the elbow, he pulled her away from the crowd.

Some of the girls were watching.

"Oh, hi, Dennis! Long time no see." She allowed herself to be steered to one side of the dance floor.

Seeing no confrontation, the girls lost interest and left for the party.

A few minutes, a few angry words, and some waving of the arms later, Dennis Cameron strode across the floor out of the ballroom. He was a sensible young man, a doctor-to-be, and knew there was no point in arguing with Eilidh; she only saw what she wanted to see. In one way he was glad to be rid of her, she had expensive tastes, *but*, he remembered, *she was fun.*

As Dennis Cameron was leaving, he took one last look at the best-looking girl he had ever met and his first real girlfriend. He saw her standing below the stage, staring up at Rob.

"Good luck, Rob McLean," he muttered. "Just don't take her too seriously."

The equipment packed, Peter asked, "Rob, Neil, would you like to come to mine for a drink?" He knew Chiara would be in bed, but he was not ready for sleep.

"I've got plans." Rob grinned and gestured to Eilidh, whose eyes, outlined in copious quantities of makeup, was staring adoringly at him, hoping he would see the resemblance to Audrey Hepburn.

Neil smiled. "Hi, Eilidh, what did you think of the band?"

"You were brilliant," she said, "especially Rob."

"Thanks." Neil laughed. "Say, have you seen Joanne Ross?"

"No, but I wasn't looking." Eilidh made it quite clear that Neil was making a mistake fancying Joanne Ross when he could have her instead.

Neil looked around again to make sure Joanne wasn't waiting somewhere, but she wasn't. *Couldn't find a babysitter*, he assumed. "Thanks, Peter, I'll take you up on that offer."

It was only a hundred yards from the ballroom to Eilidh's and Don's terrace. She and Rob ran most of the way. She locked the gate, ran to the front door, opened it, threw off her coat, kicked her shoes into a corner, threw her arms around Rob's neck, and started to kiss him so fiercely he thought his lips would bleed.

She pulled his jacket off. She pulled his shirt off. They fell backwards onto the sofa. Only on round two did they make it up the stairs.

Next morning, as Eilidh was on early shift, they woke to the alarm clock. She leapt out of bed, stark naked, and opened the big ugly cupboard that had been put together in the room when the house was built nearly two hundred years ago. He watched as, still naked, she threw clothes around, leaving them on the floor that served as an alternative wardrobe, searching for a clean uniform.

"Who was the man I saw you arguing with when I was up onstage?" Rob asked, wanting to prolong the vision of her body.

"My ex-boyfriend."

Eilidh assured him it was long finished and that the medical student she had been seeing for a few months was just being a nuisance. "He can't get over me," she finished.

"I can believe that," Rob said, meaning only to flatter her.

Eilidh took it as her due. She knew she was pretty. She knew she was different. She knew all the words of the latest songs, had seen all the latest films. She took day tickets on the train to Aberdeen and bought the latest fashions and the latest records. And she was a nurse, so she knew how to look after herself. She knew she was a catch, and if a doctor wasn't on the immediate horizon, Rob McLean would do very well as a prospect. Probably better. His family was maybe not *rich* rich, but they were certainly well off.

"How do you know Neil?" he asked.

"He came here asking if the empty house next door was for rent. I have a spare key. He looked at it, but said it wasn't his cup of tea. Pity, he's gorgeous. Would have been a much nicer neighbor than . . . Oh, no . . . look at the time. Sister will kill me if I'm late again."

He watched her hurriedly clip her stockings to the garter belt. He saw her pulling her hair into an elastic band, then checking her eyes to make sure the liner was all scrubbed off. She bounced onto the bed and kissed him. "Let yourself out. The spare keys are in the kitchen drawer."

He went back to sleep and woke at ten. The cacophony of bells reminded him he was on Church Street with three churches within spitting distance and at least three more within throwing distance.

He waited until the good folk of the town were safely inside and the first psalm sung, before dressing and leaving. He tried to lock the front door but the key was stiff. *Often happens with the spare key,* he thought, and the key to the gate worked so he didn't worry.

Walking across the suspension bridge, whistling into a biting wind, which he did not notice, whistling *Bye bye love,* which was currently his favorite, he decided Phil would be his alter ego, not Don.

Don. Don McLeod in a prison cell. Don hearing the same Sunday-morning sounds he was hearing—the tolling of church bells, the wind that had increased in the night to nearly gale force. But Don, whose house he had slept next to, his editor, his mentor, and friend, was locked up, maybe forever.

The walk home was cold. *The prison must be colder.* Rob increased his pace. Swung his arms. It didn't help.

The night before, Chiara had heard the front door. Heard the murmur of voices. She knew Peter liked occasional late nights with friends. She didn't, and had gone back to sleep.

Early next morning when Joanne collected the girls for church, Peter was in bed with a coffee and a three-day-old *Gazette,* so he missed her.

"Was that Joanne?" he asked when he came down for a refill.

"The girls were here last night—or hadn't you noticed?"

"Funny. Neil was looking for her at the dance. I thought maybe she couldn't find a babysitter."

"I told you the girls were coming here."

"Sorry, I didn't remember . . . What is it?" Peter asked.

Chiara sat down. "It's Joanne," she said. "She's in love."

Peter was about to ask *who with,* but he knew better. He would be accused of noticing nothing—which was true; a sensitive man, he could never discern quite what Joanne was thinking because, to him, she always seemed so bright, so capable. He admired her.

No, he said to Chiara, he hadn't seen Joanne at the dance. He'd noticed McAllister at the bar at the beginning of the evening, but not later. It was only Neil who had come back here for some brandy, he told his wife, Rob was off with his new girlfriend. So, no, Joanne could not have been with Rob.

At the end of this to-and-fro, Chiara worried even more.

When Joanne had called in earlier in the morning to collect the girls for church, she had no time to chat. No time to tell Chiara about the dance, too busy fussing over the children, getting their coats on, their hats, making sure they had sixpence for the collection plate, telling them to hurry or they'd be late for church.

"The rain's cold," Joanne had said, "the wind colder." She was buttoning Jean's yellow oilskin, and Annie kept repeating, "I hate this coat. We're not fishermen, you know."

She said it once too often. Joanne slapped her on the back of her leg. Chiara caught a flash of the murderous look Annie gave her mother and didn't like it one bit.

They had all rushed out with hurried good-byes and thanks, to catch one of the few buses that ran on a Sunday, leaving Chiara wondering if they would get to church on time.

Now this.

"Peter, Joanne is . . ." She stopped. *No, maybe not.* She had told Peter that Joanne was in love, but how could she explain that hopeless helpless passion, that was not love—it was obsession.

He was waiting for an explanation, and as Chiara looked at

him, she shivered. "I can't believe how lucky I am," she said and went over and pressed herself against him.

He put his arms around her and her bump and said, "Nor can I."

Church was an ordeal. And lunch. Everything seemed in slow motion. Joanne passed off her state, saying she thought she might be catching flu. Her sister looked at her, saw the feverish eyes, and agreed.

"Would you like the girls to stay here this afternoon?" Elizabeth asked. "Duncan can run you home and you can sleep."

"Aren't we going for ice cream wi' Uncle Neil?" Jean asked.

"All you think about is ice cream," Joanne snapped. She saw her daughter's lip quiver and the child looking at her, her eyes saying, *What did I do?* And she apologized. "Sorry, Jean, I'm not feeling too well."

"Well *I'd* like to stay here forever, Aunty Elizabeth," Annie declared. Elizabeth joked it was only because Annie loved her apple charlotte. But she heard the bitterness in her niece's voice.

"Thanks, Elizabeth, I'll take you up on the offer. But I'll walk back."

"In this rain? No you won't."

After her younger sister had left, Elizabeth worried about Joanne, and she too did not share her thoughts with her husband, choosing the influenza excuse.

My poor wee sister, she thought as she waved cheerio to Joanne, *you've not had much luck, have you?*

In the midafternoon Neil knocked on the front door. Joanne did not answer. The bedroom curtains were shut. *He won't know I'm home.* He knocked again, waited a moment, then left.

Her brother-in-law, the Reverend Duncan Macdonald, brought the girls home, but not until after evening service. They had had supper, were in borrowed pajamas and dressing gowns but their own Sunday church shoes. They were tired and went straight to bed without arguing.

"Hope you feel better tomorrow, Mum," Jean called out as she climbed into bed. Annie said nothing.

"Night-night, girls," was all Joanne was able to say. "Night-night."

She made tea, even though she knew it would keep her awake. She sat in her chair that felt as though it had altered its shape from Neil sitting in it, claiming it.

Feel better? No. I am terrified. I am ashamed, I am enchanted.

The ridiculous thought, that a wicked witch had enchanted her, made her smile. *I must tell McAllister . . . he would appreciate the idea of love as a wicked spell, an enchantment.* She hugged herself, remembering. *Him and his analyzing, he preferred Jung to Freud and Beethoven to Mozart. The way he would tell me his daft idea that Scotland would one day be independent again. The way he would tell me about the books he was reading. And tell me again about Spain, about camping under the pine trees, freezing cold in a forest high up in the mountains, eating olives and apricots, watching Franco's troops prepare for the assault that killed his friends. And the aftermath of the war in Paris, how the cafés and bookshops and the painters along the banks of the Seine had returned in that first magical springtime, when the war was finally over.*

"McAllister," she whispered, "talk to me."

CHAPTER 20

Monday morning and the rain had not relented; the mandatory news meeting was accompanied by the smell of damp clothing and sniffs and sneezing and girning from Hector.

"I'm never standing in the rain to watch a football match ever again," he complained. "I'll catch ma death a' cold."

"Shut up, Hector." Rob had been saying this since they were five years old in Miss Rose's class at Central School. They grinned at each other. No one else felt cheerful, especially Joanne, and the morning dragged on.

"I'm off to print up the sports shots," Hector said as he closed his bag and pulled on his black-and-white Clach supporter's scarf, "and Joanne, I'm sorry I can't do those pictures for you and Betsy, ma granny would kill me."

"What was that about?" Rob asked her.

"Mind your own business," she snapped.

Rob shrugged. He was aware Joanne was not happy, but she had Neil, so she didn't need him.

"I was looking for you on Saturday night," Neil said to Joanne when they were alone. "I really missed you."

"I was too tired," she lied.

"I came to your house on Sunday afternoon, but you were out."

"I was at my sister's," she lied.

"I'm sorry we couldn't be together," he said. "I wanted to spend time with you, but we'll have Wednesday night."

She didn't reply.

He looked at her. Head down, she was writing furiously on some notes handed in by the secretary of the Old High Church Women's Guild, an event so boring she was tempted to add to the Christmas party notice, *Saturday, two o'clock, church hall, all invited, including the Whores of Babylon*—but the phrase was overlong to be a typo.

Neil resolved to take her out for coffee whenever they had a break and tell her his news then. He gathered up some subbed copy and went to McAllister's office.

"Do you want to check these articles?" he asked.

"I'm sure they are fine." McAllister unscrewed his pen, got ink on his fingers, cursed, and signed the sheets of paper.

"I'm sorry to let you down," Neil began, "but I need to leave earlier than I expected. Next week."

McAllister said, "Sit down."

Neil sat and continued, "I know it puts you in a bit of a hole, but my ticket to Canada can't be changed, and I have to look in the archives in Glasgow library plus the *Glasgow Herald* if possible."

"I can arrange the *Herald* for you, the editor is a friend," McAllister offered. "Will you be gone before the trial?" He watched Neil, alert for a reaction.

"Rob assures me Mr. McLeod has a good chance of being found not guilty."

"Do you care?"

"I don't know the man."

"Did you know Mrs. Smart?"

"I heard she was really Mrs. McLeod."

McAllister said nothing.

"I met her once," Neil said. "Mrs. Rosemary Sokolov introduced us. I wanted to look through her family papers. She agreed. But she died before I had the chance."

"Was murdered," McAllister reminded him. "She didn't just die."

"Anyhow, I found the information I needed in Sutherland."

The reminder was painful, but McAllister couldn't dislike Neil. At first he thought him all front, but underneath the shiny smiley exterior—which was only shiny in contrast to most of the citizens of Britain still, after twelve years, recovering from the war—there was a vulnerability in Neil that made him more likable. "Where were you in the war?"

That Neil had been in the war, McAllister had no doubt; he sensed a man who had seen too much.

"The Forty-eighth Highlanders of Canada."

"Messina?"

"I was there."

"Joanne's husband, Bill Ross, was there with the Lovat Scouts."

It was on the tip of Neil's tongue to say, *So we've something else in common,* but common sense stopped him. "Like me, I imagine it is not someplace he wants to remember."

There was a pause as they both considered their own roll call of the war dead.

"We'll miss you," McAllister said and, to his own surprise, meant it. "You're a good journalist, and having you here has been a godsend."

"I'm a competent subeditor, not a journalist." Neil smiled. "I prefer archives; the dead rather than the living are easier for me to fathom."

"Good luck." McAllister could think of no more to say, but looking at Neil, seeing the way he was sitting, upright like a schoolboy before the headmaster, he sensed there was more in Neil's future than small-town newspapers.

When Neil left, McAllister tried to plow through the work

but couldn't concentrate; thoughts drifted in and out like the weather outside, and just as bleak.

Late in the afternoon, after dealing with the printers, who were complaining more and more about the lateness of the copy and constant changes to the layout, he returned to his thinking chair. He was vaguely aware of the sounds of the newspaper office winding down around him, the sounds of "cheerio" and "see you tomorrow" echoing up the stairwell. He rose once to switch on the lights—it was dark by five o'clock at this time of year, and twice he went to the filing cabinet and poured himself a dram from the bottle of Aberlour—not the Mckinlay on show for visitors.

He liked it like this—editor alone in his lair.

Footsteps coming up the stairs intrigued yet vexed him; lately, unexpected visitors had not brought welcome news.

"I'll have a drop o' the decent stuff, no' thon shite." Jimmy came in, nodding towards the visitors' whisky.

"You're welcome to it. When I heard the footsteps, I was scared it might be the police."

"I've never been mistaken for the polis." Jimmy's eyes popped open wide, mock-askance at the very idea. He accepted a decent-sized dram before asking, "How long until the trial?"

"It's scheduled to start on Tuesday, a week tomorrow." The warm single malt rolled around McAllister's tongue, reminding him of his theory that Scotland's literary and musical and philosophical brilliance, and the hardiness of her people, was because of whisky, the birthright of the nation.

McAllister hesitated before saying, "We might have to do something to help Don's cause."

"Aye, I was thinking the same. Any ideas?"

"I fancy Smart for it."

"Did he do it?"

"I can't see how—but maybe we could point a jury in his direction." McAllister was surprised by his hatred for the sergeant major.

"Unfortunately the good folk of the town love a hero, especially a legless one. But the way he treats people, he deserves a wee whiley in prison."

Jimmy looked bleak when he said this. Unlike McAllister, he knew what it was to be locked in a freezing prison cell with the hard men of Scotland. He finished off his drink. "No more for me," he said, even though it hadn't been offered. "I came by to say Ma wants to talk to you."

"When?"

"Now."

"Why?" The minute he asked, McAllister knew it was a stupid question; even if Jimmy did know, he wouldn't tell. "I'll lock up."

"Ma car's outside—and bring the bottle." Jimmy hadn't meant it as an order but McAllister did as he was told, knowing Jenny would appreciate the Aberlour single malt—one of the best of Speyside.

When Jimmy drove up Castle Street and turned left towards Crown Drive, McAllister was curious as to their destination. When the car stopped outside a house with few lights lit, Jimmy got out saying, "I won't be a minute."

McAllister did not ask for an explanation, and was not disappointed.

When Jimmy walked back to the car, with Neil Stewart in tow, he said nothing except, "Evening," and Neil nodded back. This was Jenny McPhee's show and they would know soon enough what was wanted of them.

Jenny was staying in her eldest son's house, as he and his wife were in Glasgow. Keith McPhee was at the university, and Jenny told anyone and everyone of her scholar son's achievements. *A tinker at university? Would you credit it?* she loved saying.

Now she had bleaker thoughts on her mind; although they had not seen much of each other over the years since they were young, the death of her friend Joyce was a deep wound to her soul.

"McAllister, Mr. Stewart," she nodded as Jimmy showed them in to the small airless sitting room. The fire was banked up, the windows tight shut, curtains drawn; Jenny had been feeling the cold of late, and this worried Jimmy.

She gestured to the chairs. They sat down. Jimmy did not offer a drink.

That's ominous, McAllister thought.

"Mr. Stewart, do you mind telling me your date of birth?" she started without preamble.

He stared at her, then smiled. It was a gentle smile, a smile from the eyes, and the heart. "I think you know that already, Mrs. McPhee."

"Aye." She let the word out in a long breathy drawl, "I think I do."

"When did you realize . . ."

"Who you are?" Again a long sigh, "It took a wee whiley. When I saw you, it was a shock, I couldn't take it in. Then you telling me our Chrissie was gone, and you being like ma Keith, into all them auld papers and suchlike . . . Did you come here to look for . . . ?"

"The solicitor told me where the money came from."

"So that was it."

Jimmy McPhee and McAllister were half following, and not quite making sense of all of it, but guessing. Neil was one of the stolen children. Which one was what McAllister wanted to know.

"Jimmy, we'll have a drink now." Jenny seemed to settle herself into the chair more comfortably, loosening her shawl, easing her conscience. "You've turned out a fine man," she said, "Chrissie would have been proud."

"She was. She was a good mother."

"She told you?"

"She left a letter. After her death, the solicitor gave it to me, but she kept her promise and didn't say who my birth mother is."

"It was a terrible time." Jenny nodded thanks to Jimmy as he handed her the glass. She sipped at it, and McAllister watched as her eyes took on that faraway look he had seen before, the face of the storyteller, only this time the fire was indoors, not out in the glens with the sound of running water and the sighing of the birches to add music to the telling.

"Chrissie, my mother, is she related to you?" Neil was breaking all the rules of Highland etiquette—wanting the ending, not the beginning, of his story.

"A right bonnie lass Chrissie, a lovely person." Not once did Jenny look at Neil as she spoke. McAllister thought she was scared. "She was fourteen when she went to work as a maid in the Mackenzie mansion in town. And a right good worker she was too."

Neil remembered his mother telling him of all the silver she had to polish and how she wore special gloves so as not to leave fingermarks. She said they polished the silver on rainy days when there was not much else to be done, and she loved sitting around the kitchen table blethering with the cook and the gardener, hearing their stories as she worked to make everything shine. *Shiny like her eyes when she told me about her life in Scotland.*

"Her father was in India, not many folk visited, so very few knew."

This made no sense to McAllister. *Whose father? Joyce's?*

Chrissie's? The father of Neil Stewart? But it wasn't his place to ask.

"Sergeant Major Smart's father, a drunken eejit if ever there was one, he was the gamekeeper on the estate, and there was no keeping the truth from him."

She looked into the fire. She could see the man, with his gun, shouting at the bairns, threatening the boys who were only trying to catch rabbits for the pot. He grudged them even that, although Joyce had made it clear that rabbits were there for anyone to take.

"Rabbits are a nuisance," Joyce told him. "Anyone who traps them is doing us a service."

"The man hated tinkers," Jenny continued, "and his son, Archie, even as a boy, was full o' hate, but maybe that was because his father treated him right badly. Whenever he was drunk he would beat the boy, and often as not when he was sober too, saying it would toughen him up. It did that a' right."

Spare the rod and spoil the child—McAllister had heard that excuse for brutality often enough.

"Then, one day, when Joyce saw a poor wee tinker boy who'd needed a doctor after Auld Smart beat him within an inch o' his life *for stealing rabbits*, as he put it, Joyce sacked him.

"I don't think she told her father why, just wrote that the Smart family had moved to Perthshire. We all hoped that was the last we'd see o' them—but no . . ." She did not need to continue.

"So, not long after the Smarts left, Joyce went to the town for a few days, to see to some estate business, and the men were working wi' the sheep in the hills, so I was on ma' own."

She remembered the baby at her breast. She remembered cradling his head in her hand as he looked up at her as he sucked. She remembered that that was the way it was in those days; no bottles and milk powder, whoever had milk, fed the baby that needed it. "Then the welfare came and stole you and wee Davey."

She shook her head. Even after all this time, the day haunted her.

"Stole?" Neil could not believe the word. "Stole?" he repeated.

"You heard ma Ma." Jimmy's voice was as sad and as deep and as harsh as a hoodie crow.

"Somebody reported us to the welfare saying we were not 'fit and proper parents'—and me being a widow at the time made it doubly hard." She was certain it was Auld Archie Smart's revenge, but she could never prove it.

The room was quiet, hushed—waiting for the next part of the story. But Jenny was spent.

"The welfare took tinkers' bairns." She started to rush her words. "Said they were neglected. Told us they were off to a better life."

"And they're still taking them. Even now in 1957." Jimmy was almost spitting as he spoke; he knew what this better life was: in institutions or sent to the colonies, a life far worse than a life on the road with their kinfolk. "We are despised by many people, us and the Gypsies, just because we want to be left alone wi' our own way of life. What happened in Germany to the Traveling people in the last war is forgotten by some—but not us."

"There is great ignorance and prejudice in Canada too," Neil spoke quietly, remembering John Williamson, one of his school friends. *Dirty tink was the least nasty of the names the children shouted at him.* One time, he was about seven and knew no better, he had said to his mother, *John Williamson is a dirty tink,* and she had spanked him, shouting at him to never ever say that again. Traveling people, she had told him, are good people. He never forgot because it was the only time she had given him a proper smacking.

"You were in the pram." Jimmy was waving his cigarette at Neil. "The welfare thought you were one o' us. How could ma Ma say you were the laird's grandchild? No one knew o' your birth."

McAllister stared. "Joyce Mackenzie's baby?"

"Haven't I just been telling you that?" Jenny snapped, her heart hurting from thinking back yet again to the trauma of her son vanishing forever.

"Joyce Mackenzie is my mother?"

McAllister could see that Neil was shaken. But not shocked. *Maybe it is all too huge a revelation too fast.*

"I'm . . ." Neil was searching for a word that could begin to express his feeling. "I'm completely overwhelmed." But, as ever, he could not shake the memory of that huge ship. *Where does that come from?*

"This whole story—children being stolen—shocks the life out of me," McAllister offered as a condolence.

"I searched the parish records in Inchnadamph," Neil told Jenny.

McAllister noticed he didn't say what, if anything, he had found. *That was when you went there with Joanne.* Although the thought hurt him, it did not hurt as much as he thought it would. In this moment, with Neil finally confronting his past, McAllister's principal emotion was sympathy.

Neil started to speak, filling up the empty spaces in his personal narrative.

"The children sent to Canada, I knew of two who ended up working in the mills in Halifax. I knew they were from Scotland. I heard rumors they were given away because the parents were too poor to keep them . . . but I never knew children were stolen."

As Neil was speaking, Jenny was staring into the fire, half

listening. She knew about stolen children, she'd made it her mission to find out; how they were scattered across the world, sent to the British colonies, as slave labor was how she thought of it; as children being given a chance in life was how the authorities saw it.

"Single mothers had their children taken too." McAllister remembered the stories from his days on the Glasgow newspaper.

"You were the lucky one." Jimmy pointed at Neil, taking out his anger on him, although he knew Neil Stewart was blameless. "You had a mother who sacrificed her whole life to take care o' you. My wee brother, what happened to him? Eh? Where is he?"

"No one knows." Jenny's voice made McAllister look at her, but her face was turned to the dying fire. Her body however showed her pain. *This is aging her,* he thought.

"Joyce did her best to find ma Davey, spent a fortune on solicitors. And later, Countess Sokolov, she tried an' all, but we never did find our wee boy."

"So how did I end up being with . . ." Neil hesitated. He did not know whether to call her Chrissie or Mother.

Jenny rushed the end of the explanation. She was tired. She needed them gone.

"I ran to the big house the minute thon people had left wi' the bairns and telephoned Joyce. She was out but Chrissie was in. I told her what had happened. She told Joyce. Joyce had plenty of connections. It was easy for her to find out where they'd taken you. You were both in the poorhouse in town waiting for a welfare officer to get you to Glasgow to an orphanage. Joyce told me to get to town as fast as I could but I had the other bairns to think of and it took me three days to get there wi' Davey's birth certificate.

"Joyce and Chrissie had managed to get you home. Joyce

had your birth certificate and said if they didn't agree to let you go home with her she would have the law onto them, the chief constable being friends with her father. The welfare superintendent agreed to let you go because of who Joyce was—her father, her family practically Highland royalty, they were allowed to take you home. And Chrissie, she became your nursemaid and she loved you straight off as though you were her own."

We had to sign for him like he was a piece of lost baggage, Chrissie had told Jenny.

"Joyce gave some money as a 'donation' to the poorhouse, so she told me later. Then she got one o' her lawyer friends on to it. They were going to say we were working on the estate, we had the wee house and my man was the gamekeeper even though he was gone, rest his soul. I got to town to get ma wee Davey back, but he was gone." *My wee boy,* she was thinking, *he was a right bonnie bairn.*

"We found out he'd been sent to the orphanage in Glasgow along with three other bairns. Joyce did everything she could, but it was too late, they said he had been adopted.

"'That'll be right,' I said, 'he was a right bonnie bairn.' And the woman at the orphanage agreed.

"'Aye,' she said when I got there to Glasgow on the train wi' Joyce, 'no one would take him for a tinker bairn.' And no one and no amount of money, no birth certificate, my marriage lines, none o' it mattered, he was gone, and we never could get us the records of what had happened to ma wee boy."

McAllister thought this strange; *surely it took months for a child to be adopted, not days.* But he lost the thought, caught up in the rest of the story of Joyce's baby.

"So my mother, Chrissie Stewart . . ."

"Took you to Canada. She loved you, you see. And you

didn't want to know about Joyce. You never took to your own mother. But you took to us tinkers."

Jenny laughed, but there was no mirth to it. Joyce had lost her senses after the birth, Jenny remembered. "No' her fault, poor soul, she had a bad case o' thon sadness some women get when they have a baby." *And there was the sadness of Don not wanting to know her.* But Jenny felt it was not her place to talk about that.

"So why Canada?" Neil needed to know every step of his journey to Neil Stewart, potential professor of history.

"A right brave soul was Chrissie, setting off to Canada all on her own." Jenny could see her, a wee slip of a thing, smiling into the sun when the picture was taken, the one Neil had shown her, when she had come home to say good-bye, and they never saw her again.

"So there was no Mr. Stewart?"

"No, lad, it was all made up to save Chrissie's reputation."

Didn't work, Neil almost said, *she suffered from being a single mother and never once complained.*

"It broke Joyce's heart to give you up. But she knew it was for the best."

Neil looked at her, silently asking why.

"Women's problems after you were born. No' her fault, but she wasn't up to caring for you." And the wee baby wasn't safe with her, Jenny remembered, but would never say.

A quietness fell. There was so much to take in. They would all, in their own time and way, need to take the story, nurture it, make it their own, forgive if that was needed, learn, let go.

"Joyce Mackenzie was a good woman," Jenny finished up.

"So I've heard." Neil's voice was harsh. He would never believe in the goodness of Joyce Mackenzie, the woman who had abandoned him. "But Chrissie Stewart, my real mother, was even more so."

McAllister was aware of the tension. And Jimmy. McAllister remembered, as a boy, going to a circus on Glasgow Green, watching a giant cobra sway from side to side, mesmerized by a snake charmer. He remembered the snake following the man's head and eyes, neither giving in.

What had passed between Jenny and Neil Stewart only they knew; knew completely—hearts, body, and soul.

Neil was the first to break contact. Jenny gave a brief nod.

McAllister felt the spell, the enchantment, break. He looked at Jimmy trying to gauge if he knew what had happened. But Jimmy was doing a Scottish imitation of the Sphinx.

"I made a sacred promise to Joyce—and to Chrissie, so I've said all I'm going to say." She looked up at Jimmy.

Jimmy caught the deep lines gathered around his mother's eyes and on her forehead and it made him think of thunder on the horizon, close and getting closer.

"Right gentlemen, I'll give you a lift home." He stood, giving them little choice.

Neil was reluctant to leave. He wanted, needed more. But Jimmy handed him his jacket and scarf and McAllister his hat.

They left with muttered good-byes, leaving Jenny sitting back in the chair, eyes half shut, her arms wrapped around her as though the blaze of the fire was sending out ice.

Jimmy drove to McAllister's house first. "Do you want to come in?" McAllister asked Neil.

"Another time. I need to think."

McAllister nodded. Five minutes later, as he was about to close his bedroom curtains, he saw Jimmy's car had not left. Jimmy and Neil were sitting in the front. He watched them for half a minute, and it looked like Jimmy was doing all the talking. He could not be certain, but the conversation looked earnest.

None of my business, he told himself. A sudden frisson of fear on the back of his neck made him pull the heavy dark velvet curtains, which had come with the house, tight shut. The Jimmy McPhee he knew was mostly benign, but he had seen the other side of the man, and it was terrifying.

The phone call next morning to Mr. Brodie, QC, was long. McAllister repeated the story. Brodie listened, asked few questions, mostly waiting until McAllister had finished.

"So, let me get this clear. Neil Stewart is definitely Joyce McLeod's son?"

It took McAllister a moment to think who Joyce McLeod was, until he remembered. She *was* Joyce McLeod when she gave birth.

"Yes." McAllister sounded more certain than he felt. He thought there had been something not quite right in Jenny McPhee's explanation. But he could not be sure.

"And we must suppose that Mr. Donal McLeod, the accused, is the father."

"It wasn't mentioned and I didn't ask."

"You should have."

McAllister knew he was being scolded. He did not have a chance to reply, as Mr. Brodie had embarked on an exploration of why Neil Stewart might have killed Joyce McLeod.

McAllister listened. Much as he resented Neil's relationship with Joanne, he couldn't see Neil murdering a woman. Nor *why* Neil would murder her.

"The most likely reason for the murder," the advocate summed up, "could be plain old-fashioned resentment turned to hatred."

"As an advocate, I'm sure you've seen more of that than me. But I find it hard to believe, and there is no proof whatsoever."

"I know. Though as a defense council I must examine every possibility. Does Mr. McLeod know his and his wife's past is revealed?" was Mr. Brodie's next question.

"I haven't had a chance to talk to him."

"Quick smart, McAllister"—he started to chuckle at his own pun—"And DI Dunne. Let him know everything. Then phone me with Mr. McLeod's reaction. I'll be up to the Highlands as soon as I can, but it won't be before Saturday morning. Right, if that's all . . ."

"I can't think of anything . . ." But McAllister couldn't keep up with the speed of Brodie, and the man was gone before he could say anything more.

He picked up the receiver and was about to dial the police station, when he saw the pile of work on his desk. *I'll phone later,* he thought. *Neil isn't going anywhere until next week, then Mr. Brodie, QC, can talk to him himself.*

McAllister knew the *Gazette* standards had fallen, and it hurt his pride. He knew turning out a newspaper next week without Neil was going to be almost impossible. *Deadline first,* he decided, *then I'll have a talk with Neil. Then Don. Then I'll phone DI Dunne.* Decision made, he worked quickly, clearing most of the backlog by noon.

Deadline was an hour away, and Joanne was finished her work. She was waiting for Neil, who had said *I'll be about forty minutes,* so she went downstairs to see if Betsy was still in the office.

"I'm glad you're here. I wanted to ask if you've changed your mind about our plan," Joanne said.

"No. I still want to leave the Highlands. I'm not brave like you, I'd hate it—everybody pointing me out as a shamed woman." Betsy looked at Joanne carefully as though assessing her for the first time. "Won't it be hard for the girls? You know— growing up without their father?"

"We'll manage," was all Joanne was willing to say. She would never tell anyone, even Chiara, that life without their father was what she wanted for her girls; life without violence, life without drunkenness, life without thinking they were second best because they were female and that the height of fulfillment was to marry well and produce babies, preferably male. "And of course the girls have their grandparents."

"My wee one won't."

Joanne thought Betsy would show her usual teary-eyed doe face, but no; Joanne had underestimated Betsy's determination to marry Bill, even if it meant moving to the other end of the world.

"If Bill and I can get divorced, it will all be straightforward after that." Joanne said this with such weariness, Betsy reached over and touched her arm. "Thanks, Betsy." She laid her hand on top of Betsy's. "You're the right wife for Bill. I never was."

"Thank you, Joanne. But don't say 'if.' This has to work." Betsy shut the office door and locked it and put on a scrap of a flowery confection of a hat that looked pretty but gave no warmth whatsoever. "I'm sick. I'm tired. I'm scared Bill will guess before I can give him the good news. And I'm dreading next week. With Neil leaving so soon, we'll be hard pressed to get the paper out."

"Sorry?"

Betsy looked at her and saw that Joanne had no idea what she was talking about. "I'm sorry, I thought you knew." Betsy was embarrassed. She and Joanne would never be friends, but Betsy was as soft as the baby-blue angora jumpers she loved so much. "McAllister told me to put in an advert for a subeditor. I've booked it into the Aberdeen papers, too. The ad says *immediate start*, and when I asked, he told me Neil is leaving sooner than he thought because . . ." She didn't finish, as Joanne was climbing the stairs to the reporters' room.

"Poor soul," Betsy said, "you've got it as bad as me."

Climbing the staircase that she had climbed so many times before, Joanne felt dread instead of her usual anticipation. The sound of a typewriter punctuated the claustrophobia of the stone steps and walls. The dim light from a window high above, which she always fancied had never been cleaned since the building was erected in the eighteenth century, cast shadows on the worn stairs.

"Hello."

He was intent on meeting the deadline; it took him a moment to register her presence in the high narrow room, where the reporters' table left little space between friends—or enemies.

"Oh, hello." He barely paused in his typing.

"You're leaving." When the words came out they sounded like a squawk to her inner ear.

He did not notice, or chose not to notice.

"Yep. Two days from now I'll be on the train. Then it's the transatlantic flight from Prestwick."

He looked down the length of the table. He registered her face. He saw how faded she looked, collapsing, punctured. But he could not, would not do anything; he was on deadline.

"It's been fun, but as you know I came here to finish my research and I'm finished."

I know, she thought, *I've always known. But fun?*

"Sorry, I have to get through all this." He gestured to the pile of copy paper next to the Underwood. "We can say good-bye properly when the edition has gone to press." And he grinned that grin that she had risked her reputation, her family, her job, her reason for.

"Did you ever love me?" The words were out before she knew it, and she hated herself for asking.

"Love you? Of course. You're an amazing woman. We've had a great time."

His words were unworthy of him, and her. His eyes flicked between the typewriter and the clock on the wall ticking off the minutes to deadline and the hours to his departure.

She knew she must leave. But she couldn't move. Watching him as he continued tapping the keys, torn between fleeing and begging, unaware of two fat drops of tears making tracks down her cheeks, falling and marking the high-buttoned white blouse she had bought to make her seem more professional.

"Hey. Joanne." He took a look at his watch, checking it was in time with the clock, then got up and walked to the end of the table. "Hey. Please don't cry."

"I'm not."

He laid his hand on the naked flesh of her wrist, touching her lightly with that oh-so-beloved hand with its short broad fingers and the soft down of red gold that matched his hair.

She flinched.

He stepped back. "We'll go back to your place when I've finished here. We can talk then. Please."

"No," was all she could manage to say before turning her back on him, grabbing her coat and her hat and her handbag, but forgetting her gloves, and fleeing down the stairs, running out into the early evening cold, and the stars, and the emptiness.

That night, alone in her bed, but with no tears, only a sick heaviness in her stomach and limbs and hands and feet, her throat tight, she felt a grittiness in her eyes. She remembered how once, at the seaside in Nairn, a blast of wind had sent the sand scurrying through the dunes, depositing what felt like a fair amount of the beach in her eyes.

She got up. She went to the kitchen. She rinsed her eyes. Now wide awake, she filled the kettle and made tea. Every movement, every action seemed to be in slow motion; her heart and throat hurt, she ached in her lower back, and she had a headache. Bringing the tea with her, she went back to bed. She stretched out to reach for the aspirins in the bedside table drawer when a stab of pain made her double up, clutching her stomach. It was as though a knife, a dagger, was twisting inside her, the pain horrible, excruciating, welcome. After the first wave, the pain began to recede, but her back hurt terribly. She pulled back the eiderdown and saw the stain. Deep dark red. She started to cry, but silently in case her daughters awoke.

She went to the bathroom. She dared not examine herself. She bundled up her nightie and put it into a bag, with no idea what to do other than wash. She dared not think about what had just happened. She knew it would always be there, part of her lies, part of her, part of her and Neil. She knew the overwhelming relief of this moment would haunt her. And she knew well enough to know she would have to deal with the loss one day, just not today.

After she had stripped the bed and was back under the eiderdown, the tea was cold. She drank it anyway. And as she was lying in her fresh bed, in the dark, sensing her daughters in the next room, hearing the familiar not-quite-sounds of her little home, knowing the lane and the streets and the town were asleep all around her, she once more knew that this was her life, a life she had made for herself, by herself. It gave her comfort.

She slept until Annie woke her saying, "Mum, get up. You'll be late for work."

CHAPTER 21

🖎

First thing Thursday morning, another edition of the *Gazette* safely out in the town and county, McAllister telephoned DI Dunne.

"Could you come to my office?" he asked. He had delayed calling the Inspector. *Don has gone to prison to protect his wife's past,* he thought, and discussing Joyce's secrets made him uneasy. But Mr. Brodie had been adamant that Don, although cleared, was still vulnerable. *Who knows what Smart might come up with to defend himself?*

"Tell DI Dunne all you know. Leave him to decide if it's relevant."

Next, he telephoned Angus McLean, asking him to set up a visit with Don.

"Probably not before tomorrow," Angus told him.

McAllister accepted that and put down the telephone. As he was waiting for the inspector, McAllister considered another question that had been bothering him: *If Neil was his and Joyce's son, had Don known this? And if so, was he protecting Neil? Was that what he was hiding?*

DI Dunne arrived. McAllister told him about Neil, but said nothing of his suspicions that Don might already know all this.

The inspector listened. He was interested. He said nothing until McAllister finished, then, thinking it over, said, "So, Neil Stewart is the son of Joyce Mackenzie and Don McLeod." He showed no surprise; it was a policeman's lot to uncover surprising information. "That's it? That's what makes you suspicious of the man?"

McAllister had been consumed by the "why" of it all—Don's

silence, Joyce's secrets, Neil's identity—and was still unsure of the truth. He spoke carefully as though dictating to a shorthand typist. "You'd think a man like Neil Stewart would search for his real father and mother. It's what he does, research. Then the timing—he admitted he met Joyce McLeod a day or so before she was killed. Maybe he knew she was his mother and confronted her. Motive . . . I don't know . . . anger, resentment—his childhood wasn't easy, maybe he lashed out at her . . ."

"It was a carefully planned, cold-blooded murder," DI Dunne reminded him.

"And Neil Stewart was in a Canadian regiment known for their efficiency in battle."

"All right, I'll talk to him, but I'd need some hard evidence to question him officially."

McAllister knew this, but with the trial looming, he was desperate. He was aware he was perhaps betraying Don McLeod's son. He knew Don would never forgive him if he found out. But none of that mattered to McAllister. All he wanted was to find the killer and for Don to be set free to return to the *Gazette* and return to as near as normal as possible.

Rob knew nothing of McAllister's visitor, only that when he knocked on the door the editor yelled, "Go away!"

For once Rob did as he was told. "McAllister is like a bear with a sore head," he said to Joanne. "Let's go for coffee and leave him to rage in his den."

"I can't, I lost my keys. I'm off to the ironmonger to get my spare set copied."

Rob knew Neil was leaving. He knew she was losing more than her keys, and he was scared for her. She looked terrible. "I'll give you a lift."

"It's only down the street. Besides, I'd like the walk." She was not able to face company, not even Rob. Not yet.

Only when she was gone did Rob remember he had to return Eilidh's spare keys. He took them out. Laid them on the table. A brass Yale key for the front door, a large iron key for the gate, another heavy key that looked ancient. *No wonder women need big handbags,* he thought.

Handbag. What had Mr. Brodie, QC, said? Find out what happened to Mrs. Smart's handbag. Keys. The advocate kept harping on about keys. Rob picked up the set. Two on one ring, the other big one tied to them with string. He stared. He laid them down, treating them as carefully as a hand grenade.

No, he told himself, *it can't be.* He snapped out of the daze, decision made. He zipped the keys into the inside pocket of his motorbike jacket and walked out, down Church Street, to the steps beneath the abbey wall.

He was holding his breath as he put the key into the back door of the church where Mrs. Smart had been found. It went in easily. He stopped. He was trembling. He turned the key. The lock clicked. He pushed on the handle. The door opened. He quickly pulled it shut. The noise echoed into the empty hallway. He locked the door again, put the keys back into his pocket. He ran up the stairs, almost tripping on the top step. He ran across the street. He put the other key into the courtyard gate. It worked. He shuddered. He zipped the keys back into his pocket; he had to stop himself from running up the street back to the *Gazette.*

"McAllister." He knocked on the office door. No reply.

"McAllister!" he shouted and walked in.

McAllister put down the phone. "Neil is not at his boarding-house. He left early this morning. He's gone." He was surprised there was no comment from Rob. "Neil left, he . . ." McAllister saw the normally wind-brown face was a pale shade of ill. "What's wrong?"

Rob arranged the keys on the desk, the one attached with string pointing towards the editor like a finger of fate.

McAllister looked at the keys, looked at Rob.

"I tried this one." He pointed. He couldn't bear to touch it. It had been in the hand of the murderer. "It opens the back door of the church."

"And the others?"

"This one is for Don's courtyard gate . . . The other . . ." Then he remembered. "I tried to lock Eilidh's door. It didn't work. I didn't think about it. But maybe it's the key to Don's house."

It took McAllister a moment to remember who Eilidh was. *Rob's girlfriend, Don's neighbor.* He fingered the keys. "Let's try them."

After nearly a week of horrible weather, the sky had run out of rain. And wind. McAllister and Rob strode down Church Street, men on a mission. If passersby had been asked to describe their faces they would have said they were grim.

McAllister opened the courtyard gate. They went in. He put the key in the lock of Don's house. It worked. He locked it again.

They walked across to the steps and down to the church porch. McAllister took the key tied with string. He put it into the substantial iron keyhole of the substantial wooden door. It turned with ease. He locked the door again, put the keys into his pocket, and asked, "Where did you get them?"

Rob could not answer; his words would not come, not here. He wanted to be gone from this spot, the steps where Joyce McLeod, as he now thought of her, had been murdered. By whom he was not certain, but possibly by his new girlfriend.

Eilidh is a nurse, she would know exactly where to put a knife to kill quickly, efficiently. She knew where the knife was kept. She knew of the Sunday-night get-togethers. And she had said she didn't like Mrs. Smart, but was that enough reason to kill her?

"Rob?"

"Let's get away from here."

McAllister nodded and started down the steps towards the river. They turned right. Halfway along the riverbank they had to step onto the street to avoid a crocodile of pupils from Central School. One of the girls gave a wee wave, but neither Rob nor McAllister noticed Jean Ross amongst the children smelling of chlorine after their lessons at the municipal swimming baths.

When they reached the harbor, Rob made for the Harborside Café, where the tea was strong enough to revive Lazarus. Here they had peace to talk amid the noise of customers and the clatter of dishes on tin trays. It took two mugs of tea, and three cigarettes for McAllister, before Rob finished.

"I can't figure out how Eilidh had them," he said. "There could be a simple explanation for her having the keys to Don's house, neighbors keep each other's keys, but the key to the church door?"

"It's not our job to figure it out," McAllister said. "We'll have to hand these keys in to DI Dunne, but, before we do, I'm going to call Brodie."

"QC."

Rob walked back down Church Street. *How many times have I been here today?* he wondered.

He felt the hands come up and over his eyes and knew immediately who it was.

"Guess who?" she asked.

"Oh, I don't know . . . some beautiful princess searching for her prince?"

She was pressing herself against his back, arms around his waist, giggling. He was glad she could not see his face, for he was struggling to hide the distaste, which now outweighed the lust he once felt.

"For that, you can treat me to coffee." She laughed and linked her arm through his.

It took her a good five minutes to guess there was anything wrong—she was so busy blethering away about her next trip to Aberdeen.

"There's this shop, a big one, same as they've got in Glasgow and London, and there's this dress, it's polka-dot—I've seen it in a magazine, and I'll get some new records when I'm there, so if you want anything, let me know."

He was watching her as she drew pictures in the air describing the dress, the magazine, her future shopping trips, everything. But he couldn't cover the glaze in his eyes as he stared hypnotized by the performance.

"You're quiet," she said.

"I forgot to return your spare keys." It sounded lame, but he could not think how to ask her.

"Don't worry, I have Monday off. Bring them to my house, and then . . ."

"Eilidh . . . the keys, are they yours?"

There was something of the wild animal in her; she could sense she was being lured into a trap.

"Mine? No. I found them up in the courtyard. They fitted the gate, so I kept them."

"Right." He would have believed her. The way she looked him straight in the eye. The way she smiled. He would have had no idea if it hadn't been for her coffee. She went to pick it up. It was a glass cup, with a glass saucer—very modern, Rob always thought. There was a slight rattle against the saucer. Not much. She immediately put the cup down.

"I'd better not have any more," she said, "I need my beauty sleep, I've been on night shift."

"You're a real beauty, sleep or not." He watched her preen like a wee bird fluffing up its feathers. "Eilidh, I gave Detective Inspector Dunne the keys. He'll want to ask you about them."

"Rob! What did you do that for?"

Rob saw the heads turn to look at them. "Let's talk at your house."

He put money on the table and took her arm, holding her lightly but taking no chances; *She wouldn't run away, would she?* He wasn't certain.

"I found the keys . . . honest." She was scared, but back in her own house, she was once more sure of herself.

"Eilidh, what happened that night?"

"I didn't like her, but I'd never kill her . . ." Eilidh started to cry. "You've got to believe me."

She can turn those tears on and off whenever she wants, he thought.

"Of course I believe you." Rob was speaking to her as though she were a terrified puppy.

"Dennis, my boyfriend, he was waiting in my house. He'll tell you I didn't kill her." How Dennis would know if she killed Mrs. Smart or not, she hadn't worked out.

"Eilidh, the problem is, will other people believe you? You know no one listens to anyone our age. And what will your parents think if they find out the police want to talk to you?"

This was a guess, but he was right—her wails at the mention of them were piercing.

"Eilidh, don't cry." He put an arm around her shoulder. "Tell me what happened and if you're in any trouble, we can talk to my father, he'll make sure the police believe you."

This set her off again, and Rob could feel the damp seeping through his jumper into his shirt.

"Eilidh, you'll have to explain why you have the key to the back door of the church. Don't you see? It could save Don's life."

"I can't, I can't. My parents will never let me live on my own again. They'll make me leave nursing. They'll . . . I can't."

"You can't let Don McLeod be tried for a crime he didn't commit."

"I'm sorry. I didn't mean for that to happen."

Rob kept patting her, waiting. He could feel her wanting to impress him, to prove nothing, none of it, was her fault.

"He asked me to spy on her, and I said why should I? And he said he'd tell my father I'd been having men to stay over."

Men? Rob thought. *Plural?*

"And he said if I told him about her and Mr. McLeod he'd give me money."

"A nurse's wages must be very low," Rob said.

"They're next to nothing," she said, grateful Rob understood. "Then he came round when Mr. McLeod was at work and said he wanted to borrow Mr. McLeod's knife. But I swear on the Bible I never knew he was going to kill her. He's a nice man, I never thought he could do anything like that."

He didn't want to spook her. But it took all his self-restraint not to ask who this nice man she was talking about was.

"Eilidh, I really think you should tell all this to my father. I don't want anyone putting all the blame on you."

"I don't want to talk to anyone except you! No one can make me! You're my boyfriend—couldn't you throw the key in the river like I was supposed to . . ."

"No. Don McLeod is my friend."

Somewhere in the haze of self-pity she heard the coldness in his voice. "If I tell your father everything, will he tell my parents?"

"Of course not."

"And will you still be my boyfriend?"

"Of course I will." He no longer cared how many lies he told her.

Eilidh ran upstairs and came down a few minutes later in a

tight black skirt and a periwinkle jumper that matched her eyes exactly.

Rob watched as she peered into the mirror and started to outline her eyes in black, adding layers of mascara, then a pale pink lipstick. He watched her brush her hair, fluffing it out with her fingers, and remembered the other puzzle Mr. Brodie, QC, had asked him to investigate.

"Mrs. Smart's handbag went missing. You didn't find it, did you?"

"That horrible old-lady's thing? Who cares what happened to it?"

"We'd better go." Rob stood, afraid he could no longer hide his repugnance.

She locked up. They walked to his father's office. He had his arm around her shoulder, reassuring her with murmuring nonsense, saying, "It's so good of you to help Don. It won't take long. Then you can go back and sleep. You must be exhausted. It's hard work being a nurse . . ."

They walked up the steps and into the office. He said to Mrs. Andersen, the secretary, "We'll be in the meeting room, could you tell my father? And my friend would like a cup of tea."

Forever after, he treated his father's secretary with admiration and respect—one look at him and she knew that although she had no idea what it was about, it was serious. She even brought tea biscuits with the tea.

"Dad, this is Eilidh," Rob said when his father came in.

"Pleased to meet you, Mr. McLean, I'm Rob's girlfriend."

Rob marveled how she could still turn on the charm, her voice soft and her eyes too, and that imperceptible lean towards the person she was talking to.

"Eilidh needs your help," he told his father. "She has

information about the night Mrs. Smart died, but she's really worried no one will believe her."

They went back over the story again.

"I'm so sorry Mr. McLeod is locked up, he's a really nice man." She smiled slightly at Angus McLean, her face full of concern.

"I'm sorry about Mrs. Smart too." She didn't mention her quarreling with Mrs. Smart, her being all too ready to spy on her. And she left out the payment for said spying.

"I'm really sorry I didn't hand in the keys. I didn't know it was important."

Rob watched her, marveling once again at her capacity for deception.

"I'm really sorry I gave him the knife. I swear to God I never knew what he was going to do with it."

Her eyes flicked onto Rob. "I've no idea how he knew about the knife."

She sensed his doubt. "I know he'd been in the courtyard spying on Mr. McLeod when he was at work . . ." Her voice was weakening, the energy to keep up the façade fading. "He must have seen it then, I don't know . . ."

"You're doing great, Eilidh." Rob put his hand back on her arm. "Isn't she?" He looked across at his father, who nodded and smiled. She smiled back.

Angus McLean felt it was time to intervene. "I know how painful it must be for you to recall that night. But I'm not quite clear exactly what happened." His voice conveyed the impression of some not-quite-on-the-ball-elderly uncle.

"He told me to wait inside the back gate to the churchyard. You know the place? The stone arch?"

Angus said, "You must be a brave young woman to wait

in a graveyard in the dead of night." Again he gave his elderly-favorite-uncle smile.

"No." She smiled. "I grew up in a manse next to a churchyard, I'm not afraid of ghosts. Anyway, I was waiting for Mrs. Smart to come out, she always left about the same time, quarter past nine. She walked past, but she didn't see me. A minute later he called me. I went into the churchyard, leaned over the wall, and he passed me up the knife, telling me to run and put it back in the hidey place."

How in Heaven's name did she not see the body? Angus and Rob and Mrs. Andersen were thinking.

"Didn't you *see* Mrs. Smart lying there?" Rob could hardly control his disgust. His father frowned, and Rob quickly recovered the smooth soothing voice. "But of course it must have been really dark."

"It was. It was dark, and misty and cold." She looked at him, eyes wide with gratitude. "He left me on my own, in the cemetery, with the knife, and next I knew he was gone. Then this man came down the steps. He was carrying a bicycle. I was terrified he'd see me so I hid behind a gravestone . . . it was horrible." *Nearly scared the life out of me,* she remembered.

Something must have penetrated her carapace of deceit. She looked at Rob and his father, and thought they were watching her as though she were an exhibit in the fairground freak show. "I'm so, so sorry." Tears trembled in the lower lids of her blue, blue eyes. "I never knew he'd use the knife. I thought he was only going to scare her."

Now the tears began to roll down the cheeks, making tracks in the liberal application of makeup she had so carefully applied to impress Angus McLean.

Angus said, "You're a very brave young woman."

Rob was desperately racking his brains to find a way to get her to say the name. *He? Who is "he"? She must say the name.* Then he had an idea. "Neil Stewart is going back to Canada earlier than we thought; we'll miss him."

Three pairs of eyes turned and stared at him.

"I liked him, I can't believe he was involved in a murder . . ." Rob continued.

"Was he?" Eilidh's face, so childlike, looked at Rob. There was a slight hesitation. She bit her lip, then said, "I only met him at the dancing. Mrs. Ross who works with you is his girlfriend."

Rob let that go. But he remembered Eilidh saying she had shown Neil the empty house in her courtyard. "Isn't that who we're talking about? Isn't Neil the person you gave the knife to?" Rob asked.

"Don't be silly, it was the sergeant who killed her." She stared at Rob as she said this, daring him to disagree.

"Sergeant Major Smart killed his wife?" It was Angus's opportunity to ask the question, clearly. And his secretary's opportunity to write down the answer, clearly.

"Of course." She gave a huge exaggerated sigh, shaking her head at how stupid they were. "He hated her. He's been trying to work out how to do it for at least a year now."

She went still. Her eyes flitted from one face to the other. She was trying to read their faces, attempting to gauge if they believed her story. Rob and Angus and Mrs. Andersen, who was sitting silently in a corner taking notes in shorthand, simultaneously looked down, to hide their horror.

"Of course I'm only guessing. I don't really know." There was no going back on the remark. She'd been spying, taking money, for at least a year. And everything she had told Rob and Angus McLean and the secretary was legal enough for any court of law.

The phone in the reception started to ring. The sound broke the flow. The secretary excused herself. She came back, looked at Rob. "Mr. McAllister would like to talk to you."

"And I must excuse myself for a moment," Angus rose. He wanted out of the room to breathe clean air.

"Rob, don't leave me." Eilidh was on her feet looking like she wanted to run away.

"I won't be a moment. Mrs. Andersen will look after you."

Mrs. Andersen was as intimidating as the ward sister, so Eilidh sat.

"I'm going to phone DI Dunne," Angus said when he and Rob were alone. "Then I'll phone Mr. Brodie . . ."

"QC," they chorused, and smiled. "And thank you, Rob, well done."

"Thanks, but I don't think I can face her again." He did not need to say who "she" was.

They were not a demonstrative pair, so when his father reached over and hugged him, Rob was surprised. And grateful.

"Only a few minutes more?" Angus asked his son.

Rob looked up at the ceiling, noticing how cobweb free the office was—unlike the *Gazette*. He sighed. Then, taking a deep breath, he walked back into the room.

From behind the closed door Angus could hear his son saying, "No, not much longer. Poor thing. You must be so tired."

Angus went into his office to make the phone calls, feeling even more proud of his only child.

Fifteen minutes later, DI Dunne and WPC Ann McPherson were shown in to the meeting room.

Eilidh looked at Rob. He could see her putting on her brave face, the one she must have learned as a little girl waiting for the wrath of her father to descend on her, beating her for some insignificant childish misdemeanor that he would turn into a sin.

"Hello. It's Eilidh, isn't it? I'm Constable Ann McPherson. I hear you want to help us."

Ann was an old friend; her tall strong healthy face reminded Rob that she was once the school sport's champion. And he admired the way she sat by Eilidh, putting herself at Eilidh's level, smiling as though they were old school chums who hadn't seen each other in ages.

"I want to help." The eagerness in the voice, the way Eilidh looked earnestly at Ann, mesmerized Rob. *What a little liar.* It shook his faith in his ability to read people. *She had me completely fooled.*

"It was nothing to do with me," Eilidh was confiding in Ann as though they were best friends, "and I'll help you all I can." The confidence was back; but she could tell lies upon lies and wriggle and squirm and flash her beautiful eyes and toss her beautiful hair and Ann McPherson would see through it all.

Poor Eilidh, Rob couldn't help thinking, *she's no idea how much trouble she's in.* But he couldn't forgive her. "I'm sorry, I have to go," he said.

"You'll still be my boyfriend?" Her eyes were huge and, for the first time, Rob thought, slightly mad.

"I have a deadline," he lied.

"I'll call you later." She smiled up at him, waving that little finger wave that he used to find charming.

It took him a huge effort not to run from the room.

When Rob walked into the office, Joanne was at the reporters' table. McAllister joined them and asked, "Rob, you okay?"

"For the first time in my life I understand why people drink whisky."

The bravado in his voice did not fool them. From the color of his face, pale grey; from his fingers silently tapping out the story on the table as he told them what had happened; from the way his eyes would occasionally look towards Mrs. Smart's empty seat at the head of the table as though he was filling her in on the story, they knew he was shocked to his core.

When he finished, McAllister was silent, but they could see his anger building as clearly as storm clouds gathering.

Joanne let out a huge sigh. "Unbelievable." She shook her head. "She seemed such a nice girl." Another sigh. "What will happen now?"

"I don't know." Rob meant it. The fragility in Eilidh had made it hard for him to credit she could be so involved in a murder. But the something else that he couldn't put a name to—the tough, brazen way she would flirt, the promiscuous disregard for people, having so little concern over the fate of Don McLeod, and no remorse for her complicity in the death of Joyce McLeod nee Mackenzie—shocked him to the point of disbelief. *This was the girl I've slept with*, he kept thinking.

"It's her word against Sergeant Major Smart, so, who will a jury believe?" Rob stretched and sighed. He was drained, and it was only three o'clock in the afternoon. "Don is the betting man, but I'd say the odds were even."

"Fifty-fifty—aye, I'd say that's about right." McAllister stood and without another word, he left.

When they were alone, Joanne asked, "Did you know that Neil has left?"

"What do you mean?"

"He's gone. Took the early train."

"But he didn't say good-bye . . ." Rob saw she was beyond tears. She looked so sad, so . . . older was what he saw. "I'm sorry, Joanne."

"Me too." Then she realized—"Does this mean Don will be back?"

"Hope so." Rob knew that Joanne did not want to talk about Neil. But he needed to know. "Neil was here for a reason," he started.

"To do research for his book."

"I had a feeling there was something more . . ."

"To seduce a Highland lassie? To break her heart? To murder old ladies?" Joanne slapped her hand over her mouth. "I'm sorry, I don't know why I said that."

"I know. You're hurt." He wished he could help her but he too was feeling let down by Neil Stewart's sudden disappearance. "Anyway, it was Sergeant Major Smart that killed Mrs. . . ."

"Mrs. Donal McLeod." Joanne supplied the name. "It's pretty unbelievable, isn't it?"

"Did you know Neil was adopted?"

"He told me. He told me about his childhood, and the woman he called his mother. He loved her."

"So maybe he was here to find his real mother."

"Rob, I'm past caring what Neil was here for. He's gone and . . ."

The ringing of the phone interrupted her, but she ignored it.

Rob was watching her as she struggled to hide her loss, her guilt, her anger at her self-deception.

The phone stopped for five seconds, then started again.

Rob answered. "*Gazette*." He listened. "Not again!" he hung up. "It's McAllister. He's gone to confront Sergeant Major Smart."

"The police should be there by now to arrest the sergeant . . ." Joanne was speaking to herself and to the sound of Rob running down the stairs.

Left alone, the shame of what she had done to McAllister— and of what she had lost—surfaced again; deep down, burning dark, red-hot waves of shame washed through her, momentarily paralyzing her.

McAllister. How do I face him? Just looking into his eyes was impossible.

I'll have to resign. The thought of being without her sole source of pride—and income—dismayed her.

I love my job. She was proud to say she was a reporter on the *Gazette.* It made her somebody.

She saw it was time to leave for home, to see to her children, to prepare supper, to take in the washing that had been on the line since yesterday morning because last night she couldn't summon up the energy to take it in and make a start on the ironing. There was little food in the house either; the effort to shop, to cook, to eat, to smile was beyond her.

She waited another five minutes in case McAllister and Rob returned, then gave up. *I'll find out in the morning,* she thought as she put on her coat.

As she cycled through the early dark, all she could think, again and again, was, *McAllister, I betrayed you. How can we ever be friends again?*

With McAllister, she could be herself. She never felt nervous—*not like I did with Neil.*

It came to her as she cycled under the heavy elms at the end of her lane.

Now I understand what Bill felt all these years; I made him feel the way that Neil made me feel—never quite good enough.

But McAllister? He listens, he likes me as I am.

The magnitude of her loss was beginning to sink in.

CHAPTER 22

Rob had heard the editor haring down the stairs but thought nothing of it. He was not noted for the second sight, he left that to Jenny McPhee, but suddenly he knew where McAllister was going.

He jumped on his bike and drove down to the river. No sign of McAllister. *He must have taken the footpath.* He drove up onto the path, scaring a woman pushing a pram.

He went slowly, not sure which mansion was which from the riverside view. He saw an open garden gate. He jumped off the bike and ran in.

"Hello." Beech was standing in the garden looking at the next-door house, the one belonging to the sergeant major.

"Have you seen McAllister?"

"I saw him climbing over the wall to next door . . . I'm concerned there may be trouble."

Rob did not tell him that Eilidh had accused the sergeant major of killing Joyce. Nor did he say that McAllister knew this—the explanation would take too long. Plus, he was busy examining the wall.

The moss had been ripped away from the stone. There were plenty of toeholds and a soft landing in a flower bed. He took a short run, hauled himself up and over, landed in soft earth, then snuck up on the open French doors and the loud voices, until he was sheltered in the doorway and hidden by curtains billowing out in the river breeze. He was surprised to see the former soldier standing straight and tall and confident of his artificial legs, the wheelchair nowhere to be seen.

"I'm calling the police," Sergeant Major Smart shouted.

McAllister was less than four feet in front of him, facing him, staring at him, defiant but absolutely still. "Go ahead," he said. "Call them."

Smart made a slight movement. Rob caught a glint on metal in the mirror above the fireplace. A gun was aimed at McAllister—a big, heavy, old, unreliable sort of gun, to Rob's untrained eye.

"You say I killed her." Smart was angry in the cold calm way of a man with a gun who knows how to use it. "Where's your proof, eh? You've none."

"Eilidh is making a statement to the police as we speak."

"That trollop! She's lying. Who'd take her word against mine?"

"I would."

"And if I shot you, who'd convict me, a wounded war hero, who mistook you for a burglar—"

When asked to recount what happened next, Rob couldn't, not clearly. All he remembered was the bang. It was so loud his ears were ringing. He felt the windowpane next to him shatter. There was a flurry of movement, too fast for him to see clearly. The rain of sharp needles on his skull, the noise in his ears, the fear he might be deaf, and the terror of losing control of his bowels made him stagger into the room. He leaned against the wall but slid down to the sitting room floor, where he stayed, unable to move, unable to comprehend if he was injured or not. He saw McAllister slumped in an armchair, unhurt, but looking like Banquo's Ghost.

It seemed to Rob that the banshee shriek that followed or preceded or came at the same time as the shot—for he could not be sure—had come from some unearthly creature.

Whether the scream came from Smart or McAllister—McAllister later denied it was him but he wasn't certain, or from Smart as he fell, or from Bahadur as he launched himself on the sergeant's back, one arm around his throat, the other with a knife to his ribs—Rob couldn't say.

Later, Rob decided the shriek had definitely come from Bahadur. "A Nepali war cry," he described it to Joanne. "Absolutely bloodcurdling."

He looked at the tableau of Sergeant Major Smart lying on his stomach, not daring to move, Bahadur sitting on the soldier's back, one arm around the man's neck, and in the other hand a long thin knife, the business end resting lightly on Smart's jugular vein. It must have penetrated the skin, but only slightly; a thin trickle of blood, no more than a shaving cut, had erupted, but the smell of blood, the scent of bloodlust, the discharge from the gun filled the room. When he realized Sergeant Major Smart was going nowhere, Rob was so relieved, he laughed loudly. Then stopped abruptly.

McAllister understood and gave his junior reporter a grin that made Rob think of a skeleton. *Which he may well have been if not for the Gurkha.*

"What's going on?" Beech rushed in and stood beside Rob, legs akimbo, pointing an old double-barrel shotgun, kept for deer hunting, into the room.

"Good grief, man! Put that away!" McAllister yelled. "You're terrifying the life out of me."

Pointing at Bahadur, who had managed to remove Sergeant Major Smart's legs without letting go of his stranglehold, nor removing the knife from Smart's neck, McAllister said, "Our savior."

"Well-done, Mr. Bahadur!" Beech called out. He cocked the shotgun and saluted the former Gurkha commando, who for once did not return a salute from an officer.

Rosemary Sokolov appeared, looked around, said nothing—she'd seen worse in Shanghai—went towards Rob, examined his forehead, saw the bleeding had slowed down, and told him, "The police and an ambulance are on their way."

"A doctor will do me," Rob said. "I'm not up to hospital and the sight of a nurse."

What Rob most remembered, when he and McAllister talked it over later, was that once the initial terror was over, he had been really annoyed: picking glass out of his hair; dabbing with the end of a curtain at the blood running down his forehead; seeing the pockmarks in his pride and joy, his Marlon Brando bike jacket.

Then, he remembered, he became more than annoyed—he was furious. "I'm going to be a television star one day, so if I have scars on my face, I'll kill you," Rob had yelled at the now trussed-up soldier still lying on the floor, Bahadur on one side, Beech on the other, Smart's artificial legs well out of his reach. How that had happened Rob had no idea. But he guessed it was Bahadur's doing.

McAllister, his hand shaking as he desperately tried to light a cigarette, missing the end of it at least three times before succeeding, had said, the accent pure Glasgow, "Television star! That'll be right."

Afterwards they laughed at how shock made them think of the most ridiculous things: Rob—his future television career; McAllister—although he did not say, had had a flash of Joanne laughing, as she danced with him last year, in the Caledonian Ballroom.

By the time the police arrived with a clamor of unnecessary bells that set all the neighboring dogs barking, it was dark. When they switched the lights on, the scene in the sitting room looked even worse.

When the police left with Sergeant Major Smart, Rosemary Sokolov insisted they all come next door for tea, or a brandy. McAllister politely refused. He walked to the end of the garden, needing to be alone. Whether it was the night air, or delayed shock, or lack of a decent meal for weeks, maybe a month, he didn't know, but he had to lean against the garden wall to light a cigarette.

Mr. Bahadur was watching him. McAllister saw him watching him. He nodded. The small man smiled, white teeth flashing in the dark skin and the dark night.

"Now I can go home," he said, "but only after we make a memorial ceremony for Miss Joyce."

"Amen," said McAllister.

Saturday morning, McAllister was in his office with DI Dunne. There was a knock on the door.

"Go away," he shouted. So Rob walked in.

"What's happening with Eilidh?"

He asked McAllister the question, but DI Dunne answered, "She's home, and so far only charged with obstructing the police in their inquiries. She's denying she did anything, insisting she found the keys in her courtyard."

"She told me, my dad, and Mrs. Andersen that Smart gave her the knife and she put it back in the courtyard wall." Rob was furious that she might escape prosecution. "Isn't that enough? And ask her about the Dansette, the clothes—she could start a shop with all the stuff in her wardrobe bought with the money she's been taking money off the sergeant major for months—if not longer."

"Maybe." DI Dunne looked dubious. "When her father came to take her home, she became hysterical. WPC McPherson thinks she might end up in Craig Dunain."

The mention of the lunatic asylum, or loony bin as it was

usually known, made Rob shiver. Then he remembered Eilidh's capacity for deception and wondered if it was all an act to prevent her from being charged with accessory to murder.

"I'm still puzzled as to how Eilidh had the keys," McAllister said.

"She's sticking to her story that she found them," DI Dunne said. "And she believes her boyfriend will give her an alibi. But I asked my colleagues in Glasgow to interview the medical student." DI Dunne pulled out notes of the phone call.

"The student, Dennis Cameron, remembers that night well because the next morning, he and Nurse Eilidh broke up." DI Dunne was skimming through the statement. "He's good at describing that night, good on the detail."

"He's training to be a doctor," McAllister said. "He'll make a good witness."

"On the Sunday night around the time of the murder, he was in the house, waiting for Eilidh. They had come home around six; he heard Mrs. Smart, as he calls her, arrive not much after. Sometime before nine, Eilidh went out, saying she'd only be five minutes, she needed to buy milk for breakfast."

When the Glasgow police interviewed Dennis Cameron, he told them, "It wasn't five minutes, more like half an hour. Next, I heard Mrs. Smart leave . . ."

"Did you know her, sir?" a detective asked.

"I'd bumped into her once as she was coming in, and another time I went next door to ask for shillings for the gas meter. She was nice."

"So you heard Mrs. Smart leave?"

"I heard her call out good night, their front door shut, the gate opened—it needs oil—and about ten minutes later, I heard the gate again. It was Eilidh."

"Mr. McLeod did not go out at all?"

"No, I would have heard." Dennis was embarrassed to say so, but sound carried in the wee workman's terrace, and he was grateful there was an empty house between Mr. McLeod and Eilidh. "It must be the courtyard walls—sound carries."

"What happened next?"

"I looked out the window. Eilidh was in the courtyard corner. She had a torch. When she came in I asked her what she was doing, and she said she was chasing a rat. Sounded unlikely to me—most girls run a mile if they see a rat." He did not add that Eilidh was excited and that night she had been *all over me like a rash*. He had put it down to his charm.

The fight the next morning had started when he asked where the milk was.

"What milk?"

"The milk you went out to buy last night."

"When can I come to Glasgow to live with you?" she had asked.

"The milk?" he had replied.

He was used to her nagging about Glasgow, she had asked a dozen times. He always said, *I have to finish my studies, then we can be together.* But this time she had turned on him.

"You're all the same," she had screamed, "you get what you want, then you leave."

He had never mentioned leaving. He thought he loved her. He had wanted to wait until he was a qualified doctor, then they would marry.

When he had finished giving his statement to the Glasgow police, he said, "Would you tell Mr. McLeod I'm really sorry about his wife."

"So what does the sergeant major have to say to all this?" McAllister asked.

"Not a word. No, sorry, he is saying, 'Name, rank, number, that's all you're getting out of me,' and so far, he's stuck to his word." DI Dunne was doubtful they would get more from the man.

"Look on the bright side," he added when he saw McAllister's face. "He won't get off on the charge of attempted murder. You and Rob will be star witnesses."

DI Dunne stood and began to button his coat. "Thank you, gentlemen, I'll be in touch."

"When will Don McLeod be released?" Rob asked.

"Immediately, I think. But your father will know the details." With that the policeman left.

McAllister lit a cigarette. He stood, then walked up and down the room twice, to vent his anger.

Rob waited. There was no explanation. He made a guess.

"You're furious because the sergeant major might get away with murder."

"I'm more than furious, if he were here I'd beat the hell out of him—or worse."

Rob thought about it. How could they prove it? *I haven't a clue*, he decided.

"If he gets away with it, you could always ask Jimmy McPhee to make sure his life is unbearable after he gets sent away for trying to shoot you."

"Who tried to shoot whom?" Joanne had only heard the last part of the sentence, but she saw Rob's cuts. "And what happened to your face?"

"Wasn't me Smart was aiming at, it was him." Rob pointed to McAllister, was now leaning back in his chair, smoking and smiling.

"No! What happened? When? Are you all right?" She was staring at him, horrified at the thought of McAllister being killed. "And why are you grinning at me like a demented ape?"

McAllister stubbed out his cigarette. He walked the five paces across the room. He put his arms around her, hugging her. She was embarrassed. She was laughing. She was almost in tears. "What?" was all she could say.

"Find a babysitter. I'm taking you out to dinner."

"Can I come too?" Rob was grinning so hard at the sight of McAllister with his arms around Joanne, the cut on the edge of his mouth cracked. "Ouch!"

"No," they both said.

"In that case, I'll babysit."

That evening, they were seated in the restaurant, dinner over, and in McAllister's case three glasses of wine to Joanne's one, before he had the courage to tell her.

"As Smart was pointing the gun at me, all I could think of was, I hadn't told you I love you," McAllister began.

With a table between them, he was speaking quietly, in a flat voice, choosing his words carefully—the revelation so momentous he had to suppress his emotions in case he said what he really wanted to say, which was, *Will you marry me?*

Too soon, he kept reminding himself, *much too soon.*

"McAllister, I don't know what to say . . ." She was finding it hard to look at him—her shame still consuming her.

"Don't say anything. And don't worry, you won't have to put up with me for much longer, I'm resigning from the *Gazette*, going back to Glasgow."

"But why?" She was horrified at the thought of McAllister leaving—and horrified she might lose her job if another editor was appointed.

"It will be impossible to work together, so it's best I leave." He saw her face. Don's words came back to him, *Don't do like I did.*

McAllister began, "I thought I was going to die. Smart had the gun pointed at me. I could see it in his face. He was going to kill me. There was a shot. Glass flew everywhere. Rob was at the window, blood pouring out of his head—at least that's what it looked like. I thought the bullet had hit him, but he was still standing—well, sitting. Then I saw Smart on the floor, Gurkha Bahadur on his back, one arm round Smart's neck, a knife at his neck, and I was in shock, I thought I was going to die, and I . . ." He started to laugh. "I couldn't steady my hand to light my bloody cigarette."

"So only because you thought you were going to die could you say you love me?" Her eyes were the bright green they became when she was passionate about something.

"Aye." When he smiled at her, she remembered what an intriguing man he was.

"What about . . ." She could not bear to say his name. "About what happened between me and . . ."

"Neil Stewart." It hurt McAllister as much as it hurt her to say his name, but he knew there was no running away from the memory. "I can't talk here—let's walk."

He signaled the waiter, paid the bill. They fetched their coats and once out in the street the river drew them, but McAllister instinctively walked across the bridge to the opposite bank, turning right towards the firth; he was not ready for even a distant sighting of the Smart mansion—or the abbey wall.

On the northern side, on the last half mile of the river before it reached the firth, there was a narrow gravel beach. The salmon fishermen would launch their cobles from here, rowing out with the nets, searching across the swift flow for the huge fish that spawned further upstream.

It was low tide. They walked down the slipway and onto the sandy stones. The smell of sea and river and loch and fish and drains was strong but not unpleasant. The light of stars dancing on water, a waning moon, and the dim streetlamps made it a place where, not seeing each other clearly, only sensing the space between them and perhaps a light hand on the arm, a brush against each other, they could talk. They both knew this was to be *the* conversation, the one they had been avoiding since the day they met, the one that would decide their fate. And they were afraid.

"It would be impossible to work in the same office, even the same town as you, when you know my feelings," McAllister said.

"Well, I'm not resigning from my job over a man."

"Good for you." He laughed. Then he sighed. "That's why I have to go back to Glasgow."

"Because you can't face me?"

"Because I can't be around you, loving you, without hope . . ." He picked up a stone and threw it as far as he could out across the river. It disappeared into the fast flow of water without a sound.

"I know it's impossible for you to forgive me," she started, "but I'll miss you so much . . ."

In the pause that followed they both knew it was time.

"Joanne, I love you. What happened with Neil in the last two months—is it over?"

"It's over." She sounded bitter and he hated that. "I can't believe I made such a fool of myself. Falling for him like I did, it was like I was bewitched. I knew he was going to leave. He made no promises, he didn't encourage my fantasies . . . I can't explain even to myself how I lost my senses."

"I have no right to judge you." He turned to her, took her elbow. He turned her around slightly so he could see her face, or the shadows on her face, in the streetlight above them. "But I know this: Don, Joyce, all that has happened, we have to learn from them, and as Don said, not make the same mistake."

"I can't see . . ."

"Joanne Ross." He spoke as though he was pronouncing a death sentence. "May I court you?"

"McAllister!" She started to laugh. She threw her arms around his shoulders. She leaned back and, looking into his eyes said, "That is the most preposterous thing anyone has ever said. *Court me*. And you the writer. Can't you think of a better way to put it?"

"I write. I don't know how to romance in words. But," he pointed out, "I could send you letters telling you how you paralyze me, how I can't think when I'm around you, how I can barely stop myself from kissing you."

She reached up. She touched his hair. She put a hand behind his head. She pulled him towards her. She kissed him. At first lightly. Then longer. It felt right.

"I think you should stay," she murmured.

"Persuade me."

She kissed him again.

Sunday afternoon, McAllister knocked on Joanne's front door.

"Hello." She knew she was blushing and she was aware of the girls watching them.

"I came to ask if you would all like to come to dinner at my house?"

"Do you have a television?" Jean asked.

"I do." He did not tell that he had had it delivered and installed this morning, a Sunday, breaking the Sabbath and all the rules by promising the shop owner he'd write a feature on his business.

McAllister provided soup, Joanne an apple pie. They stayed in the kitchen, the children in the sitting room, happy in front of the TV set.

"So, McAllister, what are your plans? Are you staying in the Highlands?"

"I'm courting you, remember? We'll talk, spend time together, see how it goes. Is that acceptable?"

"More than acceptable. I've never had anyone I can really talk to—except Chiara. But never a man. I loved it when we used to talk late into the night, when you shared your books; even jazz is beginning to sound more than just a cacophony of cats."

She was about to ask him if he could really forgive her for the affair with Neil. But she stopped herself. *If it really mattered to him, I wouldn't be here in his house, my children with me.*

And ever after, when Neil Stewart's name was mentioned, McAllister would feel a twinge of jealousy, but mostly gratitude to the stranger who had forced him to acknowledge that he, McAllister, who thought he knew most things, was illiterate when it came to the language of the heart.

CHAPTER 23

֎

Don McLeod had been released on Saturday at mid-morning.

As he walked out into an ordinary street on an ordinary November day, he felt the thaw beginning to melt his heart. He didn't want that; it meant facing the loss of Joyce.

"Can I give you a lift?" Beech's voice was loud and clear and most of the street could have heard him if they took an interest in the prison—which they tried very hard not to do. "I thought perhaps you would like to join us for luncheon."

"Thank you," Don said, his voice faint, unused to speaking across a space more than eight feet.

Beech drove sedately down the steep hill to the big house on the river. When they got out of the car, Don glanced at the house next door and shivered.

"Cold?" Beech asked—for it was cold, and clear and crisp with air as sharp as a rapier—or a fish knife.

Don could not reply.

They went into the kitchen, where Countess Sokolov was waiting.

"A cup of real tea would be fine," Don replied when asked if he wanted to eat.

They were sitting around the table, Don on his second cup, when he said, "I'd like your help arranging a memorial service for Joyce."

"Consider it done," Beech told him.

"I would be honored to help," Rosemary said. "And I'd like to offer you a room here for as long as you want."

"Thank you. I can't face going home—not yet." Don couldn't look at them. Their kindness was genuine, and Rosemary had been Joyce's dearest friend, and he knew they wouldn't fuss. *Besides*, he thought, *I've nowhere else to go.*

A severely depleted Monday morning news meeting was about to start. Around the table were McAllister, Rob, Joanne, and Betsy.

Rob was still feeling drained—not physically but from emotion; all he had were a few cuts that hadn't needed stitches and were healing nicely, but the memories of Eilidh were imprinted on his brain, and he would never be so trusting again.

He looked at McAllister. And Joanne. Saw lightness had begun to dawn on faces aged by the past weeks. *I hope to goodness the two of them get together*, he thought, *we could do with some good news.*

"Come off your motorbike?" Hector asked Rob when he came in.

Rob laughed. "Hector, read the paper on Thursday, that'll tell you what happened."

Hector was completely unaware of anything except the dire state of his beloved Clachnacuddin, who, having lost at home on Saturday past, were now in the bottom five of the Highland League.

Then Hector asked, "Where's Neil? We canny do the paper without him."

They had all been aware of footsteps on the stairs, but it was a newspaper office; it could be anybody.

"Now tell me Hector Bain, why would you be needing some

Canadian when you have me?" Don McLeod was looking at Hector, smiling, and for an instant, Hector failed to recognize him, he was so shrunken.

"Mr. McLeod!" Hector was whispering, his eyes so round he looked like a prehistoric bug, scared the apparition might be Don's ghost, not the real man—now minus a stone in weight, plus ten years added to his age.

"Don!" Joanne jumped off her chair. She hugged him. His face came not much higher than her breasts. He snuggled in, saying, "Now this is what I call a welcome."

He ignored the questions from Rob, *how, when, why didn't you tell me*, the squeals from Betsy of—*goodness me*, the repetition of *Jings!* from Hector.

He took the cigarette McAllister offered, examined it, gave it back, and lit one of his own.

He lifted up papers, searching, then, scrabbling around in his drawer, he found his wee red pencil, which he tucked behind his right ear. He sat in his usual chair. He did not look at the seat his late wife always occupied, which was left empty in tribute.

He looked around, and said, "Right, front page—I'm upping the font size on the heading. 'Former Soldier Accused of Murder.' That'll do nicely."

It took nearly two weeks before Don could bring himself to return to his house, and when he did, he hated the place. He unlocked the courtyard gate. He walked down the passageway. He unlocked his front door. He stepped inside. And he started to cry. He sobbed huge heaving sobs of pain of grief of loneliness. He went to sit on the sofa to recover and found he couldn't bear to be in the house a minute longer. He ran the kitchen tap, washed his face, looked around, found nothing he needed except his mother's Bible, which he put into a string bag. He walked out, not bothering to lock up—*If a burglar takes the lot, he's welcome*—and left to catch the bus to the Ferry Inn.

Jimmy nodded as Don came into the public bar. "Don. I was just leaving, but let me shout you a drink." He did not look surprised to see Don. He did not give the impression that anything of any significance was happening. He looked a moment longer than usual, taking in Don's sobriety, his new suit, his new shirt, and the haircut and the string bag.

"I'm no' drinking, thanks all the same," Don said. "I'm wondering where I can find your mother."

Jimmy did not remark on the absurd idea of a nondrinking Don McLeod. And he did not hesitate. "I'll take you."

He wanted Don to visit his mother. He knew she needed someone to talk to. And her son wouldn't do.

Jimmy took the ferry across to the Black Isle. They branched off the shore road, taking the route that climbed up and along the hillside giving a view of the firth, the mountains at the westerly end.

The fields lying fallow were dark brown—from a distance almost black. The trees were skeletons on the hillsides, marking the courses of burns, lining a driveway to a farm, in all shapes and sizes and in sharp contrast to the ubiquitous pine trees now being planted throughout Scotland by the Forestry Commission.

An abomination, Don thought, *all planted in rigid rows. What's wrong with bare empty hills?*

The car crested the spine of the Black Isle. The northern horizon was filled with the hibernating bulk of Ben Wyvis, now sporting a scattering of light snow, as though the mountain had a bad case of dandruff.

They crossed the bridge over the River Conon, took a right turn, and continued to the McPhees' winter encampment, a place not far from the distillery and a fine spot to winter the horses.

Don had been here a few times before, but never in the winter. It looked forlorn without the delicate leaves of the birch and the rowan and the hazel to soften the round, seemingly derelict benders, the rusting vehicles, the caravans that looked as though a can opener could easily slice through them, and the abandoned washing machine, the old boiler that came from a tugboat, the scrap metal and sheets of corrugated iron, all piled up in a heap next to the whisky-colored water of the burn, which was now almost wide enough to be a river.

"Afternoon, missus," Don said when he came into the warmth of the bender.

"How are you keeping?" Jenny asked.

"Fair to middling," came the reply.

"Tea?"

"Aye."

They were silent as Jenny made the tea using a huge black kettle but a new-looking gas cooker. Jimmy had left, and it took the two old friends a while to warm up to a conversation.

"So you're out for good?" Jenny asked.

"The sergeant has been charged."

"Aye." Jenny sighed. "He was always a bad lot even as a bairn."

They were sitting either side of a stove made from an old oil drum; the flue had a right-hand bend and poked out through the wall, but the joins were not tight, and an occasional backdraft sent miniature smoke signals into the room.

"I never met the Canadian," Don started, "but I heard he was a decent fellow. Clever too."

"Aye. Chrissie did a good job raising him."

"Does McAllister know? And Jimmy?"

"Aye, they know about Neil. There was no keeping it from them." She shook her head, and one of the numerous hairpins that trapped her hair in a bun came loose and fell into her lap. "But they don't know about Chrissie." Then, speaking slowly, Jenny added, "Anyhow, that's nobody's business but mine."

"But Neil knows Chrissie was your daughter?"

"I never told him. He knows who his birth mother was. And who his father is. He found the record of his christening in the parish records in Inchnadamph. I saw him one night in the Ferry Inn. He looked at me. I said nothing. But he knew I knew. And that was enough."

Neil had met Joyce, that Don knew, for she had told him not three days before she was killed. But Neil didn't know then that she was his mother. That was what he and Joyce had been talking about the night she was killed; Joyce had decided they had to tell Neil. Too late.

But after Neil discovered the truth of his birth, he never once made contact with the man he knew to be his father.

So be it, Don thought.

"It all happened a long time ago," Jenny continued, "and I could see he's done well for himself. An' that'll have to be enough." She looked across at him, looking directly at him for the first time. "The woman in the orphanage in Glasgow said our Davey had been sent away, so we'll never know what became o' him."

Don could feel her pain that had been kept alive over thirty-five years by hope.

"Aye, no one wants a three-and-a-half-year-old, 'specially a wild one who barely spoke English. But your wee laddie, he was that bonnie . . . Joyce told me she always kept his baby picture in her handbag—never went anywhere without it . . ."

Jenny stopped. She saw how Don had curled up into himself, his arms folded across his chest, holding the pain in tight, in case the genie escaped and destroyed him.

"And our Chrissie, she loved that wee boy. When she was nursemaid to him, thon time when Joyce had to go to hospital when she was no' right in her mind, and you had disappeared off the face o' the earth, baby Neil, he was left wi' Chrissie and he took to her like he never did wi' Joyce. And a fine man he turned into—so it was all for the best."

She said this like she meant it, but she wasn't sure what she believed anymore. There had been something about Neil that bothered her. *But he's gone and I doubt he'll be back.*

"I sore wish Joyce hadn't left me thon jewelry, though, I don't know what on earth to do wi' it now I have no daughter."

"You sacrificed a lot for Joyce—even your own daughter."

"And if it hadn't been for him being mistaken for a tinker, the welfare would never have taken your son."

"So that's why you let Chrissie go to Canada?"

"Partly." Jenny was remembering the sad wee soul her daughter Chrissie was before Neil came to fill her life. "There was a lad, Neil Hunter—a Dingwall lad, Chrissie never got over him being killed. The last week o' the war it was, and her only fifteen, but she'd loved him since they were bairns and was affected bad by his death. She named the baby after him. And after they got him back, and Joyce was in hospital"—Jenny refused to call it the asylum or the loony bin—"I could see Chrissie was starting to believe the baby was really hers."

And Jenny McPhee remembered that after a few months, and Joyce still not fit to care for her own child, not even showing interest in him, there was no parting her oldest child, her only daughter—born when she herself was fifteen—from baby Ian Donal Mackenzie McLeod, whom she called Neil. Neil Stewart.

Jenny knew that was why Chrissie barely kept in touch over all the years—only acknowledging the annual bank deposit through the solicitor, terrified Joyce might turn up to claim the child. But Joyce never would. She had vowed to Jenny that if her stolen child, her wee Davey, was returned, then, and only then, would Joyce travel to Canada to meet Chrissie and the boy.

Don needed to deal with one pain at a time, and the pain of his lost boy would wait, but never vanish. Thoughts of Joyce filled his days and nights; awake and asleep, it was always the same regrets and the same great big burning shame.

"I never knew, not till it was too late." Don murmured this to himself, but Jenny heard.

"She always regretted lying to you," Jenny said, although she knew there was no comfort in the thought.

"She only lied to me about defying her father. All the rest she told me when she returned from India."

Jenny had often wondered if Don had known they had a son. Now she knew.

"And it was me who threw her out and . . ."

"You were no' yourself after the war, all those burns and everything, then you was locked up in thon institution . . ."

He held up his hand to ward off the interruption from Jenny. "No, I said something unforgivable . . ."

She saw he needed to tell someone, only she wished she wasn't the one who had to listen. She wanted it over. She had had enough. But she cared for Don, so she said nothing, only nodding and inserting an *Aye*, or a *Terrible*, or a soft soothing noise as though she were hushing a frightened mare, while he recounted the saga of himself and Joyce McLeod, née Mackenzie.

"Joyce didn't show me the letter from her father—the one where he banned her from marrying me, threatening to disinherit her. She insisted we get married. So we did. But we told no one."

He wished he was drinking more than tea but held onto his vow to give up the spirits. "Then, only a couple o' weeks after the wedding, I found the letter. I was furious, and sick to the stomach. What could I give her? I had no job, not then, I had no money—only renting thon pokey wee house that's now mine. She said money didn't matter, but I was ashamed I couldn't provide for her. And I may have been poor back then, but I was rich enough for a bottle of whisky."

Many bottles, he remembered.

"Not that I'm using this as an excuse, missus." Don looked into Jenny's eyes as he said this. "But I was hurting bad, a terrible pain it was, and I wasn't sleeping . . ."

The memories of floating in a burning sea of oil and debris, of his fellow sailors, some with their hair on fire, perishing within arm's length of him, and the terrible struggle to avoid being sucked under in the whirlpool the ship created as she sank to her death in the Dardanelles, was as vivid as if it had happened yesterday, not forty years since.

"So there was I, newly married, drinking, nursing my grudge at her *making me marry her when we didn't have to*, was how I put it, and all the while not noticing what was happening." He rubbed his chin. He ran his fingers through his thick dark grey hair. He was steeling himself to say the unsayable.

And Jenny, watching him closely, could almost read his mind. Not the words, but she read that something she did not want to hear was about to be said.

"One morning, she was sick in the kitchen sink—she couldn't make it to the lavatory, which was outside in the courtyard in those days. I asked her what was wrong and she said, 'There's nothing wrong, it's wonderful news.'"

He could still hear her voice, in that posh educated accent that he so hated way back then, he could hear her saying *wonderful news*, and it had filled him with terror.

"If you're saying what I think you're saying . . ." He remembered staring at her pale face; her bright eyes, looking into his, desperate for his approval. And he remembered, could never forget, how his words—slow, deliberate—had pierced her, almost as fatally as his filleting knife that had ended her life.

"'I know an auld nurse,'" I told her. "'She can put an end to all that—for a financial consideration.'" He was sitting as he said this, watching Joyce. Watching her slump onto a wooden kitchen chair, one hand on the table to stop herself falling.

Then he had delivered the coup de grâce—*"Now I know why you were so keen to marry in spite of your father forbidding it"*—and left the house without another word.

He returned a few days later to a note saying she had gone to Assynt, to her family home. He had embarked on a drinking session that lasted seventeen days, ending up in a police cell, where a doctor subsequently had him committed as a possible suicide threat. That, along with his burns, which had not healed properly, made the doctor sign the form sending him to the Princess Louise Hospital for Limbless Soldiers and Sailors.

"Even though I hadn't lost a limb, I was crippled wi' pain and I needed the counseling. I was nearly two years in thon place. I saw so many men worse off than me that I grew right ashamed o' myself." He shuddered at the memory. "I wrote to Joyce. But there was no reply."

"She was in hospital herself that year. No' in her right mind." *And she never wanted anything to do with her wee baby,* Jenny remembered. "Then she took off to India."

"Where she, quite rightly, behaved as though the marriage had never happened," Don said.

"And where Archie Smart was waiting, his father having told him Joyce had had a bairn—and no known father for her child."

"She told me, years later, she had married him to keep the peace and avoid a scandal that would ruin her father's reputation."

"Her father was a good man. If he'd known, he'd have

stopped her." Jenny McPhee said this, not quite believing it. *You should never say you know what the dead would have wanted. Who knows what's in another's mind?* was her belief.

"The wonder of it all is how she forgave me." Don leaned back in his chair, his eyes resting on a circular gap in the canvas where the flue of the fire reached out to the heavens. He was still in awe of his late wife's capacity for forgiveness.

When he said this, *she forgave me*, Jenny heard the lifting of his voice and was glad. She too knew of Joyce's capacity for forgiveness but wished Joyce had not included Archie Smart.

Don looked across at Jenny and, for the first time, smiled. "Joyce told me that all that mattered was love and that this time we would be together—as much as was possible. When Archie came back in a wheelchair, she wouldn't abandon him, saying he was as injured as anyone."

And she didn't just mean his legs, Jenny knew, for she had once asked Joyce and received the same answer.

"And her old father sent the foreign manny to look out for his lass."

"And from what I hear, he did his best," Don added.

"Aye, he did, but I hear he's beside himself that he didn't do more." Jenny was wrung out. She wanted to be left alone. She had grieving to do. Her Chrissie, Joyce,—and Neil.

Don noticed. Joyce had taught him to.

"We're planning a memorial service for Joyce," he said.

"Let me know where and when, I'll be there." Now it was Jenny smiling for the first time in a long time. "She was a good woman, your Joyce."

"Aye. She was." He stood, settled his hat on his head, tilted it back, and said, "Thanks, missus."

And the matter of Neil Stewart would never be mentioned again.

EPILOGUE

Ten days after Christmas, a parcel arrived, addressed to Misses Annie and Jean Ross. The Canadian stamps were as fascinating to the girls as the content of the box: books, Canadian Mountie badges, and child-size beaver skin hats with earflaps.

For Joanne there was a gold chain with a gold maple leaf charm. There was no letter, just a postcard of the Rocky Mountains and one word—*Sorry*.

She did not reply and burned the parcel wrapping with the return address.

Almost six weeks had passed since Don McLeod returned to work, and Fiona felt the difference; the phone rang more, she had more classified advertising to type up, and it was brighter and lighter and easier working at the *Gazette*. Even Mrs. Buchanan seemed cheerful.

Fiona would never tell, but she knew Betsy had made at least two very expensive long-distance calls to Australia. Betsy had also told her she had good news and would be leaving the *Gazette* but not to say anything to anyone, especially not her mother.

I'm grown up now, Fiona had almost told Betsy. *I don't tell my mother everything.*

The phone rang.

Fiona answered, "*Highland Gazette*, how may I help you?" in exactly the tone and phrase their teacher had taught them at the Technical High School.

"My name is Mrs. Wilkie. Neil Stewart was my lodger. I want to . . ."

"Mr. Stewart is not longer with the *Gazette*. He . . ."

"I know that, you silly girl. I'm phoning about something he left behind."

"Perhaps you should be calling the police station," Fiona said, trying her best not to be rude, even though the woman had called her silly.

"Och, forget it," the landlady said, and hung up.

Fiona thought nothing of the call and told no one.

Mrs. Wilkie decided to keep the bicycle. And the handbag. But she threw away the photograph of a baby. *All babies look alike when they're wee*, she thought.

In late February when the first snowdrops were pushing up from the cold, cold earth in bright green shoots, Don McLeod met Angus McLean in the solicitor's office.

"I have a letter from a solicitor in Canada," Angus began. "In it is a certified copy of the birth certificate of Ian Donal Macken-zie McLeod."

Don said nothing, just waited.

"The solicitor informs me that his client, Ian McLeod, also know as Neil Stewart, wishes to claim the house in Ness Walk belonging to his late mother, Joyce McLeod, née Mackenzie, and asks that when the matter is settled, I sell it on his behalf."

Again not a word from Don.

"The letter also states that no further claim will be made on the estate of the late Mrs. McLeod, and the client, who wishes to retain the name Neil Stewart, will sign a document to that effect."

There was a pause. Angus looked at Don and waited for a response.

"Nothing else?"

"No. I'm sorry." Angus felt a surge of compassion. He looked away, not wanting to seem inquisitive.

"See to it."

Don stood, put on his hat—he was without an overcoat even though the remains of the snowstorm were still lying, and said, "Good day, Mr. McLean. And thank you for dealing with this"—he pointed to the letter—"this matter."

He walked towards the *Gazette*. Paused. Glanced down Church Street. Heard the chimes ring out eleven o'clock. *They'll be open*, he told himself.

And he walked to the Market Bar.

Highland Gazette

December 1, 1957

A memorial service to give thanks for the life of the late Mrs. Donal McLeod née Mackenzie will be held in Inchnadamph Parish Church, Sutherland, on the 15th of December.

All are welcome.

Highland Gazette

January 26, 1958

Mr. Peter Kowalski is delighted to announce the birth of his son, Andrew. The grandfather, Mr. Gino Corelli, wishes to add his heartfelt thanks to the staff of Raigmore Hospital. Mother and baby are well.

Acknowledgments

Once again I want to thank Tran Duc and Li Ly of Mango-Mango, Hoi An, Vietnam. Thank you for the coffee, the table where I write, the wonderful food, and most of all, the love.

To John Spittal of Perthshire, thanks for the company and for showing me your tree.

To Romay Macintyre of Netherton, the Black Isle, thank you for wonderful breakfasts and the room with a view.

To the Mekong writers: Jennifer, Jennifer, Ruth, and Robyn and that inspirational guide to life, happiness, angst, and writing, Jan Cornall—thank you Jan. "Lang may yer lumb reek."

Sarah Durand, editor sympathique, I really couldn't have done it without you.

All at Atria Books; Judith Curr, what a wonderful, supportive team you have.

Sheila Drummond, the Drummond Agency, sounding board, no-nonsense friend—any writer would be glad to have you on their side.

Peter McGuigan, Foundry Media, writer of enigmatic emails, a man who knows what he likes, and fights for those he believes in, I salute you, you Green-eyed Bean from Venus.

Hugh, wherever you are, you are always with me.

* * *

I wish to acknowledge all the stolen children—from the Aboriginal nations, from the Traveling people, from single mothers, from those deemed politically or socially different—stolen in the name of "doing good" or worse.

And the mothers—bless them.